## "Get your things, woman. You're coming with me."

She jerked the covers up to her chin. "I beg your pardon?"

"You'll be begging for your sorry life if you don't get a move on."

The threat in his voice struck like a whip. She didn't argue, only said, "Turn your back while I get dressed."

"I'm not fool enough to turn my back."

"Any man who bullies unarmed people is a fool," she snapped.

"Funny thing about bullies," he said calmly, using the barrel of the Colt to ease the quilt down her body. "They pretty much always manage to get what they want. Now, *move.*"

Dear Reader,

I'm so pleased that you chose to spend a few hours of your time with Leah and Jackson of *The Drifter.* These characters touched my heart in a special way—career-driven Leah who forgot to attend to her personal life, and Jackson, running from commitment and incapable of settling down. Whidbey Island, where these two fell in love, is a special place, too. The village of Coupeville still retains the charm of an old-fashioned seaside town. Life there feels a little slower, a little sweeter, and I like to think Jackson and Leah spent many long and happy years together.

The opium trade was quite active at the time, as depicted in the story. In fact, a Whidbey Island farmer once painted his barn with what he thought was a bucket of red paint, finding out later that it was $3000 worth of opium!

My affinity for the mystical Pacific Northwest remains strong, but my next book will take you to an equally magnificent place on the East Coast. Set in the rarefied world of nineteenth-century Boston, *The Charm School* (MIRA Books, March 1999) is the story of Isadora Peabody—who is anything but charming. Plain, awkward and painfully shy, she never dreams that her adventures with Ryan Calhoun, a wildly unconventional sea captain, will transform her in ways she cannot imagine. I hope, as you read her story, Isadora will steal your heart and, in the end, have you cheering her on.

Until next time, I wish you happiness and good reading!

Warmly,

Susan Wiggs
P.O. Box 4469
Rolling Bay, WA 98061-0469

# Susan Wiggs

# The Drifter

MIRA

MIRA

ISBN 1-55166-459-3

THE DRIFTER

Printed in U.S.A.

To the crew of the Sea Fox/La Tache armada:
Jay, Elizabeth, Jamie, Tucker, Ben and Kristin.

"Wherever you are it is your own friends who make
your world."
—William James, American psychologist

Special thanks to Tom McEvoy and his Jet Ski–
the Neptune of mobile marine mechanics.
Also to Alistair Cross for advice on the proper way
to sabotage a schooner.

Heartfelt thanks to landlubbers: Joyce Bell,
Christina Dodd, Betty Gyenes, Debbie Macomber
and Barbara Dawson Smith.

Thanks to Laura Shin, whose superb editorial skills
brought out the very best in the manuscript.

And finally, a big thank-you to Carol and
Don Audleman for a most convivial *tavolo comune*.

# One

```
~~~~~~~∞⟨ꞬꞬ⟩∞~~~~~~~
```

*Whidbey Island, Washington*
*1894*

"Don't scream, or I'll shoot," warned a low-pitched voice.

Leah Mundy jerked awake and found herself looking down the barrel of a gun.

Sheer panic jolted her to full alert.

"I'm not going to scream," she said, dry-mouthed. In her line of work she had learned to control fear. Lightning flickered, glancing off the dull blue finish of a Colt barrel. "Please don't hurt me." Her voice broke but didn't waver.

"Lady, that's up to you. Just do as you're told, and nobody'll get hurt."

*Do as you're told.* Leah Mundy certainly had practice at *that.* "Who are you," she asked, "and what do you want?"

"Who I am is the man holding this gun. What I want is Dr. Mundy. Sign outside says he lives here."

Thunder pulsed in the distance, echoing the thud of

her heart. She forced herself to keep the waves of terror at bay as she blurted, "Dr. Mundy does live here."

"Well, go get him."

"I can't do that."

"Why not?"

She swallowed, trying to collect her wits, failing miserably. "He's dead. He died three months ago."

"Sign says Dr. Mundy lives here." Fury roughened the insistent voice.

"The sign's right." Rain lashed the windowpanes. She squinted into the gloom. Beyond the gun, she couldn't make out anything but the intruder's dark shape. A loud snore drifted down the hall, and she glanced toward the noise. *Think, think, think.* Maybe she could alert one of the boarders.

The gun barrel jabbed at her shoulder. "For chrissakes, woman, I don't have time for guessing games—"

"I'm Dr. Mundy."

"What?"

"Dr. Leah Mundy. My father was also a doctor. We were in practice together. But now there's just me."

"Just you."

"Yes."

"And you're a doctor."

"I am."

The large shape shifted impatiently. She caught the scents of rain and brine on him. Rain and brine from the sea and something else…desperation.

"You'll have to do, then. Get your things, woman. You're coming with me."

She jerked the covers up under her chin. "I beg your pardon."

"You'll be begging for your sorry life if you don't get a move on."

The threat in his voice struck like a whip. She didn't argue. Spending three years with her father back in Deadwood, South Dakota, had taught her to respect a threat issued by a man holding a gun.

But she'd never learned to respect the man himself.

"Turn your back while I get dressed," she said.

"That's pretty lame, even for a lady doctor," he muttered. "I'm not fool enough to turn my back."

"Any man who bullies unarmed people is a fool," she snapped.

"Funny thing about bullies," he said calmly, using the nose of the Colt to ease the quilt down her body. "They pretty much always manage to get what they want. Now, *move*."

She yanked off the covers and shoved her feet into the sturdy boots she wore when making her calls. Island weather was wet in the springtime, and she'd never been one to stand on high fashion. She wrapped herself in a robe, tugging the tie snugly around her waist.

She tried to pretend this was an ordinary call on an ordinary night. Tried not to think about the fact that she had been yanked out of a sound sleep by a man with a gun. Damn him. How dare he?

"Are you ill?" she asked the gunman.

"Hell, no, I'm not sick," he said. "It's…someone else."

For some reason, his hesitation took the edge off her anger. Another thing she'd learned about bullies—they almost always acted out of fear.

"I'll need to stop in the surgery, get some things."

"Where's the surgery?"

"Downstairs, adjacent to the kitchen." She pushed open the door, daring to flash one look down the hall. Mr. Battle Douglas was a light sleeper, but despite his name, he wouldn't know the first thing to do about an armed intruder. Adam Armstrong, the newcomer, probably would, but for all she knew, the handsome timber merchant could be in league with the gunman. Aunt Leafy would only dissolve into hysterics, and Perpetua had her young son to consider. As for old Zeke Pomfrit, he'd likely grab his ancient rifle and join her abductor.

The gunman jabbed the Colt into her ribs. "Lady, don't go doing anything foolish."

Leah surrendered the urge to rouse the household. She couldn't do it. Couldn't put any of them at risk.

"You may call me Dr. Mundy," she said over her shoulder. Her hand slipped down the banister as she made her way to the foyer. The man wore a long, cloaked duster that billowed out as he descended, sprinkling rainwater on the carpet runner.

"You're not a lady?" he whispered, his mouth far too close to her ear. His voice had a curious raw edge to it.

"Not to you."

She led the way along a hall to the darkened surgery. In the immaculate suite that occupied the south wing of the house, she lit a lamp. Her hands shook as she fumbled with a match, and her anger renewed itself. As the blue-white flame hissed to life, she turned to study her captor. She noted a fringe of wet hair the color of straw, lean cheeks chapped by the wind and stubbled by a few days' growth of beard. An old scar on the ridge of his cheekbone. He pulled down his dripping hat brim before she could see his eyes.

"What sort of ailment will I be treating?" she asked.

"Hell, I don't know. You claim you're the doctor."

Leah told herself she should be hardened to doubt and derision by now. But some things she never got used to. Like someone—even a dangerous man hiding behind a gun—thinking gender had anything at all to do with the ability to heal people.

"What are the symptoms?" She lifted the flap of her brown leather medical bag, checking the contents. Capped vials of feverfew, quinine, digitalis, carbolic acid disinfectant. Morphine crystals and chloroform. Instruments for extracting teeth and suppurating wounds. A stethoscope and clinical thermometer sterilized in bichloride of mercury, and a hypodermic syringe for injecting medicines into the bloodstream.

"The symptoms?" she prompted.

"I guess…fever. Stomach cramps. Babbling and such. Wheezing and coughing, too."

"Coughing blood?" Leah asked sharply.

"Nope. No blood."

It could be any number of things, including the dreaded scourge, diphtheria. She tucked in some vials of muriate of ammonia, then took her oiled canvas slicker from a hook on the back of the door. "I'm ready," she said. "And I might add that forcing me at gunpoint isn't necessary. It's my calling to heal people. If you want to put that away, I'll still come."

He didn't put the gun away. Instead, he pushed the flap of his duster back to reveal a second gun. The holster—darkened with grease for quicker drawing—was strapped to a lean, denim-clad hip. The gun belt, slung low around a narrow waist, bore a supply of spare cartridges in the belt's loops. Clearly, he was a man unused to being given what he asked for. He jerked the barrel toward the back door, motioning her ahead of him.

They passed through the waiting room of the surgery and stepped out into the night. She could feel him behind her, his height and breadth intimidating, uncompromising.

"Is it far?" she asked, indicating the coach house, a black hulk in the sudden gloom. "Will we need the buggy?"

"No," he said. "We're going to the harbor."

A seafaring man, then. A pirate? Whidbey Island saw its share of smugglers plying the waters of Puget Sound and up into Canada. But this man, with an arsenal of weapons concealed under his long, caped coat, had the look of an outlaw, not a pirate.

As frightening as he was, he needed her. That's what was important. The oath she had taken compelled her to go. What a peculiar life she led. In the back of her mind, her father's voice taunted her: *Leah Jane Mundy, when are you going to settle down and get married like a normal woman?*

The rain drummed relentlessly on her hood. Her booted foot splashed into a puddle and stuck briefly in the sucking mud. She looked back at the boardinghouse. The tradesman's shingle hanging above the front porch flapped in the wind. In the misty glow of the gaslight Leah always kept burning, the white lettering was barely legible, but the stranger had found it: Dr. Mundy, Physician. Rooms To Let.

"Get a move on, woman," the gunman ordered.

The light in the surgery window wavered. There was nothing beyond the lamp glow but blackness. No one in sight but the stranger holding the gun on her, pushing it into her back to make her hurry.

Just who the devil was this man?

*Rising Star, Texas*
*1894*

"He called himself Jack Tower," the sheriff said, taking off a pair of ill-fitting spectacles. "Course, there's a good possibility it's an alias."

"Uh-huh." Joel Santana stroked his hand down his cheek, the skin like shoe leather beneath his callused palm. Damn. He'd been looking forward to hanging up his gun belt and spurs, and now this. Many was the evening he'd spent thinking about a parcel of green land, maybe a flock of sheep, and a good woman with broad hips and a broader smile....

He crossed one aching leg over the other and absently whirled a spur with his finger. "And you say the fugitive took off six weeks ago?"

Sheriff Reams laid his spectacles atop the hand-drawn map on the desk. "Six weeks Saturday."

"Why'd you wait to call me in?" Joel held up a hand. "Never mind, I know the answer. You and your deputies had the situation under control. This is the first time your posse ever let one get away, am I right?"

"As a matter of fact, Marshal, it's true."

"Uh-huh." It always was. These greenhorns always waited until a criminal had hightailed it across state lines and the trail had grown cold; then they called in a U.S. Marshal. "I guess we'd better get down to it, then. You say this man—this Jack Tower—murdered the mayor of Rising Star?"

Reams narrowed his eyes. "Damn right he did. Probably wasn't the first. He had a hard look about him. A mean look, like he didn't have a friend in the world and didn't care to make any."

"Who witnessed the murder?" asked Joel.

Reams hesitated just long enough to rouse his suspicions. "No one's come forward. You need to bring that desperado back and hang him high."

"Hanging folks is not my job, Sheriff." Joel lumbered

to his feet, fancying he could hear his joints creak in protest. Too many years on horseback had ruined his knees.

"What in blazes do you mean?"

Joel pressed his palms flat on the desk and glared at the map. The shape of Texas formed a mutated star, its panhandle borders so artificial—yet so critical when it came to enforcing the law. "I bring in fugitives, and I'll bring in this Tower fellow. But his guilt or innocence isn't up to us. That's for a judge and jury to decide. Don't you forget it."

"I won't."

But he would have, Santana knew. Likely if Jack Tower hadn't fled, he'd have been strung up on a high limb and left for the buzzards to pick over.

"So what've you got?"

The sheriff lifted the map, revealing an ink-drawn illustration of a man with cropped, spiky hair, a beard and mustache. A small scar marked one cheekbone. The drawing had indeed captured the mean look.

"This here's your man. He didn't leave much behind. Just a tin of Underhill Fancy Shred Tobacco and half of a broken shirt button." Reams handed them over.

"Oh—" he laid a tintype photograph in front of Joel "—and this here's the woman he fled with. Her name's Caroline. Caroline Willis."


"She's my...wife."

Leah heard a heartbeat of hesitation in her abductor's grainy voice before the word "wife."

It wasn't her place to question, but to heal. Still, she couldn't help wondering why the simple statement hadn't come easily to the stranger's lips. It had been her unfortunate lot to attend the deaths of more than a few women while the husband stood nearby, wringing his hands. There weren't many things more wrenching than the sight of a man who knew he was about to lose his wife. He always looked baffled, numb, helpless.

She glanced over her shoulder at the gunman. Even in the uncertain light of the ship's binnacle lamp, he didn't appear helpless. Not in the least. At the harbor, he'd forced her into a small dinghy. With the gun in his lap and his fists curled around the oars, he had rowed like a madman. It took him only moments to bring her out to a long schooner anchored offshore.

The twin masts had creaked in the whipping wind. She'd shivered and climbed down an accommodation ladder into the belly of the boat. The smell of damp rope, mildewed sailcloth and rotting timber pervaded the air of the once-grand aft stateroom.

An inspection hatch on the aft bulkhead flapped open and shut in the driving wind. Someone—the outlaw, she guessed—had been working on the steering quadrant or perhaps the rudder. Several bolts and cap nuts rolled along the planks. A fraying rope led out through the hatch as if he'd repaired it in haste—or in ignorance of Puget Sound gale winds.

The stranger's wife lay in an alcove bunk on freshly laundered muslin sheets, her head centered on a plump pillow, her eyes closed and her face pale. Suddenly, Leah no longer saw the run-down boat or the faded opulence of the stateroom. All her fear and anger fled. She focused her attention on the patient. Without looking at the man, she motioned for him to bring a lamp. She heard the rasp of a lucifer and a sibilant hiss as he lit one and brought the lamp forward.

"Hold it steady," she commanded. "What's her name?"

Another hesitation. Then, "Carrie," came the gruff reply.

Observation. It was the most basic tenet of healing. *First, do no harm.* Generations of doctors had violated that rule, poking and leeching and bleeding and cupping until a patient either died or got better out of sheer exasperation. Thank heaven it was more common practice these days for well-trained doctors to stand back, to observe and ask questions.

And so she observed. The woman called Carrie appeared almost childlike in repose. The dainty bones of her face and hands pushed starkly against translucent flesh. Nordic blond hair formed a halo around her small face. Her dry lips were tucked together in a thin line. Frail, defenseless and startlingly beautiful, she slept without seeming even to breathe.

And she looked as if she was on the verge of dying.

Leah unbuckled her slicker, shrugged it off, and held it out behind her. When the stranger didn't take it immediately, she gave the garment an impatient shake. It was plucked from her hand—grudgingly, she thought. She refused to let her attention stray from the patient.

"Carrie?" she said. "My name is Dr. Mundy. I've come to help you."

No response.

Leah pressed the back of her hand to Carrie's cheek. Fever, but not enough of a temperature to raise a flush on the too-pale skin. She would have no need for the clinical thermometer.

Gently, Leah lifted one eyelid. The iris glinted a lovely shade of blue, vivid as painted china. The pupil contracted properly when the lamplight struck it.

"Carrie?" Leah said her name again while stroking a thin hand. "Can you hear me?"

Again, no response. The skin felt dry, lacking resilience. A sign of dehydration.

"When was she last awake?" Leah asked the man.

"Not sure. Maybe this afternoon. She was out of her head, though. Didn't make a lick of sense." The shadows shifted as he leaned closer. "What is it? Will she be all right?" Tension thrummed in his voice.

"I'll do my best to figure out what's wrong with her. When did she last have something to eat or drink?"

"Gave her some tea with honey this morning. She heaved it up, wouldn't take anything else. Except—" He broke off, drew in a breath.

"Except what?"

"She asked for her tonic. She needs her tonic."

Leah groped in her bag for the stethoscope. "What sort of tonic would that be?"

"Some elixir in a bottle."

Elixir. Snake oil, most likely, or maybe a purgative like calomel, Leah guessed. It had been her father's stock-in-trade for years. She herself was not that sort of doctor. She found her stethoscope. "I'll want to analyze that tonic."

She adjusted the ear tips and looped the binaurals around her neck. Working quickly, she parted Carrie's nightgown at the neckline. Again, she was struck by the freshly laundered cleanliness of the garment and bedclothes. It seemed incongruous for an outlaw's lady. A gunman who did laundry?

Pressing the flat of the diaphragm to Carrie's chest, Leah held her breath and listened. The heart rate was elevated. The lungs sounded only slightly congested. Leah moved the chest piece here and there, listening intently to each quadrant. It was difficult to hear. Storm-driven waves slapped the ship's hull, and a constant flow of water trickled somewhere below.

She palpated the areas around the neck and armpits, seeking signs of infection. Then she moved her hands down the abdomen, stopping when she felt a small, telltale hardness.

"Well?" the stranger said. "What's wrong?"

Leah removed the ear tips of the stethoscope, letting the instrument drape like a necklace. "When were you planning to tell me?"

"Tell you what?" He spread his arms, looking genuinely baffled. It was probably all an act, though, she thought.

"That your wife is pregnant."

His jaw dropped. He seemed to deflate a little, sagging against the wall of the hull. "Pregnant."

She tilted her head to one side. "Surely you knew."

"I..." He drew his hand down his face. "Nope. Didn't know."

"I estimate that she's a good three months along."

"Three months."

Ordinarily, Leah loved to be the bearer of this sort of news. She always got a vicarious thrill from the joy and wonder in a young husband's eyes. Such moments made her own life seem less sterile and lonely—if only for a while.

She stared at the stranger and saw no joy or wonder in him. His face had turned stony and grim. He certainly didn't act like a man who had just learned he was going to be a father.

"So that's the only thing wrong with her," he said at last.

"It's not 'wrong' for your wife to be pregnant."

For a moment, he looked as if he might contradict her. "I meant, so that's the only thing ailing her."

"Hardly."

"What?" he asked harshly. "What's wrong?"

"What's wrong? To begin with, your boat is on the verge of sinking." She glanced pointedly at the aft hatch. The rudder seemed to be hanging by a thread—or by a waterlogged rope, to be more precise. Worm-eaten wooden bolts lolled uselessly along the deck. Big gaps separated the caulking of the hull. The line holding the post in place strained with a whining sound.

"This is no place for a patient in her condition. We've got to move her." Leah coiled the stethoscope and tucked it back into her bag. "As soon as it stops raining, bring her to the house, and we'll put her to bed—"

"I guess you didn't understand," the man said in an infuriating drawl.

She scowled at him. "Understand what?"

He stuck his thumb in his gun belt and drummed his fingers on the row of cartridges stuck in the leather loops. "You're coming with us."

A chill seized her, though she took care to hide her alarm. So that was why he'd abducted her at gunpoint. This outlaw meant to pluck her right out of her own life and thrust her into his. "Just like that," she said coldly, "without even a by-your-leave?"

"I never ask leave to do anything. Remember that."

By the time Leah had finished neatening her bag, she had worked herself into a fine fury.

With a quick movement that had him going for his gun, she shot to her feet. The old boat creaked ominously.

"No, *you* don't understand, sir," Leah said. "I have no intention of going anywhere with you, especially in this leaky hulk. I'll treat your wife after you bring her to the boardinghouse where she can enjoy a proper recovery."

Leah tried not to flinch as he trained the gun on her.

"She'll recover just fine right here with you tending her," he said.

Leah glared at the too-familiar blued barrel, the callused finger curling intimately around the trigger. "Don't think for a minute that you can intimidate me. I won't allow it. I absolutely won't. Is that clear?"

His lazy gaze strayed over her and focused on her hands, clutching the bag in white-knuckled terror. "Clear as a day in Denver, ma'am."

She hated the mocking edge to his voice. "Sir, if you hope to give your wife a decent chance to recover, you'll let me go, and after the rain you'll bring her to the house where I can treat her."

"You call yourself a doctor. So how come you can only doctor people in your fancy house?"

Fancy? She almost laughed bitterly at that. Where had he been living that he'd consider the boardinghouse fancy?

"I refuse to debate this with you," she informed him.

"Fine. I'm not fond of debating, either."

"Good. Then—"

"Just get busy with Carrie, and I'll be in the cockpit, making ready to weigh anchor."

Red fury swam before her eyes, obliterating everything, even the hated gun barrel. "You will not," she said. Her voice was low, controlled, yet he seemed to respond to her quiet rage. He frowned slightly, his hand relaxed on the gun, and he regarded her with mild surprise.

"Lady, for someone at the wrong end of a gun, you sure have a mouth on you."

"Sir," she went on, "you cannot simply pluck me from my home and sweep me away with you."

She gestured again to indicate all the damage. Her gaze followed the fraying rope across the heading of the room; the line exited through a scuttle and was tied somewhere above.

"Sugar, it's not that I *want* to sweep you away," he said insolently. "It's just that I need a doctor for Carrie."

He stepped forward, and for the first time, she got a good look at his eyes. They were a cold blue-gray, the color of his gun barrel, and his gaze was piercing, as if he saw more of her than she cared for him to see. Leah experienced an odd sensation—as if the tide were tugging her along, drawing her toward a place she didn't want to go and couldn't avoid.

*No.* She would not surrender to this man.

"You cannot force me to come with you." She looked pointedly at the flapping hatch. The wind made a sullen roar, twanging the shrouds against the mast abovedecks. "This ship is unseaworthy. Honestly, what sort of sailor are you, to be out in this tub of—"

"Shut up." In one long-legged stride, he came to her and pressed the chilly round eye of the gun to her temple. "Just...shut up. Look, after Carrie's better, we'll put you on a ship back to the island." He added under his breath, "And good riddance."

The touch of the gun horrified her, but she refused to show it. "I will not go with you," she stated. Clearly, this man had no appreciation for how determined she could be. He'd never outlast her. "I have too many responsibilities in Coupeville. Two of my patients are expecting babies any day. I'm treating a boy who was kicked in the head by a horse. I can't possibly come along on a whim as your wife's private physician."

"Right." He removed the barrel from her temple.

Relieved, she brightened and took a step toward the door. "I'm glad you decided to see reas—"

"Yeah. Reason. I know." He gave her shoulder a shove, thrusting her back into the room. "Now get busy, woman, or I'll make sure you don't *ever* see your patients again."

He stepped out into the companionway. Leah heard a bolt being thrust home as he locked her in the stateroom with his wife.

Standing in the bow of the creaking schooner, Jackson T. Underhill looked up at the sky. A white gash of lightning cleaved the darkness into eerie shards. The thunder roaring in its wake shouted a warning from the very throat of heaven. The storm came from the sea, blowing toward the shore. It was crazy to be out in this weather, crazy to sail in night so deep he could barely get a heading.

But Jackson had never been much for heeding warnings, heavenly or otherwise. He jammed his gun back into its felted holster, fastened the clips of his duster, and scowled when the wind tore at the backside of the coat, separating the flaps. The garment was made for riding astride a horse, not sailing a ship. But everything had happened in such a hurry, everything had changed so quickly, that the last thing on his mind had been fashion.

Bracing himself against the wind, he hoisted the sails. They went up squealing in protest, the mildewed canvas luffing. He hoped like hell the ship would hold together just long enough to make it to Canada. He'd been working on the rudder when Carrie had gotten sick, and had only managed to keep it from falling off with a hasty rig of lines connecting it to the helm. A sailor's worst nightmare was being swept onto a lee shore in a storm with no steering. The vessel would round up into the wind and start going backward, then go to the opposite tack as the sails backwinded. It would seesaw its way toward shore with sails flapping and no control.

Jackson set his jaw and told himself the steering would hold. Once they were out of the country, there would be time to fix the schooner up right.

Over the quickening breeze, he heard indignant thumps and muffled shouts from the stateroom below. Add kidnapping to his list of crimes. That, at least, was a first for him.

Yet when a healthy puff of wind filled the sails, he felt a measure of relief. The unplanned stop at Whidbey Island hadn't been so costly after all. He had a doctor for Carrie, and no one was the wiser. The doctor wasn't at all what he'd expected, but he'd have to put up with her.

A lady doctor. Who would have thought it? He'd never even known such a thing could be possible.

Leah Mundy was a prickly female, all pinch-faced and lemon-lipped with disapproval, and there wasn't a thing to like about her.

But Jackson did like her. He'd never admit it, of course, and would never find occasion to, but he admired her spirit. Instead of getting all womanish and hysterical when he'd come for her, she'd taken it like a man—better than most men he knew.

He felt a small twinge when he thought of the patients she wouldn't see tomorrow, or the next day, perhaps even the day after that. But he needed her. God, Carrie needed her.

*Pregnant.* Carrie was pregnant. The thought seethed inside Jackson, too enormous for him to confront right now, so he thrust it aside, tried to forget.

Dr. Mundy would help Carrie. She would heal Carrie. She had to.

Jackson pictured her bending over to examine her patient. That's when the doctor had changed, shed her ornery mantle. He'd seen something special in her manner—a sort of gentle competence that inspired unexpected faith in him.

It had been a long time since Jackson T. Underhill had put his faith in anyone. Yet Dr. Leah Mundy inspired it. Did she know that? Did she know he was already thinking of her as an angel of mercy?

He figured he'd thank her, maybe even apologize as soon as they got under way. It was the least he could do for a woman he'd ripped from a warm, dry bed and dragged along on an adventure not of her choosing. The least he could do for a woman he intended to take to Canada, then abandon.

He'd cranked in the anchor and moved to the helm when he heard a strange *thunk,* then an ominous grinding noise. The whine of a rope through a wooden pulley seared his ears. With a sick lurch of his gut, he looked behind him. The line he'd used as a temporary fastening for the rudder was slithering away.

He let go of the wheel and dove for the rope. A split second before he reached it, the rope disappeared, snakelike, through a scuttle in the hull.

"Shit!" Jackson said, then held his breath. Maybe the rudder would stay put. Maybe—

A terrible wrenching sound shattered the night. Then a quiet hiss slid through the noise of the storm. Jackson hurled himself at the aft rail and looked over.

His curses roared with the thunder. Dr. Leah Mundy, his angel of mercy, his divine savior, had just wrecked his ship.

# *Two*

*17 April 1894*

My dear Penelope,

I debated quite a bit with myself about whether or not I should relate what happened to me in the wee hours of the morning. The temptation is great to stay silent.

But since you are determined to become my partner in the practice when you complete your medical studies, I feel I owe you an unvarnished picture of what a physician's life is truly like.

Sometimes we are called upon to treat cases against our will. Such was the circumstance around three o'clock this morning when a man abducted me at gunpoint.

Somehow I managed to keep my wits about me. The scoundrel forced me aboard his ship to treat his ailing wife, who is with child. His intention was to sail away with me aboard so that I could tend to the unfortunate woman.

Naturally, such a criminal had no care whatever

for my other patients and would not listen to reason, so I took matters into my own hands. When he locked me in a stateroom with his wife, I used a scalpel to slice through a rope, thus disabling the steering and stopping our departure. After the mishap, my abductor burst into the stateroom, roaring with fury and actually threatening to use me as an anchor.

He is an uncommonly large man, broad of shoulder, with a lean and dangerous face and terrible eyes, but I refused to flinch. In my travels through the untamed West, I learned early to hide my fear. Thanks to my late father and his constant schemes and intrigues, I am no stranger to gunfighters and bullies. In my heart I knew my abductor would not harm me because I have something he needs—my skills as a physician. It is a great virtue to be needed. Greater, even, than being liked. For of course, the outlaw does not like me at all. But he *needs* me. And this prevented him from shooting me on the spot.

Instead, cursing so profusely I swear the air turned blue, he anchored his broken ship and together we bundled his wife into a dinghy. By sunup, we had her in a proper bed here at the boardinghouse in the main overnight guest room. Though her condition is still grave, I know she has a better chance to recover here. As for the husband, I can only wonder what sort of life it took to mold a man into such a hard-edged desperado.

Hoping I've not frightened you away from joining me upon completion of your ward studies, I remain as always,

Leah Jane Mundy, M.D.

Leah rolled a velvet-wrapped blotter over the page to soak up the excess ink. The heavy-barreled roller with its engraved pewter handle reminded her of earlier times.

She would have sold the ink blotter along with everything else if she could have gotten a decent price for it. But it was old and battered, and the initials stamped into the handle had meaning only to her.

*G.M.M.*

Graciela Maria Mundy. The mother Leah had never known.

A wave of sentiment washed over her as it often did when she was fatigued. She had no memory of her mother, but she felt a tearing loss all the same. Or more accurately, an emptiness. The absence of something vital.

Although it seemed nonsensical, she had an uncanny feeling that if only her mother had lived through childbirth, she would have taught Leah the things textbooks couldn't explain—how to open her heart to other people, how to live life in the middle of things rather than outside looking in, how to love.

She stared at her face in the barrel of the blotter. Her features had the potential to look exotic, owing to her mother's Latino heritage. But Leah worked hard to appear ordinary, choosing the plainest of clothing and scraping her hair well out of the way into a bun or single braid. She could do nothing to change her eyes, though. They were large and haunted, the eyes of a woman who knew someone had taken a piece of her away, and she'd never gotten it back.

Regaining a firm grip on her emotions, she thrust the blotter into a drawer, folded the letter precisely into thirds, and sealed it with a blob of red wax. "Work hard, Penny," she murmured under her breath. "I shall be glad to have your company soon."

She and Penelope Lake had never met face-to-face. Leah had contacted Johns Hopkins Medical College, newly founded the year before. The college had opened its doors to women from the very start, so Leah had asked to sponsor a promising young female medical student. Her father had sworn he wouldn't tolerate yet another woman in the practice.

In a rare act of defiance, Leah had persisted. She'd been put in touch with Miss Penelope Lake of Baltimore, who showed signs of becoming a gifted physician and who was interested in moving west. Away, as she hinted in her letters, from the cramped confines of settled society.

The correspondence grew surprisingly warm and intimate. Leah could well imagine Penny's world because long ago Leah had once been a part of it—cavernous homes like mausoleums, grim social visits, mannered conversations that went nowhere. And always, always, the unspoken expectation that any woman of worth would concern herself with home and family, not a profession.

Leah and Penelope Lake seemed to be kindred spirits. Why was it so easy to write openly to Penny, Leah wondered, when she was so guarded with the people she saw every day? She lived in a busy boardinghouse filled with interesting people, yet she could find no true friend among them. Even Sophie, her assistant, maintained a cordial distance. Leah wondered if it was simply her destiny to be alone in a crowd; never to know the easy familiarity of a close friendship or the quiet comfort of a family.

Even less likely was the possibility of intimacy with a man. Her father, always formal, demanding and distant, had made such a thing seem impossible. That was his legacy. With his pride, his expectations and his tragic shortcomings, he had left her as a creature half-formed. He had taught her that appearances were everything. He'd never shown her how to dive beneath the surface to create a rich inner life. Some parents crippled their children by beating and berating them. Edward Mundy was far more subtle, molding Leah's character with undermining phrases that slipped in unnoticed, then festered into wounds that would never heal. He sabotaged her self-confidence and he limited her dreams.

"What a charming frock," he used to say to her when she was small. "Now, do you suppose Mrs. Trotter would fix that unruly hair in order to do the dress justice?"

And later, when she was a schoolgirl: "There are a hundred ways to be mistaken, but only one way to be right. You have your mother's looks and—alas—her contempt for conventional wisdom."

When she became a young lady and a social failure, he had said, "If you cannot attract a decent husband, I shall permit you to assist me in my practice."

By the time she recognized the harm he'd done her, it was too late to repair the damage. But he was gone now, and maybe she could find a way to move out from under his shadow. Maybe the world would open up for her.

"It's not fair for me to pin so much hope on you, Penny," Leah said, shaking off her thoughts.

She placed the letter to Penelope Anne Lake on a wooden desk tray, then checked her register. Mrs. Pettygrove had sent her houseboy with a list of the usual complaints, all of them imaginary, all treatable with a cup of Sophie's mild herb tea and a bit of conversation. The Ebey lad, the one who had been kicked by a horse, had passed a quiet night.

Unlike Leah. Her own head throbbed—not from an iron-shod hoof, but from a man with an iron will.

And the most frightening eyes she had ever seen.

Just the thought of those hard gray eyes brought her to her feet. Restlessly, she paced the surgery, scanning the bookshelves and the framed certificates hanging on the walls, trying to construct her day in some sort of orderly fashion. But the extraordinary night she'd passed destroyed her concentration.

Memories of the man's bleak gaze troubled her as she stopped at the coat tree behind the door and put on a white muslin smock. The garment had been laundered and starched and fiercely pressed by Iona, the deaf-mute girl abandoned by her parents three years earlier.

Over her father's protests, Leah had taken in the girl. *Other women marry and have children of their own. But you have to adopt someone else's damaged goods.*

Leah wished she could forget her father's bitter words. But she remembered everything. Her blade-sharp memory was both a gift and a curse. In medical school, she'd been renowned for her ability to commit the most minute detail to memory. Yet the curse of it was, she also recalled every slight, every slur, and they hurt as fresh as yesterday. *Leah Mundy, too busy doing a man's job to remember she's a woman...* Her childhood friends had gone to parties while Leah had stayed home, memorizing formulae and anatomy. Her classmates had married and become mothers while Leah doctored people and delivered other women's babies.

Resolutely, she filled a small earthenware churn with vinegar heated at the kitchen stove. She added sassafras and mint, then a pinch of ground cloves, and put the container on a tray to take upstairs.

As she passed through the hallway, she heard the

sounds of clinking dishes and silver from the dining room, the clack of the coffee grinder in the kitchen. Smells of sizzling bacon and baking biscuits wafted through the house. Eight o'clock, and Perpetua Dawson would be serving breakfast.

Leah rarely took the time to sit down for a meal with the boarders. When she did, she felt awkward and intrusive anyway. She had never learned to be comfortable in company, even among people she encountered every day. For most of her life, she'd been regarded as an oddity, an aberration, sometimes an absurdity: a woman with a mind of her own and the ill manners to show it.

She paused in the grand foyer. Perhaps this was the area that had deluded the outlaw into thinking the house fancy. High above the front door was a wheeled window of leaded glass depicting a ship at sea. The colored panes with their fanciful design served as a reminder of bygone days when the owner of the house had been a prosperous sea captain. A railed bridge, reminiscent of a ship's deck, spanned the vestibule from above, connecting the two upper wings of the house.

By the time Leah's father had bought the place, it had been an abandoned wreck for many years. He'd gone deep into debt restoring it, but impossible debt was nothing new for Edward Mundy.

She went up the main staircase, noting with satisfaction the sheen of verbena wax on the banisters. Iona kept the house immaculate.

Leah stopped outside the first door on the right. She tapped her foot lightly against the door. "Carrie? Are you awake?"

No sound. Leah shouldered open the door, the tray balanced carefully in both hands. Silence. Heavy drapes blocked out the morning light. She stood still for a moment, letting her eyes adjust to the dimness. The room had a fine rosewood bedstead and, when the curtains were parted, a commanding view of Penn Cove.

Carrie lay unmoving in the tall four-poster bed. Alone. Good God, had the husband abandoned her?

Leah turned to set the tray on a side table—and nearly dropped it.

The gunman.

He dozed sitting up in a chintz-covered chair, his long legs and broad shoulders an ungainly contrast to the dainty piece of furniture. He still wore his denims and duster, his hat pulled down over the top half of his face.

Held loosely in his hand was the Colt revolver.

Leah gasped when she saw it. "Sir!" she said sharply.

He came instantly alert, the hat brim and the gun barrel both lifting in warning. When he recognized Leah, he stood and approached her, raising one side of his mouth in a parody of a grin.

"Morning, Doc," he said in his gravelly voice. "You look mighty crisp and clean this morning." Insolently, he ran his long, callused finger down her arm. The forbidden touch shocked Leah. She flinched, glaring at him. Before she could move away, he cornered her. "Uh-oh, Doc."

"What's the matter?" She forced herself to appear calm.

"You missed one." Before she could stop him, he reached around and fastened the top button of her shirt-waist.

A man should not be so familiar with a woman he didn't know. Particularly a married man. "Sir—"

"Do you always look so stiff and starched after wrecking a man's boat?"

Ignoring his sarcasm, she moved past him. "Excuse

me. I need to check on my patient." She deposited the tray on the table. "Did you find a bottle of your wife's tonic? I need to know what she's been taking."

"All our things are on the boat."

"I wish you'd remembered the tonic."

"We had to abandon ship pretty fast. It was all I could do to keep myself from choking you to death."

"That wouldn't do Carrie much good, would it?"

"Damn it, woman, you could have killed us all."

"Perhaps you'll consider that the next time you try to kidnap me." She took the lid off the medicine crock.

He crossed the room, boots treading softly on the threadbare carpet. "What's that?"

"An inhalant to clear the lungs."

"So what's wrong with her?" he asked, and she heard the anxiety in his voice. "Besides...you know."

"Yes, I do know."

"She's got the croup or something?"

"Or something." Leah folded her arms. "I'll need to do a more thorough examination. Her lungs sounded congested last night. She's in danger of developing lobar pneumonia."

His ice gray eyes narrowed. "Is that bad?"

"It can be, yes, particularly for a woman in her condition. That's why we'd best do everything we can to prevent it from happening."

"What's everything?"

"The inhalant. Complete bed rest. Plenty of clear liquids and as much food as we can get her to eat. She must regain her strength. Pregnancy and childbirth are arduous chores, and they take their toll on frail women."

He glanced at the sleeping form in the bed. So far, Leah had not seen him touch her, and she thought that was strange. None of her affair, she told herself.

"Carrie doesn't eat much," he said.

"We have to try. Since she seems to be resting comfortably, don't disturb her. When she wakes on her own, help her sit up. Have her inhale the steam and try to get her to take some broth and bread. Mrs. Dawson will have it ready in the kitchen." Leah turned to go. He stepped in front of the door, blocking her exit. He was one of the tallest men she had ever seen—and one of the meanest-looking. She folded her arms. "If you dare to threaten me again, I'll go straight to Sheriff St. Croix."

Her warning made no impression on him—or did it? Perhaps his eyes got a little narrower, his mouth a little tighter. "Lady, if you know what's good for you, then you won't breathe a word to the sheriff."

She hitched up her chin. "And if I do?"

"Don't take that risk with me."

The icy promise in his voice chilled her blood. "I don't want any trouble," she stated.

"Neither do I. So I'll be spending the day working on the boat you wrecked last night."

"That boat was a wreck long before I disabled the rudder."

"At least I could steer it." He hissed out a long breath, clearly trying to gather patience. Then he dug into the pocket of his jeans and took out a thick roll of bills. "What's your fee?"

She swallowed. "Five dollars, but—"

He peeled off a twenty-dollar note. "That should take care of the fee, plus room and board. I ought to be able to get the steering fixed today, and then we'll be off."

She stared at the paper money but made no attempt to take it. "I'm afraid you didn't understand. You have to stay here and take care of your wife. Not just for today, but until she gets better. You can't just go sailing off into the sunset.''

''But you said—''

''I said she needs complete bed rest and plenty of food and care. She won't get that on your ship. She won't get that without you. You're staying here, Mr....'' She floundered, realizing he'd never told her his name.

''Underhill. Jackson T. Underhill. And I'm not staying.''

''What's your hurry, Mr. Underhill?'' Leah demanded. As if she didn't know. He was a man on the run. A fugitive. From what, she didn't care to speculate. None of her affair. Her gaze flicked to the twenty dollars in his hand. Was it stolen?

''I don't have time to lollygag on some island.''

She felt a niggling fear that he'd go off and leave Carrie. ''You cannot abandon your duties,'' she stated. ''I simply will not allow it.''

''I've got business to take care of.''

''You've got a *wife* to take care of.''

He waved the money at her. ''That's what I'm hiring *you* to do.''

''I'm a doctor, not a nursemaid.'' Leah planted her hands on her hips and wished she were taller so she could face him down, eye to eye, nose to nose. ''Good day, Mr. Underhill. I'll look in on your wife this evening. If you need anything before then, tell Mrs. Dawson. She'll instruct Mr. Douglas to fetch me.''

She reached past him for the doorknob. He seized her wrist.

Something happened; she wasn't sure what, but his touch sparked a hot and alien sensation within her. His grip was strong, though it didn't hurt. His gaze was brutal and uncompromising. And in spite of it all, she felt a curious breathlessness, a quickening in her chest.

"If I need anything?" he repeated. "Lady, there are a lot of things I need."

She snatched her hand away, mortified by the forbidden sensations his touch had caused. "I wasn't speaking of *your* needs, but Carrie's. I'll treat your wife to the best of my abilities." She hoped he didn't hear the slight tremor in her voice. "Beyond that, I can promise you nothing."

Face flaming, she pushed past him and left the room.

The Mundy place had a real honest-to-God bathhouse, Jackson was pleased to discover. Apparently, this had been a fine estate at one time, and the previous owner had spared no expense in endowing it with luxuries. Perpetua Dawson, the small, busy woman who ran the kitchen, had shown him to the bathhouse, pointing out the deep zinc tubs and the furnace-heated water supply.

After laboring to bring the crippled boat into harbor, Jackson had looked in on Carrie, finding her listless and vague. Trying to calm the panic beating in his chest, he went to the baths to enjoy the first good soak he'd had since...Santa Fe, was it? No, there was that night in San Francisco not so long ago. A frizzy-haired whore, wet-brained from too much beer, had careered right into Jackson and landed in his lap. Laughing, Carrie had struck up a conversation with her and blurted out that they'd bought passage to Seattle. He'd thought the whore was too far gone to hear. He hoped he was right.

Carrie had cajoled him into spending his winnings on a room at the Lombard Hotel. She had exclaimed gleefully over the luxurious velvet draperies, the champagne and oysters, the tray of chocolate truffles....

But then she'd looked at the fancy grille on the window and shivered. "This is a prison, Jackson. They'll never let me out of here. I'll never be safe. Never."

"Hush now, Carrie," he'd said, repeating an age-old pledge. "I'll keep you safe."

"Build up the fire," she had begged. "It's too cold in here."

The thought ignited an old, old memory that raised a bittersweet ache in his chest. The years peeled away and he was a boy again, sitting on the wet brick pavement in the moldering courtyard of the St. Ignatius Orphan Asylum of Chicago. Through a grille-covered window he could hear a little girl sobbing, sobbing.

*Carrie.* With shaking hands, Jackson had held the bundle of sweets he'd stolen from the pantry of the refectory. The sweets were never given to the children, of course. Brother Anthony and Brother Brandon saved them for themselves.

Holding a little cloth bag of gumdrops, Jackson started to climb. His feet, in worn and ill-fitting shoes, wedged into the gaps left by crumbling mortar. His wiry arms trembled as he pulled himself up. A sliver from the windowsill stabbed into his hand. He ignored the pain. At St. I's, kids knew better than to cry over a sliver.

"Carrie," he said, finding a toehold on the rain gutter. "Carrie, it's me, Jackson."

Her sobbing hiccuped into silence. Then she spoke, her little-girl's voice clear as a crystal bell. "They locked me in. Oh, save me, Jackson. I'm so cold. I'll die in here."

"I couldn't pick the lock," he said apologetically. "I tried and tried." He pushed the bag of sweets between the rusty bars of the window. "Gumdrops, Carrie!"

"Red ones?"

The silence spun out. A distant horn blew, signaling

the end of the shift for Chicago's dockworkers at Quimper Shipyards. The swampy smell of Lake Michigan blew in on a cold wind through the courtyard. "Carrie?" Jackson strained to see inside the locked room, but spied only shadows. "You all right?"

"No," she said, the word muffled by a mouthful of candy. "What's this, Jackson?"

"Something I made for you. Carved it out of firewood."

"It's a bird."

"Uh-huh." He imagined her turning it over in her small hands. He was proud of his work, his attention to detail. It was a dove; he'd copied the stained glass Holy Ghost in St. Mary's Church. At Christmas and Easter, the brothers scrubbed the orphans up and paraded them to church, and Jackson had always spent the hour staring at the jewel-colored windows.

"Oh, Jackson." Her voice came through the barred window. "I'll keep it with me always."

"I put a hole in the back so you can wear it on a string around your neck."

"It wasn't my fault," she said, and he had the eerie impression she wasn't speaking to him. "I just wanted to hold the baby, just wanted to be warm by the fire, but they blamed it all on me, put me here in the cold. I'm scared, Jackson."

His legs began to tremble from the effort of holding himself up. "Carrie—"

"You there," barked a deep, familiar voice. "Get down from there, boy!"

Jackson didn't have to look back to know Brother Anthony stood below, flexing a knotted belt while his eyes gleamed with hell's fury and his costly ring of office flashed in the light.

"Are you deaf, boy, or just stupid? I said get down."

He tilted his head up. Just a short reach away loomed a drainpipe. If he could grab onto that, he'd climb up to the roof, maybe find a way down the other side. He leaned toward the rusty pipe, closed his eyes, and leaped. The ancient iron groaned under his weight, but it held. He began to climb, up and up, ignoring the wrathful commands of Brother Anthony. Jackson kept climbing toward the pigeon-infested ledge above him. How he wished he were a bird. He'd fly away free, soaring...

"If you won't come down, I'll give your punishment to that little devil-spawn girl you like so much," Brother Anthony promised.

Jackson stopped climbing. His brief fantasy of freedom flickered and died. He blew out a long, weary breath. He slid down the drainpipe and dropped to the cracked brick yard, stumbling a little as he turned to face Brother Anthony.

The portly warden backhanded him across the face. Jackson's head snapped to one side; he saw a spray of blood fly out. Brother Anthony's ruby ring had cut him above the cheekbone.

He knew from years of observation that the warden would go easier on him if he cried and begged for mercy. But he'd never been able to plead. Instead, he wiped his bleeding cheek with his sleeve, then clawed off his shirt even before Brother Anthony commanded it. With a cold gleam of defiance in his eyes, Jackson turned, braced his hands against the wall, and waited for the first blow to land.

In the detention room, Carrie was strangely silent.

In the bathhouse, many miles and many years away from that moment, Jackson plunged his head into the lukewarm water and scrubbed hard, wishing he could wash clean the past. But he couldn't, of course. The past would always be with him, just as the scar from Brother Anthony's ring would always be with him. Just as Carrie would always be with him.

Pregnant. God Almighty, Carrie was pregnant.

She had awakened briefly this morning. Like a petulant child, she had turned up her nose and complained about the sour smell of the vinegar and herbs, but she seemed to breathe easier after the treatment. He had managed to get her to eat a bit of bread sopped in warm milk and flavored with cinnamon and sugar.

"You're good to me," she had murmured. "You're always good to me." And she'd reached her hand out for the bottle of tonic she needed.

"I left it on the boat, honey."

He'd taken her hand in his. Her fingers tightened into a fist, and she knocked his arm away. "I need it, Jackson. I need my medicine now."

Resigned, he'd rowed out to the schooner. He planned to bring her in to dock anyway. He'd paid the harbormaster, then returned to Carrie. He should have talked to her about the pregnancy, talked about what it would mean to bring a baby into the world. *Their* world. Instead, he watched her grab the bottle, watched her drink greedily until her eyes grew dazed with a sated look.

"Save a little of that," he said. "The doctor wants to know what's in your medicine."

"I need it," she mumbled, visibly calmer. "I always do."

He'd sat with her and held her hand until she slept again. All in all, it had been an easy day with Carrie. Not every day was like that. Her moods had always been unpredictable, but lately her spirits had spiraled downward at an accelerated rate. He supposed the pregnancy explained that, but what the hell did he know of female things?

For that matter, what did he know of anything the future held for him and Carrie? He knew better than to expect love and security, a settled life, a home. That was something that didn't happen to people like them. They were too desperate, too damaged. He would simply drift along with Carrie, taking each day as it came.

He'd never done a lot of planning for the future. He'd always lived for the moment. Decisions that had altered his life had turned on a single moment. A three-year stint on a whaling ship? He'd gone simply because his bed in the flophouse where he was staying had been lumpy. Ownership of a broken-down seagoing schooner? He'd won it with a single hand of cards.

Good or bad, it was the way he had lived. If you don't expect anything out of life, he reasoned, then life won't have a chance to disappoint you.

It was enough to simply stay ahead of the law. Drifting along had never bothered him in the past, though today it preyed upon his mind. There was something about that lady doctor that made him wish he could be something more than a wanderer. Made him weary of always being on the wrong side of the law—even when he was trying to do right. If he could get Carrie away to a safe place, maybe they could start over again, settle down, get a house and some land like regular folks.

He dried himself with a clean towel and wrapped it around his waist. The timid deaf girl called Iona had set out some shaving things for him. Peering into a small, oval mirror, he lathered up. He'd gotten careless the past few days with Carrie being so sick. He had to stay clean-shaven because the Wanted poster showed him with a beard.

His mood rose a couple of notches. The likeness and its screaming headline hadn't been posted in Seattle, so he guessed the search wouldn't reach this far north. Not anytime soon, he figured.

By the time they traced him here, he'd be long gone, thanks to a lucky hand of cards dealt at a tavern on Yesler Way in Seattle. A timely quartet of queens had won him the schooner.

The thought of the boat almost brought a smile to Jackson's face. He'd always dreamed of having a boat. When he was a boy, he'd stolen a copy of *Treasure Island*—everything worth having was stolen. Late at night, burning a contraband candle in the boys' dormitory at St. I's, he had devoured the adventure story with his eyes, his mind, his heart. Against all odds, he had learned how to dream. Ever since reading that book, he'd wanted to sail away, wanted the freedom, wanted the sense that he was in control of a world of his choosing.

Jackson T. Underhill had never found that. Not yet. He was still looking.

The whaling ship had not been the answer. He'd hated the tedium, the rigid pecking order among the crew, the sick cruelty of the second mate, the grim violence of the hunt. As in all the things Jackson had done in his life, he'd gleaned important skills from the experience; then he'd moved on.

The schooner was a new—if leaky—start. But it had problems. The damage done by the lady doctor was only the beginning. Once he'd docked the boat, the harbormaster's assistant had given him a depressing litany of repairs to be made before she was seaworthy again.

If he could just get her running well enough to make it to Canada, he'd take his time, maybe make a plan. He had only the vaguest idea where he would go; all he knew was that he needed to find a place where Carrie would feel safe, where his face wasn't known, where a man could be judged by the hard work he did, not by a past he couldn't change.

He cleaned off the razor, wiped his chin, and turned to reach for the pile of freshly laundered clothes in the dressing room.

Instead of the clothes, he saw a woman's backside.

Dr. Leah Mundy was coming into the bathhouse, shuffling backward, bent over and talking softly to someone in a rolling wood-and-wicker chair. "Just a few steps more. There we are," she said.

Her voice was incredibly sweet and coaxing, devoid of the acid, scolding tone she used with Jackson.

"You'll feel like a new person when you're in the bath," Leah Mundy said. She brought the rolling chair fully into the room and swiveled it around.

"Dr. Mundy, who's that man?" asked a child's voice.

She glanced up, and her eyes grew wide and panicked, the eyes of a doe caught in a hunter's sight. "Mr. Underhill!"

He bowed from the waist where the towel was knotted precariously. "Ma'am."

He was impressed by the way she regained control without even moving a muscle. The panic in her gaze subsided to a detached authority. In her profession, she probably saw male bodies all the time. Half naked or not, he was no more than an anatomy specimen to her. She straightened her shoulders, folded her lips into a humorless line, and cleared her throat.

"I didn't expect to find anyone here," she said. Jackson could tell she was trying not to look at his tattoo. "I was bringing Bowie for his therapeutic bath. He's Mrs. Dawson's boy." Her voice softened a little as she glanced down. "Bowie, this is Mr. Underhill. He was just leaving."

The child in the chair smiled shyly. Jackson felt his heart squeeze with an odd feeling of longing and loss. Bowie had fair hair and pale skin, and a face stamped by an invalid's patient resignation. He was painfully thin, with a blanket draped over sticklike legs.

Jackson managed a friendly grin. "How do, youngster. Pleased to meet you."

He glared at Leah, his gaze never leaving hers as he gathered up his things and stepped behind a trifold screen. He whistled as he dressed, savoring the feel of clean clothes against clean skin. He noticed that his shirt button, which had been broken for weeks, had been replaced. Leah Mundy might not be all that friendly, but she employed good help.

Every so often, it was possible to feel respectable, just for a minute or two.

As he was leaving the bathhouse, he happened to glance into the bathing chamber. Leah had managed to get the boy out of his clothes except for a pair of drawers for modesty.

"Sophie's away, so it's just the two of us," she was saying. "Can you hang on to my neck?" She burrowed her arms around and under him.

Bowie complied, linking his bony wrists behind her neck. "Where's Sophie?"

"She took the side-wheeler to Port Townsend." Leah lurched as she stood up with the boy in her arms.

"Here, let me help," Jackson said gruffly, striding toward them.

A flash of surprise lit her face. She gave the briefest of nods. "Just take Bowie's legs and we'll ease him into the bath."

The legs were even paler than the rest of him, flaccid from lack of use. Jackson took careful hold and slowly bent, easing Bowie into the water.

"Too hot for you, son?" Jackson asked.

"No. Just right...sir."

"You don't have to call me sir. Call me Jackson." It just slipped out. Here he was, running from the law, and he was supposed to be keeping a low profile. Being friendly only brought a man trouble. The lesson had been beaten into him by all the hard years on the road.

The boy seemed happier once he was in the bath. He rested his head against the edge of the basin and waved his arms slowly back and forth.

"You like the water?" Jackson asked, hunkering down, ignoring Leah as she seemed to be ignoring him.

"Yup. I keep telling Mama I want to swim in the Sound, but she says it's too dangerous."

Leah scooped something minty-smelling out of a ceramic jar and started rubbing it onto Bowie's legs. "It *is* too danger—"

"Just make sure you're swimming with someone real strong," Jackson cut in.

"Don't put ideas into the boy's head," Leah snapped.

"If a boy doesn't have ideas," Jackson said, "what the hell is he going to think about all day?"

"And don't swear," she retorted.

Hell's bells, she was a bossy stick of a woman. "Did I swear?" Jackson asked. "Damn, I never even noticed."

He found a sea sponge and playfully tossed it to Bowie. The boy looked baffled for a moment, then tossed it back.

"Anyway, son," Jackson continued, "when I was your age, I was full of ideas."

"What sort of ideas?"

*Like how to escape the orphanage. How to forget the things fat Ralphie made him do in the middle of the night. How to turn a deaf ear to the cries of the younger boys…*

Jackson thrust away the memories, hid them behind a broad grin. "Ideas about sailing off to paradise. I had me a favorite book called *Treasure Island.* It was by a man called Robert—"

"—Louis Stevenson!" Bowie finished for him. "I know that book. He wrote *Kidnapped,* too. Did you read that one, Jackson? I have heaps of books. Dr. Leah always gives me books, don't you, Dr. Leah?"

"You're never alone when you're reading a book," she murmured, and Jackson looked at her in surprise.

For the remainder of the bath, he and Bowie discussed all sorts of things from storybooks to boyish dreams. Jackson couldn't believe he'd actually found something in common with a little crippled boy who spoke properly and owned a roomful of books. And all the while, Leah Mundy looked on, her expression inscrutable.

She probably disapproved. He didn't blame her. She didn't know him, and what she'd seen of him did not inspire trust. He'd taken her away at gunpoint, would have kidnapped her.

In a way, he was glad it hadn't come to that. The idea of spending days with her cooped up aboard the schooner gave him the willies. Still, a sense of urgency plucked at him. The past was nipping at his heels.

"Ever been sailing?" he heard himself asking.

"No, sir."

"It's a fine thing, Bowie. A damned fine thing." Jackson shot a glance at Leah. "Of course, you have to make sure you don't have a mutineer aboard who'd sabotage the steering."

"Who'd do a thing like that?" Bowie asked. "Pirates?"

"A crazy woman," Jackson said casually.

Bowie laughed, thinking it a great joke. Leah ducked her head, but Jackson noticed the hot color in her cheeks. She didn't look half so harsh when she was blushing.

"One time," Bowie said, "Mama was going to take me on the steamer to Seattle, but she changed her mind. Said it was too far from home."

"Maybe your daddy—"

"His father's been dead for years," Dr. Mundy said. She spoke with a peculiar icy calm that sat ill with Jackson.

He kept his eyes on Bowie. "Sorry to hear that. But be glad you have a place to call home. Maybe you'll go swimming in the Sound one of these days."

"Maybe," Bowie said, slapping his palms on the soapy surface of the water.

"I'd better go." Jackson lifted him out of the bath, and Dr. Mundy wrapped him in a towel. "You keep reading those books, you hear, youngster?"

"Yes, sir."

"Dr. Mundy."

"Good day, Mr. Underhill," she said stiffly.

He left the bathhouse, shaking his head. What the hell was it with her? She'd gotten her way, forced him to stay here on this remote green island, yet she refused to drop her mantle of self-righteousness. Something about her taunted him, challenged him, made him want to peel away that mantle and see what was underneath. He told himself he shouldn't want to know her. He wondered why her opinion of him mattered.

Damn. He'd met scorpions and prickly pears that were friendlier than Dr. Leah Mundy.

* * *

By sunset, Leah had finished with Bowie, lanced a boil for the revenue inspector, visited elderly Ada Blowers to check on her cough, and set a broken arm for a drunken lumberjack who swore at her and refused to pay a "lady sawbones" for doing a man's job.

But Leah's long day wouldn't end until she paid a visit to her newest patient. She stood for a moment at the bottom of the wide hardwood staircase, resting her hand on the carved newel post and listening to the sounds of the old house at evening.

Perpetua hummed as she worked in the kitchen, a little worker bee at the heart of the house. In the parlor, the boarders sat after supper, the men smoking pipes and the women knitting while they spoke in muted voices.

This was Leah's world, the place where she would spend the rest of her life. The light from the lowering sun filtered through the circular window high above the foyer, and to Leah it was a lonely sight, the symbol of another day gone by.

She didn't know how to talk to these people who lived under her roof, didn't know what dreams they dreamed, didn't know how to open her heart to them. And so she lived apart, working hard, keeping to herself, an outsider in her own house.

She smoothed her hands down the front of her white smock. The starch had wilted somewhat during the day, and she knew the ribbons straggled down her back.

*Have a care for your appearance, girl. No wonder you haven't found a man yet.*

Shut up. Shut up, shut up, shut up. She wished she could close out the memory of her father's voice. She had loved him with all that was in her, but it was never enough. Even at the end, when he'd lain helpless and needy on his deathbed, her love hadn't been enough. She couldn't save him, couldn't make him say the words she'd waited a lifetime to hear: *I love you, daughter.*

Pressing her mouth into a determined line, she climbed the stairs, her skirts swishing on the polished wood. She tapped lightly at the door.

"Mrs. Underhill? Are you awake?"

The sound of a male voice—*his* voice—answered her, but she couldn't make out the words.

"May I come in?"

The door opened. Jackson T. Underhill stood there hatless, his blond hair mussed as if he'd run his fingers through it. "She's awake, Doc," he said.

No one had ever called her Doc. She realized that she rather liked the homey, trusting sound of it. She found herself remembering the incident in the bathhouse. What a shock it had been to see him standing there, naked except for a towel around his middle. Even without the gun belt slung low on his hips, there was something dangerous and predatory about him. Something she shouldn't let herself think about. She forced her attention back to where it belonged—her patient.

Evening light spilled through the dimity curtains framing the bay window. The glow lay like a veil of amber upon the reposing figure on the bed. Carrie Underhill wore the shroud of gold like a mythic figure. How lovely she was, the fine bones of her face sharpened by light and shadow, her milk-pale skin and fair hair absorbing the pinkening rays of the sunset.

She turned her head on the pillow and blinked slowly at Leah.

"Mrs. Underhill, I'm glad you're awake." Leah took the slim hand in her own. Immediately, the pathologist in her took over. The first thing she noticed was how cold the hand was. Too cold. "How are you feeling?"

Carrie pulled her hand away with a weak motion. Her eyes, blue as a delft dessert plate, were wide and wounded. "I feel awful, just awful." Her gaze sought Jackson, and she seemed to calm a little when she spied him. "Is this a safe place, Jackson? You said we were going to a safe place."

"You're safe here, sugar," he said. His voice was so gentle that Leah almost didn't recognize it.

"Hurts," she said with a whimper, and her perfect face pinched into a wince of pain. "Hurts so bad."

A chill rose up and spread through Leah. Her suspicions, the ones she had been beating down since first laying eyes on Carrie Underhill, came back stronger. She moved the coverlet aside.

Carrie clutched at the quilt. "Jackson!"

"She doesn't like being uncovered," he said. "Likes being wrapped up tight."

"I need to examine her," Leah snapped. Then, collecting herself, she turned back to Carrie. "I'll be quick," she promised. As gently as she could, she palpated Carrie's abdomen through the fabric of a clean flannel nightgown.

*An outlaw who did laundry...*

What was a ruthless man like Jackson T. Underhill doing with this fey and delicate creature?

The scent of laundry mingled with something sharper, an odor that was rusty and unmistakable.

*She looks to be about three months along...*

Leah's hand touched the abdomen low. Carrie screamed. Her legs came up to reveal an angry smear of fresh blood on the sheets.

"Jesus!" Jackson grabbed Leah's arm and yanked her back. "You're hurting her."

Leah drew him away from the bed and into the recess

of a dormer window. Lowering her voice so Carrie wouldn't hear, Leah leaned toward Jackson. "When did the bleeding start?" she demanded. "Why didn't you call me?"

"I didn't know she was bleeding." Fear edged his words. "I thought she was doing better, just sleeping."

"She didn't tell you?"

"No. She— I don't think she knew, either."

"I'm afraid she's miscarrying," Leah said.

"What's that mean?" he demanded, clutching her arm, holding tight.

Leah wrenched her arm away. "She's losing the baby."

"So fix it."

The chill inside Leah froze into a ball of fear. "It's all I can do to save the mother."

"So save her. Do it now," he said, raising his voice above Carrie's high, thin keening.

"I don't think you understand, Mr. Underhill. It's not that simple. She might need surgery."

"Surgery. You mean an operation."

"I have to stop the bleeding."

His face paled. "Surgery," he repeated.

"Yes, if the bleeding doesn't stop."

"No."

She could see the shape of his mouth, but she made him say it again. "I didn't hear you, Mr. Underhill."

"No. You aren't going to hurt her anymore."

Furious, she tugged on his hand, leading him out into the corridor.

"You aren't operating on Carrie," he repeated, his voice low and threatening. "She's not some critter for you to experiment on."

"How dare you," she shot back. "I'm a healer, Mr.

Underhill. Not a butcher. Believe me, I would give anything not to have to do anything invasive to your wife, and I will try to stanch the flow as best I can. But if we ignore the problem, the bleeding will continue. Toxins will spread through her body, and she'll die. A slow, painful death.''

He pressed himself against the wall of the corridor, leaning his head back and closing his eyes. ''Damn it. God damn it all to hell.''

''Mr. Underhill, this isn't helping your wife. You have to make the decision.'' A thin wail of pain drifted from inside the room. ''You have to make it *now*.''

He moved so fast that Leah didn't even realize it until he was clutching her by the shoulders, shoving her up against the wall. The desperate strength in his fingers bit into her upper arms. He put his face very close to hers. She caught his scent of bay rum and leather.

''Look, lady doctor. You're telling me she could bleed to death?''

''That's correct.'' She tried to glare him into releasing her, but he only held her tighter. She moistened her lips, trying not to let the fatigue of a long day bother her. ''An infection could take hold, and she's too weak to battle an infection.''

''Then you fix her.'' He spoke in a low, icy undertone. ''You do it now. You stop the bleeding and you make her well. Or I swear to God I'll kill you.''

Leah and her father had argued long and loud about outfitting an operating theater in the surgery. Edward Mundy claimed to scorn the fancy, big-city ways of modern medicine. In truth, what he scorned was spending money on anything but himself. Leah rarely won an argument with her father, but when it came to her profession, she found strength in her passion for healing.

In the end, she had prevailed and was rewarded with a tiny but innovative theater adjacent to the main suite. It was nothing so grand as the busy hospital theaters where she had learned her brutal craft in Denver and Omaha, but it was an impressive facility for a small island town.

She religiously followed the antiseptic methods of Dr. Lister of Great Britain. Lister had proven beyond a doubt that sterilizing the operating theater reduced the risk of infection. Penny Lake had written to say that all the surgeons of Johns Hopkins were using rubber gloves during surgery. Leah willingly embraced the technique.

Her assistant, Sophie Whitebear, had returned from Port Townsend. With quiet competence, she sprayed the chamber with carbolic acid solution until a fine mist hung in the air. Everything—their gowns, their hair, their sleeping patient, the instruments, the walls and the floors—grew damp and acrid-smelling.

When all was in readiness—the light in place, the patient draped, the dressings and instruments at hand—Leah closed her eyes and said a quick prayer. She had done this many times, had probed dozens of bodies in search of bullets or gallstones or bleeding tumors, but each time, she was overwhelmed with the enormity of invading the sanctity of the human body.

*Dear God, please guide my hand in this. Please....*

Holding her breath and her nerves perfectly steady, she began.

# Three

There wasn't a goddamned thing he could do.

Like a caged beast, Jackson prowled the surgery. His gaze kept cutting to the enameled white door. Beyond that door, in a room lit so brightly his eyes hurt, Carrie lay bleeding. He might have looked his last at her as they brought her into the strange, foul-smelling chamber. She might never awaken again. He might never again see the color of her eyes, hear the sound of her voice, feel her hand grasping his.

Bitter guilt seared his throat. From the time they were children in the orphanage, he had promised Carrie he'd look out for her. But the deadly bleeding was a shadow enemy. He couldn't beat it in a fistfight or run away from it. He had to put all his faith in an ill-tempered lady doctor who clearly had no respect for him and not a whole lot of compassion for Carrie.

Fear had become a familiar companion to Jackson. His life had been, for the most part, a series of horrifying incidents, from the moment his mother had abandoned him on a stoop in Chicago to the moment he'd fled Texas with a man's blood on his hands. But this fear was sharper and colder than anything he'd ever felt.

He hated being in this position. Helpless. Without choices. Powerless to do anything. God, how long was this thing going to take? he wondered.

Grim silence shrouded the surgery. The lady doctor and her assistant weren't saying a word. Carrie was under ether, blessedly senseless, thank God. The only sound came from a wood-cased mantel clock. The incessant ticking pounded out a hammer rhythm to Jackson's anxiety, seized his mind and wouldn't let go.

Gritting his teeth, he forced himself to stop pacing. The outer office was snug and painfully neat with apothecary jars lining one wall and shelf after shelf of textbooks. Above a woodstove hung a picture of a misty green-and-gold island with palm trees nodding over a calm bay. For a moment, Jackson stared at it.

Paradise. He could almost smell the perfume of exotic flowers, hear the call of colorful birds. He wondered if such a place actually existed.

Hungry for a distraction, he moved into the tiny inner office. Ah. Here, at least, was a bit of evidence that Dr. Leah Mundy actually had a life. That she was not some clockwork female sawbones who snapped out orders and intimidated people into getting better. Several diplomas lined one wall. Jackson had never actually seen one up close before, and he was fascinated by the scrolling script that spelled out high honors and important degrees.

She had attended institutions that sounded both imposing and exotic—Great Western, Beauchamps Elysées, Loxtercamp Hospital. She had read books such as Delafield & Pudden's *Pathology* and *Osteology of the Mammalia*. Tucked between the medical tomes was one slim volume. He had to tilt his head to read the title: *Ships that Pass in the Night: A Tragic Love Story* by Beatrice Harraden.

An educated woman. Jackson was fairly certain he had never met one before.

He picked up a framed tintype of Leah and a bewhiskered gentleman. Jackson squinted at the image. A father. He had no idea what it felt like to have one; he'd been told he was sired by a Nordic lumberjack at a Chicago brothel.

He'd never allowed himself to care about not having a father. But he could tell from the expression on Leah Mundy's face in the picture that she cared very much. Her hand gripped his arm. Her other hand held a rolled certificate—one of the diplomas on the wall? The bearded man exuded a chilly hauteur while Leah beamed with the eagerness of a pup.

Something had happened since then to beat her down. She was smart as a seasoned cardsharp. When she did her doctoring, she exuded competence and control. But she'd lost that bright sparkle in her eye. *What happened to you, Leah Mundy?* he wondered.

Was it the death of her father, or had something else soured her spirits? Whatever it was, it had turned her from a smiling, eager young woman into a somber, authoritative physician whose only pleasure seemed to be in work.

Was that what made Leah Mundy unique? What made her seem so very sharp, so special, so competent?

Or was it that she held Carrie's life in her hands?

With a muttered oath, he started pacing again. Carrie. For years she had been his quest, his purpose; sometimes she was his only reason for getting up in the morning.

She had been no more than nine years old when he'd first laid eyes on her. He recalled the moment vividly, because it was the first time in his life that he'd dared to believe angels were real. Even standing in the dingy foyer of the Chicago orphan asylum, Carrie seemed to transcend the squalor, her eyes fixed on some point far beyond the busy roomful of orphans and wardens.

She reminded Jackson of a painting he'd once seen in church—a pilgrim filled with the quiet ecstasy of her first sight of God. The other children whispered that Carrie—as beautiful and delicate as a moth—was strangely empty, that she had no soul.

He knew he was the only one who could protect her. He had endured hell in her defense: bloodied nose, broken finger, twisted arm. The rewards were sparing, but he cherished them all the more for their scarcity. She'd smile or squeeze his hand or whisper that she loved him—just often enough to make him believe her. And with just enough sincerity to make him believe she knew how to love.

He glanced again at the surgery door. He tried to think of Carrie having a kid, but his imagination wouldn't cooperate. She wouldn't know the first thing about babies. Ever since that accident back at St. I's when an infant in Carrie's ward had died and she'd been sent in disgrace to the isolation room, she'd never spoken of babies, never looked at one, never held one.

Then one day, Carrie had disappeared from the orphanage. He remembered waiting for her outside the girls' ward as he always did, the corridor stinking of piss and borax. But she hadn't come out. Brother Anthony had informed Jackson—cuffing him on the ear for the impertinence of asking—that Carrie had been adopted.

He'd felt something implode inside him. Not from the blow; he was used to beatings. But from the news Brother Anthony had delivered. Jackson knew what it meant when a girl like Carrie was "adopted." Pimps were always on the lookout for new, pretty girls. Brother Anthony and Brother Brandon were always on the lookout for ways to line their pockets.

What happened next came back in broken images, shattered by the violence that followed. Sharp fragments of remembrance stabbed at the back of his mind.

He had lunged at Brother Anthony, seized the portly man, shoved him against the seeping wall of the corridor. "Where is she, you son of a bitch? Who took her?" Jackson's fierce, boyish voice echoed through the cavernous hallway of the tenement.

"Long...gone, damn you to the eternal fires," Brother Anthony choked out, his eyes bulging as Jackson's thumbs pressed on his windpipe. Jackson was a strapping boy despite the poor diet and poorer treatment he'd suffered over the years.

"Where?" he persisted, feeling an ugly pressure behind his eyes. Rage swept over him like a forest fire, burning out of control. The fury was a powerful thing, and his young mind absorbed its force. This, he knew then, was what drove men to murder. "Where?" he asked again. "Where? Where?"

"Already heading...down the Big Muddy—" Brother Anthony stopped abruptly. Strong arms grabbed Jackson from behind. Fists clad in brass knuckles beat him senseless. He'd awakened hours or days later—he couldn't tell which—in a windowless cell in the basement. One eye swollen shut, a constant ringing in his ears, broken rib stabbing at his midsection. It had taken him days to recover from the beating, and still longer to ambush the luckless boy who brought him his daily meal. Then Jackson had burst out into the street—to freedom, to danger, to the desperation of an outlaw on the run.

He drifted from town to town, from logging camps in the northern woods to army forts and outposts in the

West, from little farming villages where people pretended not to see him to big dirty cities where everyone, it seemed, was part of a confidence game. Jackson had mastered the trade of a cardsharp and gunfighter. He crewed on Lake Michigan yachts in the summers, learning the way of life that had captured his imagination. He was like a leech, finding a host, sucking him dry, moving on.

A six-day card game had taken place on an eastbound train, and without planning to, Jackson had found himself in New York City. He had no liking for the city, but a force he didn't understand and didn't bother to fight had drawn him inexorably eastward along the low, sloping brow of Long Island.

He'd gotten his first glimpse of the sea on a Wednesday, and he'd stood staring at it as if he beheld the very face of God. The following Monday, he signed on a whaler as a common seaman. The next three years consisted of equal parts of glory and hell. When he returned, he knew two things for certain—he hated whaling beyond all imagining. And he loved the sea with a passion that bordered on worship.

But the unfinished quest for Carrie held him captive. Eventually, he had traced her. In New Orleans, while celebrating a tidy sweep at the poker table, he'd found himself a whore for the night, oddly comforted by the mindless, mechanical way the services were rendered and received. But in the morning, he'd opened his eyes to a shock as disturbing as a bucket of ice water.

"What the hell's this?" he'd demanded, yanking at the silk ribbon around the whore's neck. "Where'd you get it?"

The whore had clutched the object defensively. "Lady Caroline left it behind, said it was a good-luck charm so I took to wearing it."

He grabbed the charm, stared at it for a long time. It was the dove he'd carved for Carrie so long ago. "Lady Caroline," he said, hope burgeoning in his chest. "So where is she now?"

"Gone to Texas, last I heard, with Hale Devlin's gang."

Texas. And that had only been the beginning.

The shattering of glass jarred Jackson out of his reverie. With a curse, he looked at the framed tintype he'd been holding and saw that he'd broken it. An ice-clear web of cracks radiated from the center, distorting the picture of Leah and her father. Her smiling mouth was severed as if by violence; the father's hand on her shoulder had been detached.

Painstakingly, Jackson removed the broken glass. The picture went back to normal—Leah, smiling, aglow with pride. Her father cold, distant. The scroll of a paper diploma clutched in her hand.

An educated woman. But could she save Carrie?

He shuddered from the memory of what he had found in Texas.

Could anyone?

Bone weary, bloodied to the elbows and filled with self-doubt, Leah peeled off her patent rubber gloves. She pressed her forehead against the damp wall of the surgery and closed her eyes.

Nearby, she could hear Sophie's movements as she placed soiled sheeting and gowns into a pail of carbolic solution, then emptied a large porcelain container into a waste pail.

"You did your best. I watched you like a hawk on the hunt," Sophie said. "Those fancy city doctors in Seattle couldn't have done better."

"Try telling that to Mr. Underhill," Leah whispered. "Oh, God, God." She forced her eyes open, made herself look at Sophie.

Her assistant was broad of face; she had wise dark eyes and an air of serenity that governed every move she made, every word she spoke. Half Skagit Indian and half French-Canadian, Sophie had been educated in boarding schools that taught her just enough to convince her that she belonged neither to the white nor the native world, but stood precariously between the two. It was an uncomfortable spot, but Leah, a misfit herself, felt sometimes that they were kindred spirits.

"It is the great curse of doctors," Leah said, "that while most people have to die only once, a doctor dies many times over, each time she loses a patient."

Sophie pressed her lips into a line, then spoke softly. "But it is the great reward of healers that each time you save a life, you yourself are reborn." She looked down at the unmoving, pale face of Carrie Underhill. "Yes, you lost the baby. But you also saved Mrs. Underhill from bleeding to death. She'll live to thank you. Perhaps to bear other children."

Leah swallowed the lump in her throat. She knew some babies were never meant to be, especially when the mother suffered such precarious health. There was something puzzling about Carrie Underhill's condition, something besides the pregnancy. A chronic complaint, perhaps. But what?

Did she drink calomel? Leah wondered. The purgative was still a popular folk remedy; it had been her father's favorite prescription. This was the sort of thing he caused, she thought resentfully. She intended to keep Carrie under close observation.

The task at hand was more pressing, though. She had to face this woman's husband. The baby's father.

With a leaden heart, she helped Sophie finish clearing up. After Carrie was clad in a clean gown and lying on clean draperies, Leah went to the door and opened it. "Mr. Underhill?"

His head snapped around as if someone had punched him in the jaw. Weariness deepened the fan lines around his eyes and mouth, yet a beard stubble softened the effect; he appeared deceptively vulnerable. "Is she all right?"

Leah nodded. "She's sleeping, but will probably awaken within the next hour."

He closed his eyes and took a deep breath. "Good," he said between his teeth. "Damn, that's...good." He opened his eyes. "Jesus. I feel like I just got dealt four aces."

Leah cleared her throat. "She might suffer a headache, possibly vomiting, from the ether. You must watch her closely in case the bleeding starts again, but I don't think it will." She forced an encouraging smile. Something tender and desperate lived in Jackson Underhill's haggard face. She wished she knew him well enough to take his hand, to hold it tight for a moment. Instead, she said, "I believe your wife will be fine. She needs plenty of bed rest and good food, and we'll see to that."

"Yes. All right." His eyes closed again briefly. His knees wobbled.

"Sit down, Mr. Underhill. I can't handle two patients tonight."

He lowered himself to the wing chair and cradled his head in his hands, fingers splaying into his thick golden hair. "Didn't know I was wound up so tight." He glanced up at her. She felt an inner twist of compassion at the turbulence in his eyes. Those gunslinger eyes. The first time she had looked into them, she had nearly fainted from fright. Now she felt a chilly reluctance to tell him the rest.

"Thanks, Doc," he said to her.

She nodded, holding the edge of the door, waiting. Waiting. Waiting for him to ask about the baby. He didn't. He didn't even seem to acknowledge its existence. She swallowed hard. "Mr. Underhill?"

"Yeah?"

She took a deep breath, sensing the harshness of carbolic and ammonia in her lungs. "I'm afraid I couldn't save the baby."

"The baby." His soft voice held no expression, no hint of what he was feeling.

"I'm sorry. So terribly, terribly sorry."

He stared at her for a long time, so long she wasn't certain he'd heard and understood. Then at last he spoke. "You did your best, I reckon."

In her travels with her father, she'd met her share of gamblers and gunslingers. They were men without souls, men who killed in the blink of an eye. Jackson T. Underhill was one of them. Until this moment, she hadn't realized how badly she'd wanted him to be different— better, more worthy, more compassionate. But his attitude about the baby proved her wrong.

"I did my best, yes," she said. "But like every physician, I have my limits. Some things just weren't meant to be." She decided not to tell him her concerns about Carrie. Not now, at least.

"I see." He steepled the tips of his fingers together.

*Mr. Underhill, you lost a child today.* She didn't say the words, but she wondered why he didn't react more strongly. Perhaps his way of coping was to deny the baby had ever existed. After all, he'd only known about it for a day.

"What about the tonic your wife's been taking?" Leah asked. "I really must know its contents."

"Yeah, I'll give you the bottle. It's some patented medicine. Helps her relax. She's always been...a nervous sort."

"I'll write off to the manufacturer and inquire about the contents." Based on the substances she'd seen her father dispense, she was not optimistic. A lot of the patented remedies contained calomel purgatives and worse. She tried to smile encouragingly. "After the recovery, there's no reason you and your wife can't have more children."

"There won't be more children." He slashed the air with his hand and lurched to his feet, the motion at once violent and desperate. "She almost died this time."

Leah had heard the same words from other frightened husbands. The vow rarely lasted, though. Once the woman was up and about again, their husbands generally forgot the terror of the miscarriage. Still, she smiled gently and said, "Make no decisions now, Mr. Underhill. Everyone's tired, and your wife has a long recovery ahead of her. You have plenty of time to think of the future."

His eyes narrowed. "What's that mean? A long recovery."

"Weeks, at the very least. She's lost a lot of blood, and she was underweight and anemic to begin with."

"I can't wait that long."

Anger hardened inside Leah. "Then you're taking a terrible risk with your wife's health, sir," she snapped. "Now, can you help bring her to her bed?"

"Doc." His voice was flat, neutral. "Dr. Mundy."

"Yes?"

"I wish you'd quit looking at me like that."

"How am I looking at you, sir?"

"Like I was a snake under a rock."

"If you see things from the perspective of a snake, that is your fault, not mine."

He muttered beneath his breath, something she didn't even want to hear, but he cooperated, helping her with Carrie.

"Will you stay, then?" Leah asked as they carefully tucked Carrie into bed. "No matter how long her recuperation takes?"

Jackson T. Underhill dragged his hand down his face in a gesture she was coming to recognize as his response to frustration. "Yeah," he said at last. "Yeah, I'll stay."

Like a morning mist, a rare, dreamy wistfulness enveloped Leah as she made her way back from the Winfield place. She had driven herself in the buggy since the weather was fine and the vehicle unlikely to get mired. Ordinarily, Mr. Douglas from the boardinghouse did the driving. But he was getting on in years, and she tried not to drag him out of bed too early.

Her father had insisted on a driver, claiming it bolstered his image of importance. The thought of her father took Leah back in time. She was nine years old again, done up in ribbons and bows, seated stiffly in the parlor of their Philadelphia house while he drilled her on her sums. Even now, she could recall the scent of wood polish, could hear the ticking of the grandfather clock in the hall. Could see the chilly glare of her father growing colder when she stumbled over a number.

"I'm sorry, Father," she'd said, her voice meek. "I'll study harder. I'll do better next time."

And she did do better the next time. She perfected everything he demanded of her, but it wasn't enough. It was never enough. Edward Mundy had done a splendid job of convincing his daughter that no matter how hard she studied, no matter how hard she tried, she would never please him.

He'd wanted her to be a doctor, yes, because he had no son to carry on in the profession. But he'd also expected her to marry, and marry well. There had been an endless parade of suitors arranged by her father, but they never stayed. The men she met had no idea what to do with a woman like her. They wanted someone who laughed and danced and gossiped, not someone who studied anatomy and voiced opinions that raised eyebrows.

Lulled by the creaking rhythm of the buggy wheels, Leah thrust aside the dark memories. Her father was gone. The past was gone. It was up to her to keep it at bay.

She watched the roadway unfold between the horse's brown ears and thought about the Winfields. The birth had been an easy one; the baby had emerged healthy and whole into her eager, waiting hands. She would never tire of the warm, slippery feel of newborn flesh. The look of wonder from the father, the triumphant tears of the mother. But most of all, she loved the first gasp of breath as the baby inhaled, the lusty cry that said, "Here I am, world, alive and hale," followed by the glorious rush of crimson as the child took on the flush of life.

Each time you save a life, Sophie had told her, you yourself are reborn.

On spring mornings like this, a week after Mrs. Underhill's miscarriage, Leah could believe it. She had been called from her bed at five to attend Mrs. Winfield. Just two hours later, the baby had made his appearance, and

Mr. Winfield, overjoyed, had paid Leah—immediately and well, a rare surprise since most of her patients tended to procrastinate when it came to settling fees.

So with pride in delivering Coupeville's newest citizen and carrying a gold double eagle in the pocket of her smock, Leah was in excellent spirits.

She practiced the most glorious profession of all, that of healing, saving lives, relieving suffering. She had been an exemplary student, studying harder than her male counterparts, performing better than her father's expectations for her, and in the end knowing the triumph of succeeding against all odds.

Yet inevitably as always, a shadow crept in on her, dimming her elation. Because even as she stood holding a newborn, the time always came for her to surrender the child to its mother. To watch the father gather them both in his arms while a glow of radiance surrounded them.

Some might claim the notion pure fancy, but Leah had seen that glow again and again. She wondered if she was the only one who recognized the magic, who realized what love and family could do. They could transform a plain woman into a vision of loveliness, could light the dark corners of the meanest lean-to hovel.

Perhaps it was her fate to be an observer, but dear God, there were times when she yearned to experience that joy for herself. Love and family. At quiet moments like this, with the clopping of hooves punctuating the silence, she could feel the fear growing inside her. It was like a fistula, a cancer. It was the horror that she would never know that kind of love. That she would grow old alone and lonely.

She released a pent-up sigh and turned the buggy down Main Street, clucking to the horse. The mare picked up her pace, but with a reluctant blowing of her lips.

Lined with shops and churches, the gravel road cleaved the hilly town in two and descended to the waterfront. Across the Sound, the rising sun burst with a dazzle over the jagged white teeth of the distant Cascade mountain range.

Some activity at the harbor caught her eye, mercifully distracting her from her thoughts. Peering through the light layers of mist, she saw Davy Morgan, the harbormaster's apprentice, come out of the small, low office at the head of Ebey's Landing. The youth stretched as he yawned to greet the day. The first rays of sunshine shot through his vivid red hair.

Davy shaded his eyes in the direction of the dock where Jackson Underhill's schooner bobbed at its moorage. The disabled rudder hung askew like a broken arm.

An unpleasant wave of guilt swept through Leah. The steerage was damaged because of her, and apparently repairing it was quite a task. Though it was none of her business, she knew Mr. Underhill had been sleeping on the boat rather than at the boardinghouse with Carrie. Perhaps he'd taken his vow to avoid having more children very seriously.

Seized by a perverse curiosity, she went to check out the boat, pulling up the buggy at the end of the dock.

"Morning, Miss Mundy." Davy Morgan bobbed his bright red head in greeting.

She nodded back. Like most people, Davy neglected to address her by the title "Doctor," but in his case, there was no malice intended. Yet when his employer, Bob Rapsilver, stepped out of the office, Leah's defenses shot up like a shield.

The harbormaster made no secret of his dislike for her, ever since she'd advised him that the liver ailment he was always complaining about would abate once he gave up his daily pint of whiskey. Instead of giving up drink, however, he'd turned on her, openly questioning her morals, her intentions and her skill to anyone who would listen.

"Mr. Rapsilver," she said with cool politeness.

"Miss Mundy." He lifted a battered sailor's cap. "You're out and about bright and early today."

"The Winfields had a fine, healthy son this morning."

"Ah. Midwifing is a proper business." He checked his pocket watch with a bored air. "Good to hear you weren't out trying to do a man's job."

"I never try to do a man's job," she countered. "I do better."

Davy snickered. Rapsilver pointed with a meaty hand. "Boy, weren't you supposed to be testing the steam engine on Armstrong's *La Tache?*"

"Already done, sir," Davy said. "And it's not safe. Almost burned my hand off trying to shut it down."

"Are you all right?" Leah asked, concerned.

Davy nodded. "Yes, thank you, ma'am. But Mr. Armstrong's not going to be too happy about his engine."

"Be careful, then." She jumped down, buggy springs squawking, and wound the reins around a cleat on the dock. She frowned at the rusty noise of the decrepit buggy. Another task to see to. Another problem to solve. Some days she felt like Sisyphus rolling a rock up a hill only to have it roll down again before reaching the summit.

Not today, she thought determinedly. She had brought a new life into the world and there were no other calls to make. She wouldn't let worries drag her spirits down.

Lifting the hem of her skirts away from the damp planks, she walked to the end of the dock and peered at the schooner. It looked to be perhaps sixty feet in length. Its once-sleek hull had dulled, the paint peeling. Jackson had told her the boat was called the *Teatime*. Some long-ago optimist had painted the name on a fancy scrollwork escutcheon affixed to the stern. Now all that remained were the letters *eat me*.

Leah walked down the length of the boat. Even in its state of disrepair, the schooner had the classic stately lines of a swift blue-water vessel. Seeing it all broken and peeling made her a little sad, reminding her of a favored patient succumbing to the rigors of old age.

She wondered who had commissioned the ship. Had it called at exotic ports in distant lands? And how had it wound up in the possession of Jackson T. Underhill? What sort of man was he anyway? Where were he and his strange, beautiful wife going in such a hurry? North to Canada, she guessed, maybe to lose themselves in the wilderness.

The fact was, they were already lost. She could see that clearly. She wondered if they knew.

She hesitated on the dock. She did need to speak with Mr. Underhill. Her patient was agitated. She knew no easy way to tell him what Carrie said during her lucid moments. Perhaps she could ease into it.

There was a danger, too, of being alone with him. He was, after all, a man who had tried to abduct her. The harbormaster would be of little help if Jackson attacked her. But why would he? He needed her. From the first moment, even holding a gun to her head, he'd needed her.

Steadying herself by grasping a ratline, she stepped onto the boat. A gentle listing motion welcomed her. Moving across the cockpit, she went up a small ladder to the midships. The deck glittered with glass prisms set into the planks to provide daylight for the rooms below. In the middle of the deck was a skylight hatch angled open to the morning.

Bending, she leaned down to see inside.

"G'damned chafer," said a furious male voice. "Chicken-bred bastard from hell—"

She clapped her hands over her ears. "Mr. Underhill!"

The hatch swung open and his head popped up. His face was flushed a dark red, brow and temples damp with sweat. "Hey, Doc."

She cleared her throat. "I'm sure whoever you're speaking to below would prefer that you keep a civil tongue in your head."

To her surprise, he gave her a crooked grin. "I'm alone, Doc. Just having a little argument with this repair."

To her further surprise, she felt her mouth quirk in amusement. "And is it working?"

"What?"

"Cursing. Is it helping to fix the boat?"

"No, but *I* feel better."

She eyed a part of the rudder lying across the main deck. Ropes and pulleys lay scattered about. She had never done a destructive thing in her life until she'd sabotaged his boat, and despite the circumstances, she felt guilty.

"I'll help you." Without further ado, she clambered down the hatch. The heel of her boot caught the bottom rung of the ladder, and she lurched forward.

"Careful there." Strong hands gripped her waist, thumbs catching just below her breasts.

He held her only a second, but it seemed like forever. Leah stopped breathing. It had been so long since anyone had touched her. His handling was impersonal, yet she couldn't help acknowledging that no one had ever held her this way before.

She saw his eyes widen.

"No corset, Doc?" he observed. His frankness embarrassed her.

"Binding is terrible for one's health."

He lifted his hands, palm out, in a conciliatory gesture. "You won't hear me objecting to a ban on ladies' corsets."

Self-consciously, she straightened her shirtwaist.

"Watch your step." He indicated a tub of pitch and masses of coiled rope on the floor. He moved back and regarded her. His attention had an odd effect on her composure. Her face grew warm, her pulse quickened, and she felt completely foolish.

"So," he said, his grin slightly off center. "You've come to help."

"You look as if you could use it."

"You're not too busy?"

"I've already made one call today. If no emergency comes up, I'm free for the time being."

"Well, thanks. That's real nice of you, Doc."

She shrugged. "I thought it was the least I could do, since…" She let her voice trail off.

"Since you're the one who broke the steering," he finished for her.

"You're the one who tried to kidnap me," she shot back.

He nodded. "You're not one to own up to things, are you?" He handed her a wood spanner.

She snatched the tool from him. "And you're not one to apologize for your actions."

"Here, hold this steady. Yeah. Just like that." He put a peg into a freshly drilled hole and tamped it tight with a mallet. "Some landlubber used iron bolts on this mast stepping and they rusted. I have to replace them with wood fastenings or the aft mast could come down." He repeated the procedure several more times, but each time he tamped down a peg, the opposite one came up. He cursed fluently and unsparingly through gritted teeth.

She watched him for a while, holding the pegs and holding her tongue until she could stand it no more.

"May I make a suggestion?"

The mallet came down squarely on his thumb. He shut his eyes, jaw bulging as he clenched it. "Shoot."

"Why don't you cut the pegs a longer length, then after they're all in, trim the wood flush with the deck?"

He stared at her for a long moment. She thought he was going to argue with her or ridicule her. That was what men always did when a woman dared to comment on their work. Instead, he said, "Good idea. We'll do it your way."

She still had to hold the pegs for him, and he had to lie on his side to reach all the fittings, but his mood lightened as the work progressed. He had a long frame, lean and sinewed, and appeared to be remarkably healthy. The human body was her calling, her obsession, and it pleased her to watch him.

More than it should have.

"So," he said at length, and she started guiltily, certain he knew she'd been studying him. "How is it you came to be a female doctor?"

She let out a relieved breath. "How I came to be a female is by accident of birth."

He laughed. "I guess I deserved that."

"How I came to be a doctor is by reading, hard work, a rigorous apprenticeship, and ward study in a hospital."

*And how did you become an outlaw?* she wanted to ask—but she didn't dare.

His eyes narrowed as he sealed one of the pegs with glue. "You sure talk a lot and say nothing."

His observation startled her. "I suppose you're right."

"So what's the real story?" He stood and brushed off his leather carpenter's apron. She liked it better than the gun belt.

"Why do you want to know?" *Why on earth would it matter to you?* she wondered.

"Just curious, I guess. Is it some big secret?"

"No. I'm just not used to being asked."

He swept a mocking bow, the tools in his apron clanking with the movement. "So I'm asking."

She caught herself smiling at him.

"You ought to do that more often," he said.

"Do what?"

"Smile. Makes you look downright pretty."

"Looking pretty is not important to me."

"That's a new one on me. You didn't have the usual kind of mama, I guess."

"Actually, I was raised by my father. Since he had no son, I suppose you could say he pinned his aspirations on me." She paused, gazing out a portal as she collected her thoughts. In the faraway past, she heard a voice calling, *"Dr. Mundy, can you come?"*

Leah, no more than ten at the time, went along with her father, holding the lamp in the buggy and then squashing herself into a corner of the sickroom at the patient's house.

She could not bring herself to admit to this stranger, this friendly man with secrets of his own in his blue-gray eyes, that her father had been the worst sort of doctor, a quack, a purveyor of questionable potions that often did more harm than good.

"I learned much from being in practice with him," she said. It was not quite a lie. She'd learned there was nothing more precious than human life. That people needed to look to a physician for hope. That a good doctor could do much to ease suffering while a bad one got rich from it. Her father had given her one gift. He had made her determined to succeed where he had failed.

She made herself remember the pain and the horror and the fact that even as he was dying, Edward Mundy had withheld his love. She swallowed hard. "He died of complications from an old gunshot wound."

He gazed at her thoughtfully. "I take it that's why you're not real fond of guns."

"A gun is the tool of a coward," she snapped. "A tool of destruction. I've seen too often what a bullet can do."

"Touché, Doc, as the Three Musketeers would say." He changed tools, selecting an awl. "So you became a doctor just like your papa."

"Not like my father." She flushed and looked away. "We disagreed often about courses of treatment." For no reason she could fathom, she added, "We disagreed about everything, it seemed."

"Such as?"

The proper way for Leah to dress. And talk. And behave.

The way to snare a wealthy husband.

Where they would flee to each time one of his patients expired due to his incompetence.

"Well?" Jackson prompted.

She already regretted the turn the conversation had taken. Yet it was surprisingly easy to talk to him. Probably because she knew that he was only here for a short time; then she'd never see him again. He couldn't use the things she told him to hurt her.

"He never quite understood my insistence on practicing medicine for the good of humankind rather than to make money. He thought I should spend my leisure time pursuing drawing-room etiquette. He was disappointed when I failed to marry well."

"What the hell's that supposed to mean—marry well?"

"My father thought it meant marrying a man who'd settle his bad debts for him."

"And you? What do you think it means?"

"Finding a man who will l—" she didn't dare say it "—esteem me."

"So why haven't you done it yet?"

"Because such a man doesn't exist." The old ache of loneliness throbbed inside her. "I've yet to meet a man who would give me the freedom to practice medicine. Men seem to want their wives to stay at home, keeping the hearth fire stoked and darning socks instead of healing the sick."

"It all sounds like a damned bore to me."

"Healing the sick?"

"No. Stoking the hearth and darning socks."

She laughed. "Did your mother never teach you a woman's place is in the home?"

All trace of pleasantry left his face. "My mother never taught me a goddamned thing."

His tone of voice warned her not to probe an old wound. We both have our scars, she thought. We work so very hard to hide them.

"So who taught you about the Three Musketeers?"

"Taught myself." His voice had gone flat, uninviting. Then he brightened, reaching up to lean the heel of his hand on a cross beam. Light from the deck prisms fell across him, striking glints of gold in his hair. "Now that I've got the *Teatime*, I can go anywhere."

"Where do you plan to go?"

"Wherever the wind takes me."

"It sounds rather…capricious. Do you never think of staying somewhere, settling down?"

He got back to work, swirling his brush in a bucket of glue. "I never think of much at all."

Letting the wood glue set around a loose bolt, Leah fell silent for a time, thinking. She wanted to ask him so many things: what he had left behind in his past, why he never spoke of the baby Carrie had lost, what he expected of the future. But she held her tongue. At an early age, she had learned caution. Watch what you say to another person. Watch what you learn about him. Watch what you feel for him.

Once in her life, she had given her whole heart and soul to a man, and he had crushed her flat. That man had been her father. He was a charlatan, but he was all she knew, all she had, and she'd given him enormous influence over her choices. Now she had nothing but broken, bitter memories.

Wishing she could forget the past, she worked in silence alongside Jackson Underhill, studying him furtively. In her profession she had seen men from all angles, yet she regarded Jackson as uniquely—and discomfitingly—interesting.

Despite a demeanor she found more charming than she should, he seemed to be a man who expected—and usually got—the worst life had to offer. Yet he still clung to hope in a way that was alien and intriguing to Leah.

"I'm curious, Mr. Underhill," she said, unable to stop

her incautious questions in spite of herself. "How is it that you came to be in possession of this boat?"

"What makes you think I didn't commission her?"

"Somehow I can't picture you christening a boat *Teatime.*"

"It said 'eat me' last time I looked."

"Then at least fix the lettering on the stern," she advised. "If you didn't name her, who did?"

He thought for a moment, no doubt weighing what it was safe to tell her. "Some English guy I met in Seattle. I won her in a card game. Her owner was down on his luck, but I'm told in her day, she sailed the Far East, plying the waters around the island groves, looking for rare teas. I mean to go there someday," he said, almost to himself.

"Go where?"

"I'm not sure. Someplace far. Exotic. Maybe I'll just follow the sunset until I find what I'm looking for."

The gruffness in his voice caught at her. "And what's that, Mr. Underhill?"

"Paradise. Like that picture in your office." His ears reddened after he spoke. "I guess. Just something I've always wanted to do." He shrugged dismissively. "Pass me that mallet, will you?"

She handed it to him, frowning a little.

"What's the matter, Doc?"

"I find you quite hard to understand," she admitted. "My profession is the motivating factor of my life. It's what gives me direction and purpose. Yet you have no plan for your life beyond sailing to the next port. You're like this ship, Mr. Underhill. You've got no fixed rudder. No fixed course. Doesn't that bother you?"

"I'm a dreamer. You're a planner. Who the hell are you to say your way's better?"

She felt a flush rise in her cheeks. "I shouldn't have said anything. I apologize."

"You don't need to." He picked up a sanding block and got to work.

"How long will these repairs take?" she asked, eager to leave the topic of planning and dreaming.

He blew out his breath. "Weeks, according to Davy Morgan who claims to know such things. He was amazed I was able to get here from Seattle. He gave me a list of repairs a mile long. I can do the work myself, but I'll have to go back to the city to earn enough money to pay for supplies."

"How will you earn the money?"

He winked. "I'm a gambling man."

"Is that why you're on the run?" she asked.

"Who said I was on the run?"

"You didn't have to." She pressed her mouth into a wry smile. "I guessed it as soon as you tried to abduct me. You confirmed it when you warned me not to alert the sheriff."

He squinted menacingly at her. "And did you?"

She forced herself to hold his gaze. "No. But if you give me a reason to, I shall."

"I'm not looking for trouble."

"I know." And she did. She'd briefly considered a visit to Sheriff Lemuel St. Croix, but she hadn't actually done it. St. Croix was a tough, humorless man who seemed out of place in Coupeville. A bachelor of middle years, he had a taste for fine things; even on his modest lawman's salary he'd managed to acquire a Panhard horseless gasoline carriage. Keeping law and order in the town did not seem to concern him overly much. This was not a problem since crimes in the area tended to be petty and few.

Lost in thought, she watched Jackson work. When he spoke of the sea, a dreamer took the place of the gunfighter. There was something compelling in his intent manner. Passion burned brightly in his gaze; she was caught by it. She couldn't remember the last time such a powerful desire had burned inside her. The rigors of everyday life had dulled her heart to dreaming, it seemed.

When had it happened? she wondered. When had all her dreams died? And why hadn't she felt the loss until now, until she looked into the eyes of a stranger and saw the lure of possibility?

She shouldn't probe into the life of this drifter. He was clearly on the wrong side of the law, clearly had much to hide in his past. The less she knew about him, the better. It was time to tell him what she'd come to say in the first place. "Your wife seemed troubled when I checked on her yesterday evening."

"She lost a baby. I guess that might trouble a woman some."

And you? she wanted to ask. Does it trouble you?

"Of course," she said carefully. "But I fear it is more than that. She said—" Leah broke off. Were they a husband and wife who shared everything, or did they keep secrets from one another? "She seems agitated."

"Yeah, well, she gets that way."

"She's been having some rather terrible attacks of panic, almost like waking nightmares. She speaks of blood and fire—a stain on the floor, a burning house. And she seems to have a horror of being closed in. Mr. Underhill, your wife suffers from a fear that someone or something is after her. Someone is hunting her down."

She wanted him to laugh it off, to joke it away as he did so many things.

Instead, his eyes took on the metallic sheen they'd had

the first time she'd beheld him. The dull gleam of gun-metal. Danger emanated from him, causing her to take a step back toward the skylight hatch.

"It's all just her talk," Jackson said. "And none of your goddamned business."

"Anything that affects the condition of my patient is my business," she retorted.

He squeezed his jaw, clearly fighting his own temper. She wondered what made him so angry, what he was hiding. She wished it could be as he said—none of her business. Unfortunately, it was.

"Carrie's had a rough life," he said grudgingly. "We were raised in an orphanage, and if she seems scared sometimes, it's because her whole life's been scary."

She felt an unexpected thickness in her throat. Life had clearly been brutal to Carrie. "I see. I'm sure the orphanage was awful for you both."

"Awful," he echoed, putting a wry twist on the word. "I guess you could say that. All right, Doc. You ready to help with the mast?"

Surprised, she followed him up on deck. He'd put his outburst behind him. It was, she realized, the boat that seemed to save him. He forgot everything else when he worked on it.

"Here." He tossed her a line. "Grab onto that. If I did this right, the top section should drop into place." He struggled for several moments with his end, breaking out in a sweat and cursing. He paused to peel off his plaid shirt and fling it aside. Leah stared, caught herself doing so, then forced her attention to the task at hand.

As the tall fir topmast responded to the ropes and pulleys, she caught her breath. Jackson experimented with hoisting the sails, and with an unexpected thrill, she took heady satisfaction in the majestic loft of the canvas. She felt a curious tightening inside her, a sort of breath-held anticipation. Then, when the sail unfurled against the sky, the sensation uncoiled with a sudden warmth that made her part her lips to utter an involuntary sound of pleasure. How had she missed the excitement of seafaring when she lived right at the edge of it?

Shading her eyes, she admitted the answer. She missed everything important because she was an outsider. It took a stranger on the run to show her the wonders right under her nose.

She lowered her hand to find him eyeing her curiously. The sun glinted off the sheen of sweat on his shoulders.

"Is something wrong, Mr. Underhill?"

"You liked that, didn't you?"

"Why, yes, as a matter of fact, I did find it... diverting."

"I mean you really liked that."

"Indeed. But how can you tell?"

He briefly touched the back of his hand to her cheek. "You look like a woman who just made love."

"Oh, for heaven's sake." She turned her back on him. She shouldn't be here, shouldn't be doing this, feeling this.

Yet her fascination with him grew each moment, became harder to cope with each day. Jackson T. Underhill was at once mysterious and seductive, shadowed by the weary indifference of a rootless drifter. She should keep a cool distance from him. Should keep her mind on his wife. Instead, she caught herself thinking forbidden thoughts, remembering dreams she had abandoned years ago, then despising herself for doing so.

"You say you did business with this Jack Tower?" Joel Santana spread the Wanted poster on the shop counter. With quick, furtive movements, the chemist swept the poster out of sight, glancing around to be sure the other customers hadn't seen it.

Ratlike, his nose twitched. "I never said that, Marshal."

Joel rested his elbow on the counter as a great wave of weariness overcame him. He'd tracked Tower across Texas and into New Mexico where the Santa Fe wind blasted a man's face with red dust during the day and chilled him to the marrow at night. "Look, mister, if I say you said it, than you damned sure did say it."

"But—"

"I don't like your kind." He glanced over his shoulder at the Indian sleeping on the boardwalk outside. "I don't like the stuff you sell."

The rat nose narrowed haughtily. "I assure you, my medicines are all of the highest—"

"Horseshit. I'm not real fond of selling folks stuff that makes them stupid, keeps them coming back for more." Squinting, Santana scanned the shelves behind the counter. Peyote, powdered psilocybe, laudanum, morphine crystals and Lord knew what else. Jail cells without bars, as far as Santana was concerned. They robbed a person of freedom, dignity and eventually life.

Reaching past the chemist's shoulder, he knocked over a stoppered bottle. The glass shattered, and a pungent herbal smell tainted the air. "Oops," he said. "I'm just a bull in a lady's parlor."

"Hey, what the—"

"Just trying to read this here label." Joel's hand shoved another bottle off the shelf. "Damn! I don't know what's got me so clumsy all of a sudden."

A matron who had been perusing an array of sleeping powders scuttled out the door.

"Now, how about this one?" Joel stretched his arm toward the shelf.

The chemist stepped back, spreading his arms, trying to protect his wares. "All right," he snapped. "I sold him something!"

Santana lowered his arm. His shoulder burned, the bursitis kicking in. Too damned many cold nights under the stars, he thought. The quicker he found Jack Tower, the sooner he could retire. A place where the weather was mild, the scenery pretty. Find a woman who'd put up with an old saddle bum's foibles.... Before his mind wandered too far, he stuck his thumb into his gun belt and regarded the chemist, waiting.

"He got me up in the middle of the night," the man said. "Woke me right out of a sound sleep."

Joel clucked in mock sympathy. "So what'd he want?"

"I couldn't even hear him at first. The woman he was with—his wife or whatever—was screaming hysterically."

Joel's blood chilled. Even though he already knew the answer, he took out the photograph the sheriff of Rising Star had given him. "This woman?"

"Yeah. Yeah, that's her."

"And what'd you sell them?"

"A tin of tobacco, Underhill Fancy Shred, I think... and a whole case of this." The chemist brought down a box of patented medicine called A Pennysworth of Peace. The label made outlandish claims of its restorative powers. The user could count on everything from a good night's sleep and regular bowel movements to perfect spiritual contentment. Joel cracked open the blue bottle and sniffed. A mixture of low-grade corn whiskey, molasses and opium, he judged.

The chill in his blood moved into his heart. Jack Tower didn't know about Caroline Willis. Didn't know what she'd done in the past, what she was capable of.

But Joel Santana knew.

He had first heard of Caroline a few years earlier in the aftermath of a fatal fire in New Orleans. One of the more notorious French Quarter cribs had burned to the ground. The victim had been a local preacher who, it turned out, had a taste for dangerous games. At the time of the fire, he'd been dressed in leather chaps and nothing else. He'd been spread-eagled and bound to the bed with leg irons. And there, on a sweltering July night, he'd come to understand the true meaning of burning in hell.

The preacher had been Caroline's client.

"Where'd they go after they left your shop?" Joel asked the chemist.

"Took the train straight out of town, swear to God. That's all I can tell you," the chemist said, clearly ready for the interview to be over. "Honest to Pete, that's all."

Joel lifted his hand to the brim of his hat. The chemist cringed, probably anticipating more breakage. "Mister, you're a pretty nervous fellow," Santana said. Spurs clinking, he walked to the door and cast an eye at the rows of potions. "You ought to take something for it."

Troubled and restless, Jackson sat on the front porch of the big house and stared up at the night sky. He'd been studying the stars because a good skipper used them to navigate by. He took out a tin of tobacco, rolled a smoke, and lit up, watching the lazy strands of gray mist weave in and out of the moonlight. He'd tried to interest Carrie in astronomy, showing her the drawings in the tattered book he'd found on board, but Carrie wasn't interested in much lately.

A small, forbidden whisper passed through his mind. *Leah Mundy would be interested.*

He shouldn't be thinking about her, not in that way, yet he felt his gaze stray to the wing of the house where her surgery was.

A light burned in the window.

He gripped the arms of the rocking chair, willing himself to stay put. But part of him wanted to go, wanted to see her, to find out why she was sleepless, too. He moved quietly across the lawn, craning his neck to see into the lighted window. What the devil was she doing up so late?

Leah held a slim glass tube up to the gaslight. Crystals formed high on the tube; lower down she discerned a layer of inert substances. Her titration had worked this time even though it was a tricky business. She was lucky she'd gotten some results at last, for the bottle of Carrie's tonic was almost empty.

Using a sterile rod, she extracted some of the crystalline substance. Now she knew for certain, but the knowledge didn't ease her mind. She had to figure out a way to tell Jackson what she'd discovered.

# *Four*

~~~⚬⚭~~~

"Mr. Underhill, if you hold that cup any tighter, you'll break it," Leah Mundy said.

Jackson glanced down at his hand, saw that the knuckles had gone white. He stood in the doorway of the parlor, watching Carrie, and he hadn't heard Leah approach him. He forced his grip to relax and turned his attention back to the parlor.

Two weeks after Carrie's illness—he'd trained himself not to think of it as a miscarriage—she appeared to be recovered. Surely she was feeling much better, for she had taken to holding court each afternoon in the parlor of the boardinghouse.

Holding court was about the only way he could describe it. She liked to put on her prettiest dresses—she had a lot of them and wanted a lot more—and sit by the window on an old-fashioned fringed chaise and talk with the people who lived at the boardinghouse.

Jackson didn't know the folks too well, but they all took a shine to Carrie. People generally did. She was as pretty as the springtime, and when she was in a talkative state, people found her entertaining. Her rapt audience consisted of Aunt Leafy, who was no one's aunt, but an avid student of everyone's private affairs; Battle Douglas, a shrinking man terrified of his own shadow; Zeke Pomfrit, the aging vigilante and miner who made Jackson nervous; and Adam Armstrong, a timber baron who was said to be fabulously wealthy. He was a guest while his steam-powered yacht, *La Tache,* was being refitted at the harbor.

Unlike Jackson, Armstrong didn't trouble himself to do the work, but had hired a local shipwright to tinker with the engine and the wood-and-steel hull. Meanwhile, Adam spent his days wrestling with the unreliable telegraph at the post office, playing cards with the other boarders, or flirting with the girls at Nellie Morse's dress shop in town.

Jackson knew the type—fat on family money and not real interested in breaking a sweat over anything. He had the polished smoothness that seemed to be bred in the bones of men born to wealth and privilege. It was as if his family money and power had been applied to him like the clear oil varnish applied to a ship's woodwork. Armstrong's hair, lacquered by bay rum, tumbled down over his forehead in an apparently casual way, but he'd probably spent an hour getting it that way.

Jackson shifted his gaze away from Adam Armstrong. The man didn't interest him. There was nothing wrong with the fellow—except his unrelenting charm.

At the center of them all, wearing an organdy gown she'd begged Jackson to buy in San Francisco, Carrie sat like a queen amid her subjects. Her eyes shone, her cheeks were flushed, and her voice had a piping, animated quality as she chattered of everything and of nothing at all.

"...I had the most beautiful gown—it was tea rose

moiré silk. And there was a woman who brought her little dog right into Antoine's."

"Imagine that," Armstrong murmured politely with a smile Jackson wanted to pound off his face.

"I believe it was in New Orleans that I first heard 'The Streets of Cairo,'" Carrie went on. "Yes, as a matter of fact, it was New Orleans, at the Wildcat Club. The Cairo dance was so scandalous, but it couldn't have been too evil, because my partner that night was a preacher. They had the most marvelous oysters there...."

New Orleans.

That was where Jackson had picked up her trail at last. Guided only by instinct and the vague recollections of a prostitute, he had followed her to Texas. And there, in the sleepy, dusty town of Rising Star, he had finally found her.

The memory still made him wince. He had barely recognized her in her dance-hall gown, spun-gold hair a brassy color, Cupid's-bow lips an angry smear of carmine. She had been standing outside a saloon, but when he greeted her, she'd pretended not to hear. She went inside and took a seat with the Devlin gang, laughing as they passed her around their table in the dim, windowless saloon.

But later that night, the laughter had stopped.

And Jackson had found himself staring across a blood-spattered room at Carrie. Between them lay the lifeless body of the mayor of Rising Star.

A door slammed.

Jackson wasn't sure why, but he vividly recalled the sound of that slamming door in the hallway behind him. The sharp noise punctuated a moment so terrible that even now he crushed his eyes shut, trying not to remember.

But he did remember. The smell of blood and spent gunpowder. The echo of a door thudding shut. The rasp of Carrie's breathing. Her stark need. Her voice as she said one word: "Jackson."

Up until that moment, he hadn't been certain she recognized him. But the minute she said his name, he knew he had no choice. He'd grabbed her hand and started running.

Ah, Carrie, he thought, willing himself to relax. Everything was so difficult with her. So dramatic, so unpredictable.

"She's doing better," he whispered to Leah, loath to interrupt Carrie's diverting chatter.

"She's certainly keeping the boarders entertained. Are you going to join them?"

"Can't. I've got more work to do on the boat. Every time I make a repair, something else goes wrong. I'm going to have to make a trip to Seattle or Port Townsend for the money. If I play my cards right." He winked at her. "Quit giving me that look."

"What look?"

"The 'you're pond scum' look. You do it all the time, Doc."

"No. No, I don't."

"So what's twisting your pantaloons today?"

"Mr. Underhill." She spoke quietly and brought her fingers to rest lightly on his arm. She had graceful, competent hands that bore the calluses of hard work. "May I speak to you in private?"

He felt a cold lick of warning somewhere deep in his chest. "Yeah. Sure." He nodded in Carrie's direction to excuse himself, but she took no notice as she laughed at some remark Armstrong made, then launched into a new tale of adventure, claiming with certainty that she had danced with the Vice President. Anything but the truth, Carrie love, he thought. Anything but the truth.

"That Leah Mundy!" Carrie's voice followed them out into the foyer. "Plain as a pigeon feather in that old-fashioned dress, isn't she?"

He hoped Leah hadn't heard. One glance at her tight mouth and the proud set of her chin told him she had. "She didn't mean anything," he said.

"No offense taken."

They went through the foyer and out onto the porch. Like the ribs of a whale's skeleton, a white railing grandly wrapped itself around the front and sides of the boardinghouse. In the distance, down the expanse of a lush, sloping lawn, the waters of Puget Sound sparkled in the late-afternoon light.

This was a place he had thought existed only in dreams. A gleaming white house on a hill, distant islands scattered like emeralds on a sapphire sea, snow-covered mountains against a hard blue sky.

He leaned against an ivory pillar and studied Leah Mundy. She wasn't a beauty, not in the eye-popping way Carrie was, yet in Leah's even features and deep brown eyes dwelt a calm serenity that he liked. Liked a lot. He caught himself thinking of the day he'd hoisted the sails on his boat. She had looked rapt. Enchanted. The way a woman should look when a man made love to her... Jesus. He had no call to be letting himself think about a woman like Leah Mundy.

"Mr. Underhill," she said.

He liked her voice, too. Low and soft. Carrie, on the other hand, was given to long, brooding silences and even longer recitations of rapid, babbling speech that said nothing.

Jackson shook himself. There was no reason for him

to be standing here like a hayseed at a barn dance, drawing comparisons between women.

"I wanted to speak to you about your wife," Leah continued.

"She's doing a lot better, Doc. I guess I owe you—"

"That's not what I want to discuss." Leah smoothed her hands down her sides and walked slowly to the porch rail. "In my estimation, she has recovered from the miscarriage."

When should he tell Leah the truth about the baby? he wondered. Never, came the answer.

"I do believe," Leah went on, "that perhaps the miscarriage was secondary to another condition."

Damn, but this woman was cautious. She was like a soldier picking a path through a minefield, each tentative inch forward hard-won and followed by a long hesitation.

"Truth to tell," he prompted, "she seems better than she's been in a long time."

Leah turned, her hands still holding the rail. In addition to the dress Carrie had made fun of earlier, she wore a clean white apron. Jackson noticed that her breasts were high and full, her waist narrow. And he caught himself remembering the time he'd held her, helping her down into the boat. No corset. By God, the woman didn't wear a corset.

"Mr. Underhill," she said, "what I'm trying to say is that I fear your wife suffers from...another affliction."

Her voice stayed calm in that low, serene way she had, so at first the words didn't sink in. He repeated them. "Another affliction." Spoken by his own tongue, he felt each one like a hammer blow. And for some reason he couldn't name, he wasn't surprised. The news wasn't unexpected. "What the hell's that supposed to mean?"

Leah's glance flickered to the door, then back to Jackson. "Please understand, I have very little experience with this sort of thing—not nearly as much as I'd like—but the symptoms are quite clear to me."

"Just say it, Doc, for Christ's sake." Apprehension buzzed through him, unpleasant, inescapable.

"I quite believe your wife is an addict."

"An addict."

"Yes."

"You mean like an ether drinker? An opium smoker?"

"Yes," she said again. "But not ether. Opium. Morphine, to be precise."

Jackson gave a bark of laughter and sagged in relief against the pillar. "Doc, you may not have much experience with this, but I've seen a few addicts in my time. Seen them puking in alleyways and begging at train depots, seen them being hauled off to jail now and then." He pictured the sallow skin, the bleary eyes, the air of complete hopelessness. "Carrie's no addict."

"I'm sorry to disagree with you, sir, but she is indeed." Ah, that voice. It was starting to get to him. "Carrie takes her elixir in copious amounts several times a day, doesn't she?"

Jackson shrugged. "The dark stuff in the blue bottle? It's mainly molasses, near as I can tell."

"It contains a great deal of morphine, which is a derivative of opium. I took the liberty of analyzing the contents. I wrote to the manufacturer and finally received confirmation of my findings."

The cold buzz intensified, freezing his limbs, clamoring in his ears. He remembered seeing the light on in Leah's surgery. She'd been hard at work with her beakers and bottles and a strange blue flame, open books strewn across a table.

"I thought the tonic helped her."

"It gave her the illusion of feeling better. But she's become a slave to it."

He shuddered, thinking of all the times he'd brought the bottle to her. "So how bad is this stuff?"

"Morphine is a powerful narcotic, and it's not always bad. I administer it to patients who are suffering unbearable pain from injury or grave illness. But when a person takes too much, and does so repeatedly, the result is addiction. Unfortunately, medical texts—even recent ones—rarely mention the potential hazards of addiction. Some even advocate opiates as a way to maintain a proper equilibrium or to cure the craving for liquor. But most modern physicians believe it's a destructive substance."

She made him feel ignorant and helpless. Worse, she made him feel he'd failed Carrie, that he'd been blind to what ailed her. He wanted to lash out, to hit something. He forced himself to stand there calmly. "You're sure about this addiction?"

"I am. Tell me, has she ever run out, ever gone without for any length of time at all?"

"Hell, yes, she has, and she does just fine—" Jackson broke off. This woman was Carrie's physician. Like it or not, he had to be honest with her. He stared at the floor of the porch. The wood planks were weathered and gray with age. "I don't guess she's ever far from a bottle of Pennysworth." Cracking his knuckles, he dragged his gaze up to Leah's eyes, those calm brown eyes. "So what's it mean, Doc?"

"An addict's dependency will commonly increase until she thinks of nothing else. Eventually, she could suffer from malnutrition, dementia and other ailments." Her unsmiling face was stark with honesty. "Mr. Underhill, it's very dangerous to let her continue taking this substance. We must set her on the road to recovery without delay."

"Yeah, all right," he agreed. But the ominous hum inside him wouldn't subside. He had to have faith in Leah's competence. He had to believe she knew what was right. "You do that, Doc."

She pushed away from the rail and looked out to sea. The sunlight shimmered like copper coins on the Sound, and a fresh breeze, redolent of the coming summer, skimmed across the surface.

Just then, Adam Armstrong came around the corner of the house, Carrie holding one of his arms, Aunt Leafy the other. The ladies looked petite and doll-like in contrast to their towering companion. Carrie waved and blew a kiss in Jackson's direction; then they continued down the sloping yard to a giant chestnut tree with a bench swing suspended from a stout branch.

His gestures smooth and gallant, Armstrong seated the ladies in the swing and gave them a gentle push. Jackson made sure Leah was watching them. "You're sure she's that sick," he said.

"I'm afraid so. I realize that at times like this, she seems as charming and healthy as any young woman. But what would happen if she ran out of medicine?"

He had a flash of memory—a night in Santa Fe when Carrie had run out of her tonic. She'd thrown a screaming fit, then retreated to her bed with cold chills and a look in her eyes that scared him. He remembered rousing the owner of the chemist's shop in the middle of the night just to get more. After that, he made sure she never ran out of the stuff.

"She doesn't like to be without her medicine," he said.

"I've never treated an addict before. From my reading

and correspondence, I understand it's a difficult and painful treatment, and the disease is not always curable.'' She turned to him, cleared her throat nervously. "I know that's not what you wanted to hear from me and..."

"And?" he prompted, irritation hardening his tone. "What else?"

She regarded him steadily, her gaze impenetrable, infuriatingly so. "She absolutely must not conceive a child while she's in this state."

If everything hadn't been so goddamned awful, Jackson would have laughed. If only she knew. "We talked about this before," he snapped. "I told you that wasn't going to be a concern."

He meant it. This was one thing he could state with perfect certainty. One of the few things. In truth, he had no clear vision of what his future with Carrie would be. He'd never thought beyond the next horizon. But he did know he wouldn't put her in danger of conceiving a baby.

"Yes...well, I just wanted to make certain. It's very important. The baby she lost—" She broke off, biting her lip.

Jackson's irritation intensified. "Just what the hell are you saying?"

"Infants born to addicted mothers often have problems."

He wanted to clap his hand over her mouth, beg her to say no more. He didn't want to hear it, didn't want to know that somewhere there was a child who would never be, never feel the wind in his face or build a sand castle or know a father's love....

"There's very little documentation," Leah went on, nervous but relentless. "The narcotic—"

"I get the idea." He didn't want to hear any more. Sweat ran down his temples as the unthinkable occurred to him. "Oh, Christ. Tell me this, Doc. Did I cause it? By giving Carrie her medicine, did I make it happen?"

Her brown eyes softened. "Her addiction made it happen. You cannot blame yourself. An addict will find a way to her medicine regardless. The craving is that strong."

Feeling sick, he tugged open the top button of his collar. "Then cure her addiction. Do what you have to do."

"I hope you'll remember that you said that."

"What's that supposed to mean?"

"What I have to do is deprive Carrie of her medicine altogether. She'll beg for it, Mr. Underhill. She'll be ill—truly physically ill—without it." She clasped her hands together nervously. "We must help her, because if she continues this way, by my estimation she could become beyond redemption."

"What do you mean, beyond redemption?" God, he couldn't handle that. His whole life had been about redeeming Carrie, keeping her safe.

"She won't be Carrie anymore," Leah said. "Just some creature who is a slave to the drug. I'm sorry to be blunt, but—"

"Then fix her," Jackson lashed out, noting with perverse satisfaction that he made her flinch. Leah, with her perfect calm and her polished shoes and her starched white apron. "You're the goddamned doctor. You heal her."

Leah knew, from the moment she told Jackson Underhill that his wife was a morphine addict, that life for all in the boardinghouse would become a living hell. But even in her wildest imaginings, she had not anticipated *this*.

For the fourth night in a row, unearthly yowls issued

from the room at the top of the stairs. Leah hauled herself out of bed, stuffed her feet into slippers, and shrugged on her robe as she hastened up to Carrie's room.

Zeke Pomfrit stood in the hall, a candle flame illuminating his cranky expression and his bent mustache. "Miss Mundy," he said, "this racket has gone on long enough. If it continues—"

"I'm sorry, I know this illness is difficult for everyone in the house."

"Difficult! Why—"

"We'll discuss it in the morning," Leah said curtly. "I have a patient to see." She knocked at the door to Carrie's room, though she knew her knock wouldn't be heard. Then she stepped inside.

Carrie sat in the middle of the bed, her alabaster throat taut as she screamed. Jackson had his arms around her, pinning her wrists to her sides. His face was pale, his mouth grim, his eyes dark with concern.

"Carrie." Leah focused completely on her patient. "Carrie, look at me. Carrie." She took her face between her hands.

"Don't you touch me!" Carrie threw off Leah's hands. "Jackson, get her away! She's trying to kill me! She knows I'll die without my medicine. I'll die. Is that what you want, Jackson? For me to die?" She ran out of breath and started to shake.

"Ah, honey, you know that's not what I want. It's not what anybody wants." Jackson's voice was amazingly gentle as he spoke into Carrie's ear. She clutched at the front of his shirt, her fists twisting into the fabric.

Leah stepped back, watching them. There was a discernable pattern to these episodes. Carrie raged madly for a while; then she subsided. But tonight she seemed different. More desperate. More determined. More filled with hate as she glared at Leah. She resembled a small child hanging on to Jackson for dear life. But the eyes she raised to Leah were anything but childlike.

"You want Jackson, don't you?" she said.

Leah was so startled that she could only say, "What?" Jackson spoke at the same time. "What?"

"You want Jackson. Women always do. They always have. But you want him so much you'll kill me in order to have him."

Leah's cheeks flamed. She couldn't help herself; she thought of that day on the boat when his touch had almost felt like an embrace. She remembered his heat, the timbre of his voice close to her ear, remembered the way the ache of loneliness seemed less fierce when she was with him. She struggled to force the thought from her mind.

"I am your doctor," she said. "I have no interest in your husband beyond the interest I have in you as a patient."

"Liar." Carrie began to rock back and forth. "Liar, liar, liar." Sweat broke out on her ashen brow, and she shivered, still clinging to Jackson. "Please, please, please get me my tonic. Just a tiny drink, Jackson. Just one little swallow. I'll be all better after that. I promise you. All better. Then everyone can go to sleep." She sounded so pitiful. Her request seemed so reasonable.

He glanced up at Leah. It was the look she expected, the look she dreaded. He wanted to give in to Carrie.

"She's in hell," he said in a low voice. "Where's the harm in a spoonful? One single spoonful. Just enough to calm her down so she can sleep." He nodded meaningfully toward the outer hall. "So we all can sleep."

Carrie stopped rocking. She held her breath, waiting.

"No, Mr. Underhill." Leah turned to meet the burning eyes of her patient. "Carrie, if you take the tonic now, you'll feel better for a very short time. But then you'll only have to start this treatment all over again."

"I never asked for your damned-to-hell treatment in the first place!" Carrie clawed at the bedclothes. "You're killing me! Jackson, oh, Jackson, please. Don't let her kill me. I'm so sick. It hurts so much."

"Honey, Dr. Mundy says you have to get it all out of your system."

"You promised." Accusation glowed in her eyes. "Way back at St. I's you promised to protect me."

"I know, Carrie, but—"

"You're breaking your promise, Jackson."

Leah could see the battle in his eyes. She understood that he was a man who didn't make promises lightly, didn't break them willingly.

He snarled at her. "Your treatment is worse than the sickness."

"Don't let yourself believe that, Mr. Underhill."

"Not one thing you've done is working. Why the hell should I trust you? All we've done is torture her. For the love of God, let her have just a little."

"One spoonful will produce a false calm. Then the craving will come back, but stronger," Leah said, "harder to fight."

"She hates me," Carrie wailed. "She hates me and wants to do away with me." She caressed her husband's shoulders, her manner suddenly fawning. "Get the medicine, Jackson. Or get the sort the doctor keeps for herself. I know where she puts it. I've seen where she puts it. There's a locked cabinet in the office. She let me see it once to torment me. Get it, Jackson. Please!"

Leah was shocked that Carrie knew of the medical locker in the surgery. She'd never shown it to her. But according to the literature, addicts were unfailingly sly and clever in discovering ways to find their narcotics.

"Hush, honey." Jackson's big hand cradled her head, fingers threading into her silky hair. Carrie couldn't see his face, but Leah could. She saw the lines of strain fanning out from his eyes and mouth, the bleak color of sleeplessness under his eyes, the twist of agony on his lips as he said, "It'll be all right. Hush... Think of something else, Carrie. Think of the place we always talk about."

"Paradise," she whispered, her hands clenching and unclenching. "Tell me about it again, Jackson. Tell me about paradise."

"Warm breezes," he whispered in her ear, "waterfalls and beaches with sand like white sugar, all the sweet oranges you can eat. Music and dancing every night..."

"I'd like that." Carrie sighed against his chest. "The warm breezes and the music."

Leah felt a lump in her throat. They were both in such pain, these two, and it was a pain only time and abstinence would heal. She so wanted to help them. Then a terrible inner voice whispered the truth in her ear: She wanted this sort of devotion for herself. She wanted to matter to someone as much as Carrie mattered to Jackson.

When he finished the story, Carrie lifted her face to his. Leah looked away, not wanting to intrude on the private moment. But they didn't kiss.

"Jackson," said Carrie, "We'll never find that place if you keep my medicine from me."

The story hadn't scratched the surface of her craving after all. Disappointed—even more for Jackson than for herself—Leah said, "You must be strong. Each moment you pass without the morphine is a moment closer to the time you no longer need it."

Carrie reared back from Jackson's embrace. "Get out!" She picked up a drinking glass and hurled it at Leah. "Get out of this room. I don't want to see you anymore. I wish you'd burn in hell. Get out! Get out!"

Leah ducked as the glass flew past her and shattered on the floor. She almost flinched at the accusation she saw in Jackson's eyes. He thought she was hurting his wife. He hated her for it. She shouldn't care, but she did.

*You want Jackson. Women always do.*

Carrie's words haunted her as she trudged back to her room to lie sleepless in the dark until the screaming stopped.

Once Carrie was quiet, Jackson stole out onto the front porch to have a smoke and try to escape the echo of her screams in his ears. He sat on the steps, letting the night enclose him, losing himself in the chorus of chirping frogs and the scent of the sea. Christ, when would this be over?

He heard a noise behind him. Leah pushed open the door. Unaware of Jackson's presence, she came out, stretched, then leaned against the wall, looking dead weary. "God, I can't do this alone," she whispered to the stars.

Jackson tossed away his smoke. "You don't have to."

"Oh!" She pressed her hand to her chest. "Mr. Underhill. I didn't see you there."

"You're not doing this alone," he said, keeping his voice low. "I'm trying to keep up with all the things you said—encourage her, get her mind on other things. But sometimes nothing works."

"I know," she said in a small voice. "And I do so want something to work. It's...what I am. What I'm about. Making things better. When I fail..." Her voice trailed off into a sigh. She looked small and alone to him just then. Not helpless, but like someone in pain. Someone he wanted to know better.

He patted the step beside him. "Sit down, Doc."

She hesitated, then joined him, leaning against the newel post and facing him. "It's hard for me to sleep after these episodes."

"Me, too."

"I shouldn't complain to you. It's you who bears the brunt of her fury."

"She hates me," he said, feeling oddly objective about the fact.

"No," Leah said quickly. "The hunger for the drug makes her say things the real Carrie would never say."

Jackson recalled Carrie's wild accusation: *You want Jackson. Women always do.* It would be funny if it wasn't so outlandish. All Leah Mundy wanted from him was— what *did* she want? When was the last time anyone had asked her?

Her shoulders looked tense. He thought about offering to rub them and soothe her burning muscles, but he talked himself out of it. Touching this woman wouldn't be right—because it wouldn't just be an impersonal touch.

"Is there a story behind that tattoo?" she asked, leaning toward him.

He angled his forearm so the moonlight illuminated the tattoo. "It's a mermaid."

"How…interesting."

"I thought so at the time. But it was a long time ago." He laughed without humor. The whaler had made port at Rio de Janeiro, and he'd lost his heart to a soft-eyed girl called Dolores. But as it turned out, his heart was worth only three days of her time. "A present from a lady to a stupid young man."

"Now that truly is interesting—"

"Dr. Mundy!" A boy on a horse galloped up the drive.

Driven by instinct, Jackson jumped to his feet, his hand going for the phantom gun he wasn't wearing.

"It's Captain Hathaway's boy," Leah said.

"We need you to come," the lad said, panting in tandem with his horse.

Leah got up. "Mr. Underhill?"

"Me? You want me to come?"

"I can always use an extra pair of hands."

The next evening, Leah came down from her room wearing her burgundy chambray suit with a cream-colored polonaise trailing down the back of the wide-pleated skirt. A pair of lace gloves and a small hat completed the outfit. She'd taken special care to dress, for Mr. Armstrong had invited her to the Good Temperance Hall to look at the moving pictures projected by Professor Newbery's Magic Lantern.

She felt a pleasant flutter of anticipation in her chest. It was past time she engaged in social diversions.

Hearing light ripples of female laughter, she stepped into the parlor. Adam waited in the wing chair by the hearth while Carrie Underhill and Aunt Leafy peered into the ornate wire cage of the old lady's pet canary.

"He's very charming," Carrie said, waggling a finger into the cage.

She was having a good day, Leah saw with relief. No temper tantrum, no sly attempt to get someone to give her the tonic, no furtive trip to Puget Race's Drugstore in town. "Carlos is my only comfort since Ambrose passed," Aunt Leafy said wistfully. "But what a mess he makes in his cage."

Carrie handed her a stack of papers. "Here, take these for the lining. I'm finished with them."

To Leah's knowledge, Carrie had never taken an interest in reading the *Island County Sun* or any other papers. She wondered what she was doing with them.

"You look lovely," Adam said, tearing his gaze from Carrie and crossing the room to bow in courtly fashion over Leah's gloved hand.

"Why, Dr. Mundy, we didn't see you come in. What a charming frock," Carrie said. "I haven't seen that style in at least ten years. I really think it should be revived."

"You put a fresh face on it," Adam said gallantly.

"Thank you," Leah murmured. "Shall we go?"

"Where are you going?" Carrie asked with a sharpness that took Leah aback. Dear God, was Carrie jealous?

Before Leah could answer, Jackson arrived, sweaty and sunburned from working on the boat. "Who's going where?"

Leah laughed at the absurdity of the moment. "Honestly, we are not running off to plot a revolution. Adam and I are going to the magic-lantern show."

"Have a good time," Aunt Leafy said vaguely, pushing a sunflower seed at the canary.

"We will indeed, Mrs. Leafington," Adam said. He held the front door for Leah. As she stepped past him, she felt the heat of Jackson's glare and made herself ignore it. She repeated to herself for the hundredth time that Adam Armstrong was as handsome a man as she'd ever seen. He was polite and well-to-do. She should be pleased by his attention.

But as they walked down the lane toward the red-painted Temperance Hall, all she could think about was Jackson and the thunderous look on his face when he'd realized she and Adam were stepping out together.

When they reached the lodge on the brow of the hill above the harbor, Adam stopped in the darkening yard. With the lightest of touches, he lifted her chin so that she was looking at him. "This isn't going to work, is it?"

Color stung her cheeks. "The lantern? But I've heard it's most interesting—"

"I'm not speaking of the lantern, but of us," Adam said.

Her cheeks burned hotter. "I'm afraid I don't know what you mean."

"Sure you do, Leah. We should make a marvelous couple, you and I. But we don't, because it's not there."

"'It'?"

"The attraction. The spark that should be there, but isn't."

She sent him a rueful smile, grateful for his understanding. "Mr. Armstrong, I can explain the anatomy of the human heart. But I certainly can't explain how it governs the emotions."

"No one can, Leah," he said with weary authority. "It makes fools of the best of us."

*16 May 1894*

My dear Penelope,

I wish to thank you most profusely for the journals and papers you sent regarding addictions. I have spent the past several nights wide-awake, poring over the new materials. Alas, there is no miracle cure. I knew there would not be, but still I dared to hope that new research would yield a way to ease this journey for my poor patient.

Each hour is a battle. The boarders at my house

are practically in revolt, but I know not what else to do. My patient, Mrs. U——, makes wild accusations during her fits of rage. Other times, she is cajoling, much like a child teasing for a sweet. But her goal is always the same. Her goal is to entice someone to get more of her tonic—that vile fluid sold by quacks—and give it to her so she can sink back into a drugged oblivion.

However, I am delighted to report that my treatment, crude and ruthless as it is, seems to be having some effect. The raging tantrums are less frequent, the nights a bit more peaceful. Each day, it seems, is slightly easier than the previous one, thank God. Some days I dare to hope that we are reaching the end of this difficult journey.

She would have succumbed to her cravings long ago if not for Mr. U——. He is the most devoted of husbands, Penny. I have seen him sit with her for hours without moving. Sometimes he tells her stories, even sings to her. She never thanks him. There are times I am given to wonder—

Leah set down her pen. What in heaven's name was she doing? Why did she think so long and hard of Jackson Underhill? It was fatigue, she told herself. Sheer and utter fatigue, because a fortnight had passed in which she had not slept a single night through. But as she'd said to Penny Lake, things were slowly improving. She glanced down at the calf-bound journal on the desk. She had to check on Captain Hathaway, whose appendix attack had been acute. At the captain's residence, Jackson had helped move furniture, drape tables, and hang lanterns to turn the kitchen into an operating theater. She'd been glad for his help, and he'd seemed grateful for the distraction. She must remember to thank him.

Through the window, she could see Adam Armstrong with Carrie. Together they walked up from the bathhouse. Carrie was gowned in a pretty lavender gabardine shirt-waist, her golden hair shining and swept up in the back, and she seemed animated, chattering away while her companion listened with rapt attention.

Leah didn't know much about Adam. He had good manners and plenty of money, which made him the ideal boarder. In truth, his attentiveness to Carrie seemed to have a beneficial effect. Still, something about their un-expected friendship bothered Leah. She wondered if it bothered Jackson. Surely Adam had heard the screams at night. Yet he was as attentive as a courting swain.

A beautiful face and a charming manner were worth more, Leah realized, than she wished them to be.

She planted her elbows on the desk blotter, closed her eyes, and massaged her throbbing temples. There were times when her calling as a doctor took so much out of her that she was certain she had no more to give. And yet she did give. It seemed her well was never dry. She wouldn't allow it to be. She was too disciplined to allow it. Too stubborn.

"I suspect that headache is my doing," said a soft voice.

Leah opened her eyes and looked up in surprise. In the doorway of the office stood Carrie, a tentative smile wavering on her face. Adam was nowhere in sight.

"Carrie dear. I saw you come in from the yard."

"The bathhouse is a godsend. And the garden is just beautiful."

Leah hastened to her feet as a cautious hope rose inside her. "Look at you. How lovely you are."

"Thank you. I thought it was time I resigned myself to being well."

Leah's heart leaped in exultation. "Oh, Carrie. I'm so very pleased for you." She took the younger woman's hands. Carrie's fingers felt slightly clammy, but she clasped Leah's hands with a friendly squeeze.

She seemed better, truly better, and even as Leah's heart exulted, she felt an evil stab of dismay. Once Carrie was better and the boat repaired, there would be no reason for Jackson to stay.

"I came to thank you." Carrie went to the window and looked out. "All along, I knew in my heart you were doing what was best for me. The things I said, screamed at you... I—I didn't mean them, Leah." She cleared her throat. "May I call you Leah?"

"Of course. And I know you didn't mean those things. It was the craving that made you speak so."

"Yes. Yes. Leah, can you forgive me?"

"There's nothing to forgive. You've done your act of contrition. I've seen how hard it's been. You and your husband—"

"My husband." Carrie gave a blithe laugh, fingering the tasseled drapery pull as she gazed out across the yard at the harbor. "All Jackson thinks of is that boat of his. We have nothing in common."

*But what about the baby?* The question burned in Leah's mind. She choked it back, telling herself that it wasn't her place to sit in judgment of a patient. "He's working hard on the repairs."

"Adam's boat isn't a wreck. His boat is ready for a cruise," Carrie said.

"Is it?" Leah asked, growing more confused by the moment. "I believe Davy Morgan mentioned a bad carbon buildup in the engine." She eyed Carrie closely, watched for the dilated eyes, the agitated movements of someone under the influence. But Carrie appeared calm and rational, perfectly in control.

"Jackson said he's going to take the steamer to Seattle soon. He's got to earn more money. He's good at that. He's always been good at that."

"I see." Leah didn't, but she had no idea what to say.

"Adam has money. Lots of money." Carrie sighed with contentment.

Adam Armstrong was one of the wealthiest men in the islands. A woman like Carrie, who seemed to crave fine things, would naturally be impressed by him.

"I'd be safe with Adam," Carrie murmured, watching out the window. In the distance, a side-wheeler nosed into the harbor. A steam whistle pierced the air.

"Your husband seems devoted to keeping you safe," Leah said. She wondered if Carrie recalled all the nights he'd sat up with her, holding her and murmuring into her ear.

Carrie rubbed her hands up and down her arms, hugging herself. "He wants adventure. He wants to go sailing off into the sunset. I'll never understand him. Never." She turned, a dazzling smile on her face. "But that is no concern of yours. You've done more than enough, Leah. I shall always be in your debt."

# Five

When Jackson went looking for Leah, Aunt Leafy told him the doctor had been summoned to the Babcock household in town. "I hear tell the whole family's ailing," the older lady had warned him with a dainty shudder. She pushed a few seeds into the cage of her pet canary.

"What's the matter with them?"

"Plenty, according to the boy who came running. And it's a crying shame for Miss Leah, because the Babcocks never pay a fee." Turning away from the birdcage, Aunt Leafy cocked her head and studied him. The sun shone on her white hair, giving it a lavender cast. "You ailing, too, Mr. Underhill?"

"No, ma'am."

"Your wife doing poorly again?"

"No, ma'am," he said with stronger vehemence. "She passed a quiet night last night. I think she's going to be right as rain."

Aunt Leafy smiled wisely. "Pretty little thing. And good company, too. I expect she'd've gotten better quicker if she had a real doctor."

"Leah Mundy is a real doctor."

"Humph. It ain't the place of a woman to go poking around the human body. Just ain't right, that's my opinion."

"Yes, ma'am, I reckon that is your opinion." This, he realized, was a prejudice Leah faced every single day. He hurried upstairs to tell Carrie he had to leave for a while. Their money had run out. God, what he wouldn't give for an ordinary workaday wage. But circumstances hadn't handed him that, not ever. He had to go to Seattle.

"You'll be all right while I'm gone?" he asked Carrie.

She smiled brightly and nodded. "I'll always be all right from now on, Jackson. I'll always be safe."

He smiled back. "I'll be going to Seattle real soon."

"You could go tomorrow," she said quickly.

That surprised him. He'd expected an argument from her. "You don't mind?"

"Why should I mind? Look at me, Jackson. I'm better. Truly."

"If the doc agrees, then I guess I'll take the steamer to the city." He bent to kiss her brow. She exuded a just-bathed softness that always roused tenderness in him. Tenderness and now hope. She was so beautiful. A twinge of desire pierced him, then disappeared as quickly as it had come. The things he wanted from Carrie had nothing to do with sex. But damn, it was good to see her smiling, to see the color back in her face. She appeared to be free of her addiction. That was why he wanted to see Leah. He wanted to know if it was true, if Carrie had her problem under control.

Funny, he thought as he walked along the waterfront, then up the hill toward the Babcock place, how quickly he'd developed the habit of checking with Leah. He'd never allowed himself to depend on anyone, least of all a mule-stubborn lady doctor. It was a new experience, relying on Leah.

As he walked through the little town, a strange feeling twisted in his gut. In just a few short weeks, he had memorized the place. There was Brunn's dry-goods store and chandlery where boaters stopped to repair and resupply, where Jackson would get provisions as soon as the schooner was fit to sail again. From the side of the hill, Jackson could see the boxy, rust-colored building in Coveland that served as the sheriff's office, with the jail annex built of fieldstone—a place Jackson casually avoided.

The Methodist church, painted pure white with a spun-sugar steeple, sat back a little from the main street. He had never ventured inside, but sometimes in the evening he stood outside the picket fence and listened as the choir practiced hymns. Over the door hung a sign: We Are All God's Children. Last Sunday, he'd had a perverse notion to go in, to see if it was true, to see if they'd let a desperado worship beside the pastor's wife.

But he hadn't gone in, of course. Church had a bad effect on him. It always made him think of the terror of his boyhood days in Chicago. The penances dealt by Brother Anthony were harsh in the extreme. Jackson was convinced that the cold-weather ache in his legs was due to the hours he'd spent kneeling on cold flagstone.

The schoolhouse in the next block bore a new coat of red paint. A bronze bell hung in a yard trampled from the children's games. Upon the brow of a hill, houses stood in rows, their porches whitewashed, their gardens starting to burst with the abundance of summer. The scent of lilacs spiced the air.

It was a town of families that worked together, played together, prayed and wept and laughed together. People made their homes here. Some of them would never leave the island. Jackson couldn't imagine it, yet at the same time he wanted it with a fierceness that made his chest hurt.

To belong somewhere. To have someone.

You belong in your boat, he told himself. You've got Carrie to look after. He wanted it to be enough. He told himself it *was* enough.

As he walked, he thought about the baby Carrie had lost. If it had lived, Jackson would have had the child to look after, as well. Life was a strange thing, he reflected. A man never knew what might happen to him next. Who would have thought a woman like Leah Mundy would fill his thoughts and make him wonder what it would be like to wake up in the same place every morning? To have friends, a job, neighbors.

He spied the Babcock house at the end of a rutted dirt lane. Apparently, there was no risk of contagion, for several neighbors had gathered on the porch. Sophie White-bear stood to one side of a strange device on a wooden table. Leah was gesturing at it and talking.

Even without hearing her words, Jackson could imagine the light, clipped timbre of her voice, the sturdy certainty that underlay her words. When she spoke of medicine, Leah Mundy exuded confidence. There were other times—when she spoke of her father and her past—that she seemed as lost as Carrie. But when it came to doctoring, there was no one smarter, and Leah knew it.

It seemed the whole town had turned out for whatever doctoring she was doing this morning. There were farmers in overalls and seafaring men in striped shirts; tradesmen with their aprons on, and even Reverend Cranney. With his clean white hands pressed together, he resembled an overaged choirboy—guileless and baffled. His plump wife, poured into a corset tied way too tight, stood gossiping with some of the parishioners.

Flanked by his two deputies, Lemuel St. Croix, the sheriff, stood to one side, watching the proceedings with only mild concern. Jackson skirted the group. He'd always avoided the law on principle; now he had a specific reason for keeping a low profile.

He didn't like the look of the St. Croix fellow anyway. Slippery. A little too fond of fancy clothes. The gun he carried—a Colt with a nickel-plated stock—was flashy, more like the piece a riverboat gambler would carry. Fortunately for Jackson, St. Croix also lacked the usual vigilance of a lawman. He seemed preoccupied by his conversation with a man in a threadbare army sergeant's shirt. Women crowded close to the house, many of them looking pale and aghast.

"She's filling your head full of lies," a man said brusquely.

Jackson craned his neck to see the speaker. It was Mr. Gillespie, the town butcher. Muscles bulged in his arms and neck, and his face was flushed with anger. Standing hardly a breath away from him was Leah Mundy, showing no signs of intimidation as she glared at him with hands on hips.

Jackson felt an absurd surge of pride. He admired the way she faced down her accuser with a mixture of defiance and audacity. She was tough and vulnerable at the same time. And even in the middle of the crowd, she seemed completely alone, like an island.

"Who're you going to listen to?" Gillespie went on. "This lady quack or James Gillespie? My family settled the island forty years ago. Our children have grown up together. You folks know me. I wouldn't sell you poisoned meat."

"I'm not saying you did it on purpose," Leah said in a clear voice that carried across the listening crowd. "But I am saying that this family is suffering from trichinosis—and the bacteria that causes it is in the ham you sold them." She gestured at a platter on the table. "It was ill prepared and ill stored. Something must have gone wrong in the smoking process."

The women began to murmur and stare at the platter, then at the butcher.

"I know my business," he said. "I been preparing hams since before you were born, missy. Don't be telling me I sold these people tainted meat."

Leah's chin lifted. "I'm certain you didn't mean to, but—"

"But nothing. This town needs a proper doctor, not some female busybody who doesn't even know how to keep house like a real woman."

Her eyes flashed, but she made a visible effort to control her temper, taking a deep breath and clasping her hands together. "Sir," she said. "It's my duty as a doctor to inform these people that you've sold them tainted meat."

"Ha! What do you expect from a lady doctor? No one will associate with you except that—that…" He gestured contemptuously at Sophie Whitebear. "She's a squaw who had too much firewater, that's what she is."

Jackson felt his hand clench into a fist at his side. Easy now, he told himself, keeping a weather eye on the sheriff. No need to draw attention to himself. While waylaid on this island, he'd best stay out of other folks' business.

Leah Mundy spoke up again. "Don't you dare cast aspersions on Sophie. You may call me anything you wish, but you will not spread lies about my assistant."

"Fine, then I'll call you what you deserve to be called.

A meddlesome female who thinks she can do a man's job. You know what I think, lady? I think you gave the whole family some tonic to make them sick, then pretended to get them better just so's you could collect a fee. You wouldn't be the first quack to do that.''

The crowd grew ugly then, muttering and glaring at Leah.

"You ought to lock her up, Sheriff," Gillespie called. "Put her someplace where she won't bother people."

St. Croix scowled beneath the brim of his fine bowler hat. It was then that Jackson noticed a shiny patch of healed skin high across his forehead. Only once before had he seen a scar like that—on the head of a man who had been scalped, but lived to tell the tale.

He gritted his teeth. None of his damned business. The deputy—a skinny Scotsman called Caspar MacPhail—leaned forward and said something to him, and the sheriff nodded. His manicured hand brushed the butt of his gun.

Jackson had had enough. Leah made him move outside himself and his own caution. She made him take risks because she was so alone. Scene or no scene, it was time to step in. "Folks," he called in a lazily reasonable voice, "what's all this?"

"Lady doctor's making trouble for this family," someone said. "And trying to ruin the butcher's reputation."

Jackson turned to Leah. She regarded him strangely, distrustfully. As if she wasn't certain whose side he was on. "Is that right?" he asked her. "I got here late. Maybe you could fill me in." He kept his voice neutral. Let her present the facts so folks could make up their own minds.

"Last night, everyone in the family ate this ham, and by morning they were all suffering from the same symptoms—violent vomiting, eruptions of the bowels. I diagnosed trichinosis."

Jackson looked at a black metal instrument on the table. "What's that?"

"A microscope. If you'll have a look, you can see the trichina bacteria in the fibers of the meat."

The butcher started forward. "Now just a doggone min—"

"Is that so?" Jackson stepped in front of Gillespie. No one saw how hard he shoved his elbow into the burly butcher's ribs, but he heard a gratifying rush of breath leave the man. "Show me how it works, Doc."

She lifted one eyebrow—he'd always wondered how she did that—but nodded at the microscope. "You simply close one eye and look down through here." She demonstrated, silky dark hair escaping her braid and falling forward.

For a fraction of a second, Jackson had a glimpse of her as an eager young student in medical school, thirsting for knowledge, earnestly pursuing her studies. How he'd longed for the things Leah had—an education, a worthy profession.

But that profession was getting her into trouble at the moment. He bent and closed one eye, looking into the eyepiece as if sighting down the scope of a rifle. He saw a small circle of...something. And even smaller somethings squirming around in it.

"The striated fibers are the meat itself," Leah said. "The little live organisms are the trichinae."

"She's double-talking us!" Gillespie objected.

"Those are the microbes that cause the bellyaches," she said in layman's terms.

Jackson gave a low whistle. "I'll be damned." There was enough fascination in his voice to rouse the curiosity of the onlookers. "You know, Dr. Mundy here didn't really get up this morning intending to put the butcher out of business. She found a sickness and she found the cause. So instead of calling her names, maybe you'd best take a peek at this and then make up your own minds about the meat.''

A couple of the women bent to look through the eyepiece. Within moments, everyone else wanted to have a look.

Gillespie the butcher fumed. ''This doesn't prove a damned thing. The ham's fine. I know my business.''

Casually, Jackson took out his buck knife and pretended to study the blade. ''Then I guess you won't mind eating a nice big piece of it right now.''

Gillespie blanched. ''This is none of your business, stranger.''

Jackson couldn't agree more. What the hell was he doing, attracting the attention of the whole town with the sheriff looking on? ''Maybe not,'' he said to the butcher. ''But it's *your* business. Now, have a bite.''

''Get away from me with that—''

His patience gone, Jackson shoved Gillespie up against the porch rail. ''You going to eat this or not?''

St. Croix took a step forward, then stopped, apparently finding the situation more interesting than dangerous.

''What were those symptoms again, Doc? Bowel eruptions?'' Jackson mused. ''We'll watch the butcher, and if he gets sick, then we'll know.''

''Mr. Underhill,'' Leah said, ''that is tantamount to poisoning.''

Christ, there was no pleasing the woman. He ignored her. ''So how about it? You going to eat this ham?'' he asked the butcher.

''I won't do a thing at your say-so.''

''Then how about ours?'' The pastor's wife gestured

with a furled umbrella. Jackson fancied he could feel the sentiment sway in his favor.

Gillespie must have sensed it, too. His shoulders sagged, and Jackson let him go. "I didn't do nothing on purpose." The butcher pushed past Jackson, scowled at Leah, and left.

"Excuse me," a woman said, hurrying away. "I've got some meat I'd better bury in the midden." Several others left with similar comments. To Jackson's relief, the men dispersed, too, the sheriff, his deputy and the army drifter among them.

Leah went into the house. He could hear her giving instructions to the patients. She spoke in a clear, authoritative tone. The lady of the house answered in a slightly angry and pain-filled voice. Hardly the grateful patient saved from doom by the compassionate physician.

By the time Leah came back out, Sophie Whitebear had cleared the table and disposed of the bad meat, and everyone else had gone. Jackson waited at the bottom of the steps. Leah didn't appear to see him as she stepped out onto the porch. She closed the door carefully behind her and then leaned against it, releasing a long, shuddering sigh. Her hand shook as she lifted it to brush a strand of hair out of her eye.

So vulnerable, he thought. But no one in the town knew that. They couldn't know that. Because they didn't look at her. They didn't look into her eyes and see the lonely soul inside.

He shouldn't, either. But he couldn't help himself.

"I'll walk you home, Doc," he said, drawing her out of her reverie.

She started. "Mr. Underhill. I didn't see you there." She came down the steps, and he stuck out his hand. She passed him her brown leather medical bag, and they fell into step together.

"Now you've seen for yourself what I'm up against," she said, a twist of irony in her voice. "Ignorance and prejudice."

"I guess," he said carefully. "But you're also up against fear."

"What do you mean?"

"How many kids does the butcher have?"

She thought for a moment. "Oh, at least five, I'd say."

"Five mouths to feed. And what you did today might run him out of business. That's why he got mean, Doc. Because he was scared. Not because he doesn't believe in female doctors."

"But I was right," she insisted. "I told the truth—"

"You did. In front of the whole town." He took her hand in his, ran his finger over her knuckles. "This is the hand of a healer," he said. "But sometimes you use words like a sledgehammer."

She stopped walking, snatched her hand away. "Dear God."

"What?"

"My God." She shook her head in disbelief. "You're right."

"I am?"

"Of course. Don't you see? *I'm* the ignorant one. I do this too often for my own good. I fail to see things from another point of view. All I saw was the bacteria making that family sick." She started walking again, quick, agitated steps. "I pilloried that poor man before the whole town. I should have gone to him in private and told him the meat was tainted. I should have given him the chance to make things right on his own. Damn."

It felt funny, hearing her swear.

"Damn, damn, damn," she said. "I'll never learn."

"Learn what?"

"To believe what Dr. van Braun once told me back in my student days. Medicine is an art, not a science." She looked helplessly at Jackson. "It's my worst failing. I don't know when to let go of facts and figures and let instinct rule."

He suppressed a smile. When it came to her work, she analyzed herself endlessly—and ruthlessly. "Sure you do," he said. "And here's your chance."

"Where?"

"Carrie. I want your opinion."

"Yes?"

"Is she really cured, or is it all just an act?"

Leah prayed for the right words to come. She sat in her office, the battered oak desk a heavy barrier between her and Jackson. His long, lanky frame dwarfed the chair he sat in. His wrists lay balanced on his knees.

"Well?" he prodded.

"The only honest thing I can say to you at this point is that I'm not certain." She pressed her hand on the sheaf of papers and journals in front of her. She'd spent hours poring over them, searching for answers that weren't there. She picked out an extract from a journal and read aloud, "'Not poppy, nor mandragora/Nor all the drowsy syrups of the world/Shall ever medicine thee to that sweet sleep/Which thou owedst yesterday.' Shakespeare wrote that. Sometimes I think he's the wisest of the lot."

"Carrie seems so much better," he insisted. "Happy, rested. Hasn't had a bad night in days."

Leah's gaze touched on the photograph of her and her father. Odd, the glass seemed to be missing from the frame. She wondered when it had broken and why she hadn't noticed it until now.

"Mr. Underhill, the allure of the drug is strong. I can't promise you Carrie won't be tempted. I've sat up night after night in this office, studying everything I could get my hands on about the disease of addiction. Dr. Penelope Lake, my associate, has supplied me with the latest extracts on the topic."

"And?"

"And the alienists who treat mental disorders claim that therapy should be sustained for a lifetime."

"Jesus Christ, Doc—"

"But the physiologists assert that once the brain chemistry is rebalanced, no further treatment is needed."

"And what do you think?" he asked.

She drummed her fingers on the stack of papers. Why was this so hard? Why couldn't she simply treat this like another medical case?

She looked into Jackson's eyes and saw her answer. She cared too much. Far too much.

"There is one point upon which all the experts agree, Mr. Underhill. The safest course for a patient like Carrie is to institutionalize her."

He stiffened as if someone had stabbed him in the back. "You mean lock her up."

"I mean put her in a place where she can rest, where she'll come to no harm. I know of a residence called Messenger House on an island to the south."

His gunmetal eyes snapped with fury, and his face grew cold as stone in winter. "A madhouse," he said.

The very word made her shudder. When she was doing her ward studies she had visited places for the insane and had been shocked by the conditions there. Too often, the disturbed found themselves in hellholes of shrieking humanity.

"No," she insisted. "There are private facilities where the treatment is humane. Places like Messenger House."

Jackson came out of the chair. "I'm not locking Carrie up."

"That's why I suggested Messenger House," Leah said. "I've visited the place myself. There are no bars. Just doctors and nurses who specialize in nervous disorders."

"But she's better, damn it. She's herself again."

Leah felt an actual physical pain in her heart. "I want it to be so, Mr. Underhill. I truly do. Please, just consider a sojourn for her at Messenger House. You can even stay with her for a while—"

"No. As soon as the boat's seaworthy, we're leaving."

"What's your hurry?"

"I'm getting tired of sanctimonious people looking down their noses at me."

"Is that what you think I'm doing?" Leah was relieved. She preferred to have him think her sanctimonious than to know the truth—that he fascinated her, made her heart beat faster, that the sun shone brighter when he was around. Dear God, what was happening to her?

"If that's what you think," she said, "then you'd better leave."

He didn't bother to reply, but turned on his heel and left the room.

Neatening the stack of already neat papers on her desk, she turned down the lamp. She couldn't read any longer, not when terrible thoughts plagued her. She couldn't shake off the feeling that some small, evil part of her wanted Carrie gone.

Gone, so that Leah could be alone with Jackson.

"No," she said aloud, jerking to her feet. It was wrong, *she* was wrong, and she shouldn't think such a thing. But all that night, it bedeviled her sleep, and when she awakened and realized what she'd been dreaming of, she buried her head in her hands and trembled with guilt.

"Just a day and a night," Jackson said. "That's all the time I'll be gone, Carrie."

She stood with him on the porch of the boardinghouse. She wore a pretty dress the color of cherries and her favorite red shoes. "I know you'll be back. You always come back."

"You're right about that, sugar." He came for her when no one else would. When no one else cared.

Her china-plate eyes regarded him solemnly. "Adam will keep me company while you're gone."

"Will he?" Jackson felt a twinge of…what? Jealousy? Guilt? "Honey, you hardly know the man."

"I know him better than I know you," she insisted, her voice rising. "During all the long days of my recovery, what do you think I did while you were off working on your boat? Talked to the walls? Talked to the furniture?" She clutched her little fringed parasol. "I talked to Adam."

"I'm sorry, Carrie. You should've said you wanted company. I would have dropped everything. I love y—"

"Don't, Jackson." She held up a dainty hand clad in a crocheted glove. "You've always said so, but you're confusing duty for love."

"Damn it, Carrie, I know my own mind."

"Yes, but do you know your own heart?" She looked at him steadily, her eyes wide and unwavering, as clear as the summer sky over Puget Sound.

"I know I spent years looking for you."

"And you found me. You kept me safe."

It always came back to that. Safety. She craved it with a desperation that Jackson knew was not normal, but he couldn't blame her. Snatched from her family at age nine, sold into prostitution at age twelve, what else could mean so much to her?

She stepped forward, putting her gloved hand on his cheek. "I'll never forget what you did for me. I'll never forget...Rising Star."

Even now, all these months later, he still felt a rush of dread. "I wouldn't think so." He tried to swallow past the dryness in his throat. "Do you think about it a lot?"

She shrugged. "Maybe."

She looked so distant, as if she sat behind a wall he couldn't penetrate. He wondered if he'd ever really know her, this icon, this woman he called wife. "Honey, do you ever think of the baby you lost?"

Another shrug. "I'm not good with babies."

The dryness in his throat started to burn. "Can you just tell me one thing, Carrie? Can you tell me who the father was?"

Her expression never changed. She was as serene as a Madonna, pale and perfect. She tapped the toe of her red shoe against the porch step. Jackson was about to apologize for asking when she said, "Don't you know?"

"I guess I don't."

"He's dead."

It all came clear to him now. The shouting, the accusations. The mayor of Rising Star in a place he shouldn't have been, with a woman he shouldn't have known. Her admission sat like a rock in Jackson's gut. It had happened the night they'd fled.

"I told Adam," she said quietly, with simple directness.

"Jesus Christ!" Jackson started to sweat. He thought about Adam Armstrong. Polite and refined, wearing clothes that cost more than an ordinary man would see in a lifetime, he exuded confidence. He took Leah to the magic-lantern show; he pushed Carrie on the bench swing in the yard. Jackson could imagine a woman wanting to confide in him. "What did you tell him, Carrie?" he asked in a low voice.

She dropped her gaze. "I told him everything."

"Everything?"

"I told him you and I were raised in a poorhouse. That we suffered many hardships, that you were forced to do some things society might not approve of."

He narrowed his eyes, remembering the reek of blood and gun smoke, the sharp sound of the slamming door. Carrie rarely talked about her time in Texas, even though it had changed the course of their lives. He was beginning to suspect that she had managed to put their final night in Rising Star out of her mind.

"Adam says I'm not responsible for misfortunes that befell me when I was young and defenseless."

"He's right about that."

She smiled softly, sweetly. "I know." She stood on tiptoe to kiss Jackson's cheek. "Thank you for everything," she whispered into his ear.

And this time he knew she meant *everything*.

It was time to go. The *Fairhaven* blew its whistle, and the skipper shouted orders. Jackson bent and kissed her lightly on the lips. "I'll bring you a present, honey."

"That would be nice. Jackson?"

He glanced over his shoulder, anxious to get aboard. "What?"

"I hope you find what you're looking for."

Not until he was aboard the Seattle-bound side-wheeler did he think it was an odd thing to say.

The sun rode high, and Jackson's pockets bulged with his winnings when he returned from Seattle the next day. His luck had been so good it was almost frightening. In the salon of the Diller Hotel, he'd played smoothly and confidently, garnering rueful admiration from the other gamblers and bawdy looks from the women.

Seattle had become the terminus for the Great Northern Railroad, and men with high ambitions flocked to the city to set up shop. Money, whiskey and grandiose plans flowed freely in the taverns, and Jackson had gotten more than his share. He could have had more than that—a fancy lady or two had offered her favors. It wasn't like him to refuse such an offer, but last night he'd said a polite "no, thank you."

It was a bit late in life to be turning decent, he reflected. And then he had a thought that wasn't decent at all. A forbidden anticipation caught at him; he was going to see Leah. *Quit that*, he told himself. *You got no business thinking like that.*

He went out onto the upper level deck. He'd never get tired of the view in these parts, and the run from Seattle to Whidbey, with a stop at La Conner, was as pleasant as anything he'd known. The undulating water was as clear and deep as eternity, and the islands had the sort of placid beauty that made a man—even Jackson—believe in everything good. Taking out a tin of Fancy Shred tobacco, he started to roll a smoke.

He felt rather than saw the *Fairhaven* change course. The big side-wheeler churned northward. In a moment, Jackson saw why.

Boots clattering on the metal steps, he rushed down to

the lower level to have a better look. Already, people were gathered around. "Damned shame," someone said. "Looks like there were no survivors."

Quiet horror settled over the passengers as they surveyed the burned-out wreckage of a pleasure boat.

"I guess there was an explosion or something," a man in Mosquito Fleet livery said. "Must've been the engine. Look at that mess."

Barrels, crate tops, decking, line, tarpaulins—they all floated helplessly through a tangle of burned timber.

"Nobody could've survived that. There ain't a piece left bigger than a splinter."

"Just as well," the Mosquito Fleet official said. "You don't want to be alive when the orcas come."

Only the aft end of the hull was visible. Jackson stared at it, mesmerized, waiting. Waiting for the steamer to chug around so he could read the name of the hapless boat.

But he already knew. Something inside him already knew. He felt no surprise when he saw the first four letters painted on the upside-down stern: *La Tache.*

That was Adam Armstrong's boat.

A woman's shoe floated by. A red shoe. One that Jackson recognized.

*"Carrie,"* he said under his breath, already striding toward the rail of the steamer. With his gaze fixed on the shoe, he peeled away his coat, kicked off his boots, and dove in. The frigid water seared him. His emotions and his extremities were already going numb as he surged toward the wreck and surfaced near the half-submerged hull. Carrie had been on this boat. *Damn it.* He should have seen it coming, should have realized she'd go off with her new friend. Faintly, he could hear people shouting to him from the steamer, but he ignored them as he

pawed through the wreckage. Her straw bonnet, torn in two. A man's waistcoat. A book, the waterlogged pages fanned out.

"Come on, mister," someone yelled. "You'll freeze to death."

A life ring splashed into the water near him. Feeling half-dead, he allowed himself to be helped aboard. Someone threw a horsehair blanket around his shoulders. Dripping wet and shivering, he stood at the rail. The truth sank in like a cold iron spike. Gone. Carrie was gone.

He spied the shoe again and fixed on it, studying the dainty ribbons that flowed out on each side like water wings. A jeweled red heel caught the afternoon sunlight like the facets of a garnet.

He kept staring at that shoe even though the steamer, its skipper certain there was no aid to be rendered, steered toward the west. The sparkling red heel kept glaring right in his eye. In his mind, he heard piano music, and he remembered a day in San Francisco.

"Of course I want to go dancing, Jackson," Carrie had said. "But I haven't a thing to wear."

"I'll get you something, honey. Don't you worry."

He'd bought her a dress and a pair of dancing shoes with satin ribbons and jeweled red heels.

Jackson wasn't sure what sort of sound he made, but people noticed, getting a look at his face, stepping out of the way.

"You all right, mister?" someone asked.

Jackson didn't answer. There wasn't any answer.

The morning after Carrie's death, Jackson had breakfast with Bowie Dawson. Fidgeting in his rolling chair, the boy peered across the table. "So what're you going to do on the boat today? Jackson? What are you going to do? *Jackson.*"

He blinked. "Oh. Sorry." He couldn't stop thinking about Carrie. Had she burned to death or drowned? Or had the orcas gotten her? For some reason, he supposed that she burned. She was hot, short-lived, a flash of lightning. She'd always been that way. He should feel crazy with horror and grief right about now.

But all he felt was empty.

For years, the search for Carrie had given shape to his life. Meaning to his existence. After he found her, caring for her had been his goal, his purpose. Keeping her safe had been his mission.

Now what would shape his life?

A Wanted poster, he thought grimly.

He used to be like a knight on a quest, and Carrie was the grail he sought. Now he had nothing to quest for. He truly was a drifter.

"Jackson?" Bowie sounded annoyed. "Are you going to be working on the boat, Jackson?"

He dragged his mind back to the present. "Yeah, I've got to fix the aft pumps."

"Can I come? Can I, Jackson? Huh?"

He ruffled the youngster's silky fair hair. "I'm going to be extra busy today. Maybe you'd better stick around here and help your ma."

Bowie's narrow shoulders sagged. "I won't get in the way—promise. You can just put my chair out of the way, and I'll watch, maybe practice my knots. I'll be quiet as a mouse, Jackson. Promise! Swear on a stack of Bibles, I'll button my lip and—"

"Right." Resigned, Jackson went around behind Bowie and wheeled his chair toward the kitchen. Maybe it wasn't such a bad idea after all, having the little mite around to fill the silences. When the steamer had docked yesterday, Leah and Perpetua and Iona had been waiting. They confirmed what he'd known all along—that Carrie had gone off with Adam.

*No survivors.*

Jackson hadn't been able to speak. He just shook off their sympathy, stalked to the *Teatime,* and got quietly drunk.

"Well?" Bowie said. "Let's *go,* Jackson."

"We'll ask your mother. If it's all right with her, it's fine with me."

They found Perpetua dressing a chicken for supper. The smell of sage and garlic filled the room. "Mama!" Bowie called. "Jackson said I can watch him work on the boat. Can I, Mama? Can I?"

"Certainly not." She didn't hesitate in her work, just kept on rubbing the chicken with sage leaves.

Jackson wondered what was so automatic with the woman—her distrust of him or her overprotectiveness of the boy. "Ma'am, he'll be fine on the docks with me. The weather's so hot, it'd be a shame to keep him cooped up indoors all day."

She aimed a grudging glance out the window and blinked as if this was the first time she'd seen such a perfect summer day.

"I'd welcome the company, Mrs. Dawson."

She fell still, looked at him. He allowed a brief smile and saw the moment she gave in. Her eyes filled; he knew she was thinking of what had happened to Carrie.

"I imagine you would," she said quietly. Then she launched into a long litany of cautions for Bowie, wrapping him in blankets and a muffler as if a blizzard raged outside. Through it all, the boy stayed quiet, clearly awed that his mother would allow such a privilege.

At last they were on their way to the harbor. Bowie chattered the whole way. "Jackson, are you sad because Miz Carrie went out on that boat and died?"

The blunt question, asked by a guileless child, ripped into him, causing a pain he wasn't ready for, wasn't used to. Damn, the kid was honest. "Yeah, I guess I'm real sad."

"Aunt Leafy says Miz Carrie wasn't fit to be a seaman's wife. Says she was too del-i-cate."

"I suppose that's so," Jackson admitted. In the whirlwind and mayhem of the life he and Carrie had led, he had never expected her to behave like a wife. It didn't seem necessary under the circumstances. He wondered what else she'd told the old busybody.

"Aunt Leafy says Mr. Armstrong was really, really rich."

"Uh-huh." Jackson didn't want to talk about it anymore. He parked the chair on the dock. Now that they were out of sight of the house, Bowie removed the plaid blanket, the muffler and the woolen cap. "It's hot as Hades out today," he remarked. He twisted around to see Jackson's reaction to the forbidden word.

Jackson merely nodded. "That it is."

He took out his tin of tobacco, and Bowie squinted up at him. "Underhill Fancy Shred," the boy read. "Underhill, just like your name, Jackson. What a coincidence, huh?"

"Yeah. A coincidence." Jackson lifted his face to the sky. The air, fresh washed by a brief shower, had a crystalline quality that was acute in its intensity. The sun brought out the colors of sea and sky, grass and wildflowers in all their eye-smarting brilliance. Jackson inhaled deeply, letting the air tingle in his chest. As he boarded the *Teatime,* preparing to tackle the repairs before him, he had an uncanny sense of well-being.

He refused to examine the reason for it.


Leah set her jaw in a grim line and faced the patient who sat on the examining table in her surgery. "Ilsa, I have other people to see today. Now, you either open your mouth and let me have a look at that tooth, or I'll have to send you home still hurting."

Ilsa Gillespie, the butcher's daughter, set her own jaw with equal obstinance. At nine years old, she already had her father's bulldog jowls and stubborn countenance. She wore two fat yellow braids crisscrossed over the top of her head and glared at Leah with eyes as blue as a bird's egg. One side of her face stood out, swollen and tender from a bad tooth, but the girl wasn't about to let Leah near it.

"If I pull the tooth," Leah said, "it'll just hurt for a minute. But if you don't let me, then it'll be hurting for days and days, maybe forever."

Ilsa's eyes widened. She clapped both hands over her mouth.

Leah folded her arms and took a deep breath for patience. After the scene at the Babcock house, Jackson had suggested a truce with the butcher. This was part of their agreement. She had tainted his reputation as surely as he had tainted his meat, and after talking to Jackson, she felt guilty. She'd gone to Gillespie in private and vowed to treat his children at no charge. On top of that, she'd made a point of going into his shop at the busiest time of day and making several purchases.

Since then, she'd seen at least one of the Gillespie children a day, treating everything from warts to a runny nose. Ilsa was actually one of the easier ones.

Though Leah rarely let her attention wander from a patient, her mind kept drifting to Jackson. Carrie was gone, gone forever. What was he feeling?

She recalled her grief when her father had died. Even now, it was hard to admit that a tiny sense of relief gleamed through the sadness. Her father, who had spent his life searching for wealth and luxury, had never attained it. Perhaps he was at peace. She remembered thinking that she was completely alone and feeling the strangeness of it. And the sense that, even in the final moments, she and her father had left something incomplete. She wondered if Jackson had those feelings today.

"Come on, honey," she tried cajoling, turning her attention back to her patient. "If you just hold your mouth open for the count of ten, I'll make it all better."

Hands still pressed protectively over her mouth, the child lifted her chin in haughty refusal.

"Would you do it for a prize? How about a shiny new penny?" Good Lord, she was resorting to bribery.

The chubby hands came down. "Make it *ten* pennies." Ilsa surely was her father's daughter.

"Five," Leah countered.

"Done," the child shot back.

A minute later, she was whimpering in Leah's arms, blue eyes fastened on the abscessed tooth in the enameled tray by the table and five pennies clenched in her fist.

Leah smiled. In the distance, the harbor bell clanged. "All better now. I'll send you home with some oil of cloves to—"

A terrified scream pierced the air. Setting Ilsa aside, Leah rushed out of the surgery. The kitchen door of the boardinghouse was flung wide open, and Perpetua Dawson, her skirts hiked up above her knees, was racing like mad across the lawn.

Aunt Leafy, on her wicker rocker on the porch, had gone white as a sheet. "Something happened at the harbor," she said. "Bowie fell into the water!"

# *Six*

~~~oᏖᎧᎧᏕᎧ~~~

Leah ran so fast that the pins came out of her hair, and her surgical smock came untied. The salty-sharp air tore at her lungs as she raced down to the harbor. Perpetua sobbed Bowie's name.

Shoved off to one side, the wicker wheelchair looked sadly empty and abandoned with a pile of clothes and blankets on it. Davy Morgan came running from the harbormaster's office. Bob Rapsilver followed close behind.

"Bowie! Where's my baby? My baby!" Perpetua teetered at the end of the dock.

Rapsilver pointed a thick finger out to sea. "Went over the side. Damnedest thing I've ever seen."

Leah froze, her gaze following the line of the pointing finger. There was Bowie, in the water just as she'd feared. But...

"Heavenly days," Perpetua panted between sobs. "What's he doing?"

A pale, thin arm rose from the water. "Swimming, Mama! Look at me! I'm swimming!" His arm came down, and he propelled himself forward with surprisingly strong—if clumsy—strokes.

"But he doesn't know how to swim." Perpetua sagged against Davy Morgan.

"He's swimming," Leah said. Her heart rate and breathing gradually returned to normal. The noonday sun beat down on her head, and she savored a sweet rush of relief.

Someone else emerged close to Bowie. Pale hair slicked back from a tanned face. Muscular shoulders and arms breaking the surface. Leah felt a smile playing upon her lips. "Mr. Underhill taught him."

"The kid's taking to it like a chum salmon leaving the river," Davy said.

Now that the emergency was over, Perpetua's anxiety turned to anger. She mopped her brow with her apron. "Bowie!" she called. "Bowie Dawson, you come here right this minute! You scared your mama half to death!"

"Aw, Mama. You'll spoil all the fun," the boy protested.

"*Now,*" Perpetua yelled. Her inflection brooked no argument.

As Bowie and Jackson paddled toward the dock, she fetched a blanket from the wheelchair. Jackson hoisted himself onto the dock with Bowie in his arms, surrendering the boy to his mother, who quickly wrapped him up, then glared at Jackson.

"This is all *your* fault," she said. "If Bowie hadn't been following you around all morning, he never would have gotten into danger. He could have died, I tell you. He might catch his death of cold—"

"Ma'am," Jackson said quietly, dripping a pool of water onto the dock. He was wearing only jeans; his chest and feet were bare. The denim clung to him, outlining a physique that gave Leah's insides a strange little twist.

It was getting harder and harder to pretend her interest

in him was limited to anatomical curiosity. The truth was, she harbored a shameful lust for this man. She wanted to touch him, to feel the texture of smooth skin over hard muscle, to feel his warmth and the beating of his heart. Good God. The man had just lost his wife. What sort of unprincipled woman was she to want him in this way?

A lonely woman, her heart answered. A woman whose needs were brought to the surface by the presence of this mysterious man.

"Well, what have you to say for yourself?" Perpetua glared up at Jackson, clearly feeling none of Leah's sensibilities.

He gestured at the Sound, clear blue and sparkling in the sun. "The kid's got to live around water all his life. I figure he'd best learn to swim."

"What about what *I* figure? I'm his mother after all."

"Then you should have taught him a long time ago." Jackson ruffled the boy's damp hair, eliciting a worshipful grin from him. "He's a strong little fellow. He did just fine. He was perfectly safe every second, I swear it. I didn't get more than a foot away from him the whole time."

Leah stood blinking incredulously. *This* was Jackson Underhill, the dangerous outlaw?

"Reckon no one ever taught Carrie to swim," he added more quietly. He spoke half to himself, gazing out to sea as he rubbed the gooseflesh on his arms.

Leah's heart lurched as she suddenly understood.

Perpetua wasn't listening. "Have you no regard at all for Bowie's infirmity?" she demanded.

Jackson tucked a corner of the blanket under Bowie's quivering chin. "Ma'am, when he's in the water, he's just like any other boy."

Leaving a wet trail in his wake, he walked down the dock and disappeared into the main cabin of his boat.

Perpetua settled Bowie into his chair and layered on another blanket, then added the ever-present muffler and hat. Each layer, Leah knew, represented Perpetua's love and her need to protect. She hadn't yet realized what was obvious to everyone else. The extra clothing smothered him.

Her heart in her throat, Leah watched Perpetua close her eyes, a reverent look on her thin face as she bent and pressed her lips to the boy's brow.

Bowie was Leah's patient, but he was so much more than that. She had watched him toddle his first steps—from Leah to his mother's waiting arms. Leah had been there when the boy sang his first song, took his first taste of watermelon, held a kitten for the first time. And she had been the first to see his little cheeks unnaturally flushed with fever, the first to know the nature of his illness. She had been charged with the responsibility of telling Perpetua that Bowie would never walk again.

"He's right, you know," Leah said before she had time to talk herself out of it.

"Whatever do you mean?" Perpetua dried Bowie's ears with painstaking care.

"Mr. Underhill. Swimming is a fine activity for Bowie."

"See, Mama?" the boy said from his pile of blankets. "Dr. Leah says it's all right."

"Yes indeed," Leah said quickly. "As Bowie's physician, I should advise you to let him swim since he's shown he has the stamina. It will be good for him. It's bound to increase his strength and his health, not to mention his self-confidence."

"No." Perpetua moved behind the chair and gripped

the handles. "You don't know what it's like to be a mother, to worry about your child—"

"With proper supervision, of course."

Perpetua stopped, looked over her shoulder. "And does Jackson Underhill provide proper supervision?" Without waiting for an answer, she walked briskly toward the boardinghouse, pushing the chair in front of her.

Leah stayed at the landing for a long time. She turned to face the water, taking in the towering sweep of clouds that gathered on the distant horizon, the sunlight glistening on the far-off mountain peaks. No one lingered at the dock. They had all gone back to work, back home, back to their families.

*You don't know what it's like to be a mother....* Perpetua's words stuck in Leah's mind. She was seized by a familiar feeling—loneliness. This was her town, her world, yet like every other place she'd been in her life, she didn't quite fit in. She used to think she simply hadn't found the right place, but now she was beginning to understand. She didn't fit in anywhere because of a lack inside her. At her father's knee, she had learned the harsh lesson of her own inadequacies. Even though, as an adult, she recognized his faults, she could never quite banish the pain of her childhood. He had been so cold he'd damaged her capacity to be loved—and possibly to love.

Why couldn't she change, just barge into the community and become one of them? She was pathetic. She couldn't even join her own boarders for a game of cribbage at night.

The McAfees had moved to the island only eight months before, and already Mr. McAfee was a church deacon, his wife a key member of the Ladies' Aid Society, the quilting circle and the garden club. Their children raced with the rest of the schoolhouse pack. Some people just knew how to "fit."

Others drifted...forever, it seemed.

Or until they drowned.

Lost in thought, she turned away from the spectacular panorama and started down the dock.

"Care for a cup of grog, Doc?" Clad in a fresh plaid shirt and dry jeans, Jackson emerged onto the deck of the *Teatime*. He held out a tin cup of amber liquid.

Leah couldn't think why she felt so relieved to see him. Why she felt as if he was rescuing *her*. "Just what exactly is grog anyway?" she inquired, taking the cup. "That's something I've always wondered."

"Take a sip and wonder no more."

She obeyed, recognizing the sweet burn of rum. "It's a bit early in the day for this, isn't it?" She tasted it again. "I feel as if I should start singing sea chanteys."

"Do you know any?"

"Not a one. And you?"

"Plenty, but you'd need to drink a lot more rum before you could tolerate my singing voice."

Leah smiled. "Thank you. For the grog."

"You looked as if you could use it. Actually, true grog is diluted with water. But I don't have to dilute it. Did all right at the card table in Seattle." He held out his hand to her.

She hesitated, studying that hand. The long, strong fingers, hands of a sailor, callused by hard work and hard weather. The nails scoured clean from his recent swim. An outlaw's hand, one that had held a gun pointed at her head. How could it be the same hand that had taken a boy from a wheelchair and taught him to swim?

Because he wasn't an outlaw, not really. Maybe he was a drifter like her, looking for a place to belong.

Aware of the impropriety of it, she put her hand in his and felt the pleasant shock of touching him. This was madness, she thought. Sheer madness, and yet she could no more resist it—or him—than she could resist the seductive warmth of a few sips of rum.

"I moved some things out of your house," he said, leaning against a newly varnished hatch cover.

She took another drink of her grog. "Oh?"

"Carrie's clothes and such."

The name hung like a gray shadow between them. Leah took her hand away from his and forced herself to speak up, to fill the silence. "I'm so sorry. So very, very sorry."

"I just don't know how I'm supposed to feel, Doc. Don't quite know what to do when folks offer their condolences. Don't know what to do with myself next."

She nodded, painfully familiar with the feeling. "Yes, well, I see you've been hard at work on the boat."

"I've gotten a lot done." He brought her down into the cockpit. He gave her a tour, pointing out the work he'd done on the inner hull and the galley, the pumps and presses. "I spent half the morning underwater with the rudder. She'll be ready to sail before too long, I reckon."

Leah told herself she should feel relieved. He was a stranger, a drifter. After he left, her life could return to normal.

She inspected the schooner with interest, murmuring approval at all the improvements. It occurred to her that he worked as hard on his boat as she did at her medical practice. There was little one couldn't accomplish, she reflected, if one was determined.

She leaned out over the stern to see that the first *T* and

the *I* were still missing from the escutcheon. "You've not fixed that, I see."

He shrugged. "She's not pretty, but she's almost seaworthy. That's all I need."

"Is it?" She drank more grog, feeling vaguely wicked for imbibing in the middle of the day. She watched him lash a neat backsplice around the tail end of a rope. He was so lean and graceful in his movements. Had Jackson Underhill ever suffered an awkward moment in his life? "I wonder," she said before she lost her nerve, "which of us will be the first to mention it."

His movements with the rope slowed, but didn't stop. "Mention what?"

"What just happened."

"Oh, the swimming? I kept telling the kid no, but he hounded me until I decided to give it a try. He took to the water like a regular guppy—you saw."

"I didn't mean Bowie. I meant...before."

This time he did stop. He froze in midmotion like a stag sensing danger. Then he seemed to come back to himself. With elaborate care and patience, he cheesed down the rope, arranging it into precise concentric circles on the deck. Unhurried, his expression unreadable, he turned to her. "Just say it, Doc. Say you're curious about how I feel now that Carrie threw me over for a rich timber baron and they died in a boating accident."

Leah already regretted broaching the subject. But she wanted to comfort him, wanted to penetrate his inscrutable veneer and let him know she cared. His chilly expression made her wince. "Mr. Underhill, if it's painful to talk about—"

"*If* it's painful?" He lifted an eyebrow. One hand still held the end of the rope, and the knuckles shone stark white. "Honey, if it's not, then I'm made of stone."

She swallowed hard, set her cup on the galley table. "I apologize. I just thought perhaps—"

"Perhaps what?"

"I could somehow be a comfort to you now that—"

"A comfort. Right." He picked up a belaying pin and stabbed it into place along the rail, then turned and went down a companionway leading to the galley belowdecks. "That's you, Dr. Mundy," he said over his shoulder. "A comfort to the afflicted."

"I understand you must feel bitter—"

"No, Doc, you don't understand. I was supposed to protect her, and I let her drown."

"You didn't let her," Leah countered, following him. "She chose to go off with Adam. What would you have done if the boat hadn't exploded? Gone after them?"

He furrowed a hand through his long, damp hair. "When Carrie gets her mind set on something, there's no stopping her." He scowled. "So why all the concern? I'm not sick."

She told herself she should shrink from the darkness that seemed to surround him. Instead, she wanted to dive into it, to succumb to the lure of his danger. "You may not be ill, but you're in pain. The shock of losing Carrie—"

"She was never mine to begin with," he said quietly. "I figure a doctor of your talent would've been able to tell. But that's not your strong point, is it?"

Her cheeks caught fire. "I do my best, Mr. Underhill. I treat the sick of this community. And if my bedside manner is not always as saintly as your own, then I more than make up for it in skill and competence."

"I wasn't attacking your bedside manner, Doc."

"That's good, because *your* bedside manner consists of holding a gun on a sleeping woman," she burst out, then caught herself. "That wasn't fair. I apologize. You were acting out of fear for Carrie."

"No offense taken. Being here, watching you, I see what you're up against with these people."

"I shouldn't get so defensive."

"Have some more grog." He refilled her cup, and she didn't object. He swept a hand toward the stern windows that framed a spectacular view from the harbor. "It's nice here, Doc. If you're unhappy, it's your fault."

"It's not my fault they think I'm harsh," she said, taking a healthy swallow. "It's not my fault they judge me out of ignorance and whisper about me behind my back." Setting down the empty cup, she clutched the opposite rail and looked away so she wouldn't have to face him. Drinking rum on an empty stomach made her give vent to an unforgivable wave of self-pity. "It's not my fault they consider me good enough to deliver their babies and lance their boils, but they wouldn't suffer me to sit at their tables for Sunday dinner. It's not my—"

She broke off as a pair of strong hands gripped her shoulders, spun her around. She had no time to think, to speak, even to breathe. One moment, her shocked gaze was fastened on Jackson Underhill's grim, furious face; the next moment, his mouth was crushing down on hers, his lips shaping themselves over and around hers, and she could taste him, could press herself against the warm wall of his chest, could feel the oddly welcome strain in her neck as she angled her head up to his.

Regrets and protests whirled through her mind and disappeared unformed, like the mist off the water. He left no room for thought, for objections, because his blunt hunger consumed her. The firmness of his lips, the sweet-rum taste of him intoxicated her. She savored the fresh scent of wind and water that clung to him, the harsh but welcome movement of his big hands over her shoulders and down her back, bringing her close, holding her as if he would never let her go.

It was the grog. It must be the grog. Otherwise she would have had the sense to resist, to pull back. It was forbidden, yes. It was improper, yes, and it meant nothing but trouble for them both.

So why didn't she care? Why didn't she protest? Why didn't she wrench herself out of his arms, run and hide until he disappeared forever?

Because, with all her heart, she wanted him to stay.

The thought gripped her like a cold iron fist, giving her the strength to break away from him at last. She made a formless sound in her throat and flattened her hands against his chest, pushing hard, pushing back with such force that she stumbled, catching herself on a bolted-down table behind her.

"Mr. Underhill." Her voice was rough and harsh with shock.

He subjected her to a long, lazy perusal, his gaze moving over her like his caressing hands had just done. "I reckon after that you should call me Jackson."

Her throat prickled with heat; then the blush moved upward until it felt as if her cheeks had been seared by flames. "I'm supposed to be comforting you."

He stuck his thumb into the top of his jeans. "It's working, Doc. I'm starting to feel real comfortable."

"That was—you were—we—you must apologize," she managed to choke out. Her blush burned hotter, for she sounded as awkward and missish as a country girl.

"Apologize?" Amusement flowed like honey through his voice. "For doing something you've wanted—something we've both wanted—for weeks?"

She clenched her hands into fists. "Sir, if I ever gave

you the impression I wanted you to k—'' She couldn't say it. She took a deep breath and said, "If I gave you the impression I wanted you to take liberties with me without so much as a by-your-leave—''

"You forgot what I told you the night I broke into your bedroom," he said, dark amusement in his eyes. "I never ask leave to do anything."

She bowed her head, doing her best to speak as Dr. Mundy, calm and professional physician. "Perhaps the fault is mine, then. For anything in my manner or conduct that invited this intimacy, I most humbly apologize."

He was silent for a long time, so long that she finally dared to look at him. And immediately wished she hadn't, for he was convulsed with silent mirth. Laughter rocked his long, lanky frame, and the smile on his face shone with infuriating brilliance.

It was too much. To Leah's horror, she tasted tears in her throat, felt them burning her eyes.

"Good day, Mr. Underhill," she managed to say through gritted teeth. Then she headed for the gangway.

He blocked her exit casually, leaning against the accommodation ladder. "Not so fast there, Leah."

It was the first time he'd called her Leah rather than Doc. That in itself was a forbidden intimacy, but not nearly so forbidden as his kiss.

"Please step out of my way."

"I can't do that."

She forced herself to look at him, tilting her chin at a defiant angle. "Why not?"

"Because I made you cry. Now I have to make you stop."

With a violent swipe of her hand, she wiped the tears from her cheeks, hating herself for losing control, hating herself for all she was feeling, and hating him for making her feel this way. "There," she said. "I've stopped."

"No, you haven't."

"Yes, I have."

In silent betrayal, a fresh tear rolled down her cheek.

"Aw, for Pete's sake." He took her wrists, ignoring her resistance. "Sit down with me."

"No."

"Then lie down with me."

"Why should I?"

He looked at her for a long time, but she saw no laziness in his gaze now, no insolence. Only acute interest—and a gentleness that made her hurt all the more.

"Because," he said, taking a corner of his shirt and dabbing her cheek, "you're breaking my heart."

Speechless with surprise, she let herself be led to a bench in the galley. He sat down beside her, never letting go of her hands.

"I figure we'd better talk about this now, because if we don't, it'll always hang between us."

She sniffed. "It will always hang between us even if we *do* talk about it."

"Maybe, maybe not. If it'll make you stop crying, I'll apologize," he said. "But I don't think that's why you're crying."

It wasn't. She acknowledged this with a shrug.

"I'm not sorry for kissing you, Leah. I could never be sorry for that." He lifted his hand and very lightly touched her lips, tracing their outline until they tingled.

*He makes my lips ache,* she thought absurdly.

"You're so soft. You taste so damned good. Hell no, I'm not sorry."

She found the strength to push his fingers away. "But it was wrong."

"What was wrong with it?"

"It can't mean anything."

"It can mean I want to hold you. Touch you, kiss you."

"Your wife just died."

"So I should spend the rest of my life beating myself up over a woman who ran off on me?" Bitterness edged his voice.

"Maybe you should beat yourself up for a day or two before grabbing the first available woman."

"Honey," he said, "you're not the first, and you're sure as hell not available. Believe me, I don't usually have to work this hard to get a woman to kiss me."

She knew he was trying to be casual—callous, even—because it was easier than feeling the hurt of losing Carrie. "Then why did you?"

"Why did I what?"

Damn him, he was going to make her say it. "Why did you kiss me?" *Why did you make me face the truth I've been hiding from ever since I first met you?*

"I wanted to," he said simply. "You wanted me to. The difference between us is, I'm not one to deny myself a basic human pleasure, and you are."

"What on earth ever gave you that idea?"

He smiled. "Your eyes, sweetheart." He placed two fingers under her chin and held her gaze. "They're so damned pretty, and they say so much."

More tears started, flowing unchecked down her face.

"Who was it, Leah? Who broke your heart? A fellow?"

"My father," she whispered. With a shaking hand, she lifted the hem of her apron and dried her face.

"You miss him that much?"

She felt the beginnings of a wobbly smile. "You've got it all wrong, Mr. Un—"

"Jackson."

She nodded, but didn't say his name. "I grieve for him, yes. I'm sorry he died. He left me…incomplete. He gave me an education, but that was for my mind, not my heart."

"What the hell's that supposed to mean?"

"I don't know how to…to feel or act like other women. There was no one to teach me."

"You grew up with a father. That's more than some folks had."

"You were probably better off on your own," she blurted, then closed her eyes, thinking of all the times her father had berated her, convinced her she had worth only as a doctor, not as a woman. "I loved him with all that I had," she confessed. "With every inch of my heart. But nothing moved him. The best I had was never, ever enough." She swallowed, opening her eyes. "I never learned how to love and be loved."

"Ah, Leah. You know."

"I don't."

"Love makes you care for Bowie Dawson day in and day out, or take the time to teach Iona how to read lips. Love makes you sit up all night with a patient when you're too exhausted to do one more thing."

"That's different. That is my profession."

He gave a low whistle. "Your father did a hell of a job on you, then. He must have been one dandy salesman to sell you that bill of goods. There's not a damned thing wrong with you, Leah Mundy. There's not a woman alive who can love better than you."

"How can you know that?" she asked. "You don't even know me."

"Honey, I know you better than you know yourself." He ran his finger down the front of her surgical apron, casually tracing the rise of her breasts. "You needed that kiss. Hell, you need another one. I know *I* do. You should quit trying to please your father and pay attention to what you really want."

That sparked her anger. "I see. The lonely spinster doctor needs a little excitement in her life, so you've decided to provide it. And when you're gone, I'll live the rest of my life on dreams of you. Isn't that right? Isn't it?"

"Leah—"

"Never mind. I know the answer." She rose stiffly. "Don't stand in my way again, Mr. Underhill."

"I wouldn't think of it." With a mocking bow, he pointed out the exit through the gangway.

She knew he wasn't backing off, just giving her a reprieve. She swept past him and left the boat. Yet as she walked back up to the house, she kept hearing his words echoing through her mind: *You needed that kiss.*

*14 June 1894*

> My dear Penelope,
> On days like today, I envy you your first glimpse of Puget Sound. The sky was never so clear, the water never so blue, nor the trees ever so green as they are here in summer. It does make the heart run wild—

Leah scowled down at the page. No. She would not let her mind wander to Jackson Underhill and what had happened between them. Not now, not ever. Resolutely, she dipped her pen and changed the subject.

Life is not without its troubles, of course. Mrs. U——, the patient for whom you so kindly sent the materials on addiction, came to a bad end in a boating accident. I find myself in need, having lost one of my boarders, as well. My buggy horse has gone lame and I don't know what I shall do for making calls on my patients—

A breeze wafted through the open window, tantalizing her with a whiff of sea air and the scent of blooming wildflowers. She should stop whining to Penny and do something with herself.

But what? She didn't pay social calls. Didn't work in the garden or play lawn tennis or anything of the sort. She just worked. Lately, she worked and she daydreamed; she couldn't help herself.

As if her yearning had conjured him up, Jackson Underhill came walking along the road with a horse in tow. He headed for the barn and carriage house.

Dear heaven, what now?

Setting down her pen, she stuck her head out the window. "Mr. Underhill, what are you doing?"

He stopped walking, raised his hat briefly. "Putting up the new horse."

"You bought a horse?"

"Nope."

"Then—"

"It's *your* horse, because the mare's lame and you need one for making your calls."

She bit her lip, admiring the beautiful animal—it was

a sleek Morgan—but common sense prevailed. "I'm afraid I can't afford—"

"It's paid for." He patted the gelding's cheek. The horse tossed its head in a spirited manner. "Captain Hathaway gave him to you. Since he claimed to be cash poor and unable to pay your fee for taking out his appendix, I told him I reckon this Morgan horse of his would just about cover it."

"Oh. Well, then. Thank you...I think." She could come up with nothing more to say. She ducked back inside before he could see her smile. Captain Hathaway, as miserly as he was prosperous, would have taken until Christmas to settle his fee. She wondered what Jackson had said to get the Morgan. Sitting back down at her desk, she began to write again.

> Sometimes we find Providence in the most unlikely of places, Penny...

Each night, Jackson paced the decks. He couldn't stop thinking about Leah Mundy, and he just didn't get it. He wanted her, and in the strangest way. To want a woman in his bed was one thing, familiar as the need to sneeze. But to want to keep company with her, laugh with her, let her weep against his chest, listen to her ideas, and tell her his deepest dreams—that was quite another, and unexplored territory for Jackson T. Underhill.

He didn't know what to make of it.

The smart thing to do would be to abandon the broken-down *Teatime,* sign onto the next Canada-bound barge or steamer, and disappear.

The notion tingled in his mind, glimmered like a distant star. He knew this feeling. He got it every time he stayed in one spot too long, every time he started noticing a place was pretty and homey and friendly. This was nature's way of telling him it was time to move on. It made sense. The only thing binding him here in these mystical isles had been Carrie. He'd spent years looking for her. Now there was nothing to hold him.

He had a huge hole in his life and just sailing aimlessly away wasn't enough. He wanted more. He wanted a life, not an existence.

He leaned into the rope webbing and heaved a sigh. The lines creaked, and the boat seemed to sigh back as she rocked gently in the harbor waters. Nothing to hold him—but he felt the strangest tug as he thought about leaving, chucking it all, taking off with no more than his gun belt and the clothes on his back.

He ran his hand along the gunwale of the boat. The wood gleamed with a fresh coat of varnish—he'd put it on with his own hand, polished it until it shone. It was just a boat, he told himself. A hulk of old timber and mildewed canvas. Broken pumps, a crooked rudder, a leaky bilge, supplies that would cost him a month of winnings. In addition to the time he'd already put in, he still had weeks of work before she was seaworthy.

"Shit," he said under his breath. He reached into his shirt pocket and took out a flat pewter flask, sucking down a generous swallow of corn whiskey and then grimacing from the harshness of it. Rum was sweeter. But the taste of rum reminded him of Leah, made him remember how velvety soft her mouth was, and that only made him more restless than ever.

A tiny red dot glowed on the dock. Davy's cheroot. "Evening, Jackson," said the harbormaster's assistant.

"Hey, Davy." Jackson held out the flask.

He shook his head. "No, thanks. The *Sea Fox* weighs anchor with the early tide, so I'd best keep my wits about me." He nodded toward the mouth of the harbor, indicating the anchored four-master. "She's bound for Java."

"I know." In addition to thinking about Leah Mundy, Jackson had also thought about the *Sea Fox*. She was headed for the vast Pacific to visit lands he'd only heard of in story and song. If he tried, he could most likely talk his way into a position as sailor aboard the big ship, and he'd be off. Disappearing forever. Into the sunset. "I ought to be weighing anchor myself pretty soon," he said conversationally.

Davy chuckled.

"What?"

"You're an optimist, Jackson. I'll give you that."

"Why do you say that?"

"Even if you get the pumps working right, there's the small matter of the leak in the bilge. And the rudder, and the lanyard pulley system, and you need a new mainsail and spanker—"

"Well now, that's real encouraging, Davy," Jackson said mockingly. "I got here from Seattle, didn't I?"

"From Seattle. Along a smooth, protected shipping lane most men could swim on a calm day. If you're going any farther, you're headed for some rough water. The Strait of Juan de Fuca's nothing to scoff at." The young man sucked on his cheroot. "I've seen ships break up like matchsticks. I grew up near the Columbia bar out at the coast. A couple of hours of heavy seas could eat a schooner alive. I've watched people drown, and you don't know how helpless that makes a man feel." He fell silent for a moment.

Jackson guessed he was thinking about *La Tache*. According to Rapsilver, the steam vessel had been sound. But something had gone wrong. Very wrong.

"Those ships I saw come apart were a lot more seaworthy than the *Eat Me*," Davy said.

"The *Teatime*," Jackson corrected.

"You still haven't repainted the name. But I guess you've got plenty of other repairs to make before you can get out of this harbor safely."

"What about unsafely?"

"Hell, you could leave tomorrow. But you'd end up swimming back."

"You're an irritating little know-it-all. And a pain in the ass to boot."

"I've been called worse. Bet you have, too."

A shiver that had nothing to do with the cool June night passed through Jackson. "Uh-huh."

He stood poised at a crossroads with Davy. The self-assured young man held out the hand of friendship. It was up to Jackson to reach out and take it. But he couldn't. Life just hadn't taught him how to be any man's friend. Or any woman's, for that matter.

"So what's it to be tomorrow?" Davy asked, clearly sensing Jackson closing up. "Test that aft pump?"

Jackson didn't say anything. He hadn't moved, yet he felt as if he were on the verge of some great precipice. He could step back now, slink away, sign onto the *Sea Fox*, and disappear. Or he could step off the edge.

And pray like hell for a net.

He wanted to stay. Wanted it fiercely. He'd never belonged anywhere in his life, but he belonged on this boat. It was the first thing that was really *his*. Not some fleabag hotel room, not a bedroll on bumpy ground. But a ship. A real, honest-to-goodness ship he'd won fair and square.

Texas was a long way away, he told himself. His route to Puget Sound had been slow and circuitous. No one would find him here. He was certain of that. Almost.

"Jackson?" Davy Morgan prompted. "You listening to me?"

"Yeah," he said at last. "I'll think about it." But he already knew the answer.

Less than an hour later, Jackson stood before the chandler of the *Sea Fox*. "Sumatra?" he said.

"Yeah, we call at Java, too." The chandler yawned. "Sometimes Bali and Fiji. It's a hell of an adventure."

The exotic names tugged at Jackson like a bright, shiny lure. "I'll sign on, then."

"I can't give you full share."

"I'll take what you've got."

The man studied him. "All right."

Jackson blinked at the swiftness of the man's reply.

The chandler took a slow pull on his bottle. "I won't ask any questions. We generally don't around here. Be aboard before the early tide. If you're not here, we won't wait."

"I wouldn't expect you to." Jackson went back to his own boat. *His own boat.* In honor of his last night aboard, he intended to get drunk and try to quit thinking about Leah.

When he bedded down in his bunk, he knew it was impossible. Tonight he couldn't drink enough to get drunk, and his mind kept wandering to Leah Mundy. When Carrie was alive, he'd worried about her, but now she couldn't occupy his thoughts anymore. His quest was over and he'd never thought beyond it, not until now. He'd just been working on surviving, not thinking.

*What would you have done if the boat hadn't exploded?* Leah Mundy made him think. The feelings she stirred in him made him ache.

It was lonely as hell on the boat, he reflected. But it was his. It was home.

Not for much longer. Not if he signed onto the four-master.

He lay awake for a long time, listening to the hush of the water lapping the hull, the trickle of a leak somewhere below, the cry of an owl on the hunt.

Leah, he thought. Leah. Her lips were so damned soft, and the rest of her... He groaned and shifted uncomfortably on the bunk. The schooner had been built to accommodate the captain's wife, the bunk in the main stateroom wide and comfortable. If he had any sense at all, he'd make love to Leah and get her out of his system.

But deep inside, he knew Leah Mundy was not a one-night adventure. She was a forever kind of woman, which meant she was not for him.

The distant thud of hooves roused Jackson. Too many months on the run had sharpened his senses, and he sat up fast, slamming his forehead on the beam above his bunk. Swearing, he opened a hatch and looked out toward the road.

A dark horseman holding a flickering lantern galloped toward the boardinghouse. Something in his manner—the flying cloak, the urgent posture as he leaned over the horse's neck—conveyed a sense of danger. Before he could even think, Jackson had jumped into his clothes, stuck a pistol into the waistband of his jeans, and was running toward the boardinghouse. He reached it just as Leah and the horseman emerged from the surgery.

"What is it?" he asked, sizing up the stranger. His anxiety subsided. The youngish man had a light beard and terrified eyes. A farmer come looking for help, not for trouble.

*Unlike me,* Jackson reflected, thinking of his first midnight visit to Leah's house.

"Mr. Amity's wife is ill. I've got to go to her," Leah said.

She was all business in a clean smock with her hair in a bun. Christ, it was the middle of the night. What did she do, use starch in her hair as well as her apron?

"Now," she said, "you can either help Mr. Douglas hitch up the buggy or stand aside, Mr. Underhill. I'm in quite a hurry."

"Then you should stop wasting time calling me Mr. Underhill," Jackson said, and he raced across the yard to the coach house.

# *Seven*

⸺◦⸺

In the coach yard, Iona stood holding a lamp and watching wide-eyed as Battle Douglas wrestled with the reins of the new gelding. Perched precariously on the high-sprung buggy seat, Battle shouted "Whoa!" and yanked with all his might. The horse backed the buggy up against a boxwood hedge at the side of the coach house.

"Hold him, Mr. Douglas, please!" Leah shouted.

"Can't!" he hollered back. "Lord-a-mercy, I might as well try to hold the wind!"

The horse shot forward. The buggy lurched, and Battle Douglas toppled off the back and into the bushes. The runaway horse lowered its head. Ears flat, it raced toward the dark field beyond the road, the buggy clattering behind it.

"So that's your new horse," Battle grumbled. "He'll do us a lot of good."

Leah's heart sank. She was no rider and didn't even care for driving after dark. But it seemed Battle's driving was limited to a well-behaved horse. Now, without the buggy, she had no fast way to reach Mrs. Amity, who'd had a troublesome pregnancy and was only eight months along.

Wishing she knew a few more swearwords, Leah helped Battle to his feet. "Half wild devil," he muttered.

Then, out of the shadows near the house burst a huge black shape, spectral and swift as a night bird. Leah stumbled back, watching it take off in the direction of the runaway gelding.

"What in tarnation was that?" Battle asked, brushing off his clothes.

Hume Amity, the farmer, came running. "That was Underhill. Grabbed my horse's reins from me, and off he went." In the lamplight, he appeared pale and shaken, his face covered in sweat.

She experienced a strange thrill at the idea of Jackson leaping astride a horse and going to her aid. Wondering if Jackson had ever looked so young and lost as this man, Leah squeezed Amity's hand briefly.

"Mr. Underhill will fetch the buggy back, and we'll get to your wife in no time." She had no idea why she spoke with such certainty. She'd never seen Jackson ride a horse or drive a buggy. Yet somehow she knew he would do it with the hard-driven competence with which he seemed to do all things. When it came to moving quickly and boldly, he had no match.

Moments later, they heard a clopping of hooves. Jackson sat astride Hume's horse, drawing the gelding along behind him. "Get in the buggy, Doc, and tell me the way." He dismounted and tossed the reins to Hume.

Slightly dazed by the speed with which Jackson had controlled the situation, Leah climbed up and took the lamp from Iona.

"You intend to drive?" Battle inquired. Relief rang clear in his voice.

Jackson glanced in the direction of the dark harbor. Leah wondered what he was thinking.

"Will we be back by early tide?" he asked.

Annoyed, she said, "People do not get well on a schedule. Now, are you coming or not?"

He hesitated, then said, "Yeah. I'll come."

"You be careful now." Battle Douglas gave the horse a wide berth. "That gelding's a devil. It's like holding the wind, I tell you."

"I've had practice at that," Jackson said, a half grin flashing across his face before he flicked the reins and commanded the horse to go.

Leah knew she should lower the lantern and look away, but instead, she found herself staring at Jackson as he drove. He had dressed in haste, she could tell. His shirt was unbuttoned, revealing a muscular chest covered by a sheen of perspiration. The gleam of lamplight on his bare flesh created a discomfiting jolt in her. She dropped her gaze lower, able to see even in the swinging lamp glow that the top button of his denim jeans was undone.

The warmth that had flooded through her earlier came back. She was glad for the cloak of night, for she knew a blush stained her cheeks. It was completely inappropriate, undoubtedly unprofessional, but in the midst of a medical emergency, she was having lustful thoughts.

"Think the patient will live, Doc?" he asked in a lazy, almost-laughing voice.

Sweet heaven, he knew. He had guessed her thoughts. She blinked, snapping her head around to face resolutely forward.

He clamped the reins between his teeth and leaned back on the seat to button his jeans and shirt. When he finished, he called to Hume, "Is your wife in a bad way?"

"I think so, yes." Hume's voice wavered as he trotted ahead on his horse.

"Real bad?"

"Real bad."

"Then why the hell are you holding that animal down to a trot?"

"So's the buggy can keep up," Hume said defensively.

"I'll keep up," Jackson promised.

Hume hesitated only an instant; then he kicked the horse with everything he had.

"Doc?" Jackson said as if only now remembering her presence.

"Yes?"

"Hang on."

"Hang on?"

*"Tight."*

Leah clutched her bag between her feet and gripped the seat rail with both hands. A snap of the reins sent the Morgan flying into the dark. The buggy bounced over ruts and potholes. Lamplight streaked past the fields of salt grass that lined the road. Long marsh reeds nodded and bowed to the wind created by their swift passage.

Leah could hear the breeze whistling through her hair, which was fast escaping its neat bun. The speed took her breath away; the sensation of hurtling into unseen darkness stunned her. Yet never once was she afraid. There was something about Jackson, some hard, dauntless competence that made her feel utterly safe, never mind that they were galloping madly into the night.

Within minutes, they had arrived at the farmstead, a little log house snug against the side of a hill, dark hulks of outbuildings on the slope behind it. The smell of manure and grain hung thick in the air.

Jackson drew back on the reins, and the gelding didn't even think about resisting. It halted and stood, head dropped in submission while he tied it to a rail in front of the house. "I'll walk both horses as soon as you get inside," he told Leah.

It seemed the most natural thing in the world for him to reach up and grasp her around the waist, to swing her down as if she weighed nothing, and then to hand her the bag. She found herself thinking, even as she rushed into the house, that with a driver like Jackson, emergencies on the island might be met more quickly.

The cabin consisted of a single room with a sagging curtain dividing the living area from the bedroom. Leah swept the curtain aside to find the area illuminated by a lantern hanging from a nail above the rope-and-timber bedstead. Marjorie Amity lay with her stomach distended, her back arched, her neck twisting at an angle. Her eyes rolled back in her head, yet she seemed strangely aware of Leah, for her hand reached out in supplication.

Convulsions, Leah realized, feeling her heart turn cold. She wished Sophie were here, but her assistant had been called away to Camano Island, where some of her people still lived. Sophie's face had been grim and tight as she'd gotten into the canoe with the silent Skagit brave. Something bad had happened, but Sophie wouldn't say what.

"Hume, I'll need plenty of hot water," Leah called over her shoulder. "Get started right away." She knelt beside the bed, taking Marjorie's flailing arm. "There now," Leah said. "Let me give you something to calm your nerves." Opening her bag, she measured out a quarter grain of morphine, thought for a moment, then increased the dose to a half grain. The convulsions were severe; she had to control them as quickly as possible.

The narcotic worked rapidly. How ironic that the substance that had destroyed Carrie could be used for good. By the time Hume came in to build up the fire, his wife lay peacefully on the bed. He paused, hugging an armload of wood to his chest. "Glory be, Dr. Mundy. You healed her."

Leah stood, brushing off her smock as he stoked the fire beneath a huge iron kettle. She went to a washstand, filled the bowl, and began washing herself up to the elbows with carbolic. "She's not healed, only sedated." This was the part of doctoring she despised—telling the bad news.

She concentrated on her washing as if it was the most important thing in the world. And it was, in a way, she reflected. Antiseptic practices had saved more lives than anyone could have imagined.

"What do you mean, ma'am?"

"I haven't healed her." Outside, she could hear Jackson dealing with the horses, probably walking them until the sweat dried. "I gave her something to control the convulsions. But I'm afraid the instructions in a case like your wife's are to empty the uterus."

"Empty the…" He stared at her, uncomprehending.

"The womb, Mr. Amity."

"You mean, take the baby?"

"Yes." Leah bit the inside of her lip, keeping her face carefully blank. Professionally detached.

"But it's too— It's early. She's got another month."

"I know that."

Leah noticed he was shaking from head to toe. The man was surely no more than twenty; his wife didn't look to be eighteen. She remembered what Jackson had told her about words as blunt instruments. She remembered his caution to her: *Sometimes you use words like a sledgehammer.*

"Hume, let's go out on the porch so we don't disturb Marjorie with our talk."

Jackson came back from the barn, a long shadow in starlight. "Found the water," he said to Hume. "Got yours all put up, and mine's been walked and watered."

"Obliged." But Hume's mind was clearly on what Leah had to say. Since she would need Jackson's help with what was to come next, she motioned for him to join them.

"Even though it's early," she said, "I have to take the baby. You see, the convulsions mean that Marjorie is suffering severe stress to her kidneys. If the pregnancy goes on, the organs could cease to function altogether."

"Is that bad?" Hume asked, though his voice hinted that he knew the answer.

"It's extremely dangerous. Your wife could die."

Hume made a strangled, hiccuping sound in his throat and turned away, his fists clenching and unclenching at his sides. Leah wanted to go to him, to touch him, but she felt awkward. Before she could make up her mind what to do or say next, Jackson stepped forward, clamping his hand on Hume's shoulder. "The doc knows what she's doing," he said gently. "Let's just hear her out."

Hume nodded, turning back as he dragged his sleeve across his tear-streaked face. "But...Margie's labor ain't started yet."

"I realize that. There is a way to dilate the uter—the womb—and take the baby. It's a serious procedure, best done in a hospital, but we'll have to manage right here."

"Now? Tonight?"

"Yes."

Jackson gave the younger man's shoulder a squeeze. "How about that? You're going to be a papa tonight."

"I'm scared," Hume said.

"Don't blame you," Jackson said. "It's a scary thing, bringing a baby before its time. But Dr. Mundy says it's a lot scarier to wait."

Leah looked at him curiously. What a fine manner he had with the young farmer, not patronizing his fear or talking over his head, but reassuring him that she'd chosen the best course of action. This sort of talk was something she'd never learned in her schooling. Strange that she was learning it from a man like Jackson.

She went inside and prepared herself in silence, praying that her skill and knowledge were equal to the task. Ideally, the baby should be taken in a hospital with an army of nurses dancing attendance. But here on the island, kitchen surgery was the order of the day.

The men came in, and she faced them calmly. "I'll need your help."

"Yes, ma'am." Hume almost dropped another load of wood, so violently was he trembling. She could tell he wouldn't be of much use.

"Keep the fire going," she told him, "and prepare plenty of hot water. Mr. Underhill, I'll need you, too."

"Me?"

"Yes."

"But—" He broke off, cast a look at Marjorie, then nodded. "Just tell me what to do."

After stacking clean linens by the bed and checking on the supply of hot water, then washing her hands again and again and insisting Jackson and Hume do the same, Leah squared her shoulders and struggled to clear her mind.

She hesitated, standing at the foot of the bed and looking at her patient. All that stood between the groggy girl and death were Leah's skill and whatever luck happened to be passing by tonight.

Dear God, it didn't seem to be enough.

"Doc?" Jackson came up behind her and whispered in her ear. He smelled faintly of the night air and carbolic. "Now what?"

She drew a deep breath. "Now…we begin."

He never balked at doing anything she asked. She anesthetized the girl with chloroform rather than ether, which tended to explode in the presence of fire. Jackson held the mask in place while Leah set herself to delivering the baby.

The husband hovered nearby, keeping the fire stoked and hot water in good supply. Each time he started to look nervous, Jackson thought of some small task for him to do, keeping him busy. Simple tasks that didn't require much thought, but that kept the hands occupied.

Leah draped Marjorie with a blanket and began a tentative exploration. The uterus contracted around Leah's hand, the powerful muscles squeezing hard. Then she felt what she had dreaded from the start—the infant's foot.

"It's breech," she said.

Jackson nodded, but made no reply. He seemed to know as well as Leah did that the position was dangerous for the baby and the mother.

With her hand growing numb from the contracted uterus, Leah managed to bring down, inch by inch, the tiny feet and legs. It took at least two hours. Hume paced a trench in the dirt floor of the cabin. Jackson said nothing, but followed instructions with the chloroform. A little box wall clock rang the time: Five in the morning.

Leah glanced at Jackson and saw him staring at the clock. "Early tide," he muttered.

"What's that?"

"Nothing, Doc. You go on with your work." He tore his gaze away from the clock and concentrated on keeping the mask in place.

At last, it was time to deliver the head. Leah moved her arm past the baby's legs and slipped her finger into the tiny mouth, which she could finally reach. It was a technique she'd heard of but never used.

The baby responded instantly, flexing its chin onto its chest and slipping right out. With a cry of triumph and relief, Leah caught it. A second later, the infant gasped for breath and let out a lusty wail. "Mr. Amity!" she said in a broken, jubilant voice. "Come and hold your daughter."

With a crooked, weary grin on her face, she looked up at Jackson. To her complete amazement, he sat perfectly still, holding the mask and staring at the baby while a single tear rolled down his cheek.


"Long night, eh, Doc?" Jackson asked as they drove slowly through the dawn toward town. He still felt light-headed and giddy from the strange new experience of assisting at a birth. His every sense was heightened. With crystal clarity he savored the ocean scent in the air and the sound of the wind through the trees, the warmth of the small woman beside him and a sense of triumph so intense it was almost frightening.

"I've endured longer," she said.

He heard the smile in her voice and slipped his arm around her shoulders. She stiffened, but didn't pull away. Damn, it felt good to hold her. To hold a woman with no thought beyond holding her. So he'd missed shipping out on the *Sea Fox*. So what? She'd given him a reason to stay.

"Can I ask you something, Doc?"

"You may."

"How do you do that without fainting?"

"Deliver a baby?"

"Yeah."

"If I faint, it does my patient no good at all. It certainly bodes ill for the baby. I don't allow myself to faint."

"So disciplined."

"Being a physician requires it." She gazed pensively at the lightening sky. "It requires everything you have."

After Mrs. Amity's ordeal, Jackson understood that. "But after you give it everything, what's left for you?"

She yawned. Somewhere, an owl hooted, sounding almost human. "A crick in the neck from sitting up all night with my hand inside a uterus." She laughed softly at the incredulous sound he made. "Surely you don't expect polite conversation at this hour of the morning."

"I guess not. And you didn't answer my question."

"What's left for me?" She toyed with the fringe of her crocheted shawl. "I just saved that woman's life. Her life, and that of her baby. I just saved Hume Amity's world from collapsing. What other reward do I need?"

"I noticed you didn't ask for a fee."

"They'll pay what they can, when they can. The boardinghouse will be swimming in butter and cream for the next year."

Damn her. Why couldn't she want more? Expect more? Dream of more? He wanted her to yearn as he yearned. To step out of her self-satisfied existence and see that there could be more for her if only she'd reach for it.

The eastern horizon had faded to a misty gray. To the north, the shadows darkened, seeming to move eerily.

"All these lives you save, Doc. Do they ever make you wish you had a life of your own?"

She drew away from him on the buggy seat. "Damn you, Jackson Underhill—"

"Doc—" He felt the danger before he understood it. He had a sixth sense for it, could feel it like the crackle of air before a lightning strike. Without even thinking, he grabbed Leah and shoved her to the floor of the buggy, then ran the horse off the road into a glade of alder trees.

"What on earth are you doing?" Leah demanded.

"Shut up," he said through his teeth, his gaze scanning the horizon.

"But I—"

"Just shut the hell up."

She went completely quiet and motionless. His chin brushed her silky hair, and he inhaled the scent of her. The misty dark quality of early dawn made it difficult to see. Then he spied a shadow moving along the rocky, cliff-topped shoreline. The dark shape wavered, then slipped up a hill and disappeared into the distance.

"Jackson?" Leah whispered. "What did you see?"

"I don't know," he admitted. "But I didn't like it." He felt trapped, hunted. It was unlikely that someone was skulking around after him, but he couldn't shake the feeling of being hounded. He took Leah's arm and helped her back to the seat beside him. "Is there much smuggling going on here?"

"I've heard there is." A sarcastic edge crept into her voice. "But remember, I have no life outside of medicine, so I wouldn't know."

"I'm sorry, honey."

"Don't call me honey."

"Excuse the hell out of me for mistaking you for something sweet."

She glared obstinately ahead. He missed her easy, satisfied smile, the camaraderie they had shared after the night of travail. But her anger was his fault.

"I had no call to say such things to you," he said. *Even if they're true.*

"Then why did you?"

"Because I want to know."

"Why?"

"Because I care."

She fell quiet, settling back against the seat with an incredulous expression on her face. Jackson kicked himself for both mistakes. He should know better than to care about a woman. He should sure as hell know better than to admit it.

He hastened to change the subject, hoping she'd forget what he'd just said. "What sort of things could be smuggled around here? Whiskey and firearms?"

"Are you thinking of trying it?"

"Doc…"

She scowled at him, then blew out a breath and cooperated. "Wool, too, or so I hear. Since we're so close to Canada, these waters are quite busy with boats trying to avoid the Revenue Service vessels. It's a fact of life."

He pointed at the distant shore. "What's over there, around that cove to the south?"

"Why, nothing. Unsettled land. It's not good for farming—too many cliffs are hazardous for the animals. Sheriff St. Croix lost a good horse off one last year. The tide pools are deep, too. Some of the caves fill up at high tide. It's a good place to pick mussels, I'm told."

Jackson wished like hell he knew what had spooked him. Now that the sky was brightening, he couldn't even tell where he'd spied the flowing shadows. He wondered why it mattered. He ought to be on his way up through

Deception Pass, past the San Juan Islands into Canada, maybe to Klondike country and beyond.

Leah Mundy and this town ought to be just another memory to him. Instead, he'd spent the night helping an ill-tempered lady doctor. And he'd enjoyed every minute of it.

As they were putting up the horse and buggy, Leah leaned her elbows on the stall door and said, "I haven't thanked you, Mr. Underhill."

"Jackson," he said automatically.

She cleared her throat. "Thank you for assisting me last night. I don't know what I would have done without you."

He grinned. "Knowing you, Doc, you'd have managed."

She tilted her head to one side. The only clue to her weariness was an untidy wisp of hair that escaped her bun. "Why do you say that?"

He hung the horse's bridle on a hook. "I guess it's just your way. Figuring things out. There are some who can barely tie their shoes in the morning without help." He shut his mouth and grabbed a curry brush. He'd said too much.

Leah went to the other side of the horse and watched him over its broad back. "You mean your wi—Carrie."

"I suppose I do."

She clasped her hands. "You've hardly spoken of her since the accident. I mean, what happened—"

"I'm all right," he said brusquely. "I'm…all right." Yet as he spoke, his vigor with the brush became violent, and the horse shied, shoving Leah against the wall. Jackson swore, yanking the horse out of the way as he reached for her. The disgruntled horse snapped, teeth biting the air very close to his ear. "Goddamn it," he said, hauling Leah out of the stall and turning to the horse. "You damned nag—"

She took his arm and gave it a tug, then closed the stall door. "Sit down!" With a none-too-gentle push, she directed him backward onto a milk crate. She put her face very close to his. "You're not all right."

"I say I am."

"Just because you say it doesn't make it so."

"I'm damned glad you know everything."

"I don't know everything. But Carrie's death hurt you. I know that. You'd be less than human if it didn't."

"What are you going to do about it? Give me chloroform? Lance me somewhere and let the pus drain out?"

"I'd like to lance that temper of yours." She sat back on her heels and glared at him. "I just thought perhaps I could help."

"There's nothing to help. She took off with a rich man and they died in a boating accident. Yeah, it's rotten. But it can't be changed. And it sure as hell can't be helped by my standing around and wringing my hands."

Her brown eyes searched his face so intently that he wanted to look away, but pride wouldn't let him. "You accepted what happened so easily. It just seems so…"

"Heartless? Cruel? I've been called worse."

She gave him a bitter smile. "So have I. But how can you hide your pain? She was your wife. She was going to have your baby."

"It wasn't m—" he blurted, then caught himself.

Too late. She'd heard. Her face softened, long dark lashes sweeping down as she blinked in surprise. "You weren't the father of her baby?"

"That's none of your goddamned business. And it's sure as hell not the reason I'm not beating my chest and tearing out my hair. If the baby hadn't—if it had been born, I'd have raised it as my own. I swear I would have.''

"Then you did love her. With more generosity of heart than most men would under the circumstances.''

He'd lain awake for hours wondering what he'd felt for Carrie. Was it love, or some stubborn sense of chivalry? Had she been his ruling passion or his cross to bear? Leah seemed to know better than he did. Why was that? Why was it that she helped him bear the unbearable?

He measured the risk, wondering what it would cost him to tell this soft-eyed, compassionate woman something about himself. He had grown so used to holding back the truth that it was difficult to find the words. But oddly, once he started speaking, the story flowed like a river. "When we were kids, Carrie and I lived—if you could call it living—in a poor school in Chicago. There was no chance of me being adopted—I'd been there too long and I'd grown plenty mean. But Carrie was a pretty thing, and when she started getting prettier—if you know what I mean—she was adopted.''

"Well, that's a relief.''

"Leah, were you born naive or is that something they taught you in doctor school?''

"What do you mean?''

"I mean, Carrie was adopted by a pimp—someone who procures young girls for bordellos.''

The color dropped from her face with amazing speed. "Oh, dear God.''

"Dear God is right. I got away from the orphanage as quick as I could, but I wasn't quick enough. People on that side of the law tend to move around, change their identities, leave no trail. Took me years to find her again.'' He looked out through the door of the coach house. The rising sun formed a burning half circle over the waters of Penn Cove.

"So that's what you did with your life? Searched for Carrie?"

"As much as I was able. I had to make some sort of living," he said. "Did plenty of cardplaying, a little roulette. Crewed on a yacht in Lake Michigan and went on a whaling ship." He thought about his gun. "Odd jobs for a fellow not afraid to get his hands dirty. But I was always looking. I never stopped looking."

"And you found her." Leah clasped her hands together. "How wonderful it must have been for you both."

"Wonderful" was not the word he thought of when he remembered their reunion. He recalled Carrie's state—the laughing red mouth and unfocused eyes, her blithe refusal to remember St. I's or acknowledge that she recognized him until she had looked across the dead body on the floor and said, "Help me, Jackson."

"I guess, all along, what I wanted was for her to be all right," he told Leah. "To be well and happy, to have someone looking after her. But Carrie never really fitted in with a regular life. No matter where I took her, what I gave her, she couldn't be happy for long. Couldn't feel safe. She was like a burning candle—bright, but gone before you know it." Feeling prickly, he got up and fetched a scoop of oats for the horse. "So, are you satisfied, Doc? Or do you want to cut me open and have a look at my heart? It's probably black as the ace of spades."

She stood, too, and glowered at him. "There's no need to be sarcastic."

In truth, he did feel the pain, but it was like the pain of having a bullet removed. It hurt like a son of a bitch, yet he knew the healing could start now. That scared him. A lot. He'd given too much of himself to Leah Mundy. He had to get it back, or he'd be lost.

"You bring out the best in me," he said with even more sarcasm.

"We're both tired. We should get some rest."

"Ah, another wise prescription from the lady doctor." He could feel his control slipping, could feel the anger building up inside him, looking for a way out. Leah Mundy gave him that way. Leah with her doe eyes and her vulnerable lips and her bright mind and soft heart. "I reckon you must've been mighty proud of yourself, getting Carrie well like you did."

"I understand now," she retorted. "You think *I'm* responsible for Carrie's leaving. That's why you're so angry. That's why—"

"Yeah, right. You know everything. Well, let me ask you this. If you're so all-fired good at healing others, why can't you heal yourself?"

She gasped as if he'd struck her. The stricken look on her face enraged him. "I don't need healing."

"So it's normal to be a lonely old maid, delivering other women's babies, poking your nose in everyone's business and pretending you don't hear when they talk behind your back?" He could see the hurt growing as he spoke, but his rage was too intense, burning out of control, and there stood Leah, a lightning rod for his anger. "You can heal others, but you can't heal yourself. You can't even figure out what's wrong."

She went white as a sheet, her lips outlined by fury. "I imagine you can, Mr. Underhill."

"It's obvious. You don't know how to associate with people unless there's something wrong with them." He hammered away at her, knowing it was his only defense against his desire for her. "You stand outside the fence, looking in, telling other folks how to live their lives, but not taking your own damned advice."

"I do worthwhile work," she said, an edge of desperation in her voice. "That's all I need."

"Yeah, well, take that to your lonely bed each night and see if it can keep you warm."

He saw the moment she snapped. She absorbed his words, and they seemed to course over her like a bucket of ice water. She balled her hands into fists and shoved at his chest. "And I suppose you have found the perfect way to live. Drifting along without wondering about tomorrow. Running away from your problems. Tell me, Mr. Know-All, have you ever truly seen anything through?"

Now it was as if the bucket had drenched him, for the truth of her words chilled him to the marrow. He never stayed. He never saw anything through. Even Carrie. He thought he'd done his duty in taking her away from Texas. But now, Leah was holding up a mirror, and he didn't like what he saw—a man who never stayed anywhere long enough to call a place home. A man who had been running all his life and would probably never stop.

Putting down roots, facing up to commitments—those notions were alien to him. He wanted them, sure. He wanted to swim with Bowie Dawson and learn the secrets of the sea from Davy Morgan. He wanted to watch another baby being born. He wanted to look at a place and say "This is home. I'm home for good." But he'd never do that. He didn't have the guts.

Even last night, as he was putting the finishing touches on the rudder, he had already been planning to sign onto a merchant ship, leaving the *Teatime* behind as he'd left behind everything that was ever worth having. He'd missed the *Sea Fox* on account of Leah. Was he sorry? He had no idea.

"I'm glad you're so damned smart, Doc. I hope all those brains keep you company in your old age." He turned on his boot heel and stalked out of the coach house.

"I can do without your lectures," she said, hurrying after him.

"Then why are you following me?"

The question flustered her. She slowed down, and he sped up, intent on getting back to the boat. Away from Leah Mundy of the soft eyes and the hard questions. Away from the truth she made him face. And most of all, away from the shameful hurt he'd dealt her.

# *Eight*

For the next week, Jackson worked on his boat. It was the damnedest thing. He'd been all prepared to hightail it. Hell, on a clear day, he could walk to the west side of the island and *see* Canada. See freedom. All he had to do was get on a mail boat or a passenger steamer, and in a matter of hours, he'd be out of the country.

But running away wasn't that simple, he was finding out. The lure of the sea wasn't so powerful anymore. Whether he liked it or not—and he didn't much like it at all—Leah Mundy had thrown down a challenge. He surprised himself by taking it up.

Her words taunted him as he tinkered and tied and stitched and varnished. *Have you ever truly seen anything through?*

Her voice ran through his head like a melody he wanted to forget, but couldn't. Damn her. Damn her to hell. Damn her for making him want to do something right for once in his life.

The *Teatime* became his challenge. By God, he would fix this old mud bucket. He would sail away on this boat that belonged to him and him alone. He would do it. He would make it work, no matter how long it took.

"Mr. Underhill?"

He had climbed the mast; a creaking leather belt beneath his hips held him in place while he fitted a block and pulley through a high mast band. Looking down, he recognized Sophie Whitebear, her broad, olive-toned face turned up to him.

"Up here," he called. "Is something wrong? Does Lea— Does the doc need something?" As he spoke, he shinnied down the mast. "Is that horse doing all right?" After the near disaster on the way to the Amity farm, he had made a point of spending an hour every evening harness training the Morgan. He landed on the deck with a barefooted *thump* and felt the boat list with his weight. "Well?"

Sophie's wide brow pleated with worry. She toyed with the end of her braid. "I came to ask you something."

He flashed her a grin and a gentlemanly bow. "Ask away."

She seemed distracted, looking left and right, a furtiveness about her manner that made Jackson's hackles rise. "The night you went with Dr. Mundy, I was away."

"She said you went to your people. There was some sort of trouble."

"A murder."

The word chilled his blood. A murder. The taking of a life. He could see his feelings reflected in Sophie's haunted eyes. The sudden shock of murder set the world on its side, yanked it around in a different direction, and no matter how hard a person tried, he could never get back to the way things were.

"What happened?" he asked in a low voice.

"On Camano Island, where many of my people live, there was a shooting. It was over something stupid. Firewater, of course. Ever since the *Franqis* trappers and the Bostons came here from the East, there has been this trouble with whiskey. It makes my people stupid and angry and careless. One man shot another over a matter no one can remember now."

"So you've told someone, right? Told the authorities?"

"The Indian agent in Port Townsend has been told."

"So I guess he's looking into it," Jackson said.

"When one Indian murders another, the white man doesn't care." Sophie spoke without malice, but with a matter-of-fact acceptance that tore at Jackson's conscience. "One man is dead," she said, "and his murderer escaped. We will never see him again. He will probably get drunk and fall to his death or drown. Perhaps he already has."

"So what is it you need to ask me?" Even as he spoke, he felt himself being drawn to the problem. He didn't like it a bit, didn't like knowing other people's business, didn't like caring about it.

She looked around briefly, then held out her hand and dropped something into his. "There is the shot that killed him," she said. "I want to know what it is."

Jackson stared at the spent rimfire, copper-headed bullet. The slug was slightly bent, and he wondered what vital part of a man's body the bullet had entered, what resisting bone had put the dent in the metal. "It's from a pistol," he said.

"But what kind of pistol?"

He turned the bullet over in his hand. "Damn," he said through his teeth. He stuffed the bullet into his pocket. "Who else have you shown this to?"

"Captain Faye, the Indian agent. And Sheriff St. Croix. That's how I know white men don't care. He said it was out of his jurisdiction, and that I should stop bothering people about a dead Indian.''

Not for the first time, Jackson felt a wave of contempt for Lemuel St. Croix. The man cared more about silken waistcoats than about law enforcement. Not that St. Croix was stupid; Jackson had always sensed a certain cold craftiness in him. He just didn't seem to care. Particularly about Indians.

Remembering the scar the sheriff always tried to hide beneath his fancy hat, Jackson figured he knew why.

"So you're not ready to let this go," he said to Sophie.

She stared at the dock beneath her feet. "I can't. The dead man is my half brother."

He brushed her cheek with his hand. "I'm sorry. But why come to me?"

"Because I thought you'd help."

"Whatever gave you that idea?"

She shrugged. "You act like a father to Bowie. You trained the new gelding for Leah. I saw you splitting wood for Perpetua. You just…help people."

"Sugar, there's a difference between chopping wood and getting involved in murder." His neck prickled with discomfort. "But you said the murderer is gone and probably drinking himself to death. So why do you need help?"

"I want to know who is supplying these man-killing guns to my people."

"The murderer probably stole the gun, and it's at the bottom of Puget Sound by now. I'm sorry as hell for your brother, but it's over for him. Best to move on, look to the future." His own advice about Carrie. He ought to heed it. "I'll keep an eye out. That's all I can do."

"I see." She turned away and walked back down the dock.

Jackson watched her for a long time. He noted the tired dignity of her posture, the plodding tread of her feet on the planks. He wished he could help her. But he knew he could help her best by keeping her from asking too many questions.

The spent bullet felt like a run of bad luck in his pocket. He'd recognized it the minute he'd seen it.

It was U.S. Army issue.

For the third time in as many weeks, Leah was summoned to the preacher's house to look after his wife. She drove Sophie and herself in the buggy with ease and assurance, the Morgan behaving beautifully, responsive to every tug on the reins. Although Jackson T. Underhill hadn't spoken to her since their quarrel two weeks earlier, he had, for some inexplicable reason, taken the horse in hand and buggy trained the gelding.

She was thinking, as she passed the wooden shop fronts that stood shoulder to shoulder along the waterfront, that she should thank him.

How simple it seemed. "Thank you, Mr. Underhill," she muttered under her breath, "for training the new horse." One sentence. That's all she had to say to him. But she knew she would choke on every word.

"Did you say something?" Sophie asked.

"Just thinking aloud."

Sophie sat on the bench beside Leah, her calico skirts handsomely arrayed with beads and shells. A few of the children playing in the street spotted her and started patting their mouths, giving war whoops.

"Don't mind them," Leah said, irritated.

"I don't."

"Well, hell's bells. I do."

Sophie gave a serene nod. "I know. You mind every

little thing. Ever since your quarrel with Jackson Underhill.''

"That's not so," Leah protested.

"Whatever you say." Sophie smoothed her hands over her skirts. "He works like a madman on that boat. He's determined to get it out to sea."

A knot of men stood on the board walkway in front of the sheriff's office. Leah gave them only a passing glance; then she noticed the tallest of them. Sun blond hair. Broad shoulders. A face she prayed each night to forget.

"Speak of the devil," Sophie said.

"What is Jackson Underhill doing with the sheriff?" Leah's heart tripped a little in her chest. Had his past caught up with him? Was he in trouble?

"I told him what happened on Camano Island. About the murder."

"I don't understand. What does it have to do with Jackson?"

"The sheriff did not answer my question about the gun that killed my kinsman. I thought Jackson Underhill might know."

Leah relaxed against the seat, relieved more than she would admit. Before turning up Main Street, she allowed herself a final passing glance over her shoulder. He wore a leather vest with no shirt beneath it, and his easy way of leaning against the peeled pine stair rail accentuated his rugged good looks.

She stared a moment too long, and he caught her. He pushed his hat up a little and raised one hand. Even from a distance, she saw a slow grin slide across his face. Cheeks aflame, she snapped herself around.

They pulled up at the preacher's house, a trim, white frame dwelling adjacent to the church. The Reverend

Cranney was well-to-do, his wife a notorious snob and the self-appointed arbiter of good taste and society. A former favorite of Leah's father, she was still a frequent patient, her ills never serious, her need for attention greater than her need for treatment.

None of which endeared her to Leah. But Leah had taken an oath, and that oath bound her to answer even the most frivolous of calls.

"I hope we have plenty of smelling salts," she muttered, clambering out of the buggy and grabbing her bag. "It's probably another fit of the vapors."

"The missus is in the back sunroom," said the maid who answered the door. "Took sick when we were out boiling laundry. She's in a bad way."

Leah followed the maid through the house, walking on carpet woven of rich wool, passing paintings of scenes in Europe she would never see, potted plants and ferns in china holders. A set of fine Irish linen draped the table and buffet in the dining room.

The beauty and opulence of the house reminded her, with unexpected poignancy, of some of the better years with her father. When things went well, they had lived in houses like this with servants and tutors. The trouble was, it never lasted.

Leah stepped into the bright sunroom and saw her patient. The brief reminiscence faded to nothing.

"Mrs. Cranney," she said, crossing the plant-filled room to a white wicker chaise where the mistress of the house reclined. "What seems to be the trouble?"

Even before the lady spoke, Leah assessed her. She was a stout woman, normally florid and active. But today she lay back against the tufted cushions of the chaise, wan and listless. Her coloring was poor; a thin layer of perspiration covered her brow and upper lip. Her eyes were dull yet contemptuous as she regarded Leah.

"There you are. It took you long enough, young lady," she said, ending on a wheeze.

Leah did not consider herself young; nor did she feel terribly ladylike in the face of Mrs. Cranney's vitriol, but she maintained a calm facade. "How long have you been feeling poorly, ma'am?" she inquired. "And have you had anything unusual to eat or drink?"

"I've been feeling poorly since I sent for you *hours* ago."

Leah didn't tell her she'd been dealing with a family in which five children had come down with the measles. The family was poor and not likely to pay her, but their need was the greater.

As Mrs. Cranney recounted, in minute detail, everything she'd eaten for the past several days, Leah glanced out the window. In the yard, one maid tended a vat bubbling over a fire, while another pegged out the washing. The clothesline displayed row after impressive row of petticoats, bustles, and corsets like suits of armor made of buckram and whalebone.

"I can hardly breathe," Mrs. Cranney complained. "When I get up, I fall right back down in a dead faint."

"Mmm-hmm." Leah took out her stethoscope. "Ma'am, I need to listen to your heart and lungs."

"You didn't do that last time."

"You wouldn't let me last time."

"Well, I won't let you this time, either. It's indecent."

Frustrated, Leah pressed her lips together. "You sent for my help. I can't help you unless you cooperate. Mrs. Cranney, I'm concerned about you. I didn't press the issue last time, but your condition has worsened."

"Your father never would have foisted such an indecency upon me."

No, just a bottle of useless syrup along with his fee, Leah thought, biting her tongue.

With slow, deliberate movements, she took off the stethoscope. "Then I'm afraid I can't—"

"Wait." Mrs. Cranney's pasty face puckered with lines of worry. "Very well, but I don't like this one bit."

"Lean forward, ma'am. Sophie will help you with your dress."

Fifteen minutes later, Leah was sweating and biting her tongue to stop a stream of swearwords that would have done Jackson Underhill proud. Mrs. Cranney had trussed herself like a Thanksgiving turkey. She wore the heaviest corset Leah had ever seen, the laces pulled so tightly that the skin was bruised, almost cut in places. Beneath the corset, a thin lawn shift lay plastered against the lady's tortured flesh. When Leah and Sophie finally managed to free the lady from her whalebone prison, Mrs. Cranney let out a huge breath, then inhaled deeply.

Sophie brought her a cup of water while Leah held the smelling salts.

"My, that's bracing," Mrs. Cranney said, some of her color returning. "You do me a world of good. Perhaps, in time, you'll be the doctor your father was."

"I certainly hope not," Leah muttered under her breath. She listened to the lady's heart and lungs, finding them quite normal now that she could actually hear something.

"Well?" Mrs. Cranney asked.

Leah regarded her soberly. "Ma'am, you are in very good health indeed. There is only one thing wrong, and that is easily remedied."

"What is that?" Mrs. Cranney asked eagerly. "Have you more of your father's calomel?"

"No." Leah refused to dispense the calomel. The purgative killed more than it had cured. "Even simpler. You see, all the years of wearing a very stiff corset have caused your inner organs some amount of harm. You are impeding your breathing with the pressure, ma'am, and placing undue exertion on the heart."

"Oh dear." She pressed her pale, soft hands against her heart.

"But the remedy is simple. You simply eschew the corset."

"You're saying I shouldn't wear the corset?"

Leah glanced at the contraption on the floor. "Exactly. You'll feel a world of good. I haven't ever worn one."

"That's immoral. And unhealthy to boot," Mrs. Cranney insisted. "Everyone knows a woman needs a corset to support her back."

"Women—like men—are born with perfectly good skeletons," Leah said. "Our bodies are wonderful machines. All the parts work as they should, for the purpose they should. They need no artificial support."

"Preposterous!" Mrs. Cranney burst out. "I won't hear of it. I won't show my face or any other part of me without a corset. Why, I even wear one to bed." She gazed reverently at the device. "Mine are imported from England. They're specially made to my particular specifications. They take months to get here."

"They're destroying your health, Mrs. Cranney. I can be no more blunt than that."

"You lie."

"No, and I refuse to give you a little purgative to make you more comfortable in your truss. If you value your health and the quality of your life, you'll simply cut your clothes to fit you without a corset.''

"Never!" She reached for the corset. "Now, help me back into this or call for my maid."

Furious, Leah grabbed the undergarment. "Do you want my help, then?''

"I sent for you, didn't I?''

"Fine, I'll give you help." She heard Sophie's gasp of surprise as she marched outside with the corset. The maids squawked in startlement as Leah walked the length of the clothesline, plucking down the other damp corsets that hung there. Her arms full of the offensive garments, she went to the fire where the laundry was boiling. "Excuse me," she said bossily to the maid standing there, agape.

Mrs. Cranney screamed a protest as she realized Leah's intent. "Don't you dare!''

Leah ignored her. She ignored the neighbors who had gathered along the picket fence to watch. She ignored the men who had sidled over from the sheriff's office to see what all the hollering was about. With a look of utter contempt, she shoved the load of corsets into the laundry fire and stepped back.

The garments smoldered for a moment, then burst into flames. Black smoke, redolent of rubberized canvas, rose from the inferno. By that time, Mrs. Cranney had found a robe and snatched it on. She came barreling out of the house. "My corsets! My corsets!''

It was too late. No one could—or would—get near them.

In all his far-flung travels, Jackson had never seen anything quite so strange. There stood Leah Mundy with a defiant Joan-of-Arc look on her face, making a bonfire of women's unmentionables while the reverend's wife flew at her, screeching like a banshee. No one standing at the picket fence and watching seemed to know quite what to do.

The preacher, who had come out of the parish office adjacent to the church, fanned his face with his flat-brimmed hat. His spectacles had fogged up, but he didn't seem to notice. The sheriff's deputy elbowed the butcher Gillespie, trying hard not to laugh aloud.

Jackson turned to the sheriff himself. Because of Sophie, he'd broken his own rule to steer clear of the law. "St. Croix?" he said. "How about a little law and order around here?"

Shrieking in outrage, Mrs. Cranney reached for a blackened corset, trying to rescue it from the fire. Leah pushed her hand away. "Ma'am, you'll burn yourself, and then I'll *really* have some doctoring to do."

"How dare you?" Mrs. Cranney demanded. "This is beyond forgivable."

"Sheriff?" Jackson prompted. It was all he could do to hold in his laughter. It had been too long since he'd had a good belly laugh, but making Leah the butt of it was probably a mistake. He elbowed Deputy MacPhail. "Caspar?"

The deputy took a step backward. "I wouldn't touch this situation with a barge pole." MacPhail gave up the effort of a dignified silence. He turned away, made the mistake of making eye contact with the butcher, and they both burst into guffaws.

"You are finished, Leah Mundy," Mrs. Cranney railed. "Do you hear me? Finished. You'll never practice your black art again. I'll see to that." Her husband scuttled back into the parish office, probably to pray for a miracle.

The laughter that had been tempting Jackson suddenly evaporated. Seeing that he'd get no help from the sheriff or the husband, he braced one hand atop a fence post and vaulted over, landing in the yard. As he approached the laundry fire, the two maids began nudging each other and whispering behind their hands.

Mrs. Cranney paused in her diatribe to pull her robe tighter. Jackson made the most of his unhurried ambling and swept off his hat with a courtly bow. "Howdy, ma'am," he said. "I just stopped by to see if there was a fire. All that black smoke looks plenty dangerous from the street. Is everything all right?"

She clutched at the front of her robe. "Why, sir... I...no, there's no danger, Mr...."

"Underhill. Jackson T. Underhill. I'm a newcomer to these parts."

"I thought I'd seen you around town."

He could feel Leah's stare drilling into him, but he ignored her. Leah Mundy's sharp tongue had a habit of getting her into hot water. He had no idea why he felt so compelled to get her out of it, but he did.

"Well, everything is fine, but thank you for stopping to check." Mrs. Cranney tilted her head coyly to one side. Hell's bells, she was flirting with him. "Will you be staying in the area very long, Mr. Underhill?"

If eyes rolling in disgust made a sound, Jackson thought, Leah's eyes were making that sound now.

"I can't be sure, ma'am. I put in for repairs to my boat." He sent her his most roguish grin. "Course, you make me wish I could settle in and join the church."

She blushed, as he knew she would. Leah made a huffy sound and turned to the fire, using a stick to poke the last of a reeking corset into the flames. Mrs. Cranney seemed to have forgotten. "Why, Mr. Underhill, really.

And here I am barely dressed in my robe, not a proper thread on me—"

"On the contrary, ma'am, you're perfect just as you are." Feigning complete innocence, he said, "You know, I always wondered why a beautiful woman would truss herself up in a hard shell, hiding all the Lord's handiwork. I know it's mighty forward of me to mention, but I'm real pleased to see you've decided not to follow that convention like some ninny sheep."

Her flush deepened. "Actually, I—"

"I'd best be going, ma'am." He bowed again and put his hat back on. "You stay just as soft and pretty as you are, you hear?" He glanced at the corsets, now charred beyond recognition. "I expect you'll start a trend."

As he walked away to let himself out through the back gate, he heard Mrs. Cranney remark, "What a delightful man."

"Isn't he, though?" Leah replied, acid in her tone.

The damnfool woman, Jackson thought. Didn't she realize he'd just saved her butt—again?

*14 July 1894*

Dear Penelope,

I worked hard at my medical studies, but now, even with a practice of my own, I realize I still have much to learn. Sometimes healing is not simply a matter of finding a physical ill and treating it.

Sometimes you must look into the heart and soul of your patient and see a need that might be masked.

Today I treated a woman for indigestion and asphyxia due to a tight corset. That was the primary, immediate problem. The true problem was that she is a lonely, neglected wife who has nothing but vanity to cling to. I thought she was wasting my valuable time. What she was really doing was calling out for help.

I would like to tell you that I saw through her and answered her need, but this is not true. It took a charming newcomer to make this lady see that she is an attractive and worthy woman, corset or not.

A simple thing.

So why was I blind to that? My temper, I suppose. I should learn to hold it in check. But honestly, I get so frustrated when I do the right thing and get kicked in the teeth. Then a stranger comes along and charms everyone into forgetting it all—

Leah sighed and rubbed her temples where an insidious headache pounded. She knew why her head hurt, and she knew what she had to do to make it stop.

She'd been too proud to thank Jackson Underhill for what he'd done. Too proud to admit that her method of dealing with her patient was inferior to his. Too proud to acknowledge the wit and intelligence of a man she considered a drifter.

Yet he'd recognized the reverend's wife for who she really was—a woman in need of a little attention and flattery. Jackson had a way of seeing people that Leah lacked.

How does he see me? she wondered.

She glanced back over the letter to Penelope Lake, then put it in a drawer to finish later. "Ah, Penny," she said. "It's so easy to tell you what is in my heart and mind. Why is it so impossible to say it to him?"

Because he was a stranger with a shady past.

Because he was leaving, never to return.

Because if she told him the truth, she'd have to admit that she was lonely, that she ached, that she feared she would never belong in anyone's life, or have anyone who belonged in hers.

She drew in a long, shuddering breath and blinked until she was dry-eyed again. Then she made a decision. She had to thank Jackson Underhill. How hard could it be anyway?

# *Nine*

❧❧❧

Impossible, thought Leah as she stood on the dock beside the *Teatime*. There was no way on earth she could look Jackson T. Underhill in the eye and say "Thank you for helping me. You were right and I was wrong." So when he began to emerge from the belly of the old wooden hull, shirtless and dazzlingly handsome in the high summer sun, she didn't say thank-you at all. She said, "I thought you might be hungry, so I brought you some lunch."

His grin widened. "Thank you, Doc. Much obliged."

She waited in heated discomfort while he extracted himself from the impossibly tiny hatch. His hair was tousled, his tanned face smudged with dark grease and sweat. He shouldn't look attractive, but damn him, he did. He angled his body slightly to fit through the opening. It was then that she feared he might be naked. Like a genie coming out of a lamp, he exited from the portal, his broad bare chest glistening in the sun, a line of golden hair leading downward from his navel. Leah told herself to look away from the indecent display, but instead, she gaped like a lingcod.

He wore jeans slung low from having the pockets over-loaded with tools. She gave an audible sign of relief.

"Doc," he said, "you'll have to excuse me while I wash up. Then I'll have lunch with you, and you can thank me for saving your butt yesterday."

"You did *not* save my butt!" Leah blurted before she quite realized what she was saying. When she did, her hand flew to her mortified mouth.

"You're mighty cute when you say butt," he declared, then disappeared into the stateroom to wash and dress.

By the time he came out, Leah had worked herself into a fine temper. "What makes you think I came to thank you?"

"Because I deserve it. The preacher's wife was planning to run you out of town, and I made her think you did her a favor by burning her drawers."

"It was her corsets, and I *did* do her a favor."

"She didn't see it that way. Not until I pointed it out."

"Ah, that you did. You're an impossible flirt, Mr. Underhill."

"It generally works on the ladies," he said.

"It doesn't work on me."

"Who said you were a lady?"

"Certainly not you."

He sauntered over, moving with lazy grace. He'd put on a clean blue shirt, but he hadn't buttoned it yet. Beads of water spangled his chest. "Then what works on you? Tell me that. What sort of flirting makes your heart beat faster?"

"No flirting works on me. I despise flirting. It's pointless and demeaning behavior."

"It's sort of fun sometimes."

"Fun?"

"Yeah, but you wouldn't know that, would you?"

"Know what?"

"Fun. You wouldn't know it if I took your fancy hypodermic needle and shot it into your arm."

"But I brought you a picnic."

Slowly, keeping his eyes on her, he buttoned his shirt. "Are we having a good time yet?"

The conversation had grown so absurd that she gave in to a smile. "I think we are, Mr. Underhill. Yes, I do believe we are." It felt alien. Yet not at all unpleasant. She looked left and right, at a loss. "So, where shall we have our lunch?"

She surveyed the boat in dismay. All the flooring had been taken up to give access to the pumps and lower compartments. A decidedly bilgelike smell came from somewhere in the bowels of the ship. To add to the atmosphere, a fisherman had just docked nearby with a reeking load of Penn Cove mussels. Gulls screeched and wheeled over the wharf area.

"Let me get some boots on, and then we'll go," Jackson said.

"Fine."

She heard him banging around in the stateroom below and started to feel faintly ridiculous. Here she was, the town's spinster physician, boldly calling on a handsome widower. The thing was, the world hadn't come to an end. That was a surprise. There had been a time when her father had convinced her that if she so much as stepped a toe outside the realm of sober study, life as she knew it would end.

Oh, Papa, she thought, why didn't I see how wrong you were? She remembered how hard she had worked all her life to please him. From the moment she awoke until the moment she fell asleep, her every act was directed at earning his love.

She'd failed, of course. She had gained his esteem, perhaps, but that was a cold substitute for the needed warmth of a father's love.

"Why the long face?" Jackson demanded.

Leah snapped to attention. "Oh! Is my face long? I didn't mean for it to be." He laughed at her, and she glared. "I don't get the joke, Mr. Underhill."

"Call me Jackson."

"I won't. I refuse to."

"Call me Jackson."

"No."

"By the end of the day, you will."

"What in the world is that supposed to mean?"

He shrugged and leaned down over the side, untying a small, weather-beaten dinghy. "Give me your hand, and I'll help you in."

She stared at the little wooden rowboat. "You expect me to go somewhere in that?"

"Uh-huh."

"But I—"

"Get in, Doc."

As she was gathering breath for a protest, he braced one booted foot on the dock, took the basket in one hand and Leah in the other. She felt her feet leave the planks, and the next thing she knew, she was in the boat. He settled her in the bow, sat astern and took up the oars. In moments, he had the boat gliding out past the cove and heading slightly northward where evergreen-topped cliffs lined the coast.

"The house looks kind of pretty from here," he said.

She had been watching the way he moved as he rowed, and his comment startled her. "My house?"

He nodded behind her. "I was just saying it looks mighty pretty."

Clutching the sides of the boat, she swiveled around and looked. The bright whitewash gleamed against the green-carpeted hills. The wraparound porch, its railings aligned like perfectly straight teeth, seemed to take on the shape of a smile. Jutting out from the roof was the front gable, its round colored window depicting the ship at sea. She couldn't fault her father in his choice of a house. The place had been a wreck when he'd gone into debt to buy it, but thanks to the boarders, Leah was slowly restoring it to its former grandeur.

"I've never looked at it from the water like this."

"Must be nice, seeing a place like that and knowing it's your home."

She thought about it for a moment. Home. Why did hearing the word spoken in Jackson's voice sound so warm and hopeful? "It was my father's choice," she said. "He always did have excellent taste."

"You sound disapproving."

"Our means rarely matched his taste." Her cheeks flamed as soon as the words were out. "I'm sorry. I should know better than to say such a personal—"

"Leah, you don't have to be so prim and proper around me. So your father lived beyond his means. He wouldn't be the first."

It was a relief to be able to admit her troubles. She nodded, heaving a sigh. "He always wanted the best, expected the best. But he couldn't afford it."

"Did he expect the best of you, too?"

"Of course. What father wouldn't?"

He shrugged. "That's not something I'd know about."

The sun sparkled on the water as he brought the dinghy ashore at a little protected beach. A family of seals lazed on the rocks at low tide, blinking at the newcomers, unafraid. Jackson stood and held out his hand to her. Gentlemanly gesture or step toward a forbidden intimacy? Leah wondered. But this time, she took it.

They walked together along the beach, a secluded stretch inhabited by no one. "How's Sophie?" he asked, scanning the area.

"Mourning her kinsman," she said. "Neither the sheriff nor the Indian agent seems inclined to find out how the murder actually came about."

"Finding out is not going to bring a dead man back to life."

"It might stop another murder from happening," she said.

They walked in silence for a while. He chose a spot in the shade of a stand of madrona trees, their bare red trunks and thick green leaves bowing over a section of the beach. "Hungry?" he asked.

She nodded, opening the basket. "I don't know what I'd do without Perpetua."

The boardinghouse cook had fixed fried chicken and flour-dusted soda biscuits, a jar of cold grapes, wedges of cheese and thick slices of peach pie topped with cinnamon. Two cold bottles of home-brewed beer provided the liquid refreshment.

With a sigh of contentment, Jackson leaned back against a rock. "I could get used to this."

"To what?"

He swept his arm out, encompassing the scenery and the lunch, as well. "All of this. Living in a place where the food's good every day, day in and day out. Where you can walk out your front door and be at the water's edge. Where you can earn an honest living. You've got it good here, Doc."

"I suppose I do."

"So what's the matter?"

She frowned. "There's nothing the matter. Why would you suggest such a thing?"

"You almost always eat by yourself. You spend your evenings with a book rather than company." He counted the examples off on his fingers. "You almost never smile, Leah. You never laugh. All you do is work."

She bristled. "Did it ever occur to you that work makes me happy?"

"I know. I've been watching you. You care so damned much. I've never heard you complain about having to get up in the middle of the night or treating someone you know won't pay you."

"I have to. I took an oath."

"You don't need an oath. You made a miracle with—" He broke off, clearly regretting the direction the conversation had taken.

"With Carrie," she finished for him. "And that was no miracle. It was hard work for all of us, especially for her, and in the end, nothing we did mattered as much as her craving for the drug." Leah forced herself to keep her gaze trained on him. "Mr. Underhill?"

"Mmm?" He took a pull on his beer.

"Do you miss her very much?"

"Hell yes, but—" He broke off again and scowled.

"But…?"

"Everyday living seemed to be wearying to her. Each day was a trial. Maybe she's in a better place."

"And what about you? Now that Carrie's gone, what are you running from?" she asked bluntly.

He looked at her for a long time, shadows of darkness flickering in his eyes. "You got no call to be asking me that."

"I think I do," she said. "I think it's time you told me why."

His face hardened, suddenly looked distant and strange. "You don't want to know."

"Why not?"

"Because telling you won't change what's done. And if anyone ever asks you about me, I don't want you to have the answer. If I don't tell you anything, you won't have to lie."

She took a long swig of her beer. "You think I'll be shocked. You think I have no knowledge of the shady side of the law. Well, let me tell you, I was raised by a man who slept with his entire fortune and a pistol under his pillow. He kept one step ahead of the law all his life."

There. She'd spoken the truth. It felt good to admit it at last—that her father, whom she'd revered from the cradle, was a charlatan. The admission hurt, yet it was liberating.

"You won't shock me," she said to Jackson.

He exhaled loudly. "Right. Because I got nothing more to say on the matter."

"I've just confessed a deep secret of the soul to you," she burst out. "You! The man who abducted me from my bed!"

His gaze probed her, caressing, touching places she shouldn't want him to touch. "I remember that night, too, Doc," he said, and his voice was low and rough as if speaking an endearment.

But he wasn't, of course. She must really be falling under his spell. Because she loved it when he called her Doc.

"Promise you won't get mad if I tell you something?" he went on.

"I'd never make such a silly promise. But tell me anyway."

"Right before I woke you up to ask for the doctor, I

looked at you. There was a storm that night, remember? When the lightning flashed, I could see you clearly.''

She shivered despite the warmth of the day, picturing Jackson standing over her with a gun, watching her sleep while lightning seared the sky. ''And...what did you see?''

''I saw what you could be if you'd relax and let go a little. Someone who could take the time to enjoy life. You're real pretty when your face is all soft and your hair's loose—''

Embarrassed, she leaped to her feet. ''I don't have to listen to this.''

''No, Doc. No, you don't. That's part of your problem. You want to know everyone else's business, but when it comes to your own, you don't lis—''

She stalked away, her feet crunching over the broken shells on the beach. She walked blindly, not heeding where she went, vaguely noting a break in the trees and heading for it. He called out to her, but she ignored him. She went into the woods and climbed a steep incline that wound through the forest of alder and cedar. She was appalled to feel a lump in her throat, the burn of tears in her eyes.

He laid her soul bare, made her see things about herself she didn't want to see. Made her want things she shouldn't want and could never have.

She heard him walking behind her, but she forged ahead. Thick shade darkened the pristine woods, and the cool green air rushed past her, welcome on her hot face. Through a gap in the trees, she saw a sunny open space, and she headed for it, knowing it led to a road back to Coupeville.

At the edge of the clearing, Jackson caught her arm. It occurred to her that he could have caught her anytime;

he was that much taller and faster than she, but he'd held back. Until now. He pulled her around to face him.

"Leah," he said, his voice gravelly and intimate. "What the hell are we doing?"

She yanked her arm away and stalked into the middle of the clearing, welcoming the battering heat of the sun. "I thought we were going to have lunch."

"We had lunch."

"Then we should go back."

"You didn't answer my question. What the hell are we doing?"

She set her hands on her hips and glared at him. "You'll have to explain that question. Or better yet, answer it yourself. You seem to know everything."

"I don't know a goddamned thing," he said, sounding harsh. "But there's something going on between us. Something that neither of us will admit to."

"Then we should keep it that way. Don't you think that would be best?" She studied him; his face in the sunlight was harsh, its angles and planes stark, the squinting eyes assessing, the color like ice in the middle. "I am bound to stay here, Mr. Underhill. In this town. With these people who need me. And you seem bound to go sailing off Lord-knows-where. So there really isn't any point in pursuing our...our...friendship, is there?" she finished lamely.

"Does everything have to have a point?" he asked.

"Doesn't it?"

He shifted his weight to one foot and looked around, studying the sweep of the clearing and the emerald fringe of the tall trees, the marbled blue sky in the distance. "Where are we?"

"North of town."

"And what's that?" He pointed to a hazy blue-green land mass to the northwest.

"Why, that's Canada. On a clear day, it looks so close you can almost touch it."

"Canada," he said, almost to himself. "That's Canada."

"Yes. Just beyond the San Juan Islands."

"I suppose I could row the dinghy there if I wanted."

She laughed. "It's not quite that close. Even if you survive the Strait of Juan de Fuca, you could encounter pirates."

"Sure, Doc."

"Well, you could. Some of the bolder crews have been known to raid towns."

He shaded his eyes and gazed into the distance. "Canada." He shook his head. "Some things look simpler than they are."

She allowed herself a small, rueful smile. "The same could be said of doctoring."

"You're a strange bird, Leah Mundy."

She relaxed enough to take a risk. "Come this way. There's something I'd like to show you."

He gave her his special half grin, a subtle lifting of one side of his mouth that made her stomach jump and her pulse quicken. She led the way across the clearing and into a grove of alder trees. Over her shoulder, she said, "I found this spot while I was out gathering medicinal herbs with Sophie."

They walked on, deeper and deeper into the woods until the grove of alders gave way to older stands of towering fir and cedar and spruce. In the middle lay another clearing, a tiny one, and in the middle of that was something extraordinary.

Jackson didn't disappoint her. "I'll be damned," he murmured, striding across the clearing.

You probably already are that, Leah thought, but she didn't say it aloud.

She watched him walk around the small structure. Ages ago—Sophie thought at least fifty years—some settler had built a cabin raised up on stumps to keep it out of the damp. But the forest had reclaimed the dwelling, trees snaking up and around the walls and over the roof, moss and ferns sprouting from the eaves. The house resembled a perfect nest in the midst of green trees. The roof had fallen in here and there and the door hung askew, but a strange, otherworldly, almost fairy-tale charm pervaded the place.

"Odd, isn't it?" Leah commented.

"Yeah," he said, half to himself.

She joined him on his slow walk circling the little house. A special enchantment haunted this spot in the woods. She'd sensed it the first time she'd come here, and the feeling persisted with each visit. Now it was stronger than ever. The tallest of the trees made arches of their branches, and the sun filtered through them in hazy-bright bars, angling down to the fine grass and moss that covered the forest floor. The light shone through the leaves, creating a cool emerald mist.

Jackson squinted up at the filtered green light. "Look, I'm sorry for what I said back there. It's none of my damned business how you live your life. I got no call to be telling people how to live."

He set one booted foot on the bottom step leading up to the nest house, testing the wood for strength. It crumbled a little at the edges, but held. He entered the house, then turned, holding out his hand for Leah.

She followed him into the house. The cabin was small

and crude, almost ghostly in the way it stood untouched, as if time itself had passed it by. Huge spiderwebs draped the corners. Where the rain came in, the floor had rotted through.

But the fieldstone hearth and chimney had sturdily endured; the iron tools hung in place and even an ancient heap of split wood lay ready, waiting to warm the place. The kitchen area was equipped with battered tin implements. A sagging bed frame stood in the corner.

"Looks like whoever used to live here just up and left," Jackson observed. "Wonder why."

"People have their reasons." She regarded him pointedly. She knew she shouldn't mention Carrie again, but she had to. She wanted to understand the woman's hold over Jackson. "Carrie was your reason," she said at last.

His posture changed the slightest bit—stiffened, sharpened. She'd seen patients do this, anticipating pain.

"I'm sorry," she said quickly. "I shouldn't have said—"

"Probably not," he agreed. "But from the time I left St. I's in Chicago until the day Carrie took off with that Armstrong fellow, finding and protecting her was the thing that gave me a purpose."

Leah felt a stirring in her chest, the beginnings of an emotion that scared her. "And now?" she asked.

He leaned back against the mantel, watching her. "Now I don't know. Now I have to ask myself some hard questions and see if I can live with the answers."

"What sort of questions?"

"Like can I live life as a workingman rather than a gambler?"

"Why not? You're a man of...varied skills."

"I can play cards and shoot straight," he said.

"Then you'd be a fine sheriff or marshal," she suggested.

"A lawman?" He snorted. "You think folks would feel safe with me?"

"I feel safe with you," she said quietly.

He stood silent for a long time, then took a deep breath. "There's something inside me, Leah, something dark and cold. It sits like a rock in my gut and it's always there. I keep thinking that if I finally get my life on the straight and narrow, the darkness will go away."

She gaped at him, stunned by his remarkable honesty. She, too, had a darkness inside her. She had made a straight and narrow life for herself, but the shadows still hung there, cool and immutable. "Then why do you run? Why not stay where you are? Or stay somewhere you can call home?"

"I never knew the meaning of the word 'home.' I never cared. Until now."

"Until now?"

"Until you."

His admission made her dizzy. She felt a jolt of emotion, something big and new, completely strange to her, yet achingly familiar. Unexpected. Exhilarating. Terrifying. "Mr. Underhill—"

"Jackson."

"Mr. Underhill, you shouldn't speak of such things."

"Why not?" He gestured around the tree house. "We're alone. There's no one to see, no one to hear."

She felt as if she had plunged into black water without knowing its depth, its treacherous shoals. She experienced the breathlessness, the heavy limbs of a drowning person. "It...it makes no sense."

"What makes no sense?"

"*We* make no sense. Forming a—an attachment. A

*tendre*. Nothing but heartbreak can come of it. You have to go. And I have to stay.''

He pushed away from the mantel and crossed the room. Instinct told her to move away, to flee, but his beautiful eyes and the sensual promise she saw there held her captive. A strange heat sparked within her, curling through her like a wisp of smoke.

"How do you know?" he asked.

"How do I know what?"

"That nothing can come of this."

"Because we have no future."

"We have right now."

"But..."

"What if 'right now' is the only thing we'll ever have?"

She stood waiting, for what she wasn't certain, but his question made a mad sort of sense. *Don't touch me*, she thought. *Don't touch me now, or I'll shatter*. The feeling was seductive, evocative, and when he reached out with both hands, she went willingly to him.

Though his arms were gentle, settling around her and drawing her against him, his lips claimed hers with a barely restrained violence that should have offended, but instead excited her. She felt the heat of desire fill her more and more completely until she was brimming over with it. She wanted the taste of him, the press of his body against hers, and just for this moment, she wanted to damn the consequences.

Her emotions were in a turmoil. She knew that, but she didn't care. He was getting too close to her heart. She should resist fiercely, but she didn't. She felt herself arching up and toward him, hungering for more, wanting to touch him everywhere, wanting him to touch her.

Passion for Jackson Underhill took her by surprise. Accustomed to a life of rigid control, she had finally found something she could not govern. All she could feel was the sensation of him kissing her, the firmness of his lips and the pressure of his arms holding her.

His kisses left her both exhilarated and frightened. She knew she was coming closer and closer to loving Jackson, and she knew there was a terrible danger in that, but for now she didn't care.

"Leah," he murmured against her mouth. "Leah, I want you. I want to make love to you."

She said nothing, only lifted herself on tiptoe and wound her arms tighter around his neck.

"Talk to me," he said with a rumbling in his chest. "Tell me you want this."

She couldn't. If she said too much, thought too much, she'd lose her nerve. "I don't want to decide."

She knew she had conceded total surrender to a man who was bigger, stronger, infinitely more powerful than her. It was a thing she'd never believed herself capable of, this unabashed giving of oneself, this leap of faith. But Jackson had brought her to the precipice. His willing victim, she teetered on the edge.

His hands slipped down, freeing the buttons of her shirtwaist. "You don't wear a corset," he whispered. "It was one of the first things I liked about you." He cupped her aching breasts. The heat flared in her, and she caught her breath with the sudden fire that roared through her at his intimate caress. She let her head drop back, baring her throat, and while all this was happening, she couldn't believe it was she, Leah Mundy, in the arms of this man, surrendering everything to him.

Due to her training and her practice, she had thought she understood the human sex act. Indeed, she'd read and studied all the literature she could find. She'd been certain she understood.

She'd been wrong. She had not even begun to understand it. She wondered what else life was hiding from her.

His mouth skimmed over the taut arch of her neck, and she brought her fingers up and into his hair. She had yearned to touch it for so long. The loosened hair felt so silky, the ends cool and curling around her knuckles.

Then he moved his mouth lower, and she felt nothing but that, nothing but the soft slide of his lips down between her breasts. His hand slipped beneath her skirts, brushing the fabric of her pantalettes. *Touch me*, she thought, knowing she could never say the words aloud. *Please, there.*

"Say it, Leah," he urged in a hoarse whisper. "Say you want this. Say you want me."

"I…" The words froze on a rush of icy fear. What in God's name was she doing, playing the whore to this desperado? She had spent years trying to build up her reputation. Yet in just a few moments it would all turn to dust and rubble around her feet.

So what if no one knew? She would be compromised. She might get pregnant.

Her hands gripped him. Take the decision away from me, she silently urged him. I want this to be your fault.

He seemed to read her thoughts. He broke the embrace with a low oath. "I won't do this unless you say you want it. All of it. A hundred percent."

And I, she thought bleakly, I can't do this unless it's forever. "But I…won't you just keep on with…what you were doing?"

His brow creased. "Honey, I'd like nothing better than to keep going. But if you can't bring yourself to admit you want me, that you want to lie down with me and make love, then I'll make myself stop." The words sounded strained, torn with reluctance from his throat. The hand he slowly withdrew from beneath her skirts trembled slightly, then fell still against his taut thigh. His other hand, which he'd held behind her, dropped to his other side.

Leah didn't just miss his touch, she ached for it.

He smiled ruefully, no doubt recognizing the tortured expression on her face for what it was. "All you have to do is ask."

She knotted her fingers and looked down. "You don't understand how hard it is for me."

A blur of regret tinged his smile. "I can't offer you much, Leah. Maybe just the chance to slow down for a minute, to taste the sweetness of life."

She felt her cheeks turn hot. "I just don't see the point."

He stared at her long and hard, seeing more of her, she knew, than anyone ever had before. "God, Leah, what the hell did your father teach you? That every damned thing has to have a point?"

Ah, anger. She almost welcomed it, a familiar old friend. "At least I *had* a father."

The barb hooked into him; she could see the change in him. One moment, he was looking at her with yearning and even compassion. But after she spoke, he turned cold and cynical and contemptuous.

She should have felt triumphant. Instead, she felt small and petty and ashamed. But she didn't know how to tell him so. Didn't know how to take back the words.

"Thanks for reminding me, Doc." He rammed his

hands into his pockets and turned to leave the nestlike little cottage.

As he strode away through the woods, she said, "Jackson," but the word came out as a broken whisper.

# Ten

Jackson stalked down to the beach without looking back to see if she followed. Leah had taught him an important lesson today, something he should have figured out a long time ago.

His scars ran too deep to risk letting another person into his life. The wounds inflicted by his mother's leaving him, by his never knowing a man to call father, would always exist. If he was fool enough to find a woman like Leah who knew just what sharp instrument to use to inflict the most damage, then he deserved to feel the hurt.

And he did feel it, all over again with brutal clarity. He had been about five years old when his mother had abandoned him. Before sunrise one morning, she had roused him from his sleep atop a smelly, bare mattress. She'd taken him to the steps of the St. Ignatius Orphan Asylum in Chicago and told him to sit there and wait for the light.

She refused to wait with him; now he knew it was because she didn't want to risk being questioned, possibly arrested and detained.

He remembered sitting there in the cold gray dawn, hearing her footsteps click on the wet brick pavement as she rushed toward the train station, never looking back. He watched and watched, shivering with cold and fear, uncomprehending. He'd never understood much that she did. At a very young age, he learned to be silent and disappear while she went about her business.

That business was always something to do with entertaining men in bed. She would giggle and whisper, and after a while, strange moans would come from behind the curtain that shrouded the bed. Once, he'd tried to look, thinking his mother was in trouble, but all he'd gotten was a cuff on the ear.

On that dark pre-morning so long ago, he sat and watched her go, watched the stringy plume that sagged from the brim of her hat, watched her feet wobble ever so slightly in their ill-fitting shoes. Though he feared a whipping if he called to her, he did it anyway. *Mama. Mama, come back. Mama, take me home.*

Her step faltered, but she didn't turn. He supposed some part of himself understood that it was the last he would see of her, but he had a child's ability to block out the truth.

Denying the truth had probably saved him from shattering more than once. But Leah wouldn't hold with denying anything. She wanted it all laid out neatly like surgical instruments on a tray. Instruments made of honed metal, designed to cut and dissect.

*If you cut me open, Leah Mundy, would you see my black heart?*

He was so wound up with his dark thoughts that at first the spectacle on the beach didn't register. Then he realized what had happened.

"Aw, shit," he said, planting himself at the top of the bluff above the spot where they'd moored the boat.

"What's the matter?" Leah came up behind him. Her

voice sounded strained, as if she found it hard to speak to him. Her gaze followed his down the bluff. "Oh dear."

"The tide came in."

"It has a habit of doing that."

In spite of himself, he smiled ruefully. "Where do you suppose the dinghy wound up?"

She looked thoughtful as she scanned the area. She had no idea that she was pretty, that her eyes were a velvety shade of brown and that her well-kissed lips were bowed and shining in a way that haunted his dreams. She wore her attractiveness like a useless old dress. He'd been inches from showing her just how powerful her attraction was, but he'd backed off.

Jackson had never walked away from seducing a woman in his life. Christ, what had he been thinking?

"It's there, see?" She pointed.

He squinted at the shoreline. Sure enough, there was the dinghy, bobbing close to a wall of jagged rocks. The bowline had snagged on something.

"How will we get to it?" Leah asked.

"Can you swim?"

"Of course. But the water's freezing. I see a better way."

"Then do it your way. I'm going after the dinghy." He peeled off his shirt, then removed his boots. When his hand went to the top button of his jeans, she gave a huffy little noise and flounced off.

If it hadn't been for that noise, he might have followed her. Instead, he scrambled down to a shallow outcropping of rock choked by gorse and yellow blossoms of Scotch broom. Damn. It was a lot longer dive than he'd thought.

He sneaked a glance over his shoulder. Leah was still stomping away toward the rocky bluff. Damn fool, stubborn woman. If he killed himself and she didn't see him do it, then it was her loss.

Without pausing to examine his own logic, he took a deep breath and dived. The shock of the water numbed him. His hands brushed the rocky bottom; then he arced upward and broke the surface. The first thing he did was look for Leah. She kept marching doggedly along the bluff. Sharp-tongued, bullheaded woman wouldn't even check to see if he'd died. With long, angry strokes he swam through the churning cold water toward the dinghy. Treacherous currents pulled and sucked him toward the rocks, but the strength of his anger sustained him. He ought to make her walk home. That would serve her right.

But instead, he found himself clambering into the dinghy by the rocks, scraping a bare foot on a barnacle-encrusted stone and feeling the sting as he bled into the salt water. Infuriated, he picked up the oars and went back for his clothes. Only then did he allow himself to look for Leah.

She had reached the crest of the bluff where the water washed into sea caves and gouges in the rock. Dainty as you please, she lifted her hand. She might have been signaling for a cab in the city.

Grumbling and rowing fast to warm himself, he went to fetch her.

"You see," she said reasonably, "if you'd walked over here with me, you could have simply gotten in this way." Sure enough, the rock grade formed a gentle incline leading to the water. She lifted her skirts and made her way down.

Just as she had one foot on land and one foot in the boat, something happened. Jackson would go to his grave swearing he did not push away too soon, that he did not smile when he saw her arms cartwheel in the air, that he did not guffaw loudly as she slammed, backside first, into the cold blue waters of Puget Sound.

But of course she would accuse him otherwise.

She came to the surface spluttering and whooping for air, her hands grabbing for the boat. Jackson held out the end of an oar and she latched on.

"You did that on purpose!" she said.

"Did what?"

"You know very well what. You—oh!" She only had time to gasp for breath before she was sucked under. Unlike Jackson, she was clearly not prepared to battle the tidal currents. Her full skirts swirled downward, dragging her along like the bell of a jellyfish.

"Leah!" He could see the white of her skirts flowing away toward a dark opening in the rock face. He rowed like a madman, one hand scooping down to clutch a handful of fabric. He could feel the tug of the current, but he fought it, dragging her up to the surface again.

She spewed out water and gulped in air. He pulled her into the boat and took her across his knees, thumping her on the back as she choked out more seawater.

It all happened in a matter of seconds, but it seemed like a lifetime, and when it was over, Jackson caught her against him, holding her cheek to his chest and saying her name over and over again. This panic was a new sensation, far different from the edgy worry he used to feel for Carrie. This feeling consumed and horrified him, took him by surprise with its intensity.

At last she drew away. "I wouldn't have fallen if you hadn't moved the boat."

"You're welcome." He glared at her.

Her teeth chattered. "Thank you for saving me."

"I'll send you a bill."

She shivered, hugging her knees to her chest. "Can we go back now? We're in danger of hypothermia."

He picked up the oars, but didn't start rowing immediately. The rogue current that had dragged Leah was now dragging the boat. They were headed for the rocks, and he knew he'd have to fight it. But he was curious, looking over Leah's shoulder at the mysterious gouged rock face. He recalled the shadows he'd seen that early dawn coming home from the Amitys' farm. This was where he'd seen them.

"What's the matter?" she asked through lavender lips.

"Are those caves?"

She swiveled around to see where he was looking. "I believe so. Why?"

"Just curious." Rather than starting back, he let the small boat drift, then used one oar as a rudder to navigate them into the mouth of one of the caves.

"What on earth are you doing?" Leah demanded.

"Exploring. It's a hot day. We won't get hypowhatever you called it."

"There are probably bats in here. Bats and—eek!" Something shadowy flickered past her head.

"Yeah, that was a bat," he said.

"Sweet heaven." She slumped down in the boat and covered her head.

Jackson wished he had a match. The afternoon light slanted into the cave, but not far enough to see. Still, he could swear he'd spotted something. A few strokes of the oars and he had his answer. Without speaking, he hefted a large wooden locker from a shelf of rock where the water didn't reach.

"What did you find?" Leah demanded.

He struggled to get the oblong box into the boat. The dinghy sat lower in the water from its weight.

"Well?" Leah demanded. "What is it?"

Jackson said nothing, but rowed out into the light.

She studied the sturdy wooden coffer. "Buried treasure?"

"Don't get your hopes up. It's probably guns." He pointed to the stenciled lettering on the side of the box. It read, Government Issue—Property Of U.S. Army.

Leah frowned. "Why would the army leave their guns in a cave out in the middle of nowhere?"

She was so naive he didn't know where to begin explaining. There were more boxes in the cave, but he wouldn't be able to get them in the dinghy. It wasn't his job anyway. He kept the one box in the boat, then took up the oars and started rowing toward home.

Home. Why did he persist in thinking of her house as home?

"Well?" she prompted.

"The army didn't leave the guns there," he said.

"Then who did?"

"Whoever stole the guns."

She gasped. "You mean they're stolen?"

"Twice stolen, now that I have a crate of them."

"Is that why you're a fugitive?" she asked. "Are you a gunrunner?"

He had to laugh. "God, no. Although it's never too late to start—"

"Don't you dare." Her expression sobered. "Dear heaven. A gun like one of these could have killed Sophie's half brother on Camano Island."

"It's real likely, Doc."

"Dear heaven," she said again. "What are we going to do?"

Joel Santana knew he was dying when he saw his mother in the desert. Only she didn't look like his mother as he'd last seen her before she died. She looked like she had many years earlier in San Antonio when Joel's father had called her *mi Rosita* and brought her bolts of red silk and baskets of ripe limes. Looming huge on the shimmering horizon, she gave Joel the beautiful smile that told him all was well with the world. Then her face shifted, transformed, and the color washed out of it, and Joel found himself looking into the lovely, soulless face of Caroline Willis. Brittle female laughter shattered the silence of the endless desert; then the woman's face went up in wavering flames.

Yet even after the mirage had trickled into empty heat shimmers on the horizon, Joel was haunted by her. Like a chimera, she moved too quickly and was too beautiful to be caught.

He suspected only he knew the past that lay like a wasteland behind her. Near as he could figure, the man called Jack Tower had hooked up with her the night of the murder. He couldn't know what she'd done in the past. He couldn't know what Joel had found out by questioning people who were in the Rising Star saloon that night.

Now maybe no one but Joel would ever know.

"I don't want to die this way," he said between cracked lips. Fatal mistakes, he reflected, happened in the blink of an eye. In the blink of an eye, he'd made the acquaintance of a Pima Indian who claimed he'd seen the yellow-hair man and the woman in the picture. In the blink of an eye, he'd agreed to ride by night with the man when the temperature was cool. And in the blink of an eye, he'd found himself stripped of his money, his gun and his food, left to die in the desert with his horse.

He'd prided himself on being an ace tracker, yet he'd

been taken in by the crafty Pima. He couldn't remember what day it was. But then, as he staggered along, he fixed his gaze on the horizon and the thought came. He wasn't supposed to die like this. There was something he was supposed to do.

Christ Almighty, he was supposed to live his damned life. He couldn't possibly die until he managed to do that. His thoughts were a muddle, but he kept thinking about a place that was cool and green, a woman who smiled a lot and bossed him around…a place and a woman he'd only ever seen in his dreams.

Jackson had wanted to avoid any dealings with the local law. He should be gone by now, lost in the wilds of Canada. So what the hell was he doing standing in the sheriff's office, the opened crate of guns at his feet?

He was doing what any ordinary, law-abiding citizen would do. If he did any less, he'd rouse suspicion. But he wasn't ordinary, and he sure as hell wasn't law-abiding. He only hoped his act was convincing.

"Well now, you're quite the hero." Sheriff St. Croix propped one foot on the crate. His tall, hand-pegged calf-skin boot gleamed with a coat of polish. "Much obliged to you."

"You'll need a big cargo boat to get the rest of the guns. There must be another dozen crates."

"I might just do that."

"When?" Jackson didn't try to hide his irritation. St. Croix was a hell of an excuse for a lawman, more interested in the cut of his clothes than in protecting folks.

"I guess as soon as I get around to it. It's a big operation—"

"Look, someone could stop in and pick up the guns at the next tide. You'd better do it now. Next high tide."

Damn, he was sounding as high-horsed as Leah Mundy. But he kept thinking about Sophie, her half brother killed by a stolen gun.

Wariness flickered across the sheriff's face, then disappeared into a look of stern agreement. "Course, you're right. I'll get right to it."

"I'll join you."

"That won't be necessary."

"I can show you where they are." Jackson narrowed his eyes. "Unless there's some reason you already know where they are."

The sheriff hesitated again. "I know my territory. But you're right. It'd be quicker if you'd just come along. High tide this evening, then."

"All right." Jackson had a strange feeling as he left the office. It was probably the dried salt water stiffening his jeans, he decided.

But he still hadn't liked the sheriff's manner.

Around midnight, Leah gave up trying to sleep. She'd lain awake for a long time, reliving the day with Jackson Underhill. Over and over again, she saw them walking along the beach and through the woods together. A quiet yearning had tugged at her heart and intensified each time she saw him lift his mouth in that maddeningly familiar half smile. When he touched her, the yearning became a conflagration—irresistible, forbidden—that consumed her.

Wanting a man, craving his touch, savoring the taste and smell of him, were new experiences to Leah. She wondered if he was aware of his effect on her. She had no idea what to do about it.

Restless, she poured herself a glass of water and went out to the front porch, barefoot, sitting on the swing and gazing up at the stars over the water. Out at the harbor where Jackson's boat lay moored, he slept. Or perhaps not.

In the evening, he'd gone with the sheriff and some men in the steamer pilot to retrieve the rest of the stolen guns. After he'd returned, he hadn't come to see her. Maybe he was confused, too. Maybe he, too, was troubled by the feelings that sparked between them.

Releasing a soft sigh, she shut her eyes and remembered the place in the woods, the nestlike house draped in lush greenery. It was a place that stood apart in time, a sanctuary. For a few moments, she had been someone else there. She had been a wanton woman desired by a seductive man. He'd wanted to make love to her. She'd wanted him to. So why had she pushed him away? Why had she denied them both the pleasure of intimacy?

Jackson was different from the prim-lipped suitors her father had paraded before her so long ago. He wasn't intimidated by the things she knew, by her ambition to succeed as a doctor. He looked at her and saw a woman, treated her like a woman. Then why was she so afraid to let him into her heart?

The fear had been planted years ago, and it had spread into her life, pervasive as a weed that wouldn't die. Instinctively, she knew she was bound to disappoint any man who dared to get close to her. Because he would look into her soul and find it empty of those virtues a woman was expected to possess.

Using a corner of her chenille robe, she wiped the tears from her face. She seemed to weep a lot these days. It wasn't like her. Before Jackson had come into her life, she'd been frozen. Now that she was thawing, she was beginning to hurt.

Damn Jackson Underhill. He wasn't good for her. This *wanting* wasn't good for her.

A small, defiant voice inside her raised a protest. Why not? *Why not?* She'd devoted her life first to her father, now to her patients. What harm in wanting something for herself?

The harm, she told herself, was in harboring a perverse desire for the wrong man. It was only a matter of time before he left. Then she'd have a broken heart on top of everything else. It was safer to keep her distance.

A breeze swept up from the Sound, and she lifted her face to the sky and silently asked for a sign that she was right to guard her heart. Better to have it empty than broken. She sat there for a long while, swinging absently, listening to the sounds of the summer night and feeling as if she were the only person alive in the world.

And then, in the middle of the deepest quiet of the night, an explosion punctured the silence.

One moment she was sitting and crying on the swing; the next she was on the floor of the porch, splinters digging into her knees as she scrambled toward the door. From the corner of her eye, she could see fire flashes at the harbor entrance. A bell began to clang—the harbormaster's bell, used to signal fog or an emergency. The sound of running feet and shouting came from the house. She rushed inside to find Zeke Pomfrit fumbling with a lamp.

"What's happening?" Perpetua asked. She held Bowie in her arms, cradling him with implacable maternal protection.

"I'm not sure. An explosion down at the harbor. Gunshots, I'm afraid."

They could hear distant bellows and then an equine scream.

"Get everyone down to the basement," Leah ordered, summoning a fierce calm from somewhere deep inside her. "Don't forget to wake Iona. She can't hear the noise."

"My canary! I won't go anywhere without my canary!" shrieked Aunt Leafy. A grumbling Battle Douglas fetched the shrouded cage.

"What about you?" Pomfrit demanded.

"I'm going to see what this is all about. Someone might be injured. The rest of you should wait in the basement."

"But—"

"Just do it, Mr. Pomfrit. You can make certain everyone's accounted for. *Please.*"

Leah scrambled into a dress, stuffing her feet into slippers as she did up the buttons. Jackson. She didn't want to believe he had anything to do with the trouble in the harbor, but she couldn't help wondering. He was so silent about his past. She left the house at a run, a single braid trailing down her back and a pounding dread in her heart.

Brunn's dry-goods store and chandlery were in flames. The roof of the telegraph and post office smoldered. People and livestock filled the street.

Leah skirted the crowd, making for the harbor. A fishing boat was also burning, as was the dock in front of the harbormaster's office. She heard a sound like crackling underbrush; then something streaked past her, sucking the air as it went. Some yards behind her, a small building went up in flames.

Sweet heaven, Coupeville was under attack. But why? *Why?*

The guns. The guns she and Jackson had found. Dear God, had they stolen from brigands or pirates? Was the entire town paying the price?

Leah made her way along the landing. A few men worked feverishly, silhouetted by the leaping flames. In the water, a canoe glided swiftly toward the mouth of the harbor.

In the deadly orange light of the fire, she could make out a ship in the distance. A steamer with sails. And it was leaving.

She found Davy Morgan. The wiry youth churned desperately at a pump attached to a fire hose while the harbormaster doused the flames.

"What on earth is happening?" she shouted.

"We were attacked!"

"Is anyone hurt?"

"Underhill." Davy dragged his sleeve across his sweating face. "I'm sorry, Dr. Mundy."

Horror. Disbelief. And finally, a searing grief. She pressed her hands to her face, amazed to feel old tears there, the tears of yearning she'd shed while sitting on the porch. Was it only moments ago?

She found him lying on the foredeck of his boat, shirtless and completely motionless. "Jackson," she whispered. "Oh, dear heaven..." As soon as she touched him, she knew. "You're not dead. Thank God, thank God..." But he was unconscious.

Working by the light of burning boats and buildings, she observed an ominous powder burn near his temple and a large bump on the side of his head.

"Jackson?" Sparing nothing for gentleness, she slapped him, then shook him by the shoulders. "Jackson, wake up. You have to wake up." She leaned over him, smelling burned powder and something elusive, something that reminded her of his kisses. She chided herself roundly for thinking of that at such a time. Mooning over a man was going to take the hardworking doctor out of her; that was a fact.

"Wake up, damn you!" She shook him again.

He rewarded her with a moan, then a foul curse.

"Same to you," she retorted, finding a wad of canvas and propping his head on it. "You scared me to death."

"What'd I do?"

"I'm not sure. You almost got yourself killed."

He blinked, squinted at the leaping flames behind her. "Oh. The pirates. Damn, I hate pirates."

"What happened? Do you remember?"

"They came into the harbor—nice steam sailer and a ballsy crew to sail in the dark—and opened fire. I saw a couple of canoes going back and forth, but with bullets flying everywhere, I didn't have much of a chance to figure out what was going on." He put up a hand, unexpectedly touched her cheek. "Hell's bells, Leah. You look like you've seen a ghost."

She was shocked that his touch had this effect on her, even here and now. "I'd be an idiot if pirates didn't frighten me." She regarded him with his wild hair spilling over the canvas, a half smile even now inching up through his pain. "And I suppose the sight of you lying senseless wasn't particularly welcome, either."

"I'll try not to lie senseless too much longer," he promised. True to his word, he braced his hands on the deck and pushed himself up, chest muscles straining. "Damn. I see stars."

"Lie back down," Leah said, alarmed. He had no idea how serious a blow to the head could be. "Jackson…"

He sank back, wincing when his head met the canvas. "I finally get her to say my name, and I'm too weak to do anything about it."

"Oh, for heaven's—"

"Dr. Mundy!" Davy Morgan's voice called out through a fog of smoke. "Dr. Mundy, can you come? Mr. Rapsilver burned himself real bad!"

She shot to her feet. "Stay still," she cautioned Jackson. "I'll be back when I can."

If he said anything in reply, she didn't hear. She raced down the dock to find the harbormaster wrapped in old blankets, the edges black and smoking. He lay on his side, teeth chattering, small moans issuing from his throat.

"He needs to be taken to the surgery to get these burns cleaned and dressed," Leah said.

Sophie Whitebear came running. "Leah, you'd better come to the surgery, too. There's a lot of folks waiting."

A cold ball of horror tightened in her gut. This was no storybook pirate adventure. This was real violence, and people were getting hurt.

"Dr. Mundy!" called a desperate voice. "Doctor, can you help?"

Feeling torn, she looked down at the man shivering on the dock. "Davy, make a litter and get him up to the house. Be very careful not to jar him."

The youth spread out a blanket. "I don't think I can carry him on my own."

Leah gritted her teeth and bent to help Davy shift Rapsilver onto the blanket.

"Here," said a gravelly voice behind her. "Let me."

She glanced up to see Jackson—unsteady on his feet, still bare-chested and barefoot. With the fire and smoke lighting him from behind, he looked magnificent. She should have protested, should have told him he was too weak and too badly injured to be up and about, but she knew he'd argue.

"Be careful with him," she said.

"We will, Doc." He nodded in the direction of the boardinghouse. "Just go."

No one in town slept that night. The able-bodied battled the flames and bore the wounded up to Leah's house. She tended the most gravely injured first; then, as dawn tinged the eastern sky over the Cascades, she cleaned and bandaged the lesser wounds.

She knew she should feel tired, but she didn't. The stress of working all the night through and into the morning sustained her.

Battle Douglas and Zeke Pomfrit tried to keep matters in hand on the porch and in the yard. "In all my born days, I've never seen a pirate attack," Battle commented, lighting his morning pipe.

Leah joined them on the porch, rubbing the small of her back and stretching. She'd spent hours bent over the examining table, teasing debris out of wounds and stitching them, dressing burns. Her eyes smarted and her neck ached.

"Why would pirates attack?" Zeke asked.

Battle nodded in the direction of the harbor. "I guess that's what the argument's about down there."

In front of the sheriff's office, Jackson and Sheriff St. Croix stood nose-to-nose, their faces red, their fists clenched. After a moment, Jackson made a frustrated gesture with his hand and stalked toward the house.

Leah leaned against a side column and watched him. Battle Douglas was saying something, but she didn't listen. She was entranced by the sight of Jackson Underhill in the morning light. He had a reddened hole torn in his trousers. He'd pulled on a plaid shirt, but hadn't paused to do up the buttons so that the edges flew back as he walked. In that moment, he was as fine to her as the rising sun.

Only hours ago, she'd sat on this porch and vowed not to succumb to his spell. Yet she couldn't help being drawn to his roguish allure, his gambler's smoothness, the dark mysteries that gave depth and texture to his charming exterior. She couldn't help feeling a physical ache for which she knew no tonic or cure.

She forced herself to put aside fanciful notions. Forced herself to fold her arms protectively in front of her and wait calmly as if his arrival was no more remarkable than seeing Iona make a trip to the well.

"It was about the guns," Jackson said, clearly having no notion of her thoughts.

"The attack, you mean?" Leah pushed away from the column and came down the stairs.

"When the stolen guns weren't where they were supposed to be, they attacked the town."

"But that makes no sense. How could they have guessed the guns were in the town?"

"I doubt there was any guessing about it."

She shuddered as a chill of suspicion swept over her. "Someone told them."

"That's what I think. I swear, this town has the sorriest excuse for a sheriff I've ever seen."

"Until tonight we didn't seem to need someone stronger."

"Yeah..." Jackson swayed on his feet.

Leah cursed herself for forgetting his head injury. "Come inside," she said. "You've been rushing around all night. You need tending." She slid her arm around him. "Lean on me."

"I thought you'd never ask." He leaned a little, then a little more until he shoved her to the ground. Battle

Douglas hurried down from the porch, pipe clamped between his teeth.

"I'll be jiggered," the older man said. "He's out cold."

"He is." Leah struggled out from under him. "Help me get him inside."

"To the main guest room?"

She was swept by unpleasant memories of Carrie's illness and treatment, the harsh words she and Jackson had exchanged in that room. "Yes," she said.

Once they got him into bed, she stood looking at him for a long time, letting relief and fear and wanting roll over her in great painful waves. He could have died last night. She could have died.

She had a number of regrets about her life. But at the moment, she could only remember one of them. She hadn't let Jackson T. Underhill make love to her.

# Eleven

Jackson awakened to find Leah Mundy bending over his private parts. Just for a moment, he felt a fine rush of satisfaction. But the pleasant feeling was quickly obliterated by a tide of excruciating agony.

"I can't say it's the first time I've been in this position," he said. "But it is the first time I've wished it could be over quicker. What the hell are you doing, Doc?"

Her attention never wandered from his upper thigh. Her hands, clad in rubber gloves bright with blood, never faltered. "Why didn't you tell me you were injured here?"

He had his teeth clamped together so tightly that for a moment he couldn't speak. "Too much going on," he managed. "You sound mad. Seems to me—ouch!—I'm the one with the right to be mad."

"You spent the night with a filthy metal splinter embedded in your thigh. That's a risk of gangrene, and a bad case of gangrene can mean you'll lose this leg."

That shut him up but good. He stared at the ceiling, recognizing the room where they'd brought Carrie. It seemed a lifetime ago. He wondered what became of a person like Carrie when she died. Did she ascend like a zephyr to the stars, or... "Damn, I'm three sheets in the wind, Doc."

"I gave you a shot of morphine."

The bed linens beneath him rustled, crisply clean, and he felt like an abomination atop them, blood and sweat and smoke and ash soiling them. Beneath his left leg, Leah had placed a thick pad, and for modesty, a sheet lay draped over his middle. Beside her was a tray of instruments that shone with a deadly glare in the mid-morning sunlight.

"So when did this happen?" she asked.

He frowned up at the white crown molding. "I heard a shot, then something exploded on my boat. More damned repairs to make."

"You'd better hope there isn't lead in this metal. I've removed about thirty slivers."

I should learn to mind my own business, thought Jackson. That was what he was best at. Getting involved with these townspeople and their storybook seaside village brought nothing but trouble.

He could feel her instrument digging deeper. To distract himself, he stared at her intently. Leah Mundy was never more beautiful than when she was totally absorbed in her work. If she would look at him that way—not just at his open wound, but at all of him—he'd be lost forever. It had almost happened yesterday. There had been a moment when he'd touched her, and he'd seen that look on her face, that near rapture...but then in a wave of self-consciousness, the look had disappeared.

"Am I naked beneath this sheet?" he asked.

"Yes."

"How did I get that way?"

"Mr. Douglas did the honors." The tiniest of smiles

pulled at her mouth. "Don't worry, Mr. Underhill, your virtue is still intact."

"Sugar, I wasn't worried about my virtue."

"Hold still," she said in a low, even voice. "Don't tense your muscles."

"I wasn't tensing them."

"You were."

"Was not."

"I'm a doctor, Mr. Underhill. I know when a muscle is tensed."

"Well, I'm the owner of the muscles, and I say they aren't tense." He propped himself up on his elbows. "I can't believe we're arguing about this."

"Lie down," she said, but it was too late. Half-sitting, he stared with dawning horror at the open wound on his thigh.

"Jesus, Doc, you're butchering me." His head felt wobbly on his neck. The sight of his own blood and sinew—and was that a glimpse of bone?—and her sharp, probing instruments nearly undid him.

"Lie down," she said more forcefully.

He sank back onto the bed. "Damn, that's a bad wound."

"You should have told me about it sooner."

"You were busy."

"I would have made time. Hold still," she cautioned. "Right now. Very, very still. There's a big sliver of something—dear God."

"Dear God? That's bad. You wouldn't say 'Dear God' if it wasn't bad."

"The sharp end of this metal is touching the bone, I'm afraid." She turned to him briskly and put a black rubber ring with a cup over his mouth and nose. "Breathe in."

"What the—"

"Breathe in, damn it," she said.

Cussing. Leah Mundy was cussing. This must be worse than he'd thought. He inhaled.

Within seconds, an airy sensation lifted him off the bed. He smiled. "What is this?"

"Nitrous oxide. Also known as laughing gas."

"I like it."

"I thought you might. But you must remember to stay still. Ready?"

"Ready for what? For you?" The fuzzy sense of well-being loosened his tongue. "Honey, I've been ready for you since the first moment I saw you."

"You were a married man."

"Was I? Funny, I don't recall getting married." There. That got a reaction out of the intractable Leah Mundy.

"I have no idea what you mean," she said.

"What I mean is, I wanted you even with the ice in your veins. And every time you put me off makes me want you more. What will it take for me to have you, Leah?"

"I need you to hold still so I can get this last sliver out. Stop moving!"

"I wasn't moving."

"You were. I'm serious."

"How serious?"

In a funny conversational tone, she said, "You know, before doctors learned to control pain, speed was of the essence. That's why surgery was so dangerous. I read of a doctor who operated with a scalpel held between his teeth. They say he once amputated a leg in two and a half minutes—and, in the rush, cut off the patient's testicles."

Jackson held very, very still. "Take your time, Doc."

"Don't worry. I shall."

His mind drifted as she worked, removing the last of the splinters. He smiled benignly into the rubber mask—until she began washing the wound with a solution of carbolic acid and linseed oil. His howl brought Sophie Whitebear running. Then came Bowie, his skinny arms pumping the wheels of his rolling chair.

"Holy cow, Dr. Mundy! Look at all that blood!" the boy blurted out.

Jackson's howls subsided to tortured moans.

"He'll be fine, Bowie," Leah said without looking up. "I just need to sew him up."

"Holy cow! That's a big needle!" Bowie exclaimed. "Why's it curved like that?"

Just what I needed to hear, Jackson thought.

"Sophie?" Leah didn't have to say more. Her assistant herded Bowie out of the doorway.

Leah stitched the wound, then put a pad over it, soaking the pad with more carbolic and covering it with tinfoil.

"Tinfoil?" Jackson asked weakly.

"To prevent the disinfectant from evaporating."

He heard a light clatter as she put her instruments into a shallow pan. As she was peeling off her rubber gloves, she seemed to be studying his face in that assessing way of hers.

What did she see? he wondered. Did she see Jackson T. Underhill, knight in tarnished armor, determined to rescue a lady who didn't want rescuing? Or did she see the outlaw Jack Tower, gambling and fighting his way to a freedom that probably didn't even exist? Or—and God help her if she did—did she see little Jackie Hill sitting on the stoop of St. I's and watching his mother walk away?

Leah touched him, her hand cool against his brow. "No fever. I must watch you for infection."

"Thanks." He wished she would keep her hand there all day.

She pushed away from the bed, piling bloody linens into a basket. "You should rest," she said over her shoulder, blowing a wisp of hair away from her brow.

"So should you." He grabbed her hand. "Lie down with me."

She pulled away. "I have things to do."

"I could make you forget them."

"That's just the problem, Mr. Underhill. Ring for Perpetua if you need anything."

Something about her dismissive tone enraged him. It blew like a winter wind through him, clearing away the blurry warmth of the laughing gas. "All I need, lady, is to get the hell out of here. I've found nothing but trouble in this town."

She dropped her soiled gloves into an enameled pan. "Perhaps that's because you go looking for it."

"I stopped here for help with Carrie."

"And you got it."

"And lost Carrie in the process," he snapped.

The color dropped from her face. Without another word, she turned on her heel and left the room.

Jackson lay still for a while, feeling the swish of powerful narcotics in his lungs and bloodstream and trying like hell to justify his behavior. The truth was, Leah Mundy scared him. She made him want a home, a family, a future. It was dangerous to want such things because he couldn't have them.

He should have figured that out a long time ago.

The day after the attack, Leah slept the sleep of exhaustion and awoke late in the morning to find everyone in the household tiptoeing around.

Before she'd come fully awake, she thought of Jackson. But as soon as her mouth began to curve into a smile, she remembered his bitter words. She was irritated but not surprised to learn that he'd gone back to work on his boat, probably tearing the stitches she'd sewn so painstakingly.

She stared at the clock on the wall opposite her bed. One minute. She would give herself one minute to think about Jackson T. Underhill, and then she would think of him no more for the rest of the day.

She failed miserably. Picking at the breakfast of porridge and marionberries Perpetua had set before her, she recalled their picnic on the beach, the way he'd unfolded his lanky length on the old blanket and savored every bite of his lunch. Later, on her way to the Rapsilver house to check on the harbormaster's burns, she caught herself gazing off between the pricked ears of the buggy horse and thinking about the day she'd helped Jackson work on his boat, how agreeable it had been to do something as mindless and undemanding as sanding a rough spot on the deck.

She pulled the buggy off by a pond so the horse could drink. She watched the wind ripple across the surface and heard the breeze sing through the high alder tops and thought irresistibly of the time at the forest house when they'd almost made love.

Even the mere memory made her flush with warmth. Her breasts tingled and she felt a sweet heaviness deep in the center of her, a throbbing summoned by the thought of his big, callused hand skimming over her breasts. She should have let him. She should have let him. The thought pulsed through her until she wanted to scream with frustration.

Stooping, she picked up a handful of rocks and flung them into the pond, shattering the pretty reflection of blue sky and clouds that had held her mesmerized.

She spanked the horse smartly and headed home. Her rounds were finished for the day, and it would soon be suppertime. She even had an hour to stop at the bathhouse for a good long soak. But the moment the silky warm water slipped over her nude body, she broke her vow yet again. She thought of Jackson.

This was getting ridiculous, she realized, hurrying through her ablutions. Purely ridiculous. She was obsessed, a lovesick mooncalf. Most girls got over this sort of affliction by the age of fifteen.

Except when Leah was fifteen, she was thinking about natural philosophy, not affairs of the heart. The only man she had thought of had been her father. Looking back, she could see that her complete adulation suited him just fine. She didn't realize it then, but his male pride had needed her unwavering worship. Not her love, though. That was something she kept hidden inside, a gift without a recipient.

In some ways, she thought, drying herself off and dressing again, she was as crippled as Bowie Dawson.

On her way in to supper, she passed through the kitchen, stopping to inhale deeply. Catching Iona's eye, she said, "Roast salmon?" Iona nodded vigorously and angled a bowl of freshly hulled strawberries so Leah could see. Her mouth started to water. She made herself ask, "Is Mr. Underhill back?" She gestured toward the front guest room.

Iona shook her head and pointed out the window at the harbor. Leah turned away quickly, hiding a scowl.

Then, with jerky, exasperated movements, she filled a tin pail with salmon and strawberries and half a loaf of bread.

"I'll have to take this down to the stubborn fool," she said.

Iona nodded, a sly smile on her silent mouth.

Leah realized just who the fool was, but she didn't stop in her dogged march to the waterfront. A new ship had arrived—a whaler, by the looks of it, but the whalers usually went on to Seattle or Tacoma after a brief stop in Coupeville. A pair of sailors ambled past, and she heard their insolent murmurs. Whether the comment was for the food or for her, she couldn't tell. She didn't care.

She stomped down the dock and dropped onto Jackson's boat, grabbing the ratlines as the schooner listed. She went down the ladder to the galley.

"Mr. Underhill," she said loudly, "you need to eat some sup—oh!"

Leah froze.

Like her, Jackson had obviously had a notion to bathe. Only on shipboard, one didn't immerse oneself in the tub. He stood with his foot propped on a low stool, scrubbing himself dry with a long yellow towel. He wore nothing but a grin.

She was a physician. She had studied anatomy. The male physique was not supposed to have this effect on her. Maybe he wasn't a man at all, she thought wildly, but a god. Some mythical being unrelated to mundane creatures.

"Hello, Doc. Brought me something to eat, did you?"

She changed her mind. He was a man. One hundred percent pure, obnoxious man. She dropped the pail, spun around, and started to scramble up on deck.

"Leah, wait!" he called.

The hem of her skirt caught on a peg. She jerked it free, tearing it a little.

"Doc, if you don't wait, I'll come up there buck naked and chase you down, and don't think I won't catch you."

He would, damn him. She knew he would. She stopped on the midships deck and called over her shoulder, "Let me know when you're decent."

"That would be a mighty long wait, honey. But I'll let you know when I'm dressed."

She waited in uncomfortable silence for a few moments. The rendering fires on the whaling ship flickered on the distant horizon. She thought of the insolent sailors she'd passed in town and pursed her lips in disapproval. She didn't care for whalers and the men who worked on them. A raucous lawlessness pervaded the big ships. Trouble often followed in their wake.

She was almost relieved when Jackson said, "I'm dressed in my Sunday best, ma'am. Come on down."

She carefully descended a companion ladder and entered the main cabin. "Actually, I came to tell you that you're not supposed to be up and about."

"My ship was damaged in the explosion. I have to fix it."

"You're supposed to be resting with a disinfectant compress on your leg."

"I washed it real well," he said, falling on the salmon and bread with an appetite she found gratifying. "Used that smelly ointment of yours. You want to have a look?"

"That won't be necessary at the moment." She picked at her supper. There was never any ease with Jackson. She was always confused or at a loss or flustered...never just comfortable. She had a notion to tell him so, but that would only make him grin at her, mock her, make her feel as gawky as a girl once again.

To distract herself, she looked around the galley. Every piece of wood gleamed with a fresh coat of varnish. It was clean and cozy, and it didn't smell bilgey.

"Well?" he asked around a mouthful of fresh bread.

"It looks...different."

"Different!"

"Much better."

"I've personally repaired and refinished every piece of this boat. It's in better shape than it was when it was new."

Which was about seventy years ago, she judged, but she didn't say anything.

"It's ready to set sail."

A phantom fist drove into her stomach. For a moment, she couldn't speak, could only stare at him. "Set sail."

"Yeah. I stayed here a lot longer than I'd planned. It was you who convinced me."

"Me?"

"Uh-huh. I was all ready to take off on a merchantman and let this boat rot in harbor, but you convinced me to stay and fix what was my own. And now I reckon it's fixed."

Leah formed the word with her lips, but no sound came out. She tried again. "When?"

"Soon."

"But your leg—"

"You fixed me up fine," he said. "I'll heal."

"You didn't finish painting the name on the stern."

"The current name is starting to grow on me." He eyed her inquisitively. "If I didn't know any better, I'd say you're stalling for time."

"Why would I do that?"

"Because you like me."

"I don't li—"

"Liar."

"Fine. I like you. But I've no business meddling in your affairs. I just want to make certain you're truly ready to leave."

He encompassed the cabin with a sweeping gesture of his arm. "Short of gingham curtains for the portholes, I'd say this boat's ready for anything."

"You certainly have worked hard," she conceded.

"Honey, this thing is varnished with my sweat." Catching her expression, he laughed. "I guess you wouldn't understand."

"Understand what?" *He's leaving. He's leaving, leaving, leaving.…* She shouldn't feel shocked, shouldn't feel anything at all. But she felt as if he'd just ripped her heart out.

"This is the only thing I have to call my own. It's the only job I've done that didn't depend on gambling and cheating. Forgive me if I'm a little excited."

"There's nothing to forgive. I understand. I have no idea why you'd think I didn't understand."

"You've had a privileged life. An education—"

"Privileged!" She laughed, though without humor. Spying an amber bottle in an enclosed shelf of the galley, she said, "May I?"

"It's grog."

"I know."

He got up and uncorked the bottle, splashing a drink into a pair of china mugs. "Cheers," he said.

"Down the hatch." She tossed back the grog, grimacing and then holding her mug out for more. She drank the second round more slowly, feeling the liquor speeding through her, rushing false courage into her heart, her limbs, her tongue. "Now, let's get back to my privileged life. I was raised by a man who hated me, and I never knew it until after he died.''

''Leah—''

''No, that's not right. I never acknowledged it. The rest of the time, I was simply pathetic, thinking if I just worked hard enough to please him, he'd love me one day. Yes, I was educated. I didn't dare be otherwise. I don't regret my education, of course, but it's not a result of privilege or even a higher calling. I was driven by fear—fear that he'd leave me, ignore me if I didn't perform.''

''He resented you because you were a better doctor than he could ever be.''

She sipped her rum, savoring the warmth as it slid down her throat. ''And what sort of education is it anyway?'' She forced herself to meet his eyes. ''I can describe the physiology of the human heart. I can map it in a drawing, dissect it down to its minutest part. If a heart falters in its beating, I can sometimes get it started again. But for the life of me, Jackson, I don't know the first thing about broken hearts.''

He sat quietly for a very long time, until she started to feel embarrassed about her frank confession. Then he said, ''It doesn't take a doctor to diagnose a broken heart. Or to mend one.''

She laughed dryly. ''Listen to us. Getting drunk and pretending to philosophize.''

''It's what drunks do best.''

She finished her second cup and held it out for more. As he poured, she said, ''We really shouldn't.''

''It does no harm, not unless it gets to be a nasty habit.''

''Have you decided where you'll go?'' She managed to ask this without letting her voice break.

He corked the bottle and put it away. "I guess that'll come to me once I set sail. You know, Doc, sometimes that's the only way to learn how to do something."

"What way?"

"Just by doing it. Not reading it in a book, but doing it. Tell me the truth. Did you really know how to set a bone until you'd actually done it on a person?"

She lifted her cup. "Touché, Mr. Underhill."

He touched the rim of her cup with his own. "So are you ready, Leah?"

"Ready for what?"

He looked at her with exaggerated patience. "To make love."

She nearly choked on her drink. *"What?"*

"That's what you came here for, isn't it?"

"What I—" With a shaking hand, she set down her mug. "I came here because you're my patient. I was concerned about your injury."

"You just happened to smell like a bouquet of flowers."

"I make a habit of bathing."

"And you just happened to have a delicious supper with you."

"Perpetua wouldn't hear of your missing supper."

"You have everything covered, then, don't you? All the excuses." He grinned. "But all the excuses in the world won't explain why you're really here."

She pressed her palms on the table. "I'm leaving."

He clamped his hands around her wrists. Sweet heaven, was he going to force her?

Alarm must have flashed in her eyes, because he laughed, his voice as smooth and melodic as a love song. "Honey, you know I won't make you stay if you want to go. But I do intend to make sure you know your own mind.''

"I...know...my own mind," she said. Her voice sounded thin. Wavering.

His hands were warm on hers, his thumbs circling her wrists, brushing over the pulse there. He didn't touch her anywhere else, just at the wrists in a gentle, circular motion, yet she started to tingle in places he wasn't even touching.

"But your body, Leah. Do you know your own body?"

"Well, of course." A pleasant lassitude buzzed through her limbs. "I'm a doc—"

"Don't give me that again. Tell me what you're feeling."

"It...tingles."

"What does? This?" He ran his hand down her inner arm.

"Yes, but...other places, too. Places you're not even close to."

He laughed softly again. "That's because I'm thinking about touching you there. And you're thinking you want it.''

"You presume a lot, Mr.—"

He leaned across the table and pressed his lips to hers, silencing her with his mouth and still not touching her anywhere but her wrists...and her lips. His were soft, bittersweet from grog, evocative with warmth. She moaned.

"That's better," he said, drawing back. "Now can we make love?"

"We can't— We shouldn't—" She felt flustered; her tongue was thick. She kept tripping over it. "No," she blurted out.

"Why not?" Leaning again, he set his lips lightly against her mouth, brushing them back and forth, back and forth, so that she was hypnotized as if by a clock pendulum. "You smell good," he commented. "Hell, even I smell good. Why waste two perfectly clean bodies that want each other?"

There was a reason, she thought. There had to be a reason. But for the life of her, she couldn't decide what that reason might be. All she knew was that she wanted him, wanted him so badly she nearly wept. She needed his next kiss as much as she needed the next breath of air.

"All right," she whispered against his mouth.

Brushing, brushing, brushing with his lips. She swooned with dizziness. "All right?"

"Yes."

"Say it, Leah. I want to hear you say it."

"I want to make love. When shall we do it?"

"What about now?"

"Now sounds...perfect."

He took her hand and helped her up from the table. She was surprised to discover that she needed help. She reeled a little. "Leah," he said, "if it's the rum and not you talking—"

"It's me. The rum just made me more truthful."

He smiled and drew her next to him. "God, Leah. Honey, I've wanted this for so long."

"How long?"

"I'll tell you later. Right now, I just want to hold you. Touch you." He reached past her and turned down the lamp, then slid open the door to the stateroom.

She hesitated in the doorway. Between waves of fear and anticipation, she remembered the first time she'd come here. The schooner had been a leaky hulk, and the room had housed Carrie. Leah pushed the memory aside. She didn't want to think about that now. She couldn't. If she did, she would lose her nerve. And then Jackson would leave, and she'd spend the rest of her life regretting the loss of this night.

"It's lovely," she said as he held up the low-burning lamp. A small writing table, a chest and a bench sat against the bank of portholes looking out the stern. The captain's bunk was above a set of drawers in an alcove. It had fresh linens on it; she could smell the clean-laundry scent of them. A wispy drape of netting enclosed the bed.

Jackson hung the lantern on a hook. "Come here, Leah." He held out his hands, palms up. "Come into my arms."

She did, and when he buried his face in her neck, she knew she was lost, lost in sensation, lost in the wonder of being held by a man for the first time in her life. It was terrible to think about it, to think how long she'd gone without this, the most elemental of human touches.

So she didn't think. She surrendered to him. To his touch, his warmth, his caresses. She let him kiss her mouth and her throat. She recalled fleetingly that she'd told him before to take the decision away from her. He hadn't done that. He'd waited. Waited for her to go mad, to promise anything, to want him so badly that she had no more pride, no more principles, nothing but a need that blazed through her like a forest fire.

He lifted his mouth from hers and stepped back. Without ceremony, without being sneaky about it, and with a frankness that she found deliciously seductive, he unfastened the row of buttons down the front of her dress.

"The day I realized you didn't wear a corset..." he whispered.

"What about it?"

"You asked me when I first started wanting you. It was that day. I started thinking about this and I couldn't stop. Damn. I just...couldn't stop."

"What day was that?"

"When you came aboard and helped me with repairs. I helped you down a ladder. Put my hands just here, like this." He demonstrated, holding her rib cage between both broad hands. "Do you remember that, Leah?"

"I remember." She'd been frightened. And fascinated. Filled with misgivings and trepidation. She still was. Jackson Underhill was a dangerous man, not quite in the way she'd thought, but treacherous still, like the sea itself, seductive and endlessly alluring.

He finished with the buttons and parted her shirtwaist, letting it hang down her back. Reaching around, he freed her of her skirt and petticoat, and she stood there in nothing but her fine lawn shift and a blush that burned so deep she was sure she must be glowing in the dark.

"Leah, you're beautiful."

"You don't have to say that."

"I know." He held her upper arms and drew her into a long, hard kiss. She skimmed her hands up his chest and behind his neck, studying the firm musculature in a way that the doctor in her never could have explained to the woman in her or vice versa.

She felt feverish by the time he stood back and took off his shirt. The lamplight gleamed across his chest and struck highlights into his damp fair hair. *He* was beautiful, but she couldn't say it, couldn't bring herself to speak at all.

"Let's lie down." He held out his hand.

She knew human sexuality from her studies. But the great irony was how ignorant she truly was. Nothing— no book, no lecture, or even a demonstration could prepare her for this: the vulnerability, the terror, the anticipation. The heady, insane sense that she was about to give all control to another person.

"I—I can't do this," she choked out.

"You mean you won't," Jackson corrected her, idly stroking one hand up and down her body, no hint of impatience in his voice. "Why not? Because we're not married?"

"No. That's not it."

"Because you might get pregnant?"

"Believe me, I've considered that. It's a risk I'm not averse to taking, since…the timing places the odds in my favor."

"Then what is it? Are you afraid?" His hand swirled downward, then up again, tantalizing the places in her that ached for him. "You've got to trust me."

"I…can't."

The hands again. Stroking, stroking… "Try."

"Why?"

"Because I'm worth the risk, honey. If it turns out I'm wrong, at least you'll know."

"At least I'll know," she echoed softly, lifting herself into his caress.

He made it easy for her, this forbidden ordeal of lovemaking. She expected clumsy, awkward groping. Timid kisses. Strangeness. Embarrassment. Instead, it was none of those things. Jackson Underhill had skills she'd never imagined. He made each movement silky smooth. Each part of her body he uncovered, he kissed and caressed until she was a little more relaxed, surrendering more of herself with each passing moment, each feathery stroke. As he uncovered each part of his own body, he took her hand and put it there, held it until the sensation felt natural and right. And so it went for endless moments.

By the time they lay together, naked, on their sides and facing each other, she was trembling.

"Cold?" he asked.

"No."

"Scared?"

"A little."

"You're a virgin, Leah?"

"Yes."

"Sometimes it hurts the first time."

*Oh, Jackson,* she thought. *With you, it could hurt every time and I wouldn't care.*

"I understand that," she admitted. "In a recent journal, I read a description—"

He stopped her words with his mouth and cupped her hip with his broad hand. She relaxed, and he lifted his mouth from hers. "Maybe it won't hurt. It'll be a medical breakthrough."

"Pain-free deflowering. I could write it up for the medical journals."

He leaned forward, nipped wickedly at her breast. "Are you going to be taking notes?"

"I don't see how I can. You keep...urging my hands to be busy."

He laughed, a low, provocative chuckle. "Then I'll just have to make sure you don't forget a single second of this."

She smiled along with him, but in her heart she knew she would never forget this night. How could she forget the warmth of his hands, everywhere touching her and invading her and teasing her? How could she forget the moist heat of her own body, arching toward him, shuddering when he touched her, shuddering even more when he stopped? How could she forget the way his mouth felt against her lips, her throat, her breasts, the backs of her

knees, the arch of her foot, and finally—shockingly—
against her woman's parts? She nearly flew to pieces, felt
herself hovering, almost there...but he left her in a fever
of wanting. Waiting. Wondering.

He wouldn't let her be timid or embarrassed even
when he made his way upward and kissed her full on the
mouth again, sharing a dizzily forbidden taste, and said,
"See what happens to you?"

"Yes," she managed.

He took her hand and guided it downward. "Now
here's what happens to me."

She trembled, not with fear or even the slightest bit of
anxiety, but because she wanted him so much, wanted
them to be together, wanted to complete whatever it was
Jackson had started with his kisses and caresses.

She stroked him, and he made a hissing sound as if
she'd burned him. She smiled into the dark. "I'm ready
for more. Are you?"

"Yes. God, *yes*."

She faltered in ignorance. The rush of power she found
by discovering her effect on him had dissipated.
"Then..."

"Then this." He moved, bracing himself above her.
She felt herself lifting toward him and they touched, and
he moved again, and they came together slowly. He
shook with the effort of restraint, and she wanted to call
out to him, to tell him that it was all right, no restraint
was necessary, that she wanted him swiftly and *now,* but
she couldn't make a sound. She hung in a thrall of such
exquisite anticipation that the breath stayed locked in her
throat.

He kept pressing himself against her in short, rhythmic
thrusts, but he didn't go deep, just rocked back and forth,
back and forth, and her nerves burned in a frenzy of

arousal. She clutched his shoulders and clenched her eyes shut, lifting toward him, lifting, lifting. Each time he thrust, he drew her closer, went deeper, and she could feel the pressure building inside her, could feel herself climbing higher and higher, holding her breath, terrified everything might come tumbling down on top of her.

Was there pain? Perhaps, but it mattered so little that she barely acknowledged it. All she felt was the sensation of reaching the top, the very crest of the invisible hill she'd been struggling up, and she hovered there for an endless moment, motionless, weightless, and then suddenly she shattered, melted down over the pinnacle, all the love-warmed parts of her languorous in their descent to earth.

She sensed his release, as well, and it surprised her, for she hadn't realized she would feel it. She took an unexpected satisfaction in the gentle ripples of his pleasure, and she savored it, hoping the feeling was almost as exquisite as her own.

He sank down carefully, breathing hard into her wildly tangled hair. "Are you all right?" he asked at length.

"Yes." The word sounded inadequate, but she wasn't certain if she was all right, and she didn't want the lie to be too big.

"Did I hurt you?"

She remembered the pressure, the bond, the pleasure. "I have arrived at an altogether different notion of what pain is. Dear heaven, your leg!" she said, remembering the wound.

"It's fine." He shook with laughter. "Damn, Leah, you're funny."

She felt the friction between them. "No one's ever said that about me before."

"Well, you are." He lifted himself up on his elbows

and kissed her forehead, her cheeks, her nose. "You're a lot of things, sugar, but I don't think you'd believe it if I told you." Then, very slowly, he eased himself away from her, and even her body was reluctant, tightening so that his eyes flew open and he said, "*Damn*, Leah!" and chuckled again.

For hours and hours it seemed, they lay side by side, listening to the sounds of the water lapping at the hull. Then, without a word, he started making love to her again, making her want him again, and they coupled tenderly, slowly, with the same shattering results. Drifting toward sleep, she was lost at sea, lost in a sea of sensation. She knew that outside their wooden cocoon, ordinary life went on, unchanged by the cataclysmic event that had transformed Leah Mundy. Everything was different. Everything. She felt as if the world had just changed colors.

And he was the reason.

At dawn, she wept, and Jackson held her close, cushioning her cheek on his bare chest. "Is this a delayed reaction?"

She nodded, closing her burning eyes when he tipped her chin up toward him.

"Open your eyes, Leah," he said.

She did, but still she wept, unable to stop the tears.

"What's wrong, honey?"

"We shouldn't have done this. We shouldn't have made love. I knew there was a reason. Before we even started, I knew there was a reason, but I wouldn't let myself think about it. But there is a reason, and I finally figured out what it is."

"And?"

She hesitated. How stupid to think she could survive

this. How stupid to realize she'd failed to recognize what she should have known right from the start.

She'd only known him a few months.

But she had loved him for as long as life.

"Leah?" he prompted. "What is it?"

"Making love for one night isn't enough for me, Jackson. It'll never be enough."

"Then I reckon," he said easily, "I'd best stay awhile."

Her heart leaped. "Really?"

"Yeah. Really."

*For how long?* she wanted to ask him. *How long will you stay?* But she wouldn't let herself question him, wouldn't let her emotions be dictated by his whims. That was the mistake she'd made with her father. She wouldn't make it again.

# *Twelve*

―◦◦◦◦◦―

"'**Be** it known that the special moral qualities of women must not be tarnished by unseemly passion.'" Reclining on the captain's bunk, Jackson eyed Leah over the top of the medical text. She lay at the opposite end, eating a plum and laughing at his absurd recitation from one of her own textbooks.

"Go on," she said.

"'...by which it is a certainty that the full force of sexual desire is seldom known to a virtuous woman.'"

The text sounded absurd to her as she relaxed against the bolsters. The captain's bunk had become her favorite spot on the boat. The little alcove, with its round porthole letting in the daylight, was more than the place she escaped to, the place where she became Jackson's woman, where she could shed her identity and simply be his lover, drowning in the lavish indulgence of his caresses. In the secret, splendid weeks since they had first become lovers, this had become her refuge, her hideaway.

Here, she was not Dr. Mundy, but just Leah, a woman whose hunger had been awakened, who knew society would frown on what she was doing, and who didn't care in the least. She sat facing him, watching the late afternoon sun play in his blond hair and feeling a warm flush of sexual contentment.

" 'The heat of the marriage bed is an unnatural obsession of voluptuaries.' " Jackson closed the book and set it aside. He ran his bare foot up the inside of her leg. "Doc, that's a hell of a way for you to learn about sex."

"Would you rather I learned it from a fast-talking gambler?"

"So long as that fast-talking gambler is me." He grinned affably, pretending he had no idea what his foot was doing under the blankets.

She frowned in mock distress. "I don't remember reading about *that* in any of my textbooks."

"It's a brand-new technique. Still in the experimental stages." He changed the movement, made it deeper, bolder. "Well, Dr. Mundy?"

"It's…working."

"Make a note of that."

She looked at the letter in her lap, the one she'd started to Penny. She hadn't gotten past the date and the greeting. With a helpless laugh, she let the paper and fountain pen drop to the floor beside the bunk. "Oops," she said.

"Never mind that." Leaning forward, Jackson slid his hands up her legs, pushing aside the covers.

She had learned long ago not to be embarrassed; he wouldn't stand for embarrassment. He'd taught her that to resist him was folly, and when she cooperated, the rewards were unimaginably sweet.

With his palms flat against her inner thighs, he eyed her frankly for a moment, then moaned. "Christ, it's hard to believe I need you again, woman." Without further preamble, without even preparing her as he sometimes spent a long time doing, he thrust inside. She welcomed him, throwing back her head and bringing her arms around his torso. "You're made for loving, Leah," he whispered in her ear. "I can't believe you didn't know that."

She raised her hips as he lowered his head to her breasts. This was what she craved—the mindless ecstasy, a feeling so powerful it would not let in anything so mundane as rational thought. She wove her fingers into his hair and inhaled the scent of him and knew that there was no sweeter sensation to be had.

He filled her completely, crying out her name, his shoulders shuddering and rippling with the movement. It was as close as Jackson Underhill ever came to surrender, and she loved it.

Her own release burst free on a pent-up rush of breath, and she floated for a few moments as if in the aftershock of an earthquake, holding still, not breathing.

The stark truth of a terrible thought raged through her. She lived for these moments. If she lost everything else in her life but this, she could still be happy.

"Ah, Jackson," she confessed, "this can't be good for us."

"What the hell is that supposed to mean?" Still joined with her, he moved back, cradled her face between his big hands.

"Just that…it…you fill my life too completely. When I'm not with you, I think of you constantly. And when I am with you, I want to be touching you. I want you inside me."

"Then I'm right where you want me."

"But what about the rest of the world? What about the rest of life?"

"It'll still be there when we decide to leave this bunk."

He didn't understand. He wasn't the sort to plan from

one day to the next. By filling her life, he drew her attention away from patients and boarders and the surgery—things that mattered to her. Did they matter still? She told herself yes, but did loving Jackson leave room for them?

"As far as I'm concerned," she said, only half-joking, "we should never get out of bed again."

"Fine with me." He shifted his hips and she felt him harden again. Her body responded with an instant spasm of welcome. "*Damn*, Leah," he said.

She smiled and started to speak, but he stopped her mouth with his own, kissing her deeply, probing and tasting until she forgot what she was going to say. And then he moved again, filling her again, and the onrush of sensation cleared her mind like a wave. Afterward, she floated, empty of thought. This was too dangerously pleasant, she told herself. She shouldn't like it so much.

Later, she snuggled against his bare chest while he read to himself from the textbook, chuckling at the sexual advice, but showing a genuine interest in diseases common to seafaring men. Leah's mind wandered. She thought about the married couples she knew, her patients and people she'd met in passing. Perhaps she had missed something, but she could not recall that any of those women appeared to experience this unholy obsession with a man.

Perhaps that was the great secret a marriage hid. The terrible ecstasy of loving someone not just with the heart, but with the body, the soul, the entire being.

And then the inevitable question snaked into her thoughts like the serpent into the Garden of Eden. Had it been like this for Jackson and Carrie?

She stirred restlessly against him.

"What?" he asked, attuned to her every nuance. "Again?"

She lifted her head to him, looked into his face—so full of mystery, so captivating. "Yes, again, but…this way," she said, and slipped downward, her kisses bold and fervent with a hunger to forget, to fill herself with him yet again, because that was the only way she could escape. She felt his breath catch when she kissed him there; it was something he had told her about but had never asked of her; something that had been written of in dry tones in a medical text; yet another matter that print had reduced to a patent absurdity. But when he groaned her name and his chest heaved with mindless pleasure, there was nothing absurd about it, and afterward she was able to disappear into sleep.

More happy than he had a right to be, Jackson curved both arms protectively around Leah as she stirred to wakefulness. She squinted at the porthole over the bunk. "What time is it?"

"Past suppertime. Are you hungry?"

"Starved."

He grinned into the gathering twilight. "I like a woman with an appetite." He handed her a plum from a bowl and took one for himself. They ate in silence for a time.

Finally, she said, "I take it Carrie didn't have much of an appetite." She spoke slowly as if considering each word.

"No." His reply was terse. He didn't want to talk about this, but he could tell from Leah's tone she wouldn't leave it be.

"The craving for the drug, and then the drug itself, tends to suppress the appetite."

She shifted, rubbing the silkiness of her bare shoulder

against him. He bent down and kissed it. Damn, she was soft, the softest woman he'd ever touched.

"Jackson?"

"Mmm?"

She took a long breath, then let out her next words. "There's something I've been wondering."

"Mmm?"

"About...you and Carrie."

He sensed a sudden chill in the air. "Yeah?"

"Did you...were the two of you...like this?"

"For chrissakes, Leah. Don't bring another woman into our bed." His voice had grown harsh with irritation.

She pushed away from him, leaving a cold spot on his chest and gathering the blanket around her. "You were man and wife. Is it any surprise that I wonder if you ever loved each other...like this?"

"Nope. No surprise."

"So did you?"

"I don't kiss and tell." He grabbed her and kissed her soundly.

Drawing back, she scowled at him from the shadows. "This is all so new to me. I cannot imagine doing this...feeling this...with anyone but you."

So that was what had been on her mind. He'd been wondering. Sometimes she'd grow silent and thoughtful, and she'd look at him with an intensity that made him think of those microscope slides he'd read about in her medical journals. She wanted to know if what they had was special, unique, a once-in-a-lifetime love that they'd never find again, that few people ever found.

He looked at her and thought, *Yes.* This thing we share, this bond. It could last a lifetime.

*Wait.* Doubts reared up inside him. All this sensual pleasure made him soft in the head. Skewed his thoughts.

Jackson started to panic. He couldn't own up to these feelings, couldn't believe in them. He knew this couldn't last as surely as he knew he was being stalked by federal marshals. He had to go. She had to stay. It was as simple as that.

And so Jackson T. Underhill did what he was best at. He lied.

"Honey, you're the doctor, so I feel sort of funny being the one to explain. But this—" he gestured at the rumpled covers heaped on the bed "—is like a drug, I guess. And a body gets to craving it like a drug, see? I don't have a damned thing some other man doesn't have, more or less. So it's just a physical thing."

Her cheeks paled. "Then why did I never feel this desire for any other man?"

"Maybe you never met one who was as persistent about it as I was."

"Maybe you're lying."

He'd rarely been caught fibbing, and he wasn't about to be snared now. "I guess I might be oversimplifying, but believe me, Leah. You're a beautiful woman. Beautiful to touch and beautiful when you touch me. But what's touching after all? A physical sensation. Surely you understand that."

"Yes, but—"

He pressed a finger to her lips, those soft, velvety lips he dreamed about every night. "I know what you want to hear. That no one makes me feel the way you do. That you're the last thought I have when I go to sleep and the first when I wake up. That I can't let a day go by without touching you, loving you." Jackson alone knew he was speaking from the heart. But it would be too cruel to let her believe it.

"Don't tell me what I want to hear," she snapped. "Tell me what's true."

"What's true is that I've been with a lot of other women before."

"With Carrie?"

"With a lot of women. And you'll find something better than we have. With someone else, someone who'll settle down with you, stay by you, give you the honor of his name."

"And you are not that person?"

"Honey, I never have been, never will be. You know that."

"Yes. I know that."

"You knew it from the start." He took away the blanket and kissed her. "So just be with me while I'm here. Let's not waste any more time talking."

"Let's not."

"Let's..." He leaned forward, whispered a suggestion into her ear. Instead of acting shocked, she laughed low in her throat. God, he loved her. What a cruel joke fate had played on him. Just when he was about to make his great escape, he fell for the one woman who would never come with him.

Or would she?

He'd never asked her. He'd never even thought of asking her...until now. Until he loomed above her and saw her dark hair spread across his pillow. Until he looked into her velvet eyes and saw paradise. Until he felt a wave of longing so huge it left him spent...yet craving more. Always more.

Tinny piano music clattered through the waterfront dance hall. The swinging half doors framed a picture-perfect view of San Francisco Bay, the water a blue mirror of the sky and the rock hulk of Alcatraz strangely ethereal, like a postcard Joel Santana had once seen of that place in France—Mont-Saint-Michel.

He had been combing the city for days, inquiring at bars and boardinghouses along the waterfront. He had a system of searching. He'd enter a place, have a drink, ask a few questions. So far, no one recalled seeing a gambling man and his lady. This was one of the last places on the busy waterfront street known as Tonquin.

He propped his elbow on the worn walnut bar and sipped cautiously at a dram of whiskey. A man had to be careful in places like this. Whiskey was always watered down to illegal levels, but some places spiked it with chloral hydrate or cocaine shavings. Not a happy combination for a man who needed to keep his wits about him.

A tired-looking whore sidled up and halfheartedly twitched the tattered hem of her red petticoat at him. He gave his head a brief shake, and she looked relieved, walking away on wobbly high heels.

Joel put down his drink, for it suddenly tasted too rough and bitter even for his trail-hardened palate. Was there ever a time, he wondered, that he'd found this job exciting? Yeah, probably, but that had been two decades ago when he was still wet behind the ears and absolutely convinced that chasing down bad guys was his calling in life.

The ensuing twenty years had taught him that there was little actual chasing to be done. Being a marshal consisted mostly of this—a tedious parade of dusty towns and stinking cities, asking questions of people who were either too drunk to answer or who had secrets of their own to hide. Waiting. Watching. Stealing sleep and gulping a meal when he could.

Joel had taken to dreaming. When he was lost in the desert of Arizona, he'd taught himself to retreat. To go somewhere inside his head where a cool green breeze blew, where a woman's soothing hand smoothed across his brow, where the smell of an apple pie greeted him at suppertime. He was convinced that his ability to create this world in his mind had saved him from going crazy in the desert and dying of thirst. The strange vision or dream or whatever it was had sustained him, made him focus on surviving, and he had. He'd come out of the desert feeling pounds thinner, uncounted years older—and a lot smarter.

The wise inner voice told him to quit now, to give up his search for Jack Tower and Caroline Willis. He could return empty-handed, report that the trail had gone cold, and still keep his pride—and his pension. The world wouldn't end if he retired without closing this last job. He'd traveled more than two thousand miles in pursuit of a pair who probably hadn't survived this far. What the hell was he doing, chasing ghosts?

He shut his eyes and tried to ignore the overly bright, off-key piano music. He moved toward that cool verdant place in his head. He started to see it, the lush greens, the blues. He started to smell the ripening apples—

"Hey, mister, you're looking a tad lonely there." A female voice yanked him back to the seamy dance hall.

Reluctantly, Joel opened his eyes. Another whore, this one tipsy and not so tired-looking. Christ, she even had dimples and ringlets of yellow hair. Young. Small bosoms, but he'd been known to tolerate small bosoms.

"Yeah?" he said.

"I seen you from across the room. You look like you done lost your best friend."

Joel reminded himself of his purpose. "I guess I have, in a way."

She cocked her head, looking depressingly vacant.

He decided to give it a try anyway. "I was supposed to hook up with a buddy of mine, and I guess I missed him. Name of Jack Tower. Tall drink of water, yellow hair, maybe a beard and mustache if he hasn't been to the barber lately. Had a scar right about here." Joel indicated the crest of his cheekbone.

She frowned, concentrating as hard as her beer-washed brain would let her. "I mighta seen someone like that."

Knowing it would probably go to waste, Joel pressed a dollar into her palm. "He was a pretty sharp cardplayer. Five-card draw was his game. And he might have been traveling with a woman. Pretty little thing, as I recall. Blond hair, blue eyes. A few years older than you."

The whore tapped her temple as if the motion would jog her memory. "Seems to me I seen a pair like that a few months ago. But it's tough, mister. I see so many folks come through the Tarnished Angel."

Fighting exasperation, he handed her another dollar.

"She liked her whiskey, as I recall. Carried it in a blue glass bottle," the woman said. She winked at Joel. "You know, mister, I can concentrate a lot better in my own private room."

"Is that a fact?" In spite of his disgust—at both the woman and himself—Joel's body reminded him that he was not as old as he felt, and she was not as bad as she looked.

"Yeah, hon, that's a fact." She took his hand and led him upstairs.

# Thirteen

12 August 1894

My dear Penelope,

I hope this reaches you before you embark on your journey west. This will be my last letter before we meet face-to-face. I never thought I would find myself in the position to confess this, but now I understand what it is to love. It is not the unhealthy attachment I had to my father, worshiping him simply because he was *there*. I've learned that there are other ways to love, better ways.

Who would have thought I'd find it with a man like Jackson T. Underhill? He is everything polite society frowns upon—he has no family and no home, though he is lately come from Texas—but I cannot help myself. When I am with him, all the colors of the world shine brighter. When we are apart, I go about with a dull feeling inside me, and there is nothing for it but to wait for our next meeting.

I am not certain where all this is leading but of one thing I am sure. I have only one life. It's time I stopped living it in fearful isolation. It's time I discovered what I've missed before it's too late.

Respectfully,
Leah Mundy, M.D.

The breeze blowing across the Sound rippled the day-old newspaper Jackson was reading. He pressed a palm down on the deck to hold it in place and stared at a small boxed article in the *Pioneer and Democrat*.

Newly appointed U.S. Marshal R. Corliss, of Port Townsend, is lately credited with the seizure of three thousand dollars' worth of smuggled opium syrup. On West Beach, a fruit grower mistook the substance for mineral paint and used it to paint his barn a deep maroon color....

The sun still held the warmth of high summer. But as he checked the *Teatime* from stem to stern, Jackson felt a slight chill. Restlessness nagged at him. He'd always had an uncanny sixth sense for danger, and that sense—coupled with the mention of a federal marshal in the area—told him he'd overstayed his welcome here on this green, too-friendly island where the town sheriff thought he was a do-gooder and the town doctor had captured his heart.

"She's looking good, Skipper," Davy Morgan said, coming along the dock, his red hair blowing out behind him.

Jackson folded the paper and stuffed it into his back pocket. "You think she's seaworthy?"

"As much as an old blue-water boat can be in these parts." His piercing blue eyes were filled with a wisdom that made him seem older than his years. He checked the row of belaying pins stuck in the fife rail and nodded in approval. "Just keep a weather eye out, follow the charts for the shoals, and you'll be fine." Lithe as a cat, he slipped up the ratlines to the midmast, aligning a pulley. "Where you planning on going anyway?"

"Do I have to know precisely?"

"It sort of helps with the travel plans." Davy shinnied down the mast and landed with a barefooted thud on the deck. "I hear the Sandwich Islands are fine."

"Yeah." Jackson pictured Robert Louis Stevenson seated under a banyan tree, writing his tales of adventure while girls with flowers in their hair brought him coconut milk. "I might go see that for myself."

"When do you weigh anchor?"

*Never,* Jackson wanted to say. But he knew better. He knew the past would find him here if he stayed long enough. Yet even that chilly certainty lost its urgency when he thought of Leah. Christ, how could he give up what they had?

"No one's going anywhere on this yet," he said. "Today I'm just hoping I can make it to the cove and back." He bent to secure a fender to a new cleat.

"Take the dinghy just in case. Is Dr. Mundy going with you?"

Jackson looked up sharply. "The doc?" He shrugged, elaborately casual. "I suppose, if she's of a mind to join me."

Davy smiled, his old-soul eyes twinkling. "I imagine the doctor's of such a mind." Since the fire, both he and Bob Rapsilver took care to address Leah as Doctor.

Jackson went on working. For Leah's sake, he was discreet about their liaison. He supposed Davy, who bunked at the harbor house, couldn't help but notice the long visits she paid to the schooner, but the youth kept mum.

Later, as he was getting ready to set sail, Leah appeared at the head of the pier. Davy conveniently slipped away, nodding courteously to her as they passed on the dock.

Damn, Jackson thought, watching her approach from his perch on the bowsprit, she was a good-looking woman. Not some pale china doll, but rock solid, her brown-eyed gaze direct and filled with an intelligence that should have intimidated him, but didn't.

As she drew nearer, his heartbeat sped up. He recognized what he was feeling now, even though he'd never felt it before. Never even thought himself capable of it. At first, he'd tried to dismiss it as lust, and he certainly felt that, but then after the lust, a quiet, settled feeling took over, reminding him of home fires at twilight, of earnest conversations and private jokes and close-knit families.

*Ah, Leah. Make me stop loving you. Do it now, before I hurt you.*

She smiled as she stepped aboard. "I finished my rounds early."

"Those rounds sure keep you busy." He looked at her hands—clean, strong, capable hands. Who had they touched today? Who had they healed?

"It was a quiet afternoon. Summers aren't usually too bad for sickness." She took in the schooner with a sweeping glance. Alarm flickered across her face. "You're ready to cast off."

"Uh-huh. A trial run."

Relief washed the tension from her face. "You were waiting for me."

"That's what Davy says." Jackson was eager to weigh

anchor, enjoy the sail, get the feel of the water under him once again. "Ready?" he asked Leah.

She smiled. "You're supposed to shout orders down the decks."

"That's only if you have a crew."

She muttered about the folly of sailing solo, but was quick enough to untie and push off into the open waters. Jackson's sense of wonder took over. The newly patched sails rode up without a hitch; he set them to the gentle summer wind, and the schooner coursed along with the grace of a seabird.

"Damn, Leah!" he shouted from the helm. "It worked. We're *sailing!*"

From the bow of the ship, she lifted her arm and waved at him. The sharp teeth of the bow cut a white-lipped wake, the sails snapped taut, wrapping around a friendly wind; the hull rushed over the rocking swells. And perched proudly on the foredeck was a dark-haired woman with her head thrown back, laughing with delight.

In that moment, Jackson knew his life was as close to perfect as it was going to get. His heart felt big, as if it was pushing up into his throat. She looked so fine and joyous just then that she took his breath away.

He experimented, tacking back and forth, setting a course and then changing it, lashing the helm in place and going below to see how the pumps were holding up. Everything worked. It was almost scary. Almost.

After an hour's sail, he came about and nosed into the cove they'd found earlier in the summer. "We'll drop anchor here," he called to Leah.

She frowned. "Why here?"

"I thought we'd check out that smugglers' cave, make sure it's not full of guns again."

"Last time we tried to interfere with the smugglers, people almost got killed and the chandlery burned."

"Yeah, and the sheriff hasn't done a damned thing about it." Jackson felt a spark of anger. He'd delivered the evidence to the sheriff's door, all but finding the culprits for him. Why hadn't St. Croix staked out this place? Why hadn't he kept a watch on the cave?

They rowed the dinghy to shore, then grabbed a pair of blankets from the boat, climbed to the top of the bluff, and checked the cave. Empty.

"I hope it stays that way," Leah said.

He thought of that night, the blood and fire and violence, and some impulse made him grab her and pull her against him. "Stay safe, Leah," he said, inhaling the fragrance of her hair.

"Of course I'll stay safe," she said, pushing back to eye him inquisitively. "Why wouldn't I be safe?"

"You live in a place where pirates attack."

Thunder pulsed in the distance.

"I think that's like lightning striking. Never twice in the same spot." She tilted her head to one side. "You're like that, aren't you, Jackson? You never go back to a place."

He kissed her temple. "Nope."

"Why is that?"

"Never had a reason to."

"Don't you think it's time you told me?"

Christ. He wanted to tell her everything. About his mother leaving him on the stoop. About Brother Anthony with his ring of office and his belt. About the endless dark nights at St. I's. About the lost years that had turned him from a desperate young boy into a man hardened by life. About the night in Rising Star when he'd sold his soul for a woman who was not worth the price.

He wanted to share it all with Leah, and then he wanted to hold her close and know she loved him anyway. The panic came again, the sense that he had no right to feel what he felt for her.

"A man like me makes his share of mistakes. And enemies," he added. "On both sides of the law."

"What mistakes?" she persisted. "What enemies?"

"I won't put you at risk by naming names," he snapped, frustrated.

She turned away to watch the boat riding at anchor.

He hated to think of her alone, living out her life here, year after year, vulnerable to the world.

It started raining, a typical summer rain swishing down in a great curtain. With an almost angry tug, he turned her toward the woods. "Let's go look at the forest house."

She balked. "I don't think—"

"Then don't think. Let's just go, Leah."

The grove had grown even more lush with summer foliage. And like the first time, a hush hung in the air as if the trees were holding their breath and waiting, waiting...for something. Fanciful as the notion was, Jackson couldn't shake it any more than he could shake the sense of awe and reverence the greenwood grove evoked.

Leah didn't speak; she kept her hand in his as they approached the strange, hidden little house. He thought of her coming here after he was gone. Would she sit inside on a rainy day and think of him? Is this the place she would come to hide from the world for a while?

They went inside, hearing a whir of wings as a thrush fled through the window. The mossy smell of the woods permeated everything. Making a heap of ancient tinder, Jackson lit a fire in the grate. Within moments, a big half-burned log caught and the flames danced, creating a cozy atmosphere as rain spattered the roof.

He spread one of the blankets in front of the hearth. Leah sat down, hugging her knees to her chest and staring at the flames. Jackson, in turn, stared at her. She was as dark and lovely as the sunset, deeply contemplative as she sat motionless. He lifted his finger, traced it from her temple down to her jaw, her chin; then he turned her face toward him.

"Leah. You know why I brought you here."

"To test the schooner. To see how she runs and to check that cave."

To Jackson's surprise, he felt nervous, too. He didn't want to hurt her. God, he didn't. But he didn't know how to avoid it. "I could have done that without you," he admitted. "But I wanted to bring you here—" he kept hold of her chin so she wouldn't look away "—to make love to you. These days, that's pretty much all I think about, Doc."

"I doubt that."

"I mean it, Leah. Can't you tell I mean it?" He took her hand and guided it down to touch him. Her eyes flared wide and her lips parted, and he couldn't wait any longer. He leaned forward and kissed her more roughly than he'd planned because the urgency inside him kept trying to claw its way out. She kissed him back just as fiercely, her hands pulling at his clothing. He forced himself to slacken his hold on her, to slow down. He pressed her to the blanket, fanning her hair out around her face. "You know what?"

"What?"

"We don't have to hurry." He lifted his head a little to glance out the door. "The rain's going to go on all afternoon. It's no fun sailing home in the rain."

"What if we get stuck here all night?"

He bent to nibble her neck. The texture of her skin was like silk, but softer, more giving. "That'd be a damned shame. I'd be forced to keep you here and do this all night long."

"Do what?"

He slipped his finger up her thigh. "This."

Her eyes widened.

"And…this." He moved his hand in a pulsing rhythm. She rewarded him with a small sound of passion, a shifting of her hips on the blanket.

He sat up and undressed her garment by garment, stopping to kiss the places he bared and pausing to hastily discard his own clothes. He lingered over her breasts, cupping the pale smoothness in his hands and then bending low to taste her until she arched helplessly toward him. Then he moved on, turning her over, massaging her back and kissing the nape of her neck and then pushing her legs apart to enter her, pulling her up beneath him and using his hands to make her cry out in dizzy surprise. When she spasmed to climax, he forced himself to wait. He turned her back and took her in his arms, letting her whimper and cling to him in a way he found curiously touching. With barely a pause, he started making love to her again, caressing her breasts and belly until she writhed against him.

"Enough," she whispered.

"It's never enough," he said, lowering his head, kissing her breasts. "I can't get enough of you."

"But I—"

He kept kissing her. His hand cupped her thigh, slid suggestively upward.

"I—"

"Hush. I tried to do this the first time we came here. You're not going to talk me out of it now."

He braced himself above her, hearing the swish of rain outside and the hiss of blood in his ears, and just before he plunged into her, he smiled. He could make her stop thinking, drive her mindless with desire and anticipation and, finally, ecstasy. He could feel the latent ripples of the pleasure they'd just shared, and like gathering waves, the strength of them revived him, and the passion started to happen all over again.

Until Leah, he would not have thought himself capable of loving a woman so long and so well. Because, he now knew, with Leah it was more than just a physical affair. His heart was engaged. His mind and his soul. It was a new experience for him. With Leah, he felt a oneness that was completely strange. He didn't understand it, didn't know what it meant, but she lifted him up, drew him close to a light source he'd never seen before. He saw it now, covering her upraised hands with his palms, then weaving their fingers together in a tight, fierce bond. She brought him up and over in a long, drawn-out moment that passed far too quickly. He lowered himself, blanketing her body with his, feeling the warmth of the fire on one side and burying his face in her silky dark hair.

"Ah, Leah. You're so soft. So damned soft."

She lay quiet, and eventually he left her, then drew a second blanket over them and cushioned her head on his shoulder. "We should go back," she murmured sleepily.

"Yeah, we should."

But they didn't. They drifted off to sleep for a time, awakened to the rain again, made love and then lay holding each other until the fire died to embers. As the feeble glow from the hearth wavered to nothingness, Jackson knew he had to quit putting off the inevitable.

"Leah." His throat felt harsh with what he was about to say.

"Mmm?"

"Honey, I have to leave."

"But it's still raining—"

"I mean for good."

She didn't move, but he felt a shifting between them, a chill, a stiffening. A long silence stretched out the tension. Then she said, "Where are you going? And why now?"

"I've been here too damned long. Best I disappear before trouble finds me."

"What makes you so certain trouble will find you?"

"Trust me, I know. If it was just me, I wouldn't much care, but I'm thinking of you. I don't want to destroy the life you worked so hard to build here. I won't do that to you. I won't take that risk."

"What if I want you to?"

"Believe me, honey, you don't."

"You *are* like the lightning," she said bleakly. "Don't deny it. You never strike in the same place."

"I can't be something I'm not, Leah. I can't be the sort of man you need."

She extracted herself from his embrace. Matter-of-factly, without any false modesty, she stood and put on her clothes with unhurried movements. He would always think of her like this—strong, slender limbs and creamy skin, a natural grace and assurance to every movement.

This was harder, he decided, than tears and hysteria. He had no idea how to cope with this dignity. He fumbled into his clothes. "Leah," he said, "I'm sorry."

"I never asked for promises, Jackson," she said. "I never asked you to stay."

*But if I could, would you want me?* He wouldn't let himself ask it aloud.

He admired the fluid economy of her movements. She was so unaffected. So pretty, with her round, dark-tipped breasts and her brown eyes. It was a daily amazement to him that men didn't line up to call on her, didn't beg for her favors like dogs after scraps.

They were afraid, he thought. Afraid of her mind, afraid they didn't have what she wanted. And, he thought in selfish gratitude, they didn't.

The rain had stopped and late sunshine shot through the glistening trees. The lowering daylight outlined her profile as she bent to draw on her stocking. In that moment, as he watched her do something so simple yet so precious to him, his heart filled and the words came up through him, unstoppable, not waiting to be thought out. "Come with me, Leah."

She froze. He recognized that complete stillness; he knew her mind was working like pistons in a steam engine. And he knew he'd just made a huge mistake.

"Leave my practice? My home? Just pick up and go?"

"You said you'd take a risk."

She nodded. "Perhaps I would. But what exactly are you offering me?"

*My heart.* But he panicked and didn't say it. Such words held a promise he couldn't keep. "Honey, it was a bad idea. But seeing you like this—" his gaze tracked over her stockinged leg "—has me thinking with something other than my head."

Instead of being offended, she turned to face him, her gaze as direct as the summer sun. "Do you love me, Jackson?"

There it was. The big test. His big chance. She was telling him what she needed from him; the one thing that could make her follow him anywhere. Away from here. Into the sunset.

With a grin that usually worked on her, he held out his arms. "Leah, come here."

She stood rigid, her hands clenched at her sides. "Answer the question, Jackson."

He couldn't lie to her and he couldn't tell her the truth. So he dropped his arms and said, "How the hell is someone like me supposed to love anybody?" Before she could comment, he added, "Leah, no matter what I feel for you, I can't give you what you already have—you're among people you can care for. Whether or not they show you the proper respect doesn't seem to matter, but you need them as much as they need you."

"Yes, but—"

He crossed the room and took her gently by the shoulders. "I dare you to deny it. I dare you to say it isn't so."

She dropped her gaze, giving him a sweet-sad smile that tore at his heart. "You know me well, Jackson. We'd better get back."

"I'll miss you," he said, taking her face between his hands and kissing her hard and deeply as if to imprint himself upon her. He wanted to say a lot more. He wanted to ask her to forgive him, to wait for him, to hold out the hope that one day he'd come back to her, a redeemed man who would fit into a place like Coupeville.

*I love you.* Say it, he urged himself. Three simple words. But he couldn't do that to Leah, couldn't give her a promise he'd never keep. Perhaps some knight in shining armor would find her one day, a respectable man who could give her everything she needed without ripping apart her life.

As they left the forest house behind, he looked back once, and a bleak feeling came over him. He had felt this queasy emptiness only one other time in his life. He had been five years old, told to sit quietly on the stoop of St. Ignatius in Chicago while he watched his mother walk out of his life forever.

Since then, he always made sure he did the leaving, not the other way around. But he'd never known this feeling before. Never known it hurt just as much to leave as to be left behind.

*Come with me, Leah.* The memory of Jackson's words—whether he meant them or not—haunted her all during the short voyage back to the harbor. The waves slapping the hull echoed the phrase. The wind, pushing at the sails, whispered it through the rigging of the schooner.

In a canvas chair on the foredeck, she sat silent because she knew if she spoke she would say, "Yes, yes, take me with you."

But she was too practical. She knew he didn't mean it. They would always have this fire between them, but eventually the pleasure would not be enough, not without the full commitment of his love. And he couldn't—or wouldn't—give her that. That was what her practical side told her.

She told herself she'd get used to his absence. But her impractical side, the side that worshiped Jackson T. Underhill, watched him working the sail and holding the wheel, knew she would love him until the end of time. He had no idea how magnificent he looked with his shirt open, painted by the colors of the sunset, the sea rising at his back. If she could be certain of his love, she would follow him anywhere.

She closed her eyes and leaned her head against the back of the canvas chair. Missionaries, she thought wildly. They could be missionaries. The natives of the Sandwich Islands needed help. They died like flies, ravaged by white men's diseases. She might be able to help them.

Would he take her there? Would he settle down?

She knew better than to ask him. He had only been here a short time, and already he couldn't wait to leave.

Ah, but if he knew how little a nudge she needed to say yes.

They sailed into the harbor and she helped him take in the sails and tie up. Davy Morgan, watching from the harbormaster's office, gave her a thumbs-up sign of approval. The westering sun spread a pink glow over the town and distant tree-topped bluffs.

She and Jackson walked up through the village. At the Coupeville cash store, she paused to look in the display window.

"See anything you like?" he asked.

"The globe," she admitted. "I've had my eye on it for a while. It was hand painted in Venice." She gazed at the enameled orb, whimsically designed with faces in the clouds and sea serpents in the oceans. Then she shrugged and moved on. "But I'd just as soon enjoy it in a shop window. I can't think what use I'd ever have for a painted globe."

It took Leah many long, sleepless hours to reach her decision. Just when she was about to admit Jackson was right about her commitment to her life here and her practice on the island, she came to a realization that would change everything.

For her, at least. It remained to be seen if Jackson could be swayed.

She looked around the quiet, orderly room and felt a shiver of apprehension. Then she squared her shoulders. Who would miss her after all, except perhaps Bowie and Iona? Those two were young, and despite their disabilities, they would get on better than most because they had one thing in abundance—a sense that they were exactly where they belonged.

She would travel light. Her medical bag, of course—she never went anywhere without that. She filled a valise with just a few things. She hesitated before a small framed photograph of herself with her father standing on the wooden walkway in Atlantic City. She wore her customary worried smile, and he wore his usual chilly hauteur.

"No," she said aloud, turning from the photo. "That part of me stays here." She felt good about the decision. She was going on a voyage to discover who she was. Who she'd been in the past had no place on this journey.

She was going away with Jackson. She pictured his face when she told him her decision. Would he feel as light with joy as she did? She closed her eyes, thinking of the way she would make love to him with passionate intensity, and imagining the two of them living on some unspoiled tropical isle. But was that the real dream? Was it the life that would fulfill and sustain them forever? It didn't matter. She couldn't let it matter.

A secret smile curved her mouth. Correction, she told herself. It would not just be the two of them.

Her hand stole down over her stomach. She had suspected it for a week or two; this morning she was sure. She was going to have Jackson's baby.

# Fourteen

Jackson awakened to the soft thump of waves against the hull of the *Teatime*. He lay still for a moment, gazing up at the curved stern end of the stateroom. The pink light of a summer dawn glimmered through the thick panes of bottle glass.

He'd been dreaming of Leah—that came as no surprise. He always dreamed of Leah lately. She consumed him, obsessed him, haunted him.

And he had to tell her goodbye.

Feeling lonely already, he rose and went to wash up, then looked longingly at the coffeepot. He had to leave. He'd delayed long enough. It was time to weigh anchor. He thought of the adventure novels he used to read as a boy, those tales of danger and excitement he used to dream about.

Finally, he was pursuing his dream. He had a boat of his own, fair weather and a brisk summer wind, and he was about to embark on an adventure he'd dreamed about all his life.

So why didn't he feel more eager to get on with it?

"Stupid question," he muttered to himself. He knew damned well why. Because of a woman.

*Women.* In one way or another, they'd made his life hell from the very beginning. His mother, abandoning him on a filthy doorstep. Carrie, leading him on a chase that had taken him years to finish. And now Leah, seeing into his heart with a velvet-soft gaze…

He would be better off without anyone, he told himself as he washed and shaved, preparing to walk into town one last time. He was a fool to even consider uprooting Leah from this place she called home and taking her to a destination he couldn't even name.

She loved him, yes, he knew that. Knew it with no vanity or pride, a mere knowledge of fact. But she needed her medical practice, too. Being a physician sustained her, fulfilled her, and he wasn't about to take her away from all that. He couldn't give her that sort of fulfillment. Couldn't give her much of anything other than his heart. And who the hell would want that? It was the ultimate vanity to think sailing off with him could take the place of saving lives, bringing babies into the world, healing the sick.

Jackson walked to the head of the landing and leaned against a hitch rail. Wisps of smoke arose from the Indian shake houses along the water across Penn Cove. Morning light gilded the town as shopkeepers and fishermen began to stir along Front Street. Deputy MacPhail stood outside the sheriff's office with its adjacent stone jailhouse, lighting a cheroot. He waved nonchalantly at Jackson, then stepped inside.

A moment later, Lemuel St. Croix came out. He wore a new black felt fedora, and a gold watch chain caught the sunlight as it dangled from the pocket of his waistcoat.

"Morning, Jackson," he said, unsmiling.

"Sheriff," Jackson said, not smiling, either. It was no

coincidence that Lemuel would come out when Jackson appeared—was it? He felt as if every nerve had caught fire. Suspicion prickled like a rash over his neck. He watched St. Croix's hands. If they so much as flickered toward the tooled gun belt, Jackson knew he was a goner. This town and what he'd found here had changed him. His own gun was no longer the first thing he put on in the morning and the last thing he took off at night. "Everything okay with you?" he asked conversationally.

"Just dandy." He pushed back his frock coat so his guns were in full view.

Narrowing his eyes, Jackson noticed a smear of light-colored dirt on the shoulder of St. Croix's coat. Ordinarily, he wouldn't notice such a thing, but he was on full alert. And the sheriff, almost comically fussy about his fine clothing, was not the sort to wear a soiled coat.

"It's about time you showed up," St. Croix said.

Jackson was about to dive for safety when someone behind him said, "Sorry I'm late, sir."

Jackson turned to see the Gillespie boy, shoeshine kit in hand, heading toward the sheriff. St. Croix took a seat on the bench outside his office, propping his tall boot on the rail for the boy to polish. He noticed the spot of dirt on his shoulder and brushed at it, but the brushing only caused the dirt to smear the crisp black fabric of his frock coat. "Damn it, boy, hand me a clean brush," he ordered, no longer paying the least bit of attention to Jackson.

Pushing away from the rail, Jackson started walking again. He was furious about his own nervousness. Hell, he'd almost given himself away thinking the sheriff was onto him. Still, his sense for danger stayed on alert. St. Croix was like a snake in hibernation—looked harmless, but he had the potential to be deadly.

Jackson didn't like the man, didn't trust him to keep

the peace and protect the citizens hereabouts. If this place, these people, were Jackson's to protect, he'd do a lot better job than St. Croix. But it wasn't Jackson's. He was pressing his luck hanging around here.

He stepped inside the cash store and greeted the shopkeeper with a nod.

"Still looking at that painted globe, eh?" the shopkeeper said.

"Today I'm not looking. Wrap it up for me." Jackson paid him and didn't even wince at the cost. It wasn't every day a man bought something that came all the way from Venice, Italy.

It wasn't every day a man said goodbye to the woman he loved.

The shopkeeper whistled as he put the heavy globe into a large, deep bandbox.

Armed with a parting gift, Jackson crossed the yard to Leah's house. He hoped he'd be able to say goodbye simply and briefly with a minimum of fuss. Even though all that he wanted in the world was to beg her to come away with him. Like a knight who had captured the Grail, he would lay his gift at her feet.

From the front drive of the boardinghouse, he saw her standing on the porch. She looked like a bride atop a fancy wedding cake, all clean and white and sweet with spun sugar.

She gave him one of those little smiles that haunted his sleep—sort of tentative, as if she wasn't used to doing it. In one hand, she held her leather doctor's bag. In the other, a carpetbag.

He frowned, sending her an unspoken question.

"I'm glad it's still early," she said. "I didn't want to get all tangled up saying goodbye to everyone."

"What the hell are you talking about?"

"I've decided to come with you. Is today a good day to leave?" She waited, an expectant look on her face.

He should have known she'd try something like this. Should have known she was too honest and too damned stubborn to stay where she belonged.

"Leah, you're not going anywhere." The words came out of him, stark, simple, emotionless. He was pleased with himself. Hearing him, she'd never guess his heart was breaking.

The timid smile disappeared altogether. "You want me to come. Don't say you don't."

"I'm not saying anything except that you can't come."

She set down her valise with a thud. "We belong together. I've never felt this way before and neither have you, even though you won't admit it."

His every instinct screamed at him to agree with her, but he wouldn't let himself. "I know my own mind, Leah. Somehow you've made me into someone I'm not. Maybe because of your father, hell, I don't know, but don't expect me to make up for his mistakes with you." Her face drained of color and he knew he'd touched a nerve. "Yeah, it hurts, doesn't it? That's all I can give you, sugar, and believe me, you don't want it."

"But—"

"There's nothing *there*." He touched his fist to his chest. "Swear to God, Leah, if there was, I'd give it to you, but…"

She took a step back, then another. A bitter smile twisted her mouth. "I thought you were a better card-player than that, Jackson. You should have known that eventually I'd call your bluff."

*I wasn't bluffing,* he wanted to tell her. But he couldn't, of course. He couldn't even kiss her goodbye. All he could do was set down the box, look up at her, and say,

"Honey, I'd give you the world if I could. But you and I both know I can't."

He turned away, shoved his hands into his pockets, and returned to the harbor. He wouldn't allow himself to look back.

Leah didn't know where she found the strength to walk back into the house, to close the door quietly behind her. She imagined the grief would come later. Could a person brace herself for heartbreak as if battening the hatches for a storm? Or would she be naked, vulnerable, letting the sorrow batter her, offering no defense?

As she crossed the vestibule, she spied Aunt Leafy in the parlor, cleaning her birdcage. The morning light streamed in on the elderly lady, suffusing the sweetly lined face with a summer glow.

Swallowing past the lump in her throat, Leah set down her bags and went into the parlor. "Morning, Aunt Leafy."

The old lady gave her a distracted smile. "Ah, there you are, dear. Could you help with this for a moment?" She slid out the bottom tray and discarded the contents in the bin. "Paper," she muttered under her breath. "I need fresh paper to line it...."

Leah knew Aunt Leafy had trouble concentrating on more than one thing at a time. She waited while the woman shuffled through a stack of old papers.

"Ah! This will do just perfectly." The little canary flitted around restlessly. "There now, Carlos, see what you've done. You've spilled your seed tray." Without turning, she held out the old yellowed paper to Leah. "Hold this a moment, dear, while I pick up the spilled seeds."

Nearly burning up with the need to be alone with her

heartache, Leah glanced down at the old newsprint. She expected it to be an edition of the *Pioneer*. Instead, it was a Wanted poster.

And the face staring up at her from the drawing was crudely rendered, yet starkly familiar.

"No," she whispered, the word feeling harsh in her throat. "Oh, God..."

"I'll only be a moment longer, dear. No need to swear at me."

Leah clutched Aunt Leafy's arm. "Where did you get this?"

Aunt Leafy looked distractedly over her shoulder. "That? Oh, the pretty young lady gave it to me."

"You mean Carrie. Mrs. Underhill."

"Yes, I believe that was her name. She was having one of her bad spells, babbling away. Sweet little thing, but a world of troubles lived inside her, I could tell." She eyed the bags. "Are you going away, dear?"

"I...I changed my mind."

With a jerky motion, Leah turned and left the room, the paper still clutched in her nerveless hands. Words leaped out at her: armed and dangerous, fugitive from justice, murderer.

*Murderer.*

She had always known he was an outlaw. She shouldn't be surprised. But as she stared down at the poster, the world seemed to crack in two.

Jackson Underhill, the man who had just broken her heart, was really Jack Tower, a ruthless killer wanted for a vicious murder.

Leah sat down on the edge of her bed. In one hand, she held the bandbox. In the other, the Wanted poster. She felt drained. Cold to the bone. Somehow she found the strength to open the box to see what Jackson had given her.

*Honey, I'd give you the world if I could.*

He had given her the world. It was the globe she'd admired in the shop window. So exquisite she'd never dared to ask the price. So extravagant she'd never dreamed of possessing it.

She held it up to the light, amazed by its weight. Whimsical dragons and blowing clouds populated the seven seas. Scrolling letters and colorful flags labeled the nations of the world. She'd never owned anything so beautiful or so whimsical.

She drew back her hand to hurl the globe at the window, compelled to destroy it, the only gift Jackson had ever given her. She wanted no evidence that she had ever known him, ever loved him.

But when sunlight through the window touched the surface, she couldn't bring herself to do it. Standing there, gazing at the colorful globe, she finally figured out what Jackson meant in giving it to her.

She stood in her painstakingly neat bedroom on the rag rug where Jackson had once stood holding a gun on her and let the knowledge wash over her like rain.

All her life, she had believed herself flawed because of her father. From the time she was old enough to speak, he'd convinced her that she lacked some fundamental quality that made her worthy. She had spent years striving to please him, trying to make up for her deficiency. And all along, there had been nothing wrong with her.

It had been her father who couldn't love.

When Jackson had rejected her this morning, she had been quick to assume she wasn't good enough, pretty enough, smart enough to please him. But the Wanted poster proved that she wasn't the problem after all.

Fierce with determination, she dried the tears from her face, stuffed the poster into her skirt pocket, and rushed downstairs. She went to the waterfront, hurrying, getting a stitch in her side, praying he hadn't left yet.

He stood in the cockpit, leaning over the back and swearing.

"Jackson."

Stone-faced, he straightened up. "Leah, there's no point in arguing—"

"I didn't come to argue." Equally stone-faced, she took out the folded paper, opened it, and showed it to him.

He didn't move a muscle, though his face paled a shade. "Where did you get that?"

"Apparently, Carrie gave it to Aunt Leafy some time ago. You know how absentminded Aunt Leafy is." Leah bit her lip. "She was about to line her birdcage with it."

He laughed harshly. "So now you know everything."

"Now I have more questions than ever."

"Well, I don't have any answers, Doc, so if you'll excuse me—"

"Jackson," she said in a steady voice, "there's something wrong here."

"What's wrong is the damned tiller broke again. I swear, you'd think someone sabotaged the thing."

"I mean about this...situation in Texas."

He narrowed his eyes. "What's wrong is a man's lying dead, and they're holding me to blame."

"That's what I mean. I don't think you did it."

He raked his hand through his hair and scowled. "A man was killed in cold blood. He was the mayor of that town. I'm to blame. That's all there is to it."

"That's *not* all there is. I refuse to believe you did this."

"Doesn't matter. You're a healer. I'm accused of murder. Can you live with that? Can you lie next to that every night for the rest of your life?" He glanced away. Her provocative, menacing outlaw, a man who thought nothing of terrorizing a woman in the middle of the night, looked as bleak and helpless as an orphan child. He turned to her, cupped her cheek in his rough hand. "You make a man dream of things he's got no call to be dreaming, Leah Mundy. I'm sorry."

She closed her eyes, wondering how she had ever survived without his touch. Then she stepped away as stubbornness rose within her. "You're innocent. I know it. I have no idea why you would simply stand back and take the blame for a horrible thing you didn't do. It's not right." She paced up and down the deck, blessing the faulty tiller that kept his boat from sailing. "You have to go back to Texas."

"What?"

"You have to go back and turn yourself in."

"For a smart person, Leah, you sometimes have some pretty stupid ideas." He shrugged. "I guess, last time I checked, stupidity was legal."

"We live in a nation built upon justice for all. You must face your accusers and prove your innocence."

He snorted. "Oh, there's an idea."

"I mean it. If you don't vindicate yourself, you'll never be free." She grasped his hand, pressed it to her chest. "You'll have to keep running all your life. And you know what you'll find out?"

"What?" he asked.

"That it's never far enough. You can never run far enough. You can never outrun injustice."

He shoved her hand away. "And you would know."

"I would." She swallowed hard, preparing to tell him something she'd never told anyone in her life. "Why do you think we left Philadelphia, my father and I? We had a lovely home, friends, many comforts. But we had to keep moving on. To Cincinnati and Kansas City and Omaha and Deadwood, and I can't even remember all the places in between. And do you know why, Jackson?" She felt almost giddy, finally shedding herself of the past. "Because we were running. My father was running, and he dragged me along. He cheated people. He was a bad doctor—dishonest, unskilled. And I was too much the dutiful daughter to bring him up on charges. Even when he caused people to die." Awash with shame, she looked back at the boardinghouse on the hill. "He would have left this place, too, and gone God-knows-where, but a bullet found him first."

"I'm not your father, Leah—"

"You're not guilty as he was. But you have more in common with him than you know."

"That's bullshit, and you—"

"You both broke my heart," she said raggedly. For the past several weeks, her emotions had been boiling below the surface. It wasn't like her to be this sensitive and weepy, but she couldn't help herself.

He stared at her, took off his carpenter's belt, and crossed the deck. "I have to go. It's way past time. I know you have no admiration for this, but it's the way I handle trouble in my life."

"You can change," she said. "You have to."

"People don't change." He repositioned the tiller and shot a bolt into place with a *thunk*. "That poster proves I can't ever stay in one spot. Even up here in the middle of nowhere, I'm too close to the law. You found out about the poster this morning. Who'll find out tomorrow? And the day after that? St. Croix? The marshal in Port Townsend?''

"That's why you must fight to prove your innocence."

"You're dreaming, Doc. Putting my fate in the hands of the justice system won't work for someone like me. If I went back to Rising Star, they'd hang me high and let the crows pick me to the bone."

"But if you're inno—"

"Honey, I haven't been innocent since the day I was born. Life does that to some people. Some, like you, stay innocent their whole lives no matter what happens. But it's not that way for me."

"I don't believe it."

"Damn, woman, you tempt me. I lie awake at night thinking about taking my chances, staying with you. Sometimes it's a risk worth taking. Leah, I want it so bad—"

She stopped him with the most wanton kiss she could summon, pushing her mouth against his as if to brand herself upon him. She could feel his brief surprised inhalation. And then suddenly, he gathered her up, and she knew her boldness tempted him beyond caution.

They half ran, half tumbled down into the stateroom, and she saw that he'd been readying the boat to leave. She thought wildly that if only she could be exciting enough, loving enough, he would fall under her spell and do her bidding. She knew it was insane, but she let herself hope anyway. She was more reckless than she'd ever been, disrobing and then pulling his clothes off.

"Leah?" He held her away from him, looking bewildered and wildly excited.

"Hush." She shoved him back against the bunk, and when he sank beneath her, she unleashed everything inside her, every tender feeling, every shred of love. She had no idea there was so much bottled up inside her. She loved him lavishly, without shame, pressing her mouth to his and sweeping her tongue inside while her hands coasted over muscular flesh. She kissed him everywhere, neck and chest and shoulders, hands and fingers, down his stomach and each leg and then up again until the madness possessed her completely and she took him in her mouth. Vaguely, she heard his helpless, amazed groan, but she showed no mercy. She wanted this, wanted to give him this, wanted to take it from him. Somehow she thought this wanton abandon would bind them in a way they hadn't been bound before. She loved him into a frenzy, and finally he lost patience and made a growling sound in his throat. Strong hands clamped around her upper arms, and she felt herself swiftly turned and parted; then he plunged into her, moving with a fast, aggressive stroke that instantly launched her into oblivion. He joined her there, calling her name and then sinking down, covering her possessively, the rasp of his breathing hot in her ear.

"Damn, Leah," he said.

She smiled into the lee of his shoulder. It was hardly a declaration of love, but she felt his need for her, heard it in his rumbling voice. Wickedly, she nipped at his earlobe. "Damn, Jackson."

He moved off her, drawing the covers up over them both. "Where'd you learn that?"

"Would you believe medical school?"

"No." He propped himself on one elbow and gazed down at her in the lowering light. "You're determined to make this difficult for me."

"Make what difficult?"

"Leaving."

She shut her eyes. She would not cry. She swore she would not cry. She'd done too much of that already and it served nothing. "Oh, Jackson. You need to find a way to stop, to say 'enough' and get on with your life instead of running all the time. Yes, I want you to stay because of me. But I want you to stay because of you, too."

"No one's ever asked me to stay."

"So I'm asking."

He took a deep breath. She held hers. Finally, he said, "I can't."

It took all her self-control not to tell him about the baby. She would not stoop to using that lure. From time to time, she'd had a patient who had "trapped" a husband with a baby. The unions were never, ever happy ones.

She lay in his arms and let hope trickle out of her. She would not cry. She would not. She understood now that she couldn't change him. She couldn't take his wounded heart and make it capable of loving again. She was a doctor, but she couldn't heal a man's basic nature.

Letting go was hard; it hurt, but at the same time she felt liberated. "You understand," she whispered, "I had to try."

Joel Santana staggered to the ship's rail, took off his battered hat, and puked one more time into the churning swells of Puget Sound. He had been in this pleasant state for days, ever since setting sail from San Francisco.

Now, even with the wooden toothpick towers of Seattle in full view, he was still at it. Heaving and reeling like a dying man.

Yeah, he wished he were dead. He'd been wishing it for a week. All during the voyage up the West Coast, through the devil's own Strait of Juan de Fuca, and now to Seattle. He gripped the rail of the four-master with one hand and wiped his face with a wrinkled bandanna, avoiding the tongue-clucking and sympathetic glances of the other passengers.

The ship belonged to the Shoalwater Bay Company, reputedly the best shipping company on the West Coast. Didn't matter. His stateroom was appointed as lavishly as any grand hotel room. Didn't matter. He was as sick as a flea-bitten mongrel dog.

Joel Santana, who had survived gunfights, capture by Indians, floods, droughts, desert sun and a dozen love affairs gone sour, was finally defeated.

By seasickness.

When the ship docked, he pushed women and children aside and half ran, half rolled down the gangway, sinking to his knees at the bottom and shamelessly pressing his lips to the dock.

"What's that man doing, Mama?" asked a child's voice.

Joel didn't even look up.

"Another victim of the demon rum, no doubt," said a stern female voice.

Joel ignored her. At length, he hauled himself up and went to wait for his baggage. There wasn't much of it—he'd turned in his horse and saddle in San Francisco. He didn't know how long he sat there before he started sizing up Seattle. A rough, rollicking town of muddy log roads winding up the hills, towering forests with trees so tall they seemed to reach into heaven, and everywhere the water, ships and barges and Indian canoes plying back and forth from hundreds of green islands.

He blinked out at the Sound, and something stirred within him. This was it, he realized with a jolt. The place in his visions in the desert. The place to which he'd escaped while he waited to die. But he didn't die. He'd struggled and puked his way to this strange corner of the country, and he knew he'd been here before. Not physically, but in his dreams.

Joel was not a superstitious man, but it had to mean something. To recognize a place out of a dream as being real just didn't happen every day.

The decision was made by his queasy stomach before consulting his head. He was staying here. This was where he would live the rest of his life. Out on one of those verdant islands—he'd get there by canoe if he had to— and he'd never leave again. Hell, maybe he'd even find an Indian wife, one with a loud laugh and a big butt—

"Here you go, mister." A ship's boy in Shoalwater Bay Company livery dropped Joel's leather bags at his feet.

He dragged himself back to reality and flipped the kid a coin. Hefting his bag, he lurched a little and then started across the sawdust flats and up a muddy hill from the waterfront. Someone—he had little recollection of who—on board had told him the J & M Hotel was the best in town. Joel wanted the best, at least for one night. Tomorrow he'd go to the telegraph office and check in with the local marshal, letting the area authorities know what progress he'd made.

Progress. He'd managed to travel across half the country without getting a glimpse of Jack Tower and Caroline Willis. He'd come to Seattle on the woozy hearsay of a whore. He was lucky she hadn't given him something he couldn't wash off. If he ever found his quarry, he'd have performed a miracle.

But that was what Joel Santana did best. Took up hopeless cases and made them work out. Any sane man would have given up by now.

He stopped walking, turned to look down at the waterfront and the Sound beyond. There was a reason he'd come here, a reason beyond the search for a wanted man. He felt a strange elation as he checked into the hotel, bathed and shaved, then went in search of the first good whiskey he'd had since San Francisco.

Compared to that city, Seattle was small and compact, the buildings crowded along the hills leading down to the waterfront. As he sampled the whiskey—most of it rotgut—Joel also went to work. Asking his questions, showing his pictures. And in the third place, dimly elegant, antlers of elk and moose decorating the bar, he got lucky.

Slipping a generous tip into his pocket, the barkeep stroked his chin. "Yeah, I seen her, but she wasn't with the guy in the drawing. It was someone different."

Suspicion dried Joel's throat. Damn. She was picking up speed. Was Jack Tower a goner already? "Well?"

The bartender poured him two fingers of Garrick's. Joel savored a burning swallow.

"Right over there," he said, then busied himself wiping down the bar.

Joel took his time over the whiskey, then turned as if to leave. At a corner table, a large man sat hunkered over an empty glass. Joel could tell from the cut of his clothes that he was a man of means. His sleeves were rolled back to reveal one burly forearm. The other arm was wrapped in white bandaging. The wrapping was frayed as if it hadn't been changed in a long while. He held his head in one hand.

"You all right?" Joel asked, moving toward the table.

The man turned to face him. Joel caught his breath. An ugly, festering gash angled across one eye, and a healing burn mark slashed the temple. The wounds weren't from your ordinary barroom brawl, Joel thought.

"What happened to you?" he asked.

"You wouldn't believe it if I told you," the man said.

"Try me."

He took a deep breath, then glared at the gold band around his ring finger. "Woman trouble."

"You fought over a woman?"

"Nope."

"A woman did this?"

"Yeah." The huge man seemed to shrink with misery.

Joel's instincts snapped to attention. "She must be some woman."

"Yeah, she's something all right."

He held out his hand. "Joel Santana. Just got into town."

The big man stuck out his good hand. "Name's Armstrong. Adam Armstrong."

# Fifteen

That evening, Jackson spread out the poster and stared at it. Not a perfect likeness, but the curved scar on his cheek would be a dead giveaway. He lived it all over again, that last night in Rising Star. The argument with Hale Devlin, who didn't want to say where Carrie had gone. The frantic search through the upper floor of the saloon. The reek of blood and gun smoke. The sound of his own racing heartbeat as he and Carrie ran for their lives.

He pinched the bridge of his nose, feeling pummeled by the images that wouldn't leave him alone. Now that Carrie was dead, he wondered if the past really mattered. He didn't have to protect her anymore. Maybe, just maybe, the truth could come out and redeem him. He had to make a decision.

*If you don't vindicate yourself, you'll never be free.* Leah's voice whispered seductively in his mind. *It's never far enough. You can never run far enough. You can never outrun injustice.*

Damn it. She was right. There had to be a way. He had to prove he wasn't this Jack Tower, this murderer.

Somewhere abovedecks, a hatch opened with a loud

thud. Jackson jumped. For a split second, he was back in the saloon, hearing a slamming door.

The door. Had it been the hot Texas wind blowing that night? Or was it a witness fleeing in terror? Then, with a flicker of pure, clear insight, he knew. Hale Devlin. He'd seen the murder. He knew what had happened.

There was no reason Devlin, who had been Carrie's procurer, should come forward. But he knew the truth. He had seen. He was the key. With Devlin's statement, Jackson would win vindication, the right to stay with Leah.

Depending on Devlin's word was risky, but Jackson was a gambler at heart. He climbed the companion ladder to see who was there.

"Jackson?" Sophie Whitebear's voice. "I need to speak to you."

He stepped out onto the deck. Summer twilight surrounded the harbor. Sophie stood waiting, her hands folded in front of her.

"It's about my people on Camano Island," she said without preamble. "They've been talking about trading for more guns."

"There's always going to be talk, Sophie."

"I think it's more than talk."

He ran a hand through his hair. St. Croix was as useless as tits on a boar. He'd let the raiders get away with the stolen guns before. They'd probably take advantage of his incompetence again.

Jackson thought of the scalping scar and St. Croix's too-large fortune. Then he looked at Sophie and knew he couldn't turn his back on her. Someone close to her had died. He wouldn't be able to live with himself unless he did something about the smuggled guns.

"I'll check the caves at the bluff," he promised. "If

there are any guns, they'll wind up at the bottom of the Sound.''

''It's not enough.''

He set his jaw, knowing she was right. Getting rid of the guns wasn't a permanent solution. Getting rid of the gunrunners was. He couldn't believe his own ears when he heard himself say, ''I'll figure out who's responsible and deal with him.''

''Then you'll stay?''

''Sugar, you're not giving me much choice.''

''You could choose to leave. But I knew you wouldn't. When will you tell Leah?''

Leah. He felt a sharp stab of yearning. She was the reason he wanted to stay. The guns were only an excuse. ''I imagine you'll take care of that for me, Sophie girl.''

''Tell her yourself. She should hear it from you.''

''Just because I said I'd deal with the gunrunners doesn't mean I'm putting down roots,'' he objected, suddenly scared again, scared of the powerful emotions that gripped him.

''I always thought you should court her,'' Sophie said as if he hadn't spoken. ''You never courted Leah.''

He blinked. ''Never...'' Sophie was right. He *had* gone straight from squabbling with Leah to making love. He'd drawn her into his life with a sweep of his arm— and as he recalled, he hadn't given much thought to courting. ''What the hell was I supposed to do? Sing songs to her? Bring her roses?''

''Yes. And other gifts.''

''Doesn't matter,'' he said. ''It's too late.''

''It's not too late,'' Sophie said. ''We'll all help you.''

''Help me what?''

''Court her.''

''Who said I was going to court her?''

"It's what you want, Jackson Underhill. It's what Leah wants."

After she left, he sat on the bow of the boat, thinking hard. Could she be right? He spent half the night mulling over his options. There had been a witness to the murder. A statement from him would clear Jackson's name.

And then he wouldn't have to run anymore.

Jackson felt as awkward as a schoolboy as he walked up the path to the boardinghouse. He held a bunch of wildflowers clutched in his sweaty hand. He'd had a busy day, though he hadn't been picking flowers. He'd been studying St. Croix, trying to get some idea of how he operated. He'd discovered a couple of items of interest. Lemuel lived in a big white house on the water with a brand-new dock jutting out into the Sound. Nothing unusual there, except that the sheriff didn't own a boat and didn't seem to be much of a fisherman. He wasn't a farming man, either, yet judging by the size of his blockhouse, he had room for hundreds of pounds of apples and potatoes.

Now what did a man with no family need with all that storage space?

Jackson hadn't decided how he'd figure out the answer to that question. Besides, it was time to turn his mind to another matter. At the barbershop in town, he got shaved and trimmed. He put on a starched shirt and boiled collar, sitting patiently while the Gillespie kid polished his boots.

It was all a bunch of nonsense, of course. He was still just Jackson T. Underhill, alias Jack Tower, a man with no place in the world. Until now. Until Leah had given it to him. Until she'd believed in him and his innocence.

He grinned nervously and waved at Bowie, who sat on

the swing in the yard, his wheelchair abandoned off to one side. Iona, who was bringing in the laundry in the back, gave him a mischievous wink. The whole boardinghouse must be in on the plan.

Well, hell, Jackson thought. Sophie had spent the day gossiping. You'd think they all knew what he was up to. You'd think they all knew he was about to ask Leah to marry him.

Alone in the bathhouse, Leah wished she could leave her hair loose to dry in the warm summer night. But she wouldn't, of course. She gave it a twist and clipped it in place with two pins. She was glad Perpetua had urged her to have a nice long soak in the tub. Calls had taken her from Admiralty Head to Oak Harbor. She'd suppurated a wound, bound a sprained ankle, checked on a case of measles, and finally had rolled in an hour before suppertime.

She thanked God for the busy day. It kept her from thinking about Jackson. But now, alone in the bathhouse, she thought of him. She remembered his touch, the way he tasted and smelled. But most of all, she thought of the way he made her feel—strong and womanly, yet dreamy and vulnerable at the same time.

Working by the light of a brilliant sunset through the frosted-glass windows of the bathhouse, she toweled her hair, then reached for her clothes. Odd, she thought, taking up an emerald dimity gown Iona had set out for her. This was a bit dressy for supper at the boardinghouse. She usually wore the dimity to church.

Giving the matter no more thought, she shook out her shift, pausing just for a moment to look down at her stomach. No change, not in the least. Ah, but she was changing. Just the mere thought of Jackson brought a maddening tingle to her breasts, and her hunger for him plagued her. There was more than nature at work here, though. She loved him to distraction. The fact that they'd made a baby merely added the stark edge of reality to her emotions.

Lost in thought, she put on her shift and bloomers. She had to see him again—if he hadn't left yet. She had to tell him, but she would do so in a way that made it clear that she expected no commitment from him. Her distaste at using the baby to hold him lingered, but Jackson deserved to know he had a child. Would he fall to his knees immediately, beg her to marry him? That hardly sounded like Jackson.

Did she even want him to?

She shook her head to shut off the haunting questions. She didn't want to marry him. She didn't need him. Perhaps if she repeated that to herself often enough, it would start to ring true. She hurried through the rest of her dressing and started up to the house.

A single candle burned on a table on the porch. Frowning, she stopped in the middle of the yard. A tall man stepped out of the house and stood beside the table, waiting.

*Jackson.*

She drew closer and caught her breath in amazement. Yes, it was him, but a Jackson she'd never seen before. He wore a crisp white shirt, formfitting trousers, a silken waistcoat. When she reached the top step of the porch, he bowed formally and held out a bouquet of flowers.

If Leah had been the swooning sort, she definitely would have swooned. Instead, she took the bouquet and lifted it to her face, inhaling the piquant spice of daisies and lupines. She peeked at him over the blossoms. Up close, he looked even more handsome and appealing. She could see comb furrows in his hair. The scent of bay rum emanated from him.

In the distance, the steamer whistle sounded.

She put the flowers on the table. "I thought you were in such a hurry to leave. What's all this about?"

He held out her chair, then scooted it in, bending to lightly nip the side of her neck. "I'm courting you."

She didn't know whether to grin like an idiot or burst into tears. Bouquets and promises one moment, tears and uncertainty the next. Love was such a giddy, mad, glorious thing. She didn't know how she'd gone without it for so long.

She picked up a goblet by its stem and took a sip. "Aunt Leafy's sherry?" she asked.

"Yeah." He took a seat. "They're all in on this." He smiled, that smile that had the power to weaken her knees. He reached across the table, drew the two pins from her hair, and let the damp sable curls tumble to her shoulders. "You should wear your hair loose more often."

"Why?"

"I just…like it. Makes you look, well, like you do when I'm making love to you."

She flushed and began to eat. For the past few days, she had vacillated between queasiness and rampant hunger. At the moment, she was starving. There was a salad of tender endive shoots, fresh salmon roasted on a cedar plank in Perpetua's big iron oven, and hot potato rolls.

But the food held only minor appeal compared to Jackson. She couldn't do much except stare at him.

"What's going on here?" she managed to ask.

"Sophie said you've never been courted."

"Sophie talks too much."

"I decided to show you what it's like."

"So this is courting," she said.

"Like it?"

She took a bite of warm bread. "I think so. But aren't we doing this out of sequence?"

"What do you mean?"

"I always thought the courtship came first. Then the seduction." She lowered her voice, leaned forward across the table. "We're already lovers, Jackson. It might be a little late for courtship."

"I sure hope not." He took a deep breath. Then he took a long drink of his sherry. "Leah."

"Jackson."

They both spoke at once. She laughed softly. "You make me nervous."

"I could say the same, Doc."

"What were you going to say?"

"Ladies first."

She hesitated. More time. She needed more time to come up with the words to tell him she was pregnant. Because deep inside she was terrified that he'd look at her in shock, tell her he didn't want a baby. "I defer to the gentleman."

He put down his goblet and reached across the table for her hand. "Leah, I want to stay. I think there's a way for me to—"

"You think I don't understand what it's like, being on the move all the time." She realized she was babbling, but she couldn't stop herself. "But I do, truly. And you're right. It's one of the truest things my father taught me. That you can't stay longer than—"

"Leah, honey, I want to marry you."

That did it. The flood tide of tears finally burst free. There was no warning, no preamble, not even for Leah herself. She simply started sobbing. She would have covered her face with her hands, but he held them fast.

He wanted to marry her. Jackson Underhill wanted to marry her. Just when she'd convinced herself that marriage was the last thing she could expect, the one thing she didn't need, out of the blue came this stunning proposal, and it was too much. He hadn't said he loved her. But that hardly mattered.

"Leah?" He got up and came around the table, sinking to one knee in front of her. "What are you crying for? Don't you want to marry me?"

She swabbed her face with her napkin. "Yes."

"So why're you crying? A simple yes will do."

"I'm afraid," she said.

"Afraid of what? The murder charge?"

How could she tell him, how could she explain? She was terrified of being this happy. Because if it ever ended, she would want to die.

She blinked away a fresh flood of tears. "Wasn't it easier just being lovers?"

He smiled. "Sugar, that's about the easiest thing I ever did."

"Then why would you want to complicate it by getting married?"

"Because you convinced me to try clearing my name. And even if I can't, I'll stay, live a decent life, deal with the past if it ever catches up with me. Unless you're saying you won't have me."

She touched his face, the smooth-shaven cheek, the slight mark where the unaccustomed collar cut into him. "I'm saying we have a lot to talk about before we make any plans."

"I'm listening."

She hardly knew where to begin. But he had been bold;

he'd come right out with what was on his mind. She owed him that much at least. "I have something to tell you, too," she said.

"All I want to hear you say is 'Yes.'"

She took a deep breath. "You're still free to change your mind when I explain this to you."

"Leah, for once in my damned life, I'm not going to change my mind. Now, just say yes and we can finish eating."

She fought the urge to smile. "This is important, Jackson. Really. I'm—"

"Jackson?" a voice called from the evening shadows.

Even before Leah's mind recognized the speaker, her instinct did. She felt a fluttering of horrified amazement in her chest, felt her lungs empty in a painful *whoosh*.

For a split second, she denied what she had heard. She looked at Jackson, at the face that owned her dreams. His smile slid away. His eyes, which had been lit with hope and confusion and the beginnings of love, changed even as she watched. Something in him died.

He straightened up and walked to the edge of the porch. "Carrie?" His voice faltered with disbelief. "My God, is that you?"

A slender shadow slipped up the hill from the front drive. She looked as fragile and willowy as a reed in the wind, a beautiful silk gown fitting her like a glove, her pale blond hair drifting around her face in loose tendrils. Wraithlike, she skimmed across the lawn toward them.

"It's me, Jackson," she called softly. "I'm back. I just came in on the steamer."

Leah saw him wince slightly, as if from a blow.

He ran down the stairs. "My God! We thought you'd died, honey."

She flung her arms around him, pressing her cheek to his chest. "Oh, Jackson, I've missed you so."

He returned the embrace, the muscles in his arms straining against the fine fabric of his new shirt.

Leah's thoughts whirled. The healer in her exalted—a patient, back from the dead! But at the same time, she wanted to look away from the forbidden intimacy of the moment. She wanted to pry them apart, to scream, to lament, to shake her fist. Everything she wanted had lain within her grasp, and now all of her dreams poured away like sand through her fingers.

All she could do was sit there and watch, wondering what miracle had resurrected Carrie, wondering about the past these two shared, the secrets they guarded in their hearts. Things Jackson had never told her, things that kept him separate from her no matter what he said.

"I had to come back," Carrie was saying against his chest. With nervous fingers, she toyed with the ribbons of her bonnet. "You're the only one who can keep me safe, the only one, Jackson."

"What the hell happened? We found Armstrong's boat, burned to the waterline."

Carrie shuddered. "We were both injured—burned." She held up her hand. Slick scars marred the milky skin.

"What started the fire?"

She turned away, though she still clung to Jackson with one hand. Her other hand still tugged absently at the bonnet ribbons. "I'm not certain. A problem with the steam engine, perhaps. Indians rescued us, can you imagine? They came out in their canoes. They must've seen the flames. And they took us to the mainland north of Seattle."

"But why didn't you come back right away, let me know you were all right?"

She lifted one shoulder demurely. "I wasn't certain you'd want me back after I ran off like I did. But I just couldn't stay away. I need you. I always, always have."

"What about Armstrong? Did he live?"

"He's not like you. He doesn't keep me safe." She pulled at her ribbon so hard the bonnet fell askew, revealing too-bright eyes and hectic spots of color in her cheeks.

Leah's skin chilled. She could hear the strained, animated tones in Carrie's voice. Could see the stark bones in her underfed body. Carrie was taking narcotics again.

"It's so good to be back," she murmured with that blurred sweetness Leah had come to recognize and dread. "So, so good to be back." Then she looked up at Leah, seeming to notice her for the first time. "Hello, Dr. Mundy. I'm back."

"I see. It truly is a miracle."

"Isn't it?" She snuggled against Jackson.

"Are you healed from your injuries?" Leah asked. Her voice sounded hollow.

"I'm fine…now." Carrie's gaze swept over the candlelit table, the half-eaten dinner.

"Are you hungry?" Leah asked. "Can I get you something to eat?"

"No, just…I'm tired, is all. Is our room ready?" Carrie clung to Jackson, addressing her question to him.

*Our* room. The words slashed into Leah's heart.

"I've been staying on the boat," he said.

"The room's vacant." Leah felt an enormous weariness come over her. "Do you have a bag?"

"A bag…" Carrie touched the tip of her finger to her full lower lip. "I left it at the steamer landing. The harbormaster's boy can bring it up in the morning." She yawned and pressed her cheek against Jackson's upper arm.

Leah watched his broad, strong hands supporting her, and she felt something vital drain out of her. Hope. She was losing hope like a patient losing blood. Jackson's marriage proposal would remain forever unanswered— unless he cold-bloodedly divorced Carrie. But Jackson would never do that.

"I'd like to lie down, if I could. Would that be all right, Jackson? And you'll come up later? I was wrong to go." Carrie spoke rapidly, hardly pausing for breath. "I'll never, ever leave you again. I'm so sorry. Oh, but it's good to feel safe with you. Jackson, my Jack—" She broke off, swaying into him.

He caught her, bringing his arm behind her knees and swinging her up. Backlit by the bruised twilight sky, they looked like a romantic painting, the willowy damsel swooning in the arms of her hero.

Without a word, Leah held the door open. Jackson stared straight ahead, his face expressionless. Together they put Carrie to bed. She smiled and sighed, giggling softly as Jackson took off her little leather top boots. Leah smelled the sweetish base of the patent tonic, turned her head in distaste, and then felt instantly ashamed of herself. She was a doctor, a healer, and to let a patient disgust her went against all of her training. Carrie was desperately ill. She needed help. It was Leah's duty to help her.

For the better part of an hour, Jackson sat unmoving at Carrie's bedside. Here she was, a living, breathing miracle. He couldn't believe she'd come back. He had reconciled himself to the death of this fragile, damaged woman. He'd convinced himself that she was in a better place, the only place she could find perfect peace. Now Carrie had come back to him as she had always come to him, right from the very first.

He remembered vividly the nights in St. I's when she would seek him out, crawl into bed with him, and sob against his chest, accusing the other children and the masters of all sorts of monstrous things, real and imagined. She always came to him. She always would.

He watched her until her hand, clinging to his, went slack and her breathing evened out. He watched her until the last of the light disappeared and the big clock in the parlor rang ten. He watched her until his eyes burned with weariness.

And then he got up and went downstairs. Battle Douglas and Aunt Leafy sat in the parlor, glaring at each other over a cribbage board. They glanced up as he passed, and he could feel their stares of disapproval jabbing at him.

"I'm not saying I'm sorry she survived, but I thought you were done with that bit of baggage," Battle remarked.

"Yeah, well, she came back," Jackson said, and went out onto the porch.

Leah was still there, seated at the table Perpetua had set so beautifully. The candle had burned to a stub, the flowers had wilted, and the meal lay forgotten.

Leah had no reaction to his arrival. She simply sat staring at the harbor lights, her chin uptilted, her back held very straight. Her stoic strength touched him more deeply than a fit of weeping.

"I'm sorry," he said.

"Don't be," she replied evenly. "We should be rejoicing. There's nothing to apologize for."

"Seems like I've been apologizing for Carrie my whole life."

Finally, she turned to him, doe eyes wide and deceptively soft. "And has it helped?"

He blinked, stung by the velvet-soft dart. "If there's nothing to apologize for, why are you so mad?"

"I'm not angry, Jackson." She got up and walked to the corner of the porch where it wrapped around to the east. "How can I get angry with a sick woman and still call myself a doctor?"

"You can, Leah, and you should."

"Because you're going to take her back." Her statement thudded into the silence. "At least I'm spared from answering your proposal."

Jackson felt a hollowness in his chest. "She's so damned helpless. Now more than ever. God knows what Armstrong put her through, but she came back to me."

"You must feel flattered."

He could tell from the slight trembling of her shoulders that she teetered on the verge of tears. Earlier in the evening, he'd made her weep from happiness. Now he was making her weep from hurt. "Leah, every single thing I've ever done in my life has turned out a failure. But with Carrie, I could actually accomplish something. Keep her safe, protect her. With her coming back so unexpectedly, it's like I've been given a second chance. I have to take that chance, Leah—"

"No!" She spun around, eyes blazing in a way he'd never seen before. "I won't listen to this! I love you with all my heart, Jackson. But I won't keep on this way. I won't go on with this never-ending Carrie problem. I can't do it. I just…can't."

She loved him. Hearing her say the words seared his soul. Yet she used that love like a blade, making him walk the razor's edge.

"Don't ask me to choose," he said in a low, gravelly voice.

"Because I'll lose, won't I?"

"What can I do?"

"She's sick. Chronically sick. She belongs in a hospital or sanitarium."

"An institution." St. Ignatius was an institution. Waves of memory swamped him, the smells, the screams, the reaching hands, the horrors in the dark. "Christ, I can't do that to her. I can't lock her up."

She watched him for a very long time. The candle on the table guttered and died. Finally she spoke. "How can you do this to *us?*"


"You look a little better today," Joel Santana said to Armstrong.

The timber baron had joined him for breakfast at the J & M. "Thanks."

"Think your wife's gone for good?"

"Oh, yeah. I never should have married her in the first place. But she…dazzled me. Had that effect on everyone, it seemed. As soon as we recovered from the boating accident, I married her." He took a cautious sip of his coffee. "I was a fool to think a spoken vow was enough to hold her."

"Any idea where she went?"

"Back to that cardsharp fellow. There was no pleasing her, but he came as close as she'd ever found, I think."

"So where will she find him?"

"Last we saw him was on Whidbey Island across the Sound."


At midnight, Jackson waited in the shadows of a brake of alder trees outside the sheriff's house. He wondered if

Davy Morgan would do his part. Earlier, Jackson had done something he never would have considered a few months ago—he'd put his trust in someone, telling Davy his suspicions and asking for his help.

He shouldn't have wondered about Morgan. The youth was as honest and reliable as a country preacher, showing up at a run and pounding on St. Croix's front door.

The sheriff took his time answering. Jackson couldn't hear what Davy said, but the kid sounded convincing, his voice low and urgent. He was supposed to say there was trouble with some of the Indians south of town. St. Croix spoke gruffly, irritably, but after a few minutes he came out, going to the barn and cursing as he cranked the Panhard to life. Davy held a lantern as the gasoline carriage lumbered along the gravel road toward the other side of the island. The youth stared straight ahead.

Jackson wasted no time entering the blockhouse. It wasn't locked; St. Croix would be smart enough to know a locked storage building would rouse suspicion. Striking a match, Jackson ducked his head and went inside.

Baskets of potatoes and apples stored in straw and charcoal. Sacks of onions and winter vegetables. Boxes of wax candles. Exactly what one would expect to see.

The match burned down and Jackson dropped it, swearing. He stood for a moment in the dark until the damp earth smell grew oppressive; then he moved toward the slanting doors. As he did, his shoulder brushed something. He frowned, lighting another match. A smear of powdery clay marked his shoulder.

He thought of the day he'd seen St. Croix in a soiled coat and recalled thinking how unusual it was for the fussy sheriff. Jackson lit one of the candles for a closer perusal. The wall where his shoulder had brushed was a false one, a thin layer of earth over a wooden door that opened outward.

He stood back, surveying his discovery and swearing between his teeth. Lemuel St. Croix was no better than the scum who sold the stolen guns to the Indians.

In the morning, there was something else Jackson had to take care of before he tackled the problem of the sheriff. He went to see Carrie, explaining that he'd spent the night on the boat. She asked him why.

"I just got used to it," he explained. "After you...left, there was no point taking up space at the boarding-house."

"I hate boats. I don't know how you can stand sleeping there." She looked as pink and white as a bouquet of roses in the morning light. She used to be like an icon to him. But Leah had opened his eyes. Carrie was sick, a spoiled girl who wheedled favors from him one moment, then forgot him the next. She was his responsibility, but not his dream.

Not in the way Leah was.

The rampant color in Carrie's cheeks gave him the first clue that she was under the influence. Until Leah had proven the truth about Carrie, Jackson had missed the signs. He'd thought the bright eyes, the dilated pupils, the manic activity were part of Carrie's naturally vivacious personality.

Ah, Leah, he thought. Was it only last night that he'd asked her to marry him? It seemed a lifetime ago. She'd had something to tell him, something to share, and he'd never even let her get the words out. He wondered what it was.

*I have something to tell you...*

Did it even matter now?

*This is important...*

He'd looked for her this morning, but Perpetua, with her lips so stiff with disapproval she could barely speak, informed him that Dr. Mundy was out calling on patients.

"So have you decided when we're going to leave? Where do we go next? Victoria would be nice. I hear it's very cosmopolitan." Carrie chattered on, inspecting her perfect fingernails. "I hope it's a short voyage, because you know how I hate that boat. Still, it was good of you to wait for me—"

"Carrie." His voice was quiet, yet some quality of tone captured her attention as if he'd shouted.

She blinked at him. China-doll eyes. He'd seen them in his dreams for years on end. "Yes?"

"I need you to listen to me, and I need you to listen real good."

She smiled sweetly. "I can do that."

"Carrie, since coming here, I've finally started to understand something. All my life I've dedicated myself to saving you. Rescuing you. Keeping you safe. It took me ten years to find you, and when I did, I was just in time."

She nodded vigorously. "Indeed you were. I still have nightmares about Rising Star. Thank God you were there to rescue me. You're my own personal dragon slayer."

"Well, that's what I've started to understand." He got up and paced the carpeted floor. One of the floorboards squeaked beneath his boot heel. He turned, made himself look at this beautiful, impenetrable woman. "There aren't any dragons after you. If there were, I could slay them."

"I know, and you'd do that for me, wouldn't you, Jackson?"

"But it wouldn't help. The demons are inside you. No matter how much I care, no matter how watchful I am, I can't live your life for you. I can't get inside you and make you better. I've tried that, and it doesn't work.''

She frowned and tilted her head to one side. A strange anticipation glittered in her eyes. ''Jackson, what are you saying?''

''I did my best, honey. I got you away from Devlin's gang before they did something permanent to you. I took care of the problem in Rising Star as best I could. I got us out of there and kept us one step ahead of the law. But I can't be with you anymore.''

''You said you'd always take care of me,'' she said.

''That was a promise made by a boy. We're all grown up now.''

''And I need you more than ever.'' Her voice rose, quavering over the words.

''No, I'm not what you need. We're just not...good together.''

''Why?'' she prompted, her fingers hooking into the crocheted pillow she held in her lap. ''Tell me why.''

He took a deep breath. Pretending hadn't helped. Maybe the truth would. ''Because there's no love. We came together out of desperation. We stayed together because I had some futile sense of responsibility. But it's not enough. The future holds no promise for us except more running. More misery. We've got to get on with our separate lives—''

''And what sort of life would that be?'' she asked, picking her words as cautiously as if she was picking berries from a thorny bush.

''Leah—Dr. Mundy—knows of a place you can go. It's safe there. They'd take care of you, better than I ever could.''

''You love her, don't you?''

''Leah?'' Jackson blinked. Carrie had been so drunk

with her tonic last night that he'd assumed she hadn't even noticed the romantic supper for two or even the fact that he'd been on bended knee before Leah.

"You love her, don't you?" Carrie asked again, her voice rising dangerously, knuckles whitening as she clutched the pillow.

"That's not what this is about," he said. He could see her unraveling, could see the fury in her eyes. "Honey—"

"You bastard!" Her high, keening scream pierced the air, making him wince.

"Now look, Carrie—"

"You fucking bastard!" The pillow flew at him, striking his chest with ridiculous softness.

He caught it and set it down. "You're making too much noise," he said.

Carrie launched herself out of the chintz-covered chair. "You want to get rid of me so you can be with her." She seized a vase from a table and hurled it at his head. Jackson ducked, hearing the glass shatter against the wall behind him. He took a step toward her, but she'd already found something else to throw—the glass chimney from a gaslight. "I won't let you," she shrieked. "I won't! I won't!" As he advanced toward her, she flung a picture frame at him, then bent and grabbed the hem of her skirt. "You'll pay for this!" she yelled. "You'll never get to be with her!"

As Jackson rushed across the room, he realized his mistake. Carrie yanked a small white-handled gun from her garter. At the same moment, the door opened, then slammed shut, then opened again. Carrie fired wildly and fled, racing down the stairs and out the door.

"Send for the sheriff!" she screamed. "Help! Help! Send for the sheriff!"

It took Jackson several seconds to realize he'd been shot. He was on the floor and he had no idea how he'd gotten there. Heat trickled down the side of his face and he put his hand there, feeling the blood and then smelling it. Dizzy, he grabbed the edge of the door and dragged himself up. Just for a second, he locked eyes with Zeke Pomfrit, who had probably come to see what all the ruckus was about.

Almost guiltily, Pomfrit went to his own room and slammed the door. Jackson didn't blame the old man for avoiding him. He took a few long breaths through his nose and staggered to the washstand. The bullet had grazed his ear. He'd survived worse.

He used a towel to wipe away the worst of the blood, then held it a minute to stanch the flow. Then the thought of Carrie, out of her head, an ivory-handled pocket derringer in hand, jolted him into action. She might hurt somebody else.

Dropping the towel, he hurried to the stairs. When he reached the top, he swayed a little and fixed his gaze on the large round window over the entryway. The ship at sea, rendered in colored glass, looked as distant as a dream.

He wrenched his gaze away and went out the front door. Carrie's screams had traveled quickly. People poked their heads out of shops and along the wharf. And Lemuel St. Croix came out of his office.

Standing on the boardinghouse lawn, Jackson reached instinctively for the gun that wasn't there. He'd given up wearing it long ago. Leah didn't like guns.

Feeling strangely detached, he watched the sheriff and deputy coming toward him. Carrie was in rare form, looking dainty and helpless and compelling all at once, waving a piece of paper Jackson recognized—a copy of the Wanted poster.

Dull bluish metal gleamed as the sheriff drew his gun.

Jackson felt himself do something he'd never done in his life—even when it was the prudent thing to do. He raised his hands in surrender.

And that was how he was standing when Leah drove up in the buggy. Hands high. Staring down the barrel of a gun.

She looked as vital as the wild land itself, her eyes big, her mouth frozen in a circle of surprise. He knew he would always remember the gesture she made as she looked from Carrie to the sheriff to him. She dropped the reins, and her arms wrapped around her middle as if she felt a terrible pain there.

It was ironic, really. He'd been at the other end of a gun when he'd captured Leah in the first place. This was how he'd come into her life. It was ironic justice that it was how he would go out.

# Sixteen

The town had never needed much of a jail. It was built of mortared fieldstone against the back of the sheriff's office. There were two cells. One was empty. The other housed Jackson Underhill.

"I'm sorry, Dr. Mundy," said the sheriff's deputy, standing in the outer office. "I got orders that the prisoner's not to have any visitors."

"Don't be ridiculous, Mr. MacPhail." Leah tried to feel something other than ice around her heart. But from the moment she'd seen the sheriff taking Jackson away at gunpoint, she had been in a state of numb disbelief.

There was nothing more devastating, she realized too late, than getting a glimpse of a dream come true only to have that dream snatched away. She wished she could turn the clock back to that magical moment on the porch. Why had she hesitated? Why hadn't she told him about the baby? She could have made him listen.

But it wouldn't have changed anything, she conceded. Carrie would always be first with Jackson.

She craned her neck to see beyond the deputy's burly shoulder. "You know me. Why on earth you would consider me a threat is—"

"Ma'am, that's not the problem. I got strict orders. This Jack Tower character is a dangerous man."

"By whose estimation?" she demanded.

"You seen the Wanted poster yourself, ma'am."

Everyone had by now.

"And you've seen Jackson Underhill for yourself," Leah stated. "You've seen him help fend off a pirate attack. You've seen him settle disputes, buggy train my horse, help me heal people. I ask you, are those the acts of a dangerous man?"

"According to the poster, he's a master of deception and escape. All I know is, I got my orders."

"He does." Sheriff Lemuel St. Croix stepped into the office, brushing a bit of dirt from the sleeve of his coat. "We apprehended the murderer just in time and wired the authorities." His swaggering self-importance grated on Leah.

"A little late to start acting like a lawman, isn't it?" she asked.

His face paled and hardened like stone. "What do you mean by that?"

"Just that you haven't shown much interest in enforcing the law until now."

"I keep this town clean," he shot back. "A federal marshal will be here soon to take the prisoner to trial."

"I certainly hope he knows a terrible mistake has been made," Leah said. "Because he is innocent."

"Don't get your hopes up, ma'am," St. Croix said. "Fact is, the law wouldn't go to all this trouble for a man who wasn't a danger to decent folks."

"And you'd know about that," she snapped, marching out of the office. Yet St. Croix's words scared her. She wanted to believe Jackson would be cleared and set free.

But he needed proof of his innocence, and she didn't know whether or not he had that.

She felt a wave of nausea and wondered erratically if Penny Lake, due to arrive any day now, had much experience tending expectant mothers.

"Dr. Mundy, you all right?" the deputy asked, following her out of the office. "You look a little green around the gills."

"Injustice has that effect on me."

MacPhail awkwardly put a hand on her shoulder. "No one's done anything but apprehend a wanted man."

"Uh-huh."

"Look, if you want me to give the prisoner a message..."

Leah couldn't help herself. She laughed aloud at the magnificent irony of it all. Give the prisoner a message. *I never got to answer the question you asked last night. The answer is yes, I want to marry you, and not only that, I'm going to have your baby.* Her whole life she'd been waiting to find someone like Jackson, and she didn't even know she'd been waiting until she met him.

"No message," she said quietly. "When did you say the next steamer from Seattle gets in?"

"Sorry, sir," the clerk at the Mosquito Fleet office informed Joel Santana. "Last boat's already left. Next one's the midnight packet."

Joel nodded, hiding his irritation. In all his years of duty, he'd learned it was futile to rage against things like schedules and tight-assed timetable clerks.

There were worse things than spending another day in Seattle. He sort of liked the creaky wooden town. The J & M Hotel was as fine as any he'd stayed in, and more than that, he'd found someone directly connected to his quarry—Adam Armstrong.

Joel wasn't big on getting civilians involved with his affairs, but Armstrong himself had insisted. He'd survived an extraordinary ordeal with Caroline—or Carrie as he called her—and now he wanted to see this to the end. He would be taking the steamer over to Whidbey Island, too. Joel turned to go outside and tell Armstrong about the delay.

But instead of walking across the cracked tile floor of the waiting room, he stopped and stood rooted in amazement.

He was looking straight at her.

And *she* was looking back.

A jubilant voice inside Joel raised itself in song. *It's her, it's her, it's her...*

The woman from his dreams. A big smile and broad hips. A frank, open look that invited him to lift his hat, to say, ''Ma'am, I hope you don't think I'm being too forward or anything, but I want to introduce myself. Name's Joel Santana.''

She gazed at him with placid gray eyes, considering. Then she nodded briefly, the curled plume from her hat sweeping down her plain, honest face. ''Mr. Santana. My name is Penelope. Dr. Penelope Lake.''

Leah had taken an oath. She had lived by that oath, had inhaled it with every breath she took, had embodied it in some perverse hope that she could make up for her father's flaws. But when she stood outside Carrie's room in the boardinghouse, she could only think that the woman in the room, the woman she had worked so hard to care for and to heal, was a sick, manipulative creature not worth saving. Leah's own anger horrified her. She struggled to find compassion within herself. But still she had no idea how she would behave with Carrie.

What did one say to the thief of one's dreams?

Then she realized it wasn't Carrie at all, but herself who was in charge of her dreams. Carrie just made the problem more difficult. It was up to Leah to meet the challenge.

She rapped lightly at the door.

"Come in." Carrie's voice sounded soft from the effects of narcotics; Leah could hear the listlessness.

She pushed the door open and stepped inside. "Carrie—"

"All gone." Like a broken doll, she sat upon the bed, her feet stretched out in front of her, a blue glass bottle cradled in both hands. "It's all, all, gone."

"Carrie, you have to stop. You did so well last time. You can do it again. I'll help you."

Carrie held the bottle out and upended it. A curious blankness dwelt in her eyes as if whatever lay behind them was gone. "All finished. Not even a drop left."

"You're going to stop. For the moment, it's best you go to sleep." Leah took the bottle, turning her head away from the thick, sweetish scent, and unlaced Carrie's boots. She wanted to ask Carrie why she'd betrayed Jackson.

But in her current state, Carrie would have no answers that made sense. Resigned, Leah helped her undress, putting aside clothes far finer than anything Leah had ever owned.

Carrie bestirred herself to lift the shift up and over her head, baring her breasts. A fading burn marred her skin. "Adam said I had a beautiful body," she murmured with a slight giggle. "Do you think I have a beautiful body?"

"I think the human form is beautiful. I made its healing my life's work."

"Jackson always thought my body was beautiful."

An icy chill seized Leah's shoulders and spine. She didn't want to hear this, didn't want to think about it, didn't want to know what had occurred between Jackson and Carrie in the long past they shared.

"Poor Jackson." Carrie let Leah drop a white lawn nightdress over her head. "Poor, poor Jackson." She blinked owlishly. "A wanted man."

Leah saw a chance to learn more about the incident that had turned him into an outlaw. Maybe Carrie held the key to the secrets he carried inside him. "Because of what happened in Rising Star," she said.

"Yes. Godforsaken place anyway."

"Was that when he found you?"

Carrie sighed indulgently. "You should've seen the way he rode into town, his duster flapping, his horse all sweaty and foaming at the mouth. He looked like something out of a dream."

Leah could imagine it too well. "You must have been overjoyed to see him."

"Not at first. He came at sunset. I was standing on the boardwalk in front of a saloon waiting for someone."

"Who were you waiting for?" Leah asked, trying to sound neutral.

Carrie made no reply, and Leah feared she'd lost her in a fog of opium and whiskey. Then Carrie smiled slyly. "He thought I didn't recognize him."

"Jackson?"

"Yes, but I did recognize him. You know how handsome he is. How could any woman forget? Besides, he had a peculiar expression on his face. He always looked like that, even when he was a kid."

"Like what?"

"Like he'd do anything for me. Die for me."

*Kill for you?* Leah didn't let herself ask it. She felt as if she stood on the edge of a discovery. This might be her only chance to hear the truth from Carrie's lips, and she didn't want to push too hard. She had to draw on all her expertise, all her knowledge of human nature in order to keep Carrie talking.

"You're very lucky he's so devoted," she said. "Did he greet you right away?"

Carrie hugged her knees up to her chest. "Mmm-hmm. Took off his hat and just stood there for a minute. Just stood there and said, 'Carrie. My God, it really is you.' But I didn't speak to him. I marched right inside the saloon and sat on Hale Devlin's lap. You should have seen Jackson's face." She laughed softly. "Poor Jackson."

Leah shivered. "Hale Devlin," she said, her mouth dry with apprehension. "That's the name of the man who died?"

"No. Hale didn't die."

Leah struggled to make sense of Carrie's listless talk. "Who was it, then?"

"Max Gatlin. The mayor." She shuddered delicately.

"And what happened with the mayor?"

"Hale made me go with him."

"Go where?"

Carrie leaned back against a bank of pillows. She waved her arms as if making a snow angel. "Upstairs," she said with an excess of patience. "I know what you're doing. You're trying to figure out what happened that night."

Leah cautiously touched Carrie's hand. "I know there

are two sides to every story. Maybe no one ever listened to your side before.''

Carrie blinked slowly, sleepily, but in the depths of her eyes, anger flickered. ''He was an animal.''

''Max Gatlin? He hurt you?''

She shuddered, pulling her hand away from Leah. ''He deserved what he got. Deserved to be shot like a dog.''

''So that's what happened?'' Leah helped her lie down and tucked the covers beneath her chin. ''You're sure that's what happened?''

''I was there,'' Carrie said. ''I *saw.*''

''What, Carrie? What did you see? Do you remember what the wounds looked like?''

''Of course I do. Once right in the chest.'' She started to shiver, and Leah knew she was losing her to the oblivion of the drug.

''A bullet wound.''

''Yes. Blood. All that blood. I'm tired. So tired...''

''Just one.''

''It's only a single shot.'' Carrie's trembling increased and tears filled her eyes.

Leah thought of what Zeke Pomfrit had told her earlier—Carrie had a gun. A little .41 pocket derringer. A single-shot weapon.

''Did anyone else see?'' she asked, whispering.

Carrie crawled under the covers, shivering violently. ''I need more medicine. Need more.''

Leah put a hand on her shoulder. ''Finish telling me, Carrie. You'll feel better after that.''

Carrie lay silent for a long time. Thinking she'd drifted off to sleep, Leah went to the door.

''I'm glad the baby didn't live,'' she said, her voice muffled by the quilts and pillows.

Leah stopped short at the door. "Oh, Carrie. You mean——"

"Yes." She hid lower beneath the covers. "He made me pregnant that night."

"So you've come all the way from back East." Joel Santana eyed his supper companion with amazement and growing conviction. *It's her, it's her, it's her...* "That's a long way for a lady to come alone."

"It's a long way for anyone, Mr. Santana." Dr. Penelope Lake helped herself to a second roll, slathered it with butter, and took a bite.

He even liked her way of eating. None of this pretending she had a bird's appetite. She'd had a long trip, she was hungry, and by God she was going to eat.

"True enough," he said, thinking of the trek across Texas, the desert, up through California. "True enough." He cut into his steak. "But what's even truer is you make me as nervous as a schoolboy at an ice-cream social, ma'am."

She laughed. "Do I?"

"That's a fact." *You scare the hell out of me.*

"I suppose I should be intimidated by you, as well," she admitted cheerfully. "I've never known a man who carried such a variety of weapons on his person."

He tried to be discreet, but she had noticed everything—the pocket pistol in his vest, the gun belt, the knife strapped to his thigh, the dagger in his boot. "Truth is, I'd prefer to pound all this hardware into plowshares, so to speak. In fact, I intend to one day soon."

"How soon?"

*How soon will you marry me?* He couldn't believe the thought that whirred through his mind, yet once established, the notion wouldn't leave him alone. In all his years of travel and struggle, he'd come across plenty of women, good and bad, and not a single one of them had ever inspired such an idea.

"Soon's I find a spot to farm."

"Oh. Is that why you're going over to Whidbey Island?"

He hesitated, hating the thought of his mission. Then he said, "I guess I'll be looking around."

"It's supposed to be lovely. My friend, Dr. Mundy, swears it's heaven on earth." She sampled her steak, nodded appreciatively. "I'm joining Dr. Mundy in Coupeville. We've been corresponding for some time."

Joel's heart sank. That could only mean one thing. She was going to marry this Mundy fellow. "Congratulations," he said dully. "I wish you both great joy."

"Thank you. Leah and I have been planning this partnership for over a year."

"Leah?"

"Leah Mundy. She's going to be my partner." Penelope Lake spoke slowly, enunciating every word as if she was speaking to an idiot.

Which of course she was, Joel conceded. "Another lady doctor," he said.

"Do you disapprove?"

"Hell—er, heck no, ma'am." He glanced ruefully down at his gun belt. "World needs more healers in it, if you ask me."

She smiled, her plain face lighting up with a brilliance that warmed his heart. "That's terribly sweet, Mr. Santana. And you know, you won't be the only fellow from Texas to stop in at Whidbey Island." With a playful wink, she said, "I believe Dr. Mundy is being courted by a Texan."

Joel almost choked on a bit of potato. "From Texas, you say?"

"Yes. Really, I shouldn't gossip, but I'm hopeful that it's happy news. In her last letter, she was avidly hoping Mr. Underhill would stay."

Underhill. Joel relaxed, but just for a moment. He was after Jack Tower. Not some Underhill fellow.

Then he remembered something. It was one of the few clues the fleeing pair had left behind in Rising Star. A tin of Underhill Fancy Shred Tobacco.

"Mr. Santana, are you all right?" Penelope Lake asked, leaning forward, her ample bosom brushing the edge of the table.

He used his napkin like a gentleman, as his mama had taught him forty years before, dabbing at his lips and then setting the cloth aside. "No, ma'am," he said grimly, "I don't guess I am."

Unable to sleep that night, Leah turned down the lamp and left her bedroom, tiptoeing to the surgery. This time of the night had always been hers alone, a stolen time when all the house was quiet and even the midnight breeze seemed to be holding its breath. It was time she could give to herself with nothing to interfere.

She had plenty on her mind. The man she loved was in jail on false charges. Yet he refused to say anything in his own defense. She was carrying his child, and Carrie had emerged from the past more beautiful and more dangerous than ever before. Though Carrie's conversation had been disjointed, Leah had gotten a glimpse of that night. Blood and fire and panic. They seemed to follow Carrie wherever she went.

Leah sat down at her desk. Ordinarily, she would put her thoughts in order in a letter to Penelope Lake. But

Penny had been traveling across the country, would be here soon.

"Oh, Penny," Leah said aloud into the night quiet, "I've revealed so much of myself to you."

She kept thinking of Carrie, of the eerie blankness in her eyes, the hollow laughter of a person with no soul. And she thought of Jackson all alone in a cold stone cell, neither admitting to his crime nor denying it.

*Once right in the chest...it's only a single shot...* Carrie's words nagged at Leah. She heard them over and over in her head like a melody that wouldn't go away.

*Once right in the chest.*

Leah's fist clenched around the pen she was holding. She swept aside the notes she'd been making. With a trembling hand, she took out a fresh sheet of paper imprinted at the top with Leah Mundy, M.D. Coupeville, Whidbey Island, Washington.

It was Carrie. There could be no doubt. Carrie—not Jackson—had committed the murder. But Jackson had shouldered the blame, and true to form, he would not accuse her in order to save himself.

He would not. But Leah had no such compunction. Trying to calm her racing pulse, she dipped her pen in ink and began to write. If St. Croix could be trusted, she would have gone straight to him, but he—like everyone else—seemed blinded by Carrie's beauty, her childlike manner. In the morning, Leah would send the message by telegraph to Seattle and Olympia. She would—

The sound of breaking glass startled her. She jumped, spilling ink like black blood across the desk. "Who's there?" Clutching the neckline of her robe, she stood up quickly. She raised the flame of the gaslight, then opened the door. "Who is it?" she asked.

The soft white light illuminated Carrie standing next

to the medicine cabinet. Its door hung askew, pried open. A large bottle lay broken at her feet. The slender woman stood with a tiny white-handled derringer in one hand and a steel wagon iron in the other. Her golden hair tumbled in disarray down her back, and her pretty features were blurred by sleep.

"There you are, Leah," she said. "I went to your room to find you, but you weren't there."

Leah kept her gaze trained on the pistol. *My baby,* she thought. *Please don't hurt my baby.* "Are you…ill? Do you need something?"

Carrie looked down at the shattered glass on the surgery floor. Her feet, bare and bleeding, stood amid a seeping dark pool of liquid. "It's broken," she said. "I didn't mean to break it."

Judging by the smell, Leah realized the liquid was camphor. She smelled something else, too. *Smoke.* "What are you doing, Carrie?" she asked, her voice steely calm.

Carrie tossed her head and took a step forward. Leah winced as glass cracked beneath Carrie's bare foot, but she didn't seem to notice. "Where do you keep the morphine?—There must be another medicine cabinet somewhere."

Leah realized that she'd known, from the moment she'd heard breaking glass, what was happening. Carrie's craving consumed her. She would not rest until she got what she wanted.

Warring instincts raged inside Leah. The doctor she had trained all her life to be wanted to reach out to the patient. But the woman Jackson had made of her felt a primal need to protect the baby growing inside her.

The baby won out.

"I'll get it for you," she said. Yes, that was the thing.

Buy time, then summon help, figure out where the smoke was coming from, send the telegraph she knew could save Jackson. Lord, so much to do. So much depended on Leah's ability to handle this disturbed woman.

"You keep it locked in your desk?" Carrie brushed past Leah, shoving her aside with surprising strength. She walked to the desk, glancing down at the spilled ink, then frowning intently at the letter Leah had been writing.

Leah took a step forward. "Carrie—"

"You're writing to the authorities about me." The snub nose of the derringer came up. It was a Colt Number 3 with a sheathed trigger. *A single shot.* That, at least, was in Leah's favor.

Holding the gun rock steady, Carrie leaned over the desk, overturning the small candle stub. A pool of wax gathered on the letter, but the candle flame didn't go out.

Leah forced herself to hold firm. "You can't let Jackson hang for something you did."

"He keeps me safe. He promised he'd always keep me safe." Ignoring the widening pool of flame on the desk, Carrie broke the lock with a one-handed blow of the wagon iron and jerked open the cabinet, her eyes widening when she saw the hypodermic needles Leah used on rare occasions. "I'll take the morphine through a needle," she said.

Leah felt sick, keeping her eye on the gun in Carrie's hand. Bit by bit, Carrie was coming apart at the seams. It was like seeing a perfect tapestry unraveling before her eyes, and she was powerless to stop it. "Let me put out the flames. There are people asleep upstairs. If you were to cause a fire—"

Carrie laughed, that hollow, hungry sound that was more malice than mirth. She grabbed something else from the cabinet. A clear bottle. "Is this it? Is this the morphine?'' Still holding the gun, she uncorked it with her mouth.

"That's ether," Leah said quickly. "Be careful, it's flammable—"

Even as she spoke, Carrie hurled the bottle away from her. The liquid spewed out, covering the desk, then meeting the flames from the candle and exploding upward.

# Seventeen

Night was never darker than in a jail cell.

Jackson lay wakeful, staring at nothing while thoughts tumbled over and over in his mind. The thin, straw-filled ticking covering the rough wooden bench was too short to contain his height. He had progressed beyond discomfort, though. If physical torment was all he had to face, he'd count his blessings.

But he was alone in the dark, and the torment came from within, closing in like nightmare demons, circling him, choking him. Everything lay in ruins—his life, his plans, his hopes. It had seemed so simple all those years ago. He would find Carrie, rescue her from her dangerous way of life, take her somewhere safe, and reinvent himself as a man who could hold his head up, who could sail the seven seas with nothing but the wind at his back.

Somehow everything had gotten mixed up, like metal poured into a crucible and then reemerging, made of the same substance yet immeasurably different. It was wrong, all wrong. Nothing had turned out as he'd planned. He'd discovered things about himself he'd never suspected—honor, ambition, commitment. And a love so great it made his chest hurt just thinking about it. Leah made him want things he'd never even considered before—a home, a family, respect.

He could have none of it because the past wouldn't leave him alone. He thought of Carrie, thankful beyond measure that she was still alive, but at the same time wincing as he recalled the wide-eyed, needy way she had stared at him. Maybe she had never healed because he hadn't cared enough, hadn't loved her the way she so desperately needed to be loved.

Could you *make* yourself love someone?

No. He knew that now. A man couldn't make himself love someone any more than he could make himself *not* love someone.

*Leah.* She had known the truth long ago—that all the love and commitment in the world couldn't fix what was wrong with Carrie. Jackson realized now he'd grown up with a skewed, romanticized view of love. Lacking it all his life, he had idealized the notion as some sort of spiritual balm that healed all ills. Leah had taught him differently. She had taught him that love was difficult. It didn't just rain down on a man, bathing him in a mist of perfect happiness. It brought pain as well as joy.

But Christ, he wanted it, wanted *her*—wanted those quiet moments awakening with her beside him, looking up at the supper table and seeing her face, sitting across from her in the parlor and peering over the top of a book to find her smiling at him.

These were not thoughts a man should be having when he was about to die. Jackson knew he'd be better off if he just resigned himself to his fate. His future had been sealed that rainy night in Rising Star, and nothing he could say or do would change the outcome. Only Leah had faith. Leah, Leah. But it wasn't enough to have her believe in him. He had to believe in himself.

He'd never been able to do that.

He squeezed his eyes shut, but the darkness made no difference. He couldn't sleep, couldn't eat, didn't want to think or dream. He almost welcomed the loud thumping sound that brought him leaping to his feet.

Caspar MacPhail, assigned to guard duty for the night, started bumping around outside. MacPhail seemed a little sheepish around Jackson, as if he should have known better than to consort with him. Every lawman harbored the conviction that he had a sixth sense for spotting criminals. Jackson was living proof that he was mistaken. Living, hah. He was dead meat.

"MacPhail!" Jackson called out. "What's all the ruckus about?"

"Never you mind, Jackson." Another thump, as if he was stomping his foot down into his boot. Clearly, MacPhail had been sleeping on the job.

Shouts and clanging came from the street. Jackson gripped the rough iron bars of the cell. "Give me a break, partner. What's going on?"

The door opened, and yellow light from a kerosene lamp crept across the floor in an elongated triangle. MacPhail was jamming a Stetson hat down on his head. "Fire," he said.

Jackson felt a jab of fear. "What's burning?"

"The Mundy boardinghouse." MacPhail took his gun belt from a hook and held it, preparing to strap it on. The rawhide thigh strings hung down into the pool of light.

Acting on an instinct that struck as swiftly as lightning, Jackson snaked his arm between the bars. He grabbed the rawhide laces and yanked the gun belt out of the deputy's hands. The heavy leather clanged against the bars as he unholstered one of the pistols. The gun felt weighty and familiar in his hand as he aimed and cocked it.

The deputy stood motionless with shock, but just for a moment. He inhaled deeply, no doubt gathering breath to shout for help.

"Now, MacPhail," Jackson cautioned, "I'm probably not going to shoot you. I sure as hell don't want to. But I need you to let me out of here."

"Damn it, Jackson—"

"Do it now. I'm in a hurry."

MacPhail flexed his hands as if readying himself for a fight. "If you shoot me, you'll *never* get out of there," he said.

"If I shoot you, you'll never do a lot of things, my friend. Like kiss your wife in the morning or see that baby she's expecting—"

MacPhail bolted.

Jackson squeezed off a shot before the deputy reached the doorway.

MacPhail froze, shoulders tucked up against his ears. Then he relaxed. "You missed."

"No, I didn't, MacPhail."

"What—"

"Look at your hat."

With a shaking hand, the deputy snatched off his hat. A bullet hole pierced the crown, front and back.

"That was a warning," Jackson explained. "It's the only one you'll get. Unlock the cell."

The deputy's hands shook so badly that he couldn't fit the key in the hole, and Jackson had to help him. He felt almost apologetic as he shoved MacPhail into the cell and locked him in.

Smoke clawed at Leah's throat. Though barely able to see, she could discern Carrie standing in the middle of the office, watching the flames devour the drapes and roar along the hall carpet runner. She didn't flinch as glass bottles and vials exploded from the heat.

A flying splinter of glass stung Leah's cheek. She lifted her hand to cover her eyes, shouting, "Carrie! We've got to get out!"

"It's so beautiful, seeing the fire like this," Carrie said dreamily. "Just like on Adam's boat."

Leah plunged toward the door, but she wasn't quick enough.

Carrie lifted the derringer. "You can't drive me away. You can't keep me from getting my medicine. You can't lock me up in some hospital."

"Carrie, please." Leah eyed the gun; she sensed the racing fire behind her. "We can talk about this after we get everyone out of the house."

"By then it will be too late."

Leah took a chance, grabbing for the derringer. She caught Carrie's wrist, managed to drag her out of the burning office and slam the door. Smoke poured beneath it in a boiling river.

Carrie wrenched herself away, keeping hold of the gun. "You wanted me gone," she shrieked.

"You left of your own accord. Jackson would have looked after you forever, no matter what the cost. He'll still keep that promise. You're his wife, no matter what."

Carrie chuckled. "I was never his wife. We just pretended. Now, Adam really did marry me."

Leah absorbed the knowledge. Jackson was free. *Free.* But it was too late for that to mean anything.

"Adam didn't take care of me," Carrie complained. "Didn't give me what I need." Her eyes glittered at the hypodermic needle clutched in her free hand. "Do it, Leah. I'm ill. This will make me feel better."

Feeding the appetite of an addict went against all of

Leah's instincts and training. But when she glanced at the door to the outer office, the paint on the wood was blistering and melting, sliding down. "Give me the gun," she ordered.

With her hungry gaze fastened on the syringe, Carrie placed the barrel against Leah's temple. "The needle first."

Leah took the hypodermic, grasped Carrie by the arm and turned it wrist up. With one well-aimed jab, she pierced a vein and plunged down with her thumb, shooting the milky drug into Carrie's bloodstream. Swiftly, Leah removed the needle, dropping it on the desk. "Hold your elbow closed like this. You'll feel better in a moment." Carrie stumbled, dropping the gun. Leah kicked it out of the way and guided her toward the exit. "Come. *Now.*"

"Why should I come with you?"

Something in Leah snapped. It was everything at once—the years of living in her father's shadow. The grinding frustrations of medical school. The unending prejudice of the townspeople. And the fact that this one crazed, charmed woman stood between her and the only man she had ever truly loved.

*"Move, damn you!"* she yelled, shoving Carrie with all her might.

As she forced Carrie out through the back door, Leah barely recognized herself. How different she was from the spinster physician Jackson had stolen from her bed. He had guided her into a new understanding of herself—she was someone who could love and be loved. Someone who could let out her anger, who could take action rather than observing life from the fringes. The ordeals, the peaks and valleys of the past few months had transformed her utterly.

Carrie fell to her knees outside. Instantly forgetting her, Leah went to the front of the house.

"Fire!" she screamed, running up the stairs of the front porch, yanking open the main door. Soaring flames surrounded the doors and passageways. "Everyone wake up!" Leah yelled. "There's a fire in the house!"

She headed for the back of the main floor first, where Perpetua and Bowie slept. Thick, hazy smoke layered the corridors. Holding her sleeve over her mouth and nose, Leah raced to Perpetua's room. She wrenched open the door to the suite of rooms the cook and her son shared.

"The house is on fire!" Leah called. "Get Bowie out—quickly!"

Perpetua sprang out of bed, long braids trailing down her back. Within seconds, she'd scooped up Bowie, who made no more than a groggy protest, then clung to her neck as she dashed from the room. Leah followed, choking on the thickening smoke in the hall.

Hot yellow tongues of flame licked up along the wooden rail and the bridge that spanned the second story. Praying the stairwell would be safe another few moments, Leah lifted the hem of her robe and pounded upstairs.

Battle and Zeke had taken charge in the upper quarters, moving swiftly along the hallway and rousing the boarders.

The threadbare carpet smoldered underfoot. Leah went to the room at the end of the hall, passing a disoriented-looking Aunt Leafy, who stopped in the middle of the hallway and squinted.

"Ambrose, is that you? Ambrose Leafington!" She called the name of her dead husband.

"Battle!" Leah yelled. "Get Aunt Leafy out. I'm going for Iona."

The girl slept in a small room at the end of the hall. When Leah burst in, she was still asleep, though an ominous fog of smoke hung suspended from the ceiling. Leah took her by the shoulders, giving her a firm shake.

Iona opened her eyes.

"Fire!" Leah exaggerated the shape of the word and gestured at the smoke.

Iona made a strangled sound and started to dash out. Leah pointed her toward the stairs. The fire had climbed, eating along the beams overhead. Flames devoured the outer edges of the risers, but if Leah and Iona descended swiftly enough, they'd avoid getting burned. Leah followed Iona—but hesitated halfway down the stairs.

Out of the corner of her eye, she'd seen...something.

She glanced fearfully back up the stairs. The flames danced underfoot. But...something had moved in one of the rooms she'd passed in the corridor.

At the foot of the stairs, Battle met Iona. Together the two ducked their heads and made for the front door.

"Battle!" Leah screamed.

He stopped and squinted through the fog of smoke.

"Where's Aunt Leafy?" Leah shrieked.

She could tell by his posture the moment he realized Aunt Leafy was still inside. "I guess she didn't come down!"

Leah heard a groaning of timber. Her scalp and shoulders stung from falling sparks. She spun around and went back upstairs to Aunt Leafy's room.

The elderly lady stood in the middle of her chamber holding the shrouded cage of her pet canary. "I nearly forgot Carlos," she said wonderingly. "Can you imagine, forgetting my little precious?"

"Aunt Leafy, you must come—*now!*" Leah grabbed the cage in one hand and Aunt Leafy's wrist in the other.

She dragged them both to the stairs. The old lady made some noises of protest, but Leah ignored them and hustled her along. "Battle!" she called. "I've got her! I've got Aunt Leafy!"

In the mere seconds it had taken for her to go back for Aunt Leafy, the bottom four stairs had been consumed by the flames. Battle and Zeke stood with their hands outstretched.

"Come, Aunt Leafy, there you are," Leah said, using all her strength to push her toward Battle's waiting arms.

The woman was frightened into near inertia. She managed to gasp, "Carlos first. I won't move a muscle unless you save Carlos first."

Leah borrowed one of Jackson's oaths. She swung the birdcage in an arc, then let go. Zeke caught it and handed it to someone outside.

"Your turn, Aunt Leafy. You'll have to jump past those bottom steps."

"I can't!"

"You haven't any choice." With a decisive nod at Battle, Leah gave her a shove. The old woman shrieked as she lurched over the gap.

In the next second, Leah saw a blur of movement that made her think the world was coming undone. Battle Douglas caught Aunt Leafy and stumbled out the door. The next set of stairs caved in beneath her feet. She jumped back in the nick of time, landing on the bridge that spanned the foyer. Sparks showered down on her like a hot, lethal rain.

A great uprush of flame stole all the oxygen from the air around her. She heard a thundering sound and glanced up to see the ceiling collapsing.

# *Eighteen*

⸙

Joel Santana thought Dr. Penelope Lake looked mighty pretty in the moonlight. She didn't realize he was watching her as she sat on the railed upper deck of the steamer *Intrepid,* getting ready for the early crossing to Whidbey Island. He stood on deck, feeling the wind in his face, his feet braced apart while he prayed to high heaven he didn't puke in front of her.

Just a few quick steps and he'd be beside her. If the boat didn't roll, he might be all right. She was a powerful motivation, her warm reddish hair neatly coiled at the nape of her neck, her hands folded politely in her lap, and her face raised to the night sky as she waited for the sunrise. She was that rarity, a woman who seemed completely at home in her body. She wasn't concerned about trussing up her stoutness or binding her feet into shoes that were too small.

Joel liked that.

He took a deep, steadying breath and carefully planted one foot in front of the other, making his way across the deck to her. "Enjoying yourself, Dr. Penny?" he asked.

She glanced his way, and a smile lit her face. He had taken to calling her Dr. Penny and she seemed to like it.

"Very much, Marshal Santana. I declare, I've never seen anything quite so pretty as the islands of Puget Sound. I can't wait to see them in the sunlight."

"I hear tell it gets even prettier up Canada way." Joel was halfway to her side when a swell rolled the steamer. The movement was subtle, but to Joel it felt like a tidal wave.

"Marshal Santana?" She stood up. "You've gone quite pale all of a sud—"

"'Scuse me, ma'am," he managed to grumble. He reached the rail in time to aim his morning coffee over the side. He was tempted to follow it and drown himself in the clear, cold waters far below. Here he was trying to make a good impression on the lady, and instead, he almost upchucked on her patent leather boots.

To his mortification, she touched him, putting a gloved hand at the nape of his neck. "Hold very still, Marshal," she said, pressing her thumb beneath his left ear. "I'm not certain this will work, but sometimes a strong pressure right here will help the equilibrium. Keep your eyes open. Just stare at the horizon line."

A few moments later, he put his hand back and covered hers. "Dr. Penny?"

"Yes, Marshal?"

"It's working. You're a miracle worker."

"Oh, I wouldn't say that, but I'm very pleased when I'm able to ease someone's suffering."

They stood that way for a long time, her thumb pressing near his ear, his hand covering hers while the night faded into misty gray dawn. The white cliffs of the lower end of Whidbey Island hove into view. It looked just like a picture postcard, green and moist, lines blurred by a silvery haze.

"I'm looking at my new home," she said. "This is where I shall live. It's lovely, isn't it?"

"That it is, ma'am." Joel's next words came even before the conscious thought. "I aim to stay here, too."

"What?"

"I'll be retiring from service soon's I finish my business up here. I mean to find me a little farm, maybe homestead a place on the island." His own words shocked him as much as they seemed to shock her. "Maybe we'll be…friends."

Dr. Penny dropped her hand, turning to face him. "Maybe we'll be more than that," she said, her gaze level and direct.

Joel found himself grinning like a greenhorn at a barn raising. He settled back to enjoy the rest of the voyage. "Yeah," he said, "we might."

Jackson had broken out of jail before. More than once. The first thing to do was to get the hell out of town, out of sight. But this time he didn't revel in a sense of freedom. His thoughts were consumed by Leah.

"Be safe, honey," he said beneath his breath as he ran up the hill toward the burning house. "Please be safe."

Townspeople were creating a minor stampede in their rush to help. Men and women armed with buckets surged up the lawn. None of them seemed to notice Jackson, or if they did, they didn't think it odd that he was among them.

The entire lower floor was burning. Flames leaped out of the windows and climbed steadily up the walls. In the yard, Carrie sat on a garden bench, her knees drawn to her chest as she rocked back and forth and watched the fire as if spellbound. Battle Douglas had organized a bucket brigade from the outdoor pump to the front porch.

"Is everybody out?" Jackson asked.

"Everybody but Dr. Mundy," Battle said grimly. His face was stained coal black, with a black mustache of soot beneath his nose. "I tried to go in after her, but she's trapped upstairs."

Jackson didn't wait to hear more. He grabbed a bucket from someone's hands and doused himself with it, shouldered a coil of rope, then raced for the house. As he ran, he tied his wet neckerchief over his mouth and nose, *bandido*-style. He heard shouted warnings and protests, but ignored them. Leah was inside. It was the only thought he allowed himself to have as he entered the house and slammed smack into a wall of flame.

The fire was alive. Leah could hear it roar like a wild animal. Heated tongues licked her feet and legs, her arms, her hair. She had retreated to the end of the hallway only to find the area engulfed in flames, as impassable as the front of the house.

Her oxygen-deprived brain must be playing tricks on her. For deep within the lethal bellowing of the fire, she could hear Jackson calling her name.

She knew then she was only moments from death, for she heard the voice of her beloved. "Leah!" How close he sounded. How frantic. "Leah! Where the hell are you?"

Even though she knew Jackson was in jail and she'd never see him again, Leah thought of the baby and felt hopeful. Perhaps this was one final blessing before eternity—to hear his voice. Hope swept her up like a wave, and she began to move toward the faint, frantic voice. She ran down the burning corridor, beneath flaming rafters, to the bridge that spanned a gaping hole where the staircase used to be.

When she saw his face, she knew he was not a vision. In the unholy light of the fire, he looked so wonderful that she ached, and it hurt more than the heat, more than the smoke starving her lungs. There were worse things, she decided, than having a last glimpse of something so beloved. "Jackson," she said. He reached for her, but he stood too far below. He might as well have been in another world.

She didn't want him to stand there and watch her burn, but she knew he wouldn't leave. Of all the things in the world she could have taught him, it had to be that. To stay. She had taught him to stay, no matter what the risk, no matter how much it hurt.

What an idiot she'd been. He'd tried to leave so many times. She should have let him.

He took a coil of rope from his shoulder. Tossing the end up, he missed his target a few times. Leah kept screaming for him to get out, but he ignored her, throwing the rope with grim concentration. Once, twice, three times... He finally managed to loop it over a spurting water pipe high in the burned-out ceiling. He passed one end of the rope through the loop and then began to climb. She saw the strain in his face, saw his muscles bulge and glisten with sweat as he climbed.

His hand stretched toward her, reaching, reaching. "Jump, Leah!" he bellowed, his voice even louder than the flames.

She clutched the railing. "It's too far!"

"Do it anyway, damn it—"

A beam collapsed, falling with unnatural slowness to the floor of the foyer. It lay like a felled tree, blocking the front door. Jackson swore through his teeth. Water from the pipe hissed down on him.

Through smarting eyes, Leah stared at the beam. They

would burn in here. This place that had once been her father's dream would be her tomb.

"Jump, goddamn it!" Jackson yelled. "Trust me for once in your goddamned life!"

He had never said "I love you," but she knew in that instant that he did. More than she'd ever imagined possible. She looked at him and at the flames below like the pit of hell, then at the one escape route left to them—the round colored window over the foyer. If only they could get to it.

But if not... She looked at him one last time, then closed her eyes, and jumped.

From the deck of the steamer, the town resembled a toy village made of pastel-colored blocks, its harbor filled with boats of all sizes.

"Leah Mundy lives in the big house on the hill," Dr. Penny said. "I imagine that's the one." She paused, squinted at the sight. "Good Lord, it's on fire!"

Joel Santana stared at the ugly tower of black smoke issuing from the large house. "Reckon it is, Dr. Penny," he said, hitching up his gun belt. "Reckon it is." As passengers lined the rail, mouths agape, Joel shifted his weight from foot to foot. "Can't they get this tub into harbor any faster?"

"Not unless they want to cause an accident," Adam Armstrong said, joining them at the rail.

Santana stared at the burning house. "Hell of a thing, isn't it?"

"What on earth happened?" Dr. Penny put her hand on Joel's arm.

He covered her hand with his. "I aim to be the first one to find out, soon as we land."

"I'm right with you," Armstrong assured him.

"So am I," Dr. Penny said.

"That's too dangerous. You stay away from the fire."

"I'm a doctor. They might need me," she said stubbornly.

Though he hardly knew her, he knew better than to argue. The moments seemed like hours as the steamer docked, even though the crew worked with frantic haste to tie up and lower the gangway.

True to his word, Joel went first, hurrying to the fire. Adam and Dr. Penny followed, racing up the hill. She matched him stride for stride, and they reached the house at the same time.

Adam made a strangled sound in his throat. "Carrie!" He sank to one knee beside a slim young woman with yellow hair.

By God, it *was* her, Joel realized. Carrie. Caroline Willis.

"Is she all right?" Dr. Penny asked, bending to look at her.

"My wife is going to be fine," Adam said. "Aren't you, honey?"

"This is your wife?" Penny asked.

Carrie looked up unblinkingly. "I used to want to marry Jackson, but we only pretended. I wish he would burn in hell, he and that bossy Leah Mundy." She released a thin, eerie laugh. "My wish is coming true."

"They're inside?" Joel demanded.

"Trapped." Her strange, fey laughter echoed in his ears as he ran toward the house.

He almost made it into the inferno. But the moment he put his foot on the bottom step to the front porch, something inside collapsed in a deadly rush of heat and a shower of sparks.

"Get back, mister!" A man wearing a badge grabbed his arm. "No way to get in now. It's too late."

"You're just going to let him burn?" Joel demanded.

"He was scum anyway. Too bad about the doc, though." The sheriff flinched as smoke belched from the front door.

God, thought Joel. To come all this way—

The round window above the door exploded outward. Joel jumped back and shielded his eyes. The crowd on the lawn raised a chorus of amazed babbling. Through the window, clinging to a burning rope, came Jackson Underhill clutching a woman in a nightgown.

They landed heavily on the lawn in a heap of smoldering clothes. People rushed forward with blankets and buckets of water. "It's Dr. Leah!" a boy in the crowd yelled. "He saved her."

"Let me through!" a voice called. "Let me through. I'm a doctor!" Dr. Penny had her skirts hiked up over her plump knees as she ran toward them. Her unmistakable air of authority parted the crowd, and within seconds she had the two victims laid out, examining them for mortal wounds.

The man groaned and stirred, restless until his hand touched the woman's cheek. Then his eyes opened to slits. The woman coughed and inhaled with a harsh gasp.

"Amazing," Penny said, gingerly checking them. "They're both exhausted and bruised. He's probably broken some ribs. Minor burns and asphyxiation from the smoke. But I don't see a mortal injury on either of them."

Joel swallowed hard, stunned to feel his eyes smarting. His hand went automatically to his gun even though he knew he didn't need it. His other hand went to his badge and credentials, kept as always inside his leather waistcoat.

"I'm Joel Santana," he said, his gaze fixed on the man's sooty, sweating face, "U.S. Marshal. You're under arrest."

The hard landing on the lawn had knocked the wind out of Jackson, but his hearing was fine. The old desperado instincts reared up, but he knew he wouldn't fight his way out of this one. Wouldn't even try.

A babble of voices started after the marshal made his statement. Leah choked violently, then clung to him, her eyes looking huge in her soot-stained face. "Jackson," she whispered so only he could hear, "run for your life! I can create a diversion, and then you can run—"

"Honey, save your breath." Jackson's voice was quiet with weary resignation. He felt something worse than physical pain when he had to let go of her, had to stand on his own two feet.

"I guess you'd be the marshal who tailed me all over kingdom come," he said.

"That'd be me. I tracked you all the way from Texas." Santana looked battle worn and tired the way Jackson felt. He studied the serious-eyed, craggy-faced man who had followed him across the country only to have him—almost literally—drop into his lap. Santana had a reputation; Jackson wondered if he knew that.

"Now what happens?" he asked.

"We have a lot of talking to do." Santana clearly took no joy in the prospect. "It's my job to do this by the book. But if you dare to try one blamed thing, I'll forget what's in that book and hang your sorry ass."

Jackson heard Leah begin to weep softly. He caught the eye of the red-haired woman who had declared herself a doctor. "See to the lady," he said. "You take damned good care of her, you hear?"

* * *

"Leah Mundy, you get right back in that bed," Dr. Penelope Lake scolded.

Clutching the edge of the door frame, Leah heard a pounding noise and thought it was her throbbing head. "Where am I?"

"In the coachman's quarters over the carriage house."

"How long have I been asleep?" She pushed a mass of tangled hair out of her face and stumbled to the window. Amber light streamed through the wavy glass. "Is that sunrise or sunset?"

"Sunrise. You slept through the day—and then through the night."

"What is that pounding noise?"

"They're repairing your house and surgery."

"They?"

"The whole town. From your letters I got the impression folks weren't too neighborly toward you. But everyone's pitching in." Penny led Leah back to the bed. "Sit down, Leah. Honestly, I never dreamed my very first patient would be you."

The moments after the fire flowed through Leah's mind in a blur. Both of her hands stole to her midsection.

"I think the baby's all right," Dr. Lake said. "I've been watching that more closely than anything."

A lump formed in Leah's throat. "Did you tell anyone?"

"Of course not. It's your baby. Your business."

Leah managed a dry-lipped smile. "I like you already."

"I would say the feeling is mutual, but you're a terrible patient. Wouldn't calm down for a minute until you finally collapsed."

"They arrested Jackson. Took him away." Leah

plucked at the unfamiliar robe she wore. "Are there some clothes here? I've got to go to him."

"Of course you must." Leah liked the tall red-haired woman even more. Most people would have argued with her; Penny Lake seemed to understand what was important as she rifled through a carpetbag. "My things will be far too big on you—"

"They'll do." Leah put on a shift and a plain cotton gown. She winced at the ache in her muscles. Pain seared her burned hands and arms, but she didn't hesitate. Penny bit her lip and said nothing.

In the lower part of the coach house, Leah found a pair of paddock boots and put them on. Hearing Penny behind her, she turned.

"I look a mess."

"You had a bad night."

She almost smiled at the wry understatement. "I never even asked how your journey was."

"Long. And hot. I'll tell you all about it after we straighten out the business with Jackson and Joel."

"You call him Joel?"

Penny's plump cheeks flushed. "We've been... traveling companions since Seattle."

Leah studied her partner, whom she knew only through their long correspondence. Penny had the look of a woman in the first flush of new love. Leah knew it, recognized it, because not so very long ago she had looked at herself in the mirror and seen that very same starry-eyed expression.

"Joel Santana is the man who placed Jackson under arrest," Leah said. "I cannot possibly approve of any association with such a person."

"He is doing his duty."

"He is taking an innocent man to be hanged!"

Together they walked outside and started down the road toward town. "If Jackson Underhill is innocent, then Joel won't allow him to be hanged," Penny stated.

Leah set her jaw and plunged on, past the houses of people who had scorned her and only embraced her when Jackson had forced Leah to see her own worth. God, what would she do without him? What in heaven's name would she do?

The sheriff's office was a hive of activity, men rushing back and forth between the telegraph office and the jail, a reporter from the city nagging everyone with questions.

Leah pushed past Deputy MacPhail, Joel Santana and Marshal Corliss from Port Townsend. "Dr. Mundy!" MacPhail said loudly.

Instant silence blanketed the area. She stopped in the middle of the office, craning her neck to peer toward the jail cell. She could see the silhouette of a man sitting on a bench behind bars.

With a strangled cry, she stumbled toward him.

He looked up in weary resignation.

Jackson's name died on her lips. "Sheriff St. Croix," she said dully. He merely grunted and hung his head. Santana took Leah by the arm. She wrenched away. "Where's Jackson?"

The marshal lifted his hat and raked a hand through his salt-and-pepper hair. "He took off."

Thank God he was free, she thought. But pain shot through her gratitude. The inevitable had finally happened. He was gone from her life.

"His boat is missing, isn't it?"

"That's what they tell me." He rubbed his jaw, which was swollen and livid with a bruise.

Grim satisfaction tasted bitter in her mouth. "You didn't really think you could hold him, did you?"

"Dr. Mundy, I did my best, but he wouldn't listen. He—"

"Nothing can hold Jackson Underhill," she said cuttingly as she turned to leave. "Not a blessed thing, and anyone who dares to think otherwise is a fool."

"I will not break bread with that man," Leah said to Penny later that evening.

"I think you should," Penny insisted. "I think you'll want to hear what he has to say."

"What can Mr. Santana possibly say to me to convince me that running Jackson off was the right thing to do?"

"He didn't run Jackson off. Jackson punched him unconscious and escaped."

"Because Joel would have locked him up, for God's sake," Leah said in exasperation.

Penny sat down on the bed beside Leah. "You used to write to me about how frustrating it was sometimes, being a doctor in a town full of people who wouldn't give you a chance to prove yourself." Penny's broad hand patted her knee. "Give Joel a chance, Leah. If you don't like what he has to say, then you can condemn him."

Leah let out a sigh and placed her hand over Penny's. "I started out liking you. Don't make me change my mind."

"You're the only one who can do that. Now, you're sure you don't want to rest?"

"I'm starved."

"Then the pregnancy is fine."

Leah swallowed past the thickness in her throat. This was Jackson's baby. She would take such good care of it.

She and Penny Lake walked across the lawn. Long

boards had been set up on sawhorses and a huge feast
had been laid out for the workers. Her heart filled as she
greeted them all, the people who had come to help re-
build her house: Mrs. Cranney, gossiping and cutting pies
and looking plump and lovely without her corset; James
Gillespie the butcher, whose children were busy serving
ham and smoked salmon to everyone; Hume Amity, up
on a ladder while his wife looked after their baby. Even
Bob Rapsilver greeted her properly, calling her Dr.
Mundy loudly enough for everyone to hear. Countless
others took the time to say hello and promise her house
would be back in order in no time.

Jackson had given her this, she realized, her throat
tight once again. He'd come to town a stranger, a drifter,
and had shown her how to be a part of the heart and soul
of the community, not just an outsider looking in.

Joel Santana was just putting the finishing touches on
a new rolling chair for Bowie when Leah found him. She
felt torn. It was hard to hate a man who was busy helping
a little boy.

Santana saw her coming and sent Bowie off to show
his new chair to the boarders. "Dr. Mundy," he said,
seating her at a small table rescued from the parlor.

Leah took a sip of lemonade. "Penelope says you
wanted to speak to me."

"Yes, ma'am. First to say how sorry I am about Jackson Underhill or Jack Tower—he went by both names. I
tried to explain to him that he didn't have to worry—"

"Didn't have to worry? You were hauling him off to
jail."

"Well, yes and no. But he coldcocked me before I
could explain."

Leah sat mute and numb, absorbing the shock of what

she'd just heard. She swallowed hard, then found her voice. "I knew he couldn't have killed anyone."

"You were right."

"But if you knew he was innocent, why did you hunt him down?"

"Because that's my job."

"Why did you arrest him?"

"So he'd quit running. Some marshals I could name prefer to bring their fugitives in dead. I didn't want that to happen in this case because I knew I was chasing an innocent man. Christ, I thought I'd never catch up with him. And then once I did, I made the mistake of thinking he'd thank me for finding him before it was too late."

Leah refilled her lemonade glass from the pitcher. Her hand shook, and some of the liquid spilled. "Too late for what?"

"He didn't know Caroline Willis. He didn't understand what she'd done, what she was capable of."

"So why didn't you arrest *her*?" Leah said, exasperated.

"Because I had to follow the letter of the law. But there'll be a warrant for her soon enough. She had a reputation. Killed four men that I know of, maybe more I don't. That night in Rising Star, it was Carrie who did the shooting."

Leah leaned back against her chair. "She all but admitted it to me before she set the fire."

"That's one of her favorite things, setting fires."

"But Jackson has no faith in the justice system. He thinks he'll be condemned and convicted regardless of what really happened."

"That might have been true, except for a couple of things. The weapon used was a single-shot pocket pistol.

Not the sort of gun you'd expect from a man like Jackson.''

"It was Carrie's gun," Leah said. "I figured that out myself."

"And another thing." Joel took a paper from his vest pocket and unfolded it. "A sworn statement from a witness named Hale Devlin. He saw Carrie do the shooting. Saw it all."

"So why was Jackson held responsible?"

"The witness didn't come forward. He and Carrie go back a ways, and he didn't want to draw any suspicion on himself. So it took some convincing to persuade him that it was the right thing to do."

Leah studied Joel's big, callused hands and figured she knew how he'd done his convincing. "But why arrest Jackson? Why shame him in front of everyone the way you did?"

"Because I knew he'd get spooked and take off before I could explain." He shaded his eyes northward. "I just wasn't quick enough. Why would he believe a lawman anyway? What with the sheriff and all…"

"What about St. Croix?"

Joel blew out a weary breath. "When we got to the jail, we found him loading up his gasoline carriage with more money than he could explain having. Turns out he's a gunrunner. In the scuffle to stop him, Jackson nailed me and took off."

"And what will become of Carrie?"

"She'll be taken to Texas. Her husband, Mr. Armstrong, will go with her."

Leah's head throbbed with all the new information. She felt satisfaction but no joy in the fact that Jackson had been vindicated, that he was free of the law and of Carrie and even of the past, because there was a hole in her heart. Jackson didn't know any of this. If he was as good at running as he had been in the past, he might never find out.

Joel selected a slice of ham and chewed thoughtfully. "How many islands are out there?"

She looked out across the water where the islands rose, dozens of them, tree spiked and growing smaller with the curve of the earth. "No one knows. Hundreds, really. Most of them don't even have names."

"Would you excuse me, Dr. Mundy?" He paused, watching her expectantly.

She hesitated, studied the rock-faced older man until she saw it—the spark of complete, decent honesty in his eyes.

"You're excused, Mr. Santana."

# Nineteen

30 October 1894

"Don't scream or I'll shoot," warned a low-pitched masculine voice.

Leah Mundy jerked awake and found herself looking down the barrel of a gun.

Sheer panic jolted her to full alert.

"I'm not going to scream," she said, dry-mouthed. In her line of work she had learned to control fear. Lightning flickered, glancing off the dull blue finish of a Colt barrel. "Please don't hurt me." Her voice broke, but didn't waver. After the extraordinary events of the summer, nothing could frighten her.

Thunder pulsed in the distance, echoing the thud of her heart. She squinted into the gloom. Beyond the gun, she couldn't make out anything but a dark shape.

Yet her heart knew the truth before her mind was fully awake. *"Jackson."*

"Yeah, honey. It's me."

She almost laughed. Or wept. Or screamed. She pushed the gun away. "That's not funny."

Leather creaked as he holstered the weapon. "It's not loaded."

She blinked into the darkness. "I can't believe it's you."

"Lightning does sometimes strike twice in one place."

Leah swallowed. She felt frozen, immobile. She didn't remember how to be intimate with him anymore. Two months had passed since she had seen him, heard the sound of his voice, kissed him, touched him. Two months that felt like forever. She'd spent an eternity wondering if he'd ever realize he could stop running. An eternity trying to forget him, because that was the only way she could live without him.

Rain hissed on the windowpanes. A loud male snore drifted down the hall, and he turned his head toward the noise. "House looks good," he commented.

"There's still a lot of finishing work to be done. But everyone cooperated in rebuilding it. The whole town. It was extraordinary."

He shifted restlessly. She caught the scents of rain and brine on him. Rain and brine from the sea and something else... She just didn't know this man anymore.

She jerked the covers up under her chin. She should be bubbling over with elation. But losing him had made her wary of loving someone as much as she loved him. "Are you still running?"

"Would it matter to you if I was?"

She swallowed hard. He was a man who couldn't stay. That was one thing that would never change about him, no matter what had happened in the past. No matter how hard she loved him.

"Leah, come with me," he said. "To the boat."

The *Teatime*. She had spent the past two months trying

not to think about it. She didn't want to remember the time she'd spent there, the dreams she'd dreamed.

"No," she whispered, clutching the covers tighter.

"Please. Trust me. Just one more time."

She was terrified because so much was at stake now. She had resigned herself to staying here, raising her baby alone. Now Jackson had come along to threaten the quiet world she'd built for herself. But she knew she had to see him. She was braver now, more sure of herself when it came to matters of the heart.

"Turn your back while I get dressed," she said.

"Isn't that like closing the barn door after the horse ran off?" he asked, the old teasing note lifting his voice a little.

Hoping the darkness would conceal her condition, she yanked the covers off and shoved her feet into the sturdy boots she usually wore when making her calls. Then she wrapped herself in a robe, tugging the tie snugly around her waist—or what was left of her waist.

She tried to pretend this was an ordinary call on an ordinary night. Tried not to think about the fact that a man she had given up on was back, that he still had the power to make her knees weak and her mind swirl with colors and hopes more vivid than the brightest dream.

"We have a lot to talk about," she said over her shoulder, her hand on the banister, making her way into the darkness of the foyer.

"We need to do more than talk," he whispered, his mouth enticingly close to her ear as he helped her into an oiled slicker. His voice had a curious raw edge to it.

She stepped out into the wind-driven rain. In the flash of a lightning strike, she turned to look at her captor. Lank hair the color of straw, lean cheeks chapped by the wind and stubbled by a few days' growth of beard. A wide, unsmiling mouth. He pulled down his dripping hat brim before she could see his eyes.

Yet she knew that face, those eyes. They were more dear to her than life itself. She had died a thousand deaths thinking she'd never see him again.

She could feel him behind her, his height and breadth intimidating, uncompromising. The rain drummed relentlessly on her hood. Her booted foot splashed into a puddle, stuck briefly in the sucking mud. She looked back at the boardinghouse. What a wonder it had been, watching the whole town pitch in for weeks on end to make the house livable once again.

A new tradesman's shingle hung above the front porch. In the faint gaslight, the lettering was barely legible: Drs. Mundy & Lake, Physicians. Rooms To Let.

A shiver passed over Leah as she approached the schooner. A lamp burned low in the stateroom porthole.

Just what the devil did Jackson Underhill want now?

Nervously, Leah made her way onto the ship. It was cozier and better kept than she remembered. She sat on the bunk and looked up at him. "Now can you tell me where you've been?"

"I've been to hell and back. It's hell without you, Leah."

Her breath caught. "Is that why you came back?"

"Yeah. And that's why I plan to stay." He swallowed. "If you'll have me."

She felt the tears start and blinked fast to keep them at bay. "I won't, Jackson. Not unless I know it's forever."

"It's forever. I swear it, honey. Forever and ever." Wearily, he drew his hand down his face. "It took what amounted to a war party to make me understand that I didn't have to run anymore."

Leah frowned. "A war party?"

"Skagits. They found me at the Inside Passage in Canada."

She blinked in wonderment. "Sophie's people."

"Yep. Joel and Davy were with them."

"Sweet heaven." She knew Santana and Davy Morgan had gone off somewhere, but she'd had no idea they were searching for Jackson. "So they're back?"

"Yeah. They told me what I didn't stick around to hear the day I took off."

"That Joel Santana knew it was Carrie all along."

"Yeah." He looked miserable.

"You couldn't keep trying to protect her."

"I know. Damn." He leaned back on the bench seat. "I spent so many years of my life chasing a dream, Leah. Chasing an illusion. What the hell does that make me?"

"A dreamer," she said softly.

He sank onto one knee in front of her and took her by the shoulders. "You're my dream now. You. You always have been. I just didn't know you were real until I met you."

"Jackson..." She couldn't say anything else. Her heart was in her throat. And in her hands as she stroked his face and his damp hair. And in her lips as she leaned forward to kiss him at last, to taste him, sobbing against his mouth.

"It's all right, Leah," he whispered, pulling back, his own smile wavering. "It's all right now." He began kissing her again. His hands threaded into her hair and then moved down, cradling her cheeks before dropping lower. She felt his thumbs skim along her collarbones and wondered how she had survived without him, without this touch, without the precious taste and scent of him near her every moment.

A slight chill slid across her when he parted her robe. He bent to kiss her breasts and then moved lower...and then he stopped.

"*Damn*, Leah." He looked up at her with eyes full of pain and wonder. "When the hell were you going to tell me?"

She tucked her knees up against her chest. "I told you we had a lot to talk about."

He bristled. "You might have been a little more specific. Christ, you're pregnant!"

She remembered his reaction to Carrie's pregnancy. He'd been terrified, furious. But this was different, she told herself. This had to be different. Still, she didn't like his harsh tone. "You say that as if you had nothing to do with it."

He unwound her hands from her knees and pressed her back onto the bunk. He slid his hand down along her belly, cradling the small rise in his palm. "My Leah," he said. "My beautiful Leah. What a beautiful baby you'll have."

"We," she corrected, then lifted herself against him, undoing the buttons of his shirt. The unfamiliarity and awkwardness started to dissolve. She remembered the texture of his tongue as he outlined her lips. She remembered the sound he made deep in his throat when she stroked him. She remembered the exquisite delicacy of his large hands as moved them over her body, touching her breasts and her thighs, cupping her against him.

He hovered over her, the lines of his face taut. "I can't...wait much longer."

"No one asked you to."

He sank into her as he had in the past, sinking into the

middle of her life where everything felt so right. She nearly wept with the unhurried tenderness of their love-making. Their rhythm and their release spoke of forever.

Afterward they slept, replete, in one another's arms. The rain stopped, and the sun came up just as they awakened.

Jackson nuzzled his face into her hair. "Doc, that was the first good night of sleep I've had in weeks."

She stretched, sliding her body against his. "I was almost afraid to wake up. I thought this might be a dream."

"It is." He reached under the bunk and took out a jug of water and two fresh apples. "But it's a dream that just came true." A fresh wind sang through the shrouds, and he handed her an apple. "What do you say to a sail?"

She thought of the agenda she'd planned today. Penny was making the calls, but Leah had planned to work at the surgery on the endless, tedious task of restoring the books and records damaged in the fire. The old Leah would have clung to duty, insisted on keeping to her schedule. But Jackson had changed everything. Today was for them, a stolen time, a time to heal from the past two months of separation.

"Perfect," she said.

The *Teatime* cut cleanly through the hard autumn swells of the Sound. The schooner was truly a thing of beauty and power. No wonder Jackson loved it so. No wonder he kept sailing away.

They made love during the day, feeling decadent and spoiled under an Indian summer sun. In the late afternoon they lay against each other in the cockpit, warm and languorous with the intimacy they'd shared. Jackson held one hand lazily on the helm while his other one caressed her bare shoulder.

"Leah?"

"Hmm?"

"You never answered my question."

"Which one is that?"

"The one I asked on the porch two months ago." He kept his eyes on the horizon. "Will you marry me?"

The haze of sexual contentment cleared away. She drew back, forced herself to look at him, really look. "That depends."

He gave her a crooked smile. "On what?"

"On what you mean."

"I mean I want to marry you." He skimmed his thumbs lightly across her cheeks, catching the tears she didn't realize she was shedding. "I love you, Leah. I always will. Just showing up and saying the words doesn't seem like enough. I wish I could have come back on a white charger, bringing you the whole world."

"Don't you see?" she said, her voice breaking as she thought of the day he'd set the painted globe at her feet and walked away. "You've already given me the world."

He was quiet for a long time. He adjusted his course so that they were sailing due west. Into the sunset.

"Where are we going, Jackson?"

"To Coupeville. I reckon we have to, seeing as how I've been appointed sheriff."

The tears fell freely now; she didn't try to stop them. "You? Sheriff?"

"Hired on the recommendation of a recently retired U.S. Marshal." Letting go of the helm, he turned and took her in his arms. In his eyes she saw the reflection of clouds and sunset. She saw all she had ever dreamed of.

She bit her lip, tasting the salt of tears and of the sea.

"But you wanted to sail to paradise. You talked so much about it. Remember the picture in my office?"

"Yeah, I remember. Back then I thought it was a place in the middle of the ocean. Or a place on a map."

"And now?" She hardly dared to breathe.

"It's here, honey." He tightened his arms around her. "With you. Only I don't call it paradise anymore." He set a course for the harbor, and the newly painted boardinghouse hove into view. "I call it home."

Available in May!

National bestselling authors

# JENNIFER BLAKE
# EMILIE RICHARDS

Welcome to the Old South—a place where the finest women are ladies and the best men are gentlemen. And where men from the wrong side of town have more honor than all the blue bloods combined! This is a place where everyone has their place and no one dares to cross the line. But some rules are meant to be broken....

# Southern
# GENTLEMEN

Sweeping romance and sizzling passion...
and you will soon discover that
**NOT ALL MEN ARE CREATED EQUAL.**

Available in May 1998 at your favorite retail outlet.

MIRA

Available in
May from
*New York Times*
bestselling
author

# TESS GERRITSEN

He emerged from the mist, right in front of Cathy
Weaver's car—running from killers who were closing
in. Victor Holland's story sounded like the ravings of a
madman, but his claim to be a fugitive was confirmed
by the haunted look in his eyes—and the bullet hole
in his shoulder. As each house brought the pursuers
ever closer, Cathy had to wonder: Was she giving her
trust to a man in danger...or trusting her life to a
dangerous man?

Available in May 1998 wherever books are sold.

MTG468